Diary of a Wimpy Vampire

BECAUSE THE UNDEAD HAVE FEELINGS TOO

TIM COLLINS

Michael O'Mara Books Limited

First published in Great Britain in 2010 by
Michael O'Mara Books Limited
9 Lion Yard
Tremadoc Road
London SW4 7NQ

A CIP catalogue record for this book is available from
the British Library.

Papers used by Michael O'Mara Books Limited are natural,
recyclable products made from wood grown in sustainable forests.
The manufacturing processes conform to the environmental regulations
of the country of origin.

ISBN: 978-1-84317-458-5
10

www.mombooks.com
Designed and typeset by Envy Design

Illustrations by Andrew Pinder
Printed and bound in Great Britain by CPI Cox & Wyman, Reading, Berks

Diary

ACKNOWLEDGEMENTS

Thanks to Lindsay Davies, Ana McLaughlin,
Sarah Sandland and everyone at Michael O'Mara Books.
Thanks to Andrew Pinder for the illustrations. Finally,
thanks as ever to Collette.

SATURDAY 1ST JANUARY

I shall turn 100 this year, so I thought it was about time I kept a diary. Perhaps you're reading this in the future when some idiot has rammed a stake through my heart or chopped my head off. Perhaps you're a professor who's studying my poetry. Either way, welcome to my first ever diary!

Just because I said that I would turn 100 this year, don't imagine me as an ancient old man. To your eyes, I would look fifteen years old, as this is the age I was turned into a vampire by the people I call my parents. They transformed me along with the girl I call my sister, as they felt like starting a family. And did they ask me about my feelings on the subject? Of course they didn't.

You might think that being undead is a non-stop thrill ride. Well, think again. Today was boring as hell and I've got another day to go until school starts again. I can't believe I'm looking forward to going back to that place. That should tell you how exciting things are round here!

Diary of a Wimpy Vampire

SUNDAY 2ND JANUARY

It's quite hard to get the hang of writing diary entries. Humans probably start by saying what time they wake up, but I never sleep. I suppose I should start with what happened from midnight onwards. Or maybe make 4 am the cut-off point. It won't make much difference anyway, as all I ever do at night is play computer games.

If you're wondering why I don't run around all night sucking the blood of humans, it's because Mum and Dad have to do all that stuff for me. When you transform into a vampire, your strength and speed are supposed to increase to superhuman levels. But guess what happened to me? Oh, that's right. Absolutely nothing. If anything, I got even weaker and slower than ever.

The annoying thing is, I still need blood to survive. But as it's too difficult for me to hunt, I have to rely on Mum and Dad to get it for me. Every few days, they travel to a different town to get a fresh supply, because if they did it right here in Stockfield, everyone would realize we were vampires and put us in a zoo or something.

I hate being dependent on Mum and Dad, but I don't feel guilty about making them get the blood. After all, I didn't ask to be transformed. They got me into this mess, and fetching my meals every day is the very least they can do.

MONDAY 3RD JANUARY

A new girl has joined our school. She is called Chloe and her family has just moved to town. She has pale skin, black eyes and dark hair in a ponytail, showing off her long neck. She sat on her own in History, so I think she's scared of meeting new people. It will be interesting to see if she ends up making friends with the popular gang, the tough gang or the goths.

I'm sort of part of the goths but I don't hang around with them outside school or anything. I'm a bit of a mysterious loner, really.

Anyway, other than the new girl joining, it was a rather uneventful first day back. We had Maths with Mr Wilson and he said that we weren't concentrating enough because

Diary of a Wimpy Vampire

we were still too full of Christmas pudding. He made the same joke last year and I didn't laugh then either. Nobody likes to ask him for help because he leans right over your shoulder and his breath smells of rancid coffee. People say the smell of garlic is lethal to vampires. Well take it from me, it's got nothing on Maths teacher coffee breath.

Had some type A+ blood for dinner. It was quite bitter. You're supposed to say 'Bless the sacred life force' before you drink it, but I'm too much of a rebel to bother with tradition.

TUESDAY 4TH JANUARY

I sat next to Chloe today in Art and I could smell that she had type O- blood, which is rare but especially tasty (my dad calls it the champagne of blood). I told her about the goths, the tough gang and the popular gang, and she said she wouldn't want to be in the popular gang anyway. She is a girl after my own heart.

I told her about the rumour that Mr Byrne was a millionaire before he lost all his money and had to become an English teacher, and about how Darren from our class came in on No Uniform Day wearing his PE kit because he's so poor that these are the only clothes he owns. She didn't laugh at this and said she felt sorry for him, and I agreed, to make myself look caring and sensitive.

4AM

I am in love with Chloe! I know this because I've been thinking about her since half past ten. I can't stop picturing her dark eyes and her lovely pale neck.

I've had crushes on various girls before, but this is the real thing. Even if I could eat or sleep I wouldn't be able to eat or sleep right now!

WEDNESDAY 5TH JANUARY

I sat next to Chloe in the library at lunchtime. Every time I stared at her she looked down at her book instead of making eye contact. By rights, I should have mesmerized her with my intense, brooding beauty, but there was no sign of that.

Basically, I got the worst deal ever when I became a vampire. Every other vampire in history developed a supernatural level of attractiveness when they transformed. But not me. When I look in the mirror,* I just see a pasty, tired, fifteen-going-on-100-year-old looking back at me.

It's so unfair that I didn't get vampire beauty. I thought that was part of the deal. How am I supposed to attract humans to feed on? With my bubbly personality?

Diary of a Wimpy Vampire

Anyway, I've resigned myself to the fact that I can't snare Chloe in with my vampire good looks, so I'm going to have to do this the hard way, through seduction.

*Yes, vampires can see themselves in mirrors. Don't believe everything you see in horror films. Why would becoming a vampire mean that you couldn't see your reflection any more? If they're going to make up lies about us, they could at least make sense.

THURSDAY 6TH JANUARY

A policeman showed us a road safety video in assembly this morning. It was really gory, and upset some of the younger pupils, but it just made me feel thirsty. Sometimes I am ashamed of myself.

At lunchtime I went back to the library to sit next to Chloe. I wanted to talk to her, but I was too nervous. It was so humiliating. My kind has struck fear into the hearts of female humans for centuries. Why should I be the nervous one?

I can't even ask my parents for advice. They possess vampire beauty, so they wouldn't understand. I just wish they'd had the courtesy to pass it down to me.

Tonight I asked Dad what the best way to impress a girl is and he said you should save her from death. But how am I supposed to do that without vampire strength? Buy her a cycle helmet? Give her an anti-smoking leaflet? As ever, he's totally failed to appreciate what it's like for me.

FRIDAY 7TH JANUARY

An embarrassing thing happened today. I was sitting behind Chloe in History, and my fangs extended.

When you're a vampire, your fangs are supposed to grow longer when you're about to feed on a human. As I don't hunt, this doesn't happen to me very often. But today it happened when I looked at Chloe, which was quite alarming.

I was getting bored listening to Mr Morris droning on about the Second World War, so I looked over at Chloe. As I focused on her, I began to hear the sound of blood pumping around her veins and I thought about what a wonderful relief it would be if I could pierce her jugular vein and have a refreshing sip. Then I ran my tongue

Diary of a Wimpy Vampire

across my teeth and I realized that my fangs had grown to twice their normal length!

To make the whole situation even more awkward, Mr Morris then accused me of paying no attention, and quizzed me about what he'd been saying. I know all about the Second World War, because I remember it well, but I couldn't speak in case anyone saw my fangs, so he went nuts at me.

It's official – even my own body has decided to make things difficult for me now.

SATURDAY 8TH JANUARY

After all the stress of last week I wanted nothing more than to lie in bed today and think about Chloe and her pretty neck. No chance of that, though. Dad barged in at six this morning and announced that we were going for a hike.

I hate family hike days.* As I lack vampire strength and speed, I'm always trundling along behind the rest of them as they bound back and forth like undead labradors.

Even my little sister runs ahead of me on family hikes. She has vampire strength and speed, but good luck getting her to admit this when Mum and Dad want her to do something round the house.

Today's hike was around the wild countryside north of Stockfield and the three of them kept zipping around and telling me about the lakes, hills and forests I was missing out on. Like I even cared.

We came across a wide river and they crossed it by leaping hundreds of feet up in the air. Dad offered to carry me across on his back, but I told them I'd wait in the car.

And it's in my dad's Volvo that I reside now, Dear Diary, thinking about my sweet sweet Chloe. I have been waiting for three hours now, and gazing at the tempestuous, turbulent clouds racing across the windswept landscape. So this is what being in love is like!

*Technically they're my 'coven' rather than my family, and we live in a 'lair' rather than a house. I don't see the point in these formal terms, though.

SUNDAY
9TH JANUARY

Annoying things about my sister Part One Million: she's decided that she wants to drink animal blood rather than human blood from now on. She says she's doing this for 'ethical reasons'. One of her friends must have taught her that phrase because she's used it about fifty times today.

17

Diary of a Wimpy Vampire

What ethical reasons? Feeding on humans doesn't kill them, unless the vampire in question is so greedy that they drain every last drop of their blood. It won't even turn them into vampires if you don't mix blood with them.

All that happens to humans is they're mesmerized, drained of a couple of pints of blood, left feeling a bit woozy and have to take a couple of days off work. When you think about it, vampires are no more evil than a case of flu.

Anyway, my sister says she only wants to drink animal blood now, so today they've all driven off to gather it from cows and sheep. Needless to say, I'm refusing to take any part in this charade. My sister is only going to make herself ill by refusing to drink proper blood. As long as she doesn't come crying to me when she's weak with hunger, it's of no interest to me.

Note: If you are actually my sister and you're reading this, I don't care if I've upset you. It's no less than you deserve for reading the secret words of others.

Update: I have decided that every night I will tape a hair over the end of my diary. If the hair is broken I will know my sister has been looking in here.

Diary of a Wimpy Vampire

MONDAY 10TH JANUARY

12:20PM

I am sitting opposite Chloe in the library writing this. She's always here at lunchtime. This either means she doesn't have any friends yet or she's a swot. I hope she's a swot, because that way none of the other boys will fancy her and I'll have a better chance. Perhaps in a minute she'll look over and ask me what I'm writing.

12:55PM

Lunch is coming to an end now and Chloe has not yet asked me what I'm writing. I think I need to be more proactive. I shall find out more about her interests. She is currently looking at a book about animals, so I shall pretend I'm interested in them, even though the truth of the matter is that I hate them because they freak out if I go anywhere near them.

2AM

Mum and Dad were playing funeral marches at full volume tonight, which made it really hard for me to concentrate on learning animal facts. When they finally went upstairs, they left all the candles on. I must have told them a thousand times that this could cause a fire.

Diary of a Wimpy Vampire

TUESDAY 11TH JANUARY

I think I'm bonding with Chloe. Perhaps she'll yield to my immortal allure soon.

I reeled off my animal facts in the library this lunchtime. She seemed quite impressed, and we had a good chat.

Later on she offered me one of her boiled sweets. It was supposed to be lime-flavoured, but like anything that isn't blood, it tasted of coal dipped in sick to me. When she wasn't looking, I spat the rotten thing into the bin. But I kept the wrapper as a relic of my love.

I shall tell her about this when we're married and we shall laugh.

To get rid of the taste of the sweet, I went to the toilets for lunch. I understand that this might sound rather unpleasant, but this is the only way I can feed at school. Every day, I take a flask of blood to school as a packed lunch. As I can hardly sit in the canteen with blood dribbling down my chin, I have to lock myself in a toilet cubicle to enjoy it. I understand that as dining experiences go, this is unlikely to get a Michelin star, but it's the only safe place for me to drink. I once tried it crouching down behind the wheelie bins, but someone saw me with blood all around my mouth and I had to pretend I'd fallen over.

WEDNESDAY 12TH JANUARY

6PM

I couldn't find Chloe at lunchtime, so I went to the steps at the back of the gym and hung around with the goths instead.

The goths are called Brian, John and Si, and if you call them the goths they say they're emos really. I think Brian only joined the group because he's fat and it doesn't show as much when you wear black. I think Si joined because he's a ginger and he can dye his hair black. It's hard to tell why John joined because he never says anything. As for me, I don't really hang round with them out of choice. It's just that my pale skin and black clothing sort of automatically place me in their gang.

Brian has a girlfriend who goes to another school. I thought he might be lying until he showed me a picture of her. Nobody would pretend to have a girlfriend who looked like that.

4AM

I have been lying in bed all night and thinking about Chloe. Is it normal for a vampire to be this attracted to a human? I wish there was someone I could talk to.

Diary of a Wimpy Vampire

THURSDAY 13TH JANUARY

Our Science lesson today was about the heart and the teacher kept going on about how blood pumps around the atria and ventricles. Needless to say, I got so thirsty that my fangs extended for the entire lesson and I had to bury my head in my textbook in shame.

At the end of the lesson, we were given colour handouts with explicit pictures of hearts, veins and blood cells. I took mine home and hid it underneath my mattress.

I sat with Chloe again at lunchtime, and she told me she's agreed to be a prefect. Her duties will include reporting people who run in the corridors or cause disruption in assembly. I doubt this will win her much popularity, but I respect her maturity, and fully intend to defend her against those who tease her for it. As long as I don't have to fight anyone.

FRIDAY 14TH JANUARY

Chloe fell over and cut her knee on the way to the library today, and a small trickle of delicious type O- ran down her leg. I was so overpowered by the desire to lick it off that I had to run to the toilets and gulp down the contents of my flask.

As I ran away I could see that Wayne from my class came to Chloe's aid. What must she think of me for running away like that? Why am I cursed with these desires? How

Diary of a Wimpy Vampire

can I explain myself? Perhaps I should pretend that I have a phobia about blood rather than a thirst for it. Either way she's going to think I'm a weirdo.

SATURDAY 15TH JANUARY

Today I offered to help Mum and Dad tidy the house. We only moved here six months ago, and it already looks like a ruined gothic castle. I know they feel more comfortable surrounded by thick velvet curtains, golden candelabras and ancient oil paintings, but the place is too gloomy and dusty. I bet social services wouldn't be too impressed if they paid a visit.

My parents rejected my offer, saying that I'd only throw something expensive away by mistake. So what should I do then? Wait for them to tidy up themselves? Let's just say it's a good job we've got the rest of eternity for that!

This afternoon my sister asked me if I wanted to play football with her in the back garden. I said no, just like I did the last thousand times she asked. I don't know why she thinks I'm suddenly going to change my mind.

All that happens is that we take turns to do penalties while the other goes in goal. It's all very one-sided, thanks to my sister's speed and strength. I'll take five penalties, which she'll save in the unlikely event that they go near the goal, and then she'll take five penalties. Even if I do catch the ball, the force of it whacks me into the back of the net and she counts it as a goal. We even broke the conservatory at our last house, when the force of one of her penalties dragged me through it.

So even if I was remotely interested in football, getting beaten at it by a ten-year-old girl would hardly be my idea of fun.

SUNDAY 16TH JANUARY

My stupid sister is upset because she wants to change her name and Mum and Dad won't let her. Her name is Mavis (and has been since she was born in 1916), but now she's being teased in school for having an old-fashioned name and wants to change it to something modern.

Quite sensibly, Mum and Dad have told her that she

Diary of a Wimpy Vampire

has to wait until next time we move rather than suddenly announcing to her class that she's changed her name. They might have been more likely to give in if her ideas had been less ridiculous, though. Her list of suggested names in order of preference was:

Twist
Princess
Jet
Sailor
Melody
Orchid
Manhattan
Angel

Like she wouldn't draw attention to herself with that lot!

Anyway, Mum and Dad put their foot down with her for the first time in a century, and now she's stormed off to her room. I am resisting chanting the name 'Mavis' outside her door, because I'm too mature to care. I might just go and shout it a couple of times, though.

MONDAY 17TH JANUARY

I sat next to Chloe in the library at lunchtime so I could apologize for dashing off on Friday, but she didn't say anything about it, so I let it go.

I wanted to talk to her, but whenever I tried I kept getting thirsty and could feel my fangs growing again. Why does my body insist on betraying me like this? It's not like I only want to sink my teeth into her neck. I want to get to know her and have meaningful conversations with her and take her for long moonlit walks. Obviously, it would be nice if she let me drink her blood too, but that's not all I'm interested in.

I'm so confused by my feelings.

Tuesday
18th January

12:05pm

I'm in the library sitting next to Chloe once again. Perhaps I'm putting her off by smiling too much. I once read that humans are attracted to the smouldering intensity of vampires. I will now make an effort to pout.

12:10pm

It's actually quite difficult to pout. I probably should have practised in front of the mirror.

Look up from your textbook, Chloe, and see the doomed longing of the decades etched upon my melancholy features!

Diary of a Wimpy Vampire

Look up from your textbook and yield to icy bliss! Look up from your textbook because my face is starting to hurt now!

12:15 PM

Chloe looked up from her textbook and asked if I was feeling ill. Pouting attempt deemed a failure.

WEDNESDAY 19TH JANUARY

Mum dropped me off at school today and it was a very embarrassing experience. Like all vampires except me, she appears overwhelmingly beautiful to humans. Which is all well and good when she's catching prey, but not great for me if I want to get through the school day without being teased.

I told her to stay in the car, but she insisted on kissing me on the cheek in front of everyone. Craig from my class shouted out that he'd like my mum to kiss him on the cheek too.

By lunchtime, the whole pathetic school was buzzing with the news that I had a 'hot mum' and I couldn't walk down the corridors without some idiot asking if they could go on a date with her.

Diary of a Wimpy Vampire

It would serve them right if I did set them up with her. They'd be lying in an alley drained of blood after five minutes.

Why can't I just have normal parents like everyone else?

THURSDAY 20TH JANUARY

Today was cold but bright and I got a couple of unpleasant spots on my chin. It's sometimes said that sunlight kills vampires, but this is another myth. Bright sunlight makes the skin of vampires burn, but it's only a mild irritant, not much worse than someone with ginger hair would experience. This is the real reason we avoid hot countries and prefer to go out at night, and the origin of all those silly ideas about us turning to ash if we forget the clocks have changed and open the curtains at the wrong time.

As usual, I got a particularly bad deal as the sun gives

Diary of a Wimpy Vampire

me terrible acne as well as a rash. In the summer, I cover my face in high-factor sunblock every few hours and that gives me decent protection. But there are days like today when rays unexpectedly hit my face and I get a nasty cluster of whiteheads. It's annoying, but it beats turning into the contents of an overturned ashtray, I suppose.

I was too ashamed to sit next to Chloe at lunchtime with my hideous spots so I went to the toilets to squeeze them instead. I shall cover them up with white foundation tomorrow.

Mum barged into my room while I was looking at my Science handout about the heart tonight. I wish she would learn to knock.

Friday 21st January

Mum and Dad have gone down to London today to do boring bank stuff. Sometimes I go down with them but I couldn't today because I had school.

Although London is an exciting city, it makes me feel sad when I see how much it's changed since we lived there in the thirties. The neon adverts at Piccadilly Circus have changed from Player's Cigarettes to Cinzano to Skol to McDonald's. And in all that time I still haven't got a girlfriend. I need to sort my life out.

My parents don't need jobs because we live off the interest of the many bank accounts they've opened over the years. However, we're not allowed to spend too much in case it draws attention to us. I only get ten pounds a week pocket money, which is grossly unfair when you consider I'm the son of millionaires.

1 AM

My sister is so annoying! She's got her music on at full blast and she won't turn it down! Mum and Dad are still out, and she won't obey me.

For a vampire, her taste in music is an absolute disgrace. She's listening to some dreadful pop song about how true beauty is on the inside written by cynical old songwriters for a manufactured teen starlet. Vampires are supposed to like funeral marches, dirges and haunting

Diary of a Wimpy Vampire

piano pieces. If we must listen to modern music we should at the very least listen to emo, goth or death metal. Teen pop is surely inappropriate for the undead.

Plus, if these songwriters really believe that true beauty comes from within and not from physical appearances, why didn't they get someone ugly like Brian's girlfriend to sing it rather than a sixteen-year-old starlet who looks like she's been created from scratch by a plastic surgeon?

SATURDAY 22ND JANUARY

Mum and Dad are back from London, but they are both unwell. I don't know what kind of blood they drank down there, but they look pale, even by vampire standards. I suspect they fed on someone with a high level of alcohol in their blood, which we're supposed to avoid. In theory, the smell of alcohol should have been enough to repel them, but I bet they went right ahead and glugged away anyway, the greedy pigs.

And what happens to me in these situations? Oh, that's

right, I miss out on meals altogether. They know I'm not strong enough to hunt humans myself, and yet they merrily stuff their faces with dodgy blood, not caring about the consequences. I wish they'd think about someone else for once in their lives.

SUNDAY 23RD JANUARY

Mum and Dad are still ill and now I'm feeling weak due to lack of blood. I can't stay off school next week, as I shall miss the chance to seduce Chloe, and someone will steal her from me.

Wait, my true love! I shall find my strength!

MONDAY 24TH JANUARY

I went into school today, although I'm still weak from lack of blood. If any of the teachers were observant enough to notice my condition, I'd get taken into care.

Chloe smiled at me in Maths today, but this made my fangs come out so I couldn't smile back. If only I could express my true feelings for her. I might write a poem.

2AM

Dad has finally seen fit to go out and get us some more blood. He even had the cheek to tell me off for not thanking him when he brought it to me. I would have thanked him if I'd had the strength, the selfish old corpse!

Diary of a Wimpy Vampire

4AM

I have written my poem now, and I think it shows how deep my feelings are. It's a symbolic poem as it uses actual light and dark to stand for the lightness and darkness of my moods. I considered posting it to Chloe, but I've decided to wait before sharing it. Perhaps I will read it to her on our wedding night.

I WALK IN SHADOW

I walk in shadow
Shielding my dark desire
You walk in sunlight
Your eyes afire
To join you in the light
Oh how I long
But it gives me spots
And my skin feels all wrong

TUESDAY 25TH JANUARY

Mrs Maguire did an assembly about religious tolerance today, and I went home sick.

She started her talk by showing us a crucifix on the overhead projector, which wasn't great for me. Although it's not true that crucifixes make vampires recoil in terror, they can give us headaches. And it's not just crucifixes either. I can get a stinking migraine from any religious symbol. Which is why I began to feel queasy when Mrs Maguire proceeded to show us the symbols of every other major religion. I got as far as the Star and Crescent and the Yin and Yang before I had to make a dash for the exit, reeling like I was on a ferry in a storm.

I've been lying down for a while and feel better now. At least I've got PE to look forward to tomorrow. I don't think.

Wednesday 26th January

PE was hell on earth as expected. I didn't want anyone to notice my pale skin while I was getting changed, so I tried to get into my PE kit really quickly and ended up tripping onto the floor.

We then had to go to the gym and jump over a vaulting horse. I couldn't manage it, so Mr Jenkins said I had to do

press-ups on the crash mat as punishment. I really hate Mr Jenkins. I hate him more than any other PE teacher I have ever had, which is saying a lot, as I must have had about forty over the years and they tend to represent the absolute lowest form of humanity.

Diary of a Wimpy Vampire

Luckily for me, Chloe is in a different PE class. If she'd seen my humiliation at the hands of the evil Mr Jenkins, there's no way she'd ever fancy me.

THURSDAY 27TH JANUARY

11AM

We got our Science homework back today and I got a 'C'. It's not a very good mark, but it's not bad enough to get me put down to the bottom set.

You'd think that after studying a subject for over eighty years, I'd be better at it. But the weird thing is that I can't apply myself because I know that soon we'll move towns and I'll start the school year all over again and get another chance to learn it. As long as I do enough to coast along, my parents don't tell me off. I'm pretty good at History, especially the bits that happened in my lifetime. I'm also really good at playing the piano, which I learned before we had a TV, but Dad won't let me study Music at school in case it draws attention to us. Anyone would think he would be proud of his son's talent.

5PM

Mr Wilson went out of the room in Maths this afternoon and Wayne showed everyone a sexist magazine. It had things about football and fighting in it, but it was the pictures of girls without many clothes on that caused the most excitement. I had a look, but I couldn't understand what all the fuss was about. The pictures had been airbrushed so much that you couldn't even see the veins in their necks. I pretended to be interested nonetheless, so I didn't get accused of being a weirdo.

Friday 28th January

Mrs Maguire told me off after assembly today for refusing to sing along with the hymns. I wasn't doing it to break the rules, I was just worried that I would get a bad headache again like when I looked at the crucifix. At any rate, it's better not to sing at all than to sing obscene alternative words like Wayne and Craig did.

In the library at lunchtime, Chloe said she admired me for sticking to my principles as an atheist, so at least some

Diary of a Wimpy Vampire

good came out of it. She gave me another boiled sweet, and her hand touched mine for a brief, forbidden moment. Like all vampires, my body temperature is very low, and Chloe seemed surprised by how cold my hand was. It's easier to get away with this in January than it will be in summer, but by then we shall be lovers, and she'll know of my true nature.

I need to make a move on Chloe. When I'm back in school on Monday, I'll invite her out on a date. Or I might wait until Tuesday.

SATURDAY 29TH JANUARY

Today we had our annual family trip to Whitby. It's really boring, and I've been there loads of times before. It's the place where Mum and Dad first lived when they came over from France, so they go back there to talk about dull nostalgic things every year. It's also the place where Dracula first arrives in England in Bram Stoker's novel, which has led Dad to speculate that the character was based on him. Personally, I think it's just a coincidence. Dracula does lots of silly things in that book, like transforming into a bat, a dog and even some fog, so it's clearly a work of wild fancy written by someone who's never even met a vampire.

On the way back from Whitby, Mum and Dad tried to strike up a conversation, but I didn't feel like talking. I heard them muttering something about how I'm just going through a phase. I was going to explain to them that when something goes on for eighty-five years it hardly counts as a phase, but I couldn't be bothered. They wouldn't understand.

Mum and Dad wanted to play Scrabble when we got back, but I wasn't interested. They always cheat by making up words like 'zaqox' and pretending they were really popular in the nineteenth century.

SUNDAY 30TH JANUARY

Today I looked on the Internet for tips about asking girls out, but when Dad saw that I was on the computer, he got really annoyed.

He thinks that all computers are dangerous, even though he doesn't understand them at all. He barely got the hang of typewriters before they went out of fashion.

Dad's convinced that someone or other is going to trace us all through the Internet. What does he think I'm doing, tagging a photo of him drinking blood on Facebook? And who is he so worried about anyway? He's always told me that we are the last four vampires left on earth, so it can't be any of our own kind that he fears. And as for human enemies, anyone he's offended in the past must surely be too old to be a threat by now.

I tried to show Dad the fun side of the Internet by showing him a clip of a panda sneezing, but I don't think he understood it was supposed to be funny. If anything, I think it just made him hungry.

Dad's so out of date he makes me cringe. Once, when Mum was planning a surprise party for my sister, he suggested that we get some hunchbacks with bells on to dance for her. I can't believe he thought that would be appropriate. That's not been considered an acceptable form of entertainment for centuries now.

MONDAY 31st JANUARY

12PM

I've decided to ask my parents to buy me a car to compensate for the extra speed I should have got when I became a vampire. It's the least they can do really. I know they can afford it, so they have no reason to refuse me other than spite. Based on observations I've made of older boys, I've decided that Chloe would be more likely to go out with me if I had a car.

7 PM

My parents won't buy me a car, as they say I don't look old enough to drive it and it will draw too much attention to us. I even offered to wear a false beard every time I drive, but they still refused.

I told them that I don't care what they think because they're not my real parents anyway, and then ran up to my room and slammed the door.

It's so unfair. My sister gets absolutely everything she wants, but they refuse me simple requests like this.

Diary of a Wimpy Vampire

12AM

I spent tonight feeling really angry with my parents for refusing to buy me a car, but I've calmed down now. I know I get annoyed with them, but I should at least be grateful that I'm not one of those vampires with parents who are younger than them.* Then it would be really annoying if they were strict with you.

*This might sound impossible, but it's quite simple really. Imagine if my dad had been born as a human a few years later than me, but not transformed into a vampire until he was in his thirties or forties. To the eyes of a human he would look older than me, but I would know he was younger. And ignore everything he said.

TUESDAY 1ST FEBRUARY

10AM

I looked in the bathroom mirror this morning and noticed that my spots have got worse. Sometimes I wish vampires really couldn't see their reflections.

1PM

Chloe was upset today when the girls from the popular gang wouldn't let her sit on their table because she reported them for talking in assembly. I agreed that they were being completely unfair, as she was only doing her duty as a prefect.

We then had a good chat about a ghost-hunting show that was on TV last night. They had some actors from a soap opera staying in an old country house and it filmed them listening to strange noises. Chloe thought it was fake and I agreed with her.

I can remember getting scared of ghosts when I was at school in the fifties. We used to think that one of the corridors was haunted by a pupil who drowned, and we would always run down it so he couldn't get us. Looking back, it was a bit hypocritical of me to be so scared of a supernatural entity despite being one myself, but I was much more easily swayed back then.

5PM

I sat with Craig and Wayne in Maths but it was really boring as they kept going on about how low cut Mrs Thomson's top was. They were talking like they were experienced international playboys rather than spotty adolescents from a small town. I found it difficult to care about the subject, as all tops seem low cut to me if you can see a girl's neck. Unless a girl is wearing a polo neck, I regard her as provocatively dressed.

It's PE again tomorrow. I can't face another lesson with that idiot Mr Jenkins so I'm going to ask Dad for a note to get me out of it. I'll get him to write that I've got a bad back, and that I can't do it for three months.

WEDNESDAY 2ND FEBRUARY

At first Dad refused to give me a note to get out of PE. He said it was the best lesson in school, and I should be looking forward to it. That's easy for him to say, with his vampire strength and speed. PE might well be fun if you can run a marathon in five minutes and leap over hurdles as if they were paperclips. I can't even do a forward roll!

In the end he agreed to write the note, but still managed to make it embarrassing. He went off into his study and wrote on ancient parchment with a quill. That might have been acceptable in the seventeenth century, but it isn't now. I wish he would make at least some effort to get with the times.

Mr Jenkins almost had a heart attack when I gave him the note, but he accepted it nonetheless, and I enjoyed a blissful PE-free afternoon in the library.

THURSDAY 3RD FEBRUARY

We had a Science test this morning that I'd completely forgotten about. I hadn't done any revision and I got it all wrong. It's so horrible when you scan through the questions on a test and realize you can't do any of them. I don't know why humans think vampires are scary. Tests are much worse.

This afternoon I found out that the girls from the popular gang have given every boy in the class a mark out of ten for looks. I don't care what the popular gang think about me, but I hope I didn't get less than seven. I'm supposed to be a beautiful, aristocratic immortal. I'd be the first to admit that I'm not the best-looking vampire of all time, but I'd still like to think that I'm better than average-looking.

Jay from the tough gang waited outside the school gates tonight and gave everyone a dead arm on the way home (this is when he hits you so hard at the top of your arm that it goes numb). I didn't mind because I can't feel pain. Technically, the whole of me is dead, so a dead arm isn't a big deal.

Diary of a Wimpy Vampire

FRIDAY 4TH FEBRUARY

Craig has seen the list of marks out of ten and apparently I got a four! According to him, only three people in the class got a worse score than me! And they include Darren, who has fleas.

Why do none of the girls fancy me? I'm a vampire, I should be the class heart-throb. Judging from my score, I'm more Quasimodo than Count Dracula.

I have thick black hair and deep-set eyes, although I'm not good at eye contact. My skin is pure white when it's not plagued with rashes or acne. I'm also quite tall for my age, and I would surely have grown to over six feet if I'd stayed human longer.

Why don't these elements combine to produce the deadly, hypnotic beauty that's rightfully mine?

Diary of a Wimpy Vampire

Perhaps one day they will, and all the girls in the popular gang will be begging to go out with me. And I will laugh in their silly little faces.

SATURDAY 5TH FEBRUARY

I asked Dad today about why I don't have the same attractiveness as other vampires and he suggested it was to do with the age I transformed. He said that supernatural beauty is something grown-up vampires need to attract prey, but vampire children don't need it because they have their parents to get food for them.

Could he be any more patronizing? For a start, I wasn't a child when I transformed, I was fifteen, and mature for my age, so you'd think that the laws of vampire biology would have made an exception.

He also said that you don't hear my sister complaining about it. Of course she doesn't. She hates boys and would be happy enough to spend the rest of eternity getting pampered by my indulgent parents. All I can say is that she'd better hope they don't bump into any vampire slayers, as I have no intention of looking after her if they aren't around.

He did make one useful suggestion, though. He said that to humans, vampires smell of the thing they most desire. He suggested that I might be stifling my natural vampire aroma with deodorant. I know he dislikes the smell of the

Diary of a Wimpy Vampire

Lynx I spray on every morning, so he might just be saying this to make me stop using it, but I'll try cutting it out next week and see if it makes me more alluring.

SUNDAY 6TH FEBRUARY

Today we had a family outing to the seaside. My sister insisted that we all go on the ghost train even though it always makes her frightened. She had to bury her head in Mum's gown when the carriage went past a luminous skeleton (or 'skellington' as she pronounces it). It was so pathetic.

The man in the ticket booth was dressed as a vampire, though he wasn't putting much effort in. In fact, he was the first vampire I've ever seen who looked even more bored than me! He was also seriously overweight, which wouldn't be possible for a real vampire. We live off human blood, not deep-crust pizzas.

Diary of a Wimpy Vampire

MONDAY 7TH FEBRUARY

As suspected, Dad was talking nonsense about the whole vampire smell thing. I've been off the deodorant since Saturday, but far from attracting anyone, I ended up sitting on my own in every lesson today.

In Maths, I even stretched out my arms to see if the smell of my untreated pits would get the humans flocking round. Instead, everyone in the row behind me pulled their jumpers up over their noses to protect themselves from the pong like they do when Darren sits next to them.

I concluded that my natural smell is probably not attractive to humans, so I avoided Chloe for the rest of the day. I clearly don't smell of the thing humans most desire. Unless the thing humans most desire is a cheese sandwich that's been accidentally left in a locker over the summer holidays.

TUESDAY 8TH FEBRUARY

Today I heard a piece of news that pierced my heart like a stake dipped in garlic and holy water. Wayne fancies Chloe!

I must act soon! I'll never forgive myself if she starts

going out with that fool. I'm sure she won't be interested in him, though. He hangs around with the popular gang, and he's quite good at football, I'll admit. But he's got bad teeth and a downy moustache and he's in the bottom set for English where they let you watch DVDs instead of reading books. My wonderful Chloe couldn't possibly fall for anyone that stupid.

If only I could tell you the truth, Chloe! When he's middle-aged and bald, I'll be here for you just as young and attractive as ever. Or at least, just as young as ever.

Tomorrow, my beautiful prey, I shall reveal all.

Wednesday 9th February

10pm

I went to the library to reveal the truth about my nature to Chloe, but I was too nervous to say anything, so I went to the steps at the back of the library to hang around with my annoying friends the school goths instead.

They were talking about a new vampire show that started on TV last night, and weren't they just the world's leading authorities on the subject? Si got the ball of ignorance rolling by trotting out the myth that vampires can transform themselves into bats. Oh, can they now? And what happens to our bones when we do this? Do they magically shrink and then expand again? And what about our clothes? Do they somehow appear again when we transform back to human form, or are we naked? It would hardly be worth using your bat power if it meant having to spend the rest of the day with your privates on display.

Next, Brian said that he wished he was a vampire. I was so incensed by this that I was tempted to sink my fangs into his ample neck right then and show him the dull reality behind his childish fantasy. He'd be bored out of his mind in minutes, with no extra large pizza or afternoon nap to look forward to.

Then, worst of all, John said that he preferred zombies anyway. Zombies? What have those stinking corpses got to do with vampires? How is this a legitimate comparison? And if even zombies did exist, what kind of cretin would prefer them to pale, beautiful immortals?

I utterly despair of these idiots I am forced to call my friends.

3AM

I've been having a think about what it would be like if I really could transform into a bat and fly into Chloe's bedroom. Sometimes I wish the myths about vampires were true!

Diary of a Wimpy Vampire

THURSDAY 10TH FEBRUARY

10AM

The girls from my class all fancy the actor from the vampire TV show, and they've covered their exercise books with pictures of him in serious and moody poses. How blind of them to obsess over this manufactured image of vampirism when they have the real thing right under their noses.

Sometimes I think these shallow humans don't deserve my company.

6PM

In Art today I drew a charcoal picture of a girl fleeing in terror from a vampire in a graveyard. The girl was wearing a thin white dress and looked like Chloe, while the vampire was wearing a cape and looked like me. It was a very corny and inaccurate depiction, but I must admit I found it rather thrilling.

I got worried that Chloe would notice the drawing so I went over it until it turned into abstract shapes. My artistic talent, like my musical talent and my literary talent, must remain cloaked for now.

The art teacher asked me what the abstract shapes represented and I said 'Desire'. I think she was quite impressed.

Diary of a Wimpy Vampire

Friday 11th February

2pm

We did cooking in Home Economics today, which is always boring for me because I don't eat. I only took the subject in my options because the alternative was Design and Technology and I've heard that includes smoothing down wooden poles on the lathe. Imagine if I tripped over and pierced my heart on one of those things! I'm surprised they even allow it.

We were supposed to be making spaghetti bolognese, and Mrs Molloy told me off for not draining the water before I added the tinned tomatoes. Why would I care? It's going straight in the bin anyway.

Later I told Chloe about how much I hate cooking, and she said she hates it too! We have so much in common we must be soulmates.

Chloe said that she doesn't care about cooking because she doesn't want to end up as a housewife. She wouldn't have to do any cooking if she was my wife. Or any housework at all if she didn't want to. All she would have to do is stand on a moonlit balcony wearing a flimsy white dress and offer her perfect white neck to me.

4pm

The headmaster has announced that there will be a special

Diary of a Wimpy Vampire

Valentine's postal service on Monday. I have just seventy-two hours to compose a message to write in my card to Chloe. Let's just say that my Maths textbook will go ignored this weekend!

SATURDAY 12TH FEBRUARY

This morning I went to the newsagents near the station and bought the biggest card they had. It's over fifty

centimetres high, and features a love heart and a border of red roses. I'm not sure why humans think that particular shape resembles the heart, as it doesn't look like one to me. Personally, I'd prefer the image of an actual pumping heart, like you'd see in Biology textbooks.

Anyway, I'm guessing that the card is the kind of thing that female humans find appealing. Now to compose an appropriate message...

Have a nice Valentine's Day. (Too weak.)

Sending you sincere wishes on this Valentine's Day. (Too formal.)

I've been watching you but you don't know. (Too creepy.)

Roses are red, violets are blue, I've waited a century for a girl like you. (Too corny.)

I've searched through the frozen mists of eternity for you. (Too vampirey.)

Yield to the forbidden music of my soul. (Way too vampirey.)

Dear Chloe, please can I sink my teeth into your neck and drink your blood? (One step at a time, Nigel.)

SUNDAY 13TH FEBRUARY

I have chosen the message for my card...

In eternal admiration, love from ?

As you can see, it has a clever double meaning, because my admiration really is eternal, as I'm immortal.* I have practised writing the message ten times in fancy handwriting and now I shall put it in the card.

Diary of a Wimpy Vampire

Soon you shall join me in my world of darkness, frightened mortal lamb.

* Some pedants complain when this word is used to describe vampires, as we can be killed if you ram a stake through our hearts or lop our heads off. But I'm happy to use it because it sounds cool. Anyway, I'd like to see those pedants heal broken bones in a matter of minutes.

MONDAY 14TH FEBRUARY

A worrying development today.

Although my card was the biggest, Chloe got a total of three Valentine's cards! Three! I know she's beautiful, but I presumed nobody else would fancy her because she's a prefect.

How am I going to fend off two love rivals?

I was so worried I hardly noticed that I didn't get a single card myself. But just imagine the scene if I possessed the vampiric good looks that should be mine. A desk piled high with cards, every pair of female eyes in the room fixed on me, my dark hunter's eyes meeting Chloe's expectant gaze, and my voice burning with ancient desire as I proclaim my love for her.

Instead, I get one less card than flea-ridden Darren. I am truly a creature of the damned.

TUESDAY 15TH FEBRUARY

Though it annoyed me to do so, I sat on a table with the girls from the popular gang in Maths to catch up on the Valentine's gossip. Based on their information, I've compiled a table of suspected love rivals:

Name	Likelihood	Threat level
Wayne Cross	Very high – told Peter Ellen he fancied her, and Peter told Samantha Jackson.	Low – he has bad teeth and even more spots than me, and is from a rougher area of town than Chloe, so there would be a class barrier like in *Wuthering Heights* (which we're doing in English).
Gary Martin	High – Walked her home once.	Low – he has rich parents but attends lunchtime chess club and smells of disinfectant.

Diary of a Wimpy Vampire

Name	Likelihood	Threat level
Craig Hopper	High – posted eight cards in total.	Medium – he is the best-looking boy in our year, but he says he's a ladies' man and doesn't want to commit himself to one woman.
Sanjay Bhatti	Unknown.	High – his parents live on the same street as hers, so he would have ample opportunity to make a move.
Darren Riley	Unlikely – cannot afford card.	Moderate – although girls don't usually fancy him because he has fleas, Chloe is very caring and feels pity for social outcasts.
John the Goth	Unknown – too quiet.	Low – too quiet.

I feel slightly better about the situation now I've completed my table. Although there are some potential threats out there, I am convinced Chloe will be mine if I act fast.

WEDNESDAY 16TH FEBRUARY

Jay from the tough gang charged me 50p just to walk past him in the corridor this afternoon. It was so humiliating. I should be striking fear into the hearts of mortals, not unwillingly contributing to their next pair of trainers.

I attempted to talk to Chloe about Valentine's cards in the library at lunchtime to see if she'd worked out that I sent the best one. I tried to steer the conversation round to the topic by asking her if she'd had a good week and if anything unusual had happened. She wasn't taking the bait, so in the end I had to come right out and ask her if she got any cards. She said no, and then looked down at her book, blushing a deep red. Her delectable blood filled her cheeks and in my head it sounded like stormy waves crashing on a beach. Needless to say, my fangs extended and I had to clamp my mouth shut. We stayed in this awkward stalemate for the rest of lunch, with her staring down at her textbook and me drawing on every ounce of self-restraint to prevent myself from tucking into her neck in front of everyone.

It was actually quite a relief when she had to go to Business Studies.

Diary of a Wimpy Vampire

THURSDAY 17TH FEBRUARY

There's been a vampire attack right here in town! I'm so angry with Mum and Dad, the greedy pigs! Why can't they hold back from their blood-drinking urges?

The worst thing is, they wouldn't even own up to it. I only found out because Mr Talbot the school caretaker was looking a bit pale and I asked him about his health. He said he'd collapsed on the way back from the pub at the weekend and blacked out for a couple of hours. Although his wife didn't believe him, he said that he'd only drank two lagers. He had to stay in bed for a couple of days, but just as he was about to see a doctor, he started to feel better again. He kept scratching his neck, and when I looked closely, I saw a couple of telltale fang marks on it.

I confronted Mum and Dad about their behaviour as soon as I

got home, but they insisted that they'd only been feeding in towns over twenty miles away, which was our agreement. I don't know why they insist on lying to me. It's obvious that they were too thirsty to wait until they were further away, and fed off poor old Mr Talbot instead. So just because they couldn't contain their urges, they risked exposing our identity and forcing us to flee this town, meaning that I would never see my dear Chloe again. In other words, they put their own stupid thirst above my first ever chance of happiness! How can I trust them again?

FRIDAY 18TH FEBRUARY

8:30AM

We don't have to go to school today because it's snowing. My sister ran into my room at six to announce this like it was the most exciting thing that had ever happened. She must have opened her curtains to see snow a million times by now, but it still makes her giddy with excitement.

She's so stupid that I wonder if she even knows she's been alive for almost a century. Perhaps she has no sense of time passing at all, like a goldfish swimming around a bowl.

When you're as dense as my sister, living forever is a breeze. But when you're as sensitive and intelligent as me, it's not easy. Not that I expect anyone to understand.

From the excited laughter I can hear outside my window,

Diary of a Wimpy Vampire

I'm guessing that everyone else shares my sister's idiotic joy that a snow day should occur just before the half-term break. All it means to me is that I have to wait ten long days before I see my darling Chloe again.

10AM

My sister has built a snowpire using carrots for fangs and a bin bag for a cape. I thought my parents would tell her off for exposing our identity, but they seemed to think it was the most adorable thing they'd ever seen. As ever, it's one rule for me, and one rule for my sister.

Dad said it was the only vampire he'd ever seen that really would be destroyed by sunlight and then he laughed at his own stupid joke.

1PM

I am so bored I am now watching *Sesame Street*. I have to say, I find the character of The Count somewhat offensive. He has a huge nose, pointy ears and a ridiculous Eastern European accent. They wouldn't get away with doing this about any other minority group.

Diary of a Wimpy Vampire

If they insist on showing all the usual clichéd stuff like castles and bats, they could at least balance it out by showing the positive side of vampirism as well, like our unnatural beauty and strength.

Plus, if they're going to show a vampire with a rank of nobility, why does it always have to be a count? They would find that vampires have also been archdukes, barons, knights, margraves, viscounts and kings if they spent more time researching and less time making up silly jokes about us counting things.

SATURDAY 19TH FEBRUARY

7AM

Mum and Dad are out hunting, and I'm expecting a bumper harvest of blood. They always get loads when it's snowing, as it makes humans much easier to trap and mesmerize.

I can't wait to see what kind they bring back. If you're a human and you're reading this, you might think it must be boring for me to drink blood all the time. But I think it must be boring to eat food all the time.

There are so many different flavours and textures of blood that it never feels like you're having the same thing over and over again. Sometimes, if it's a special occasion such as a transformation day, we even have a three-course meal, starting with a glass of something light and thin like type A-, tucking into hot bowls of thick, nourishing type B+, and finishing with a sweet dessert blood from someone with high blood-sugar levels.

5PM

Good news! Mum and Dad have brought back loads of lovely type O-. And the best thing is, they've harvested so many flasks of it they couldn't even fit them in the fridge, and they've let me take some up to my room for a feast!

7PM

Having a good time getting through the blood. Starting to feel a bit stuffed, but it would be a shame to waste all this lovely stuff. I imagine this is what humans feel like on Christmas day.

9PM

Still getting through the flasks. Have decided to teach myself dancing.

Diary of a Wimpy Vampire

10PM

Why won't Mum and Dad admit they attacked the caretaker? Why do they insist on lying to me? What else are they hiding from me?

11PM

My parents are alright really. I shouldn't be so suspicious of them. They're not so bad when it comes down to it.

12AM

Why doesn't Chloe love me? Nothing ever goes right in my life. What does anything even mean?

1AM

Feeling ill now.

SUNDAY 20TH FEBRUARY

I would like to apologize for the haphazard nature of yesterday's entries. When vampires drink too much blood, it produces a state that is similar to drunkenness in humans.

   I have been lying in bed with a thumping headache today. It's at times like this that I wish vampires could sleep.

Diary of a Wimpy Vampire

In future, I will be more careful about how much blood I consume. It's said that if vampires regularly drink too much, they become bloodoholics. You used to hear about drifter vampires who lived in a constant state of thirst, becoming too slow and clumsy to hunt, and leading a miserable existence of sneaking into blood banks through windows. By the time they were caught and destroyed by irate mobs, they were usually relieved.

MONDAY 21st FEBRUARY

I am feeling better today and have decided to limit myself to three flasks of blood a night.

I went down to the shopping precinct today and sat on a bench. I noticed that a nearby group of older teenagers were smoking, so I asked them to stop but they refused. I can't believe how anti-social they were. Don't they know they could kill someone with those things? Obviously, they couldn't kill me with them, but they could have damaged the lungs of a human. What if my precious Chloe had been walking past?

I know I wouldn't like it if someone went out in public and did something harmful to me, like throwing holy water and garlic everywhere. If I had vampire speed, I would have snatched their cigarettes and thrown them away in a rapid blur of motion. As it was, I had to make do with tutting and shaking my head, but I think I made my point.

Diary of a Wimpy Vampire

TUESDAY 22ND FEBRUARY

10AM

Dad told me off this morning for hogging the bathroom when I brush my teeth. He said that vampires don't even need to do it, as our teeth can't decay. That may be true, but I still need to keep my breath minty fresh. After my experience with the deodorant, I'm not taking any chances.

1AM

If you think half term can be boring, you should try going without sleep for the whole thing.

There's nothing to watch on TV and I'm stuck on an end-of-level boss in my current PlayStation game. Welcome to the shadowy, fiendish realm of the undead. I don't think.

I will now try and count up to 10,000 just to pass the time.

2AM

I got as far as 148 before I realized how much I resembled The Count from Sesame Street. I refuse to conform to these vicious stereotypes.

Diary of a Wimpy Vampire

WEDNESDAY 23RD FEBRUARY

8AM

How can it only be Wednesday? This half-term holiday has already felt longer than most summer holidays. What if Chloe has moved again to a different town? What if another boy has stolen her from me while I languish here? What if she's dead? And I don't mean dead in a cool way like me, but actually a dead body.

I must stop torturing myself with these possibilities.

7PM

I tried to shave my upper lip tonight because I've heard that it makes a moustache grow quicker so you look older.

I kept cutting my lip and having to wait for it to heal, so I got bored. I don't really want a moustache anyway, because Dad has one, and it's not cool to look like a miniature version of your parents. In the nineties I had a human friend whose dad used to make the entire family wear matching orange tracksuits. He said it would make it easier for them to find each other in the event of a fire, although why he chose such easily flammable items of clothing for this, I have no idea.

1AM

Why has this forbidden desire taken over my life? Why

did I have to fall in love with a mortal? I am the predator stalking over moonlit hillsides, and she is the sheep for whom I burn with desire.

That last bit came out wrong.

THURSDAY 24TH FEBRUARY

I think something very odd happened to me today, but I'm not sure if I was imagining it. I was walking down the road to the shopping precinct when a coach full of old people drove past. I caught the eyes of one of the old ladies in it, and I thought for a second that she was Caroline Blake, a girl I used to fancy in the fifties. As the coach drove away, I tried to work out if it was possible. If she was fifteen in the early fifties, then I suppose she could be in her seventies now.

I've got so used to moving around that I forget humans get older. Since I knew Caroline, she's probably got married, had kids, had grandkids, bought a house, moved house, got a job, lost a job, got another job, got ill, got better and gone grey. And what have I done in all this time? Nothing.

Even my heroic attempt to memorize all the statistics on Supercars Top Trumps seems trivial and pointless in this light.

Friday 25th February

The experience that I might or might not have had yesterday has made me realize I have to declare my love to Chloe soon. I can't let her slip away and watch her go past in a coachload of old folk in the 2070s. Today I shall reveal that I'm immortal and announce my everlasting love for her.

On second thoughts, I might start by asking her to come to the cinema with me.

SATURDAY 26TH FEBRUARY

Tomorrow my sister and I will celebrate our transformation day, which is the vampire equivalent of a birthday.

It's celebrated because we're supposed to believe that the day you became a vampire is more important than the day you were born as a human.

We were both transformed in East London on 27th February 1927. Mum and Dad fed on our necks until we were weak, and then mixed vampire blood into our veins. A few moments later we effectively 'died' and then came back to life as vampires. A transformation isn't always a pleasant thing to watch, but then again neither is human childbirth if we're being honest.

My parents took us from the crowded orphanage where we lived to a comfortable town house, so they've got nothing to feel guilty about. But I still find it arrogant of them to assume that we want to celebrate the end of our human lives. They've been vampires for so long now that all their human memories have gone, but every now and then I still get an echo of how it felt to enjoy a satisfying roast dinner or drift off to sleep with the rain falling on the window.

I haven't forgotten the actual day I was born on, either. It was 14th May 1911. This is how I know I'm nearly 100 years old.

Diary of a Wimpy Vampire

Note to self: One way or another, I must win Chloe's heart before my 100th birthday. I can't turn 100 without having had a girlfriend. That would just be tragic.

SUNDAY 27TH FEBRUARY

My sister came bounding into my room at six this morning to remind me about our transformation day. I don't know why it still thrills her so much. I admit I used to find it exciting, but after a while it begins to serve as a depressing reminder of how long you've been undead, and how little you've achieved in that time.

I was quite happy lying in bed and thinking about Chloe, but my sister insisted on dragging me downstairs. For breakfast Mum took a flask of type AB+ out of the fridge that she's been saving for a special occasion.

After we drank it, we opened our presents. I got a Fabergé Egg, some original Leonardo da Vinci sketches and a smoking jacket that once belonged to Lord Byron. I would have preferred Guitar Hero, but I made an effort to pretend that I got what I wanted. Mum and Dad are being suspiciously nice to me at the moment. They must be trying to win back my trust after I found out about their attack on the caretaker.

My sister got a Stradivari violin, a crystal skull and a ballgown that once belonged to the young Marie Antoinette. She seemed overjoyed with her presents, although I can't imagine what use she'll make of them. You can bet that skull will be broken this time next week.

I'm back at school tomorrow, and I've promised myself that I'll ask Chloe to come on a date with me.

MONDAY 28TH FEBRUARY

I went back to school today, and am happy to report that cruel fate has not yet snatched Chloe from me. I had a good chat with her in the library at lunchtime, although I didn't ask her to come on a date with me as I'd promised myself. I think I spent too long talking to her about the questions on fish farming we had to do for Science. It wasn't a very seductive topic, in retrospect.

I tried to think of something I did in the holidays to tell her about, but the only things I could thing of were the time I drank too much blood and my transformation day, and that side of my life must remain cloaked for now.

Diary of a Wimpy Vampire

But soon you shall know the truth, flower of the
mortal realm.

TUESDAY 1ST MARCH

10AM

Craig was giving everyone a pinch and a thump this
morning, saying 'Pinch, punch, first of the month'. I didn't
mind because I don't feel pain, but Wayne looked rather
angry.

1PM

Craig has given Susan from our class (who looks like a
troll) a note saying that he fancies her. Except he hasn't
really, because the note was a fake written by Wayne to
get revenge, and now Craig has found out that there will
be a fight in the playing fields after school. Chloe and I had
a chat about how childish all of this behaviour is. We have
chosen to attend the fight nonetheless.

7PM

The fight was a disappointment to say the very least. We
all stood around in a circle chanting the word 'fight' and
then Craig and Wayne pushed each other a bit until Mr
Morris came along and broke it up.

It's times like this when I wish there were still a few

vampires around to give us some proper entertainment. Although all vampires would face permanent exclusion if they killed one of their own kind, they could formally challenge each other to duels. These duels were epic physical struggles of vampire martial arts that often went on for days and crossed several continents. Which sounds more entertaining than a couple of teenagers shoving each other until a teacher turns up.

After the non-fight, I walked Chloe home for the first time. She lives on Heywood Lane, the poshest road in Stockfield, as her dad works in insurance. We could afford to live there if we wanted, but Dad won't spend money on anything because he says it will draw attention to us. Yet he lets Mum hang her ancient ballgowns and corsets on the washing line where everyone can see them. Could he be any more of a hypocrite?

If you ask me, we're much more likely to draw attention to ourselves by living in a semi-detached house. If someone with better hearing than Mr Perkins ever moves in next door, they might wonder why we stay awake all night every night.

WEDNESDAY 2ND MARCH

We had a lesson about food chains in Science this morning, and it was one of those occasions where I have to keep quiet even though I know the teacher is wrong. Mrs Jones claimed that humans are 'apex predators' because they reside at the top of their food chain. I know this is nonsense because vampires feed on them, so we're the ones who really sit at the top of the food chain. But I managed to keep quiet as she spewed out the misinformation.

I'm still off PE on Wednesday afternoons on account of my imaginary bad back. Whenever I walk past Mr Jenkins he really glares at me to see if I'm ill. I know he can't wait for me to go back to his stupid lessons so he can find some new way of humiliating me.

Usually, when I'm feeling angry about a human, I just remind myself that they'll get old and die one day, and then I begin to feel sorry for them. Not in the case of Mr Jenkins, though. I can feel no pity whatsoever for that fiend.

THURSDAY 3RD MARCH

We had an assembly about global warming today.
Apparently, the polar ice caps are melting, and everywhere
will be underwater soon. Mrs Maguire kept going on
about how we mustn't leave our TVs on standby to save
the planet. Why should she care? She'll be dead by then.
How does she think I feel? I'm immortal, and I'll be around
to see the whole stupid thing. And the worst thing is,
I hate swimming.

I wouldn't mind spending eternity on a watery planet
with Chloe, though. We could live on a mountain together,
and feed on the people swimming past. It would be
really romantic.

Diary of a Wimpy Vampire

This afternoon we had fire alarm practice, and Craig sent all the younger pupils into a frenzy by pretending it was a real fire. I got told off by Mr Morris for not being quick enough, but I didn't care. A real fire wouldn't do me any lasting damage anyway, unless somebody accidentally chopped my head off in the panic.

Friday 4th March

I spent today avoiding Craig because he was showing off his new camera phone and I'm under strict instructions to stay away from cameras.

The idea that vampires don't show up in photographs is just another silly myth, of course. But like many of these misconceptions, it has a basis in truth. Vampires have to stay out of photographs because they make it obvious that we don't age. The last thing you want is for someone to produce a photo of you looking exactly the same twenty years ago.

This is more of a problem for Mum and Dad, as their vampire beauty draws attention even if they're in the very background of a shot. Whereas I'm so instantly forgettable you could live next door to me for years without noticing that I've always been fifteen.

Overall, we've been quite good at avoiding photos over the years, but every day it gets harder to duck out of the way of digital cameras, speed cameras and CCTV. The only bright side is that our mantelpiece isn't cluttered with embarrassing childhood snaps.

SATURDAY 5TH MARCH

Mum is upset with Dad because he never uses the mobile phone she bought him. I told her not to buy it, as he always mistrusts new technology. He wouldn't even buy us a washing machine until about twenty years after everyone else had one because he thought it would shrink his capes.

Mum says that she just wants to be able to ring him and make sure that he's safe, but I don't know what she thinks is going to happen to him. Unless he falls heart-first onto an upright wooden stake, I doubt he'll be in too much danger.

An update regarding the stupidity of my sister: She has announced that she no longer wishes to kill animals for their blood, and will now only consume the blood of animals that have died by accident. Again, she has said she wants to do this on 'ethical grounds'.

For once, my parents drew a line at her idiocy and refused to cave in.

They explained that the blood of dead animals would be stale and make her poorly. And how did she react to this sensible advice? By kicking a hole in the kitchen door and stomping off to her room, of course.

I have to say I'm surprised that they finally put their foot down with her. I expected them to indulge her until it got to the point where she refused to drink anything except the sap of plants.

SUNDAY 6TH MARCH

12PM

I have come up with a new plan to make Chloe fancy me. I shall work out at the gym until I force my body to unleash its vampire strength. I'm off to the leisure centre right now to put my scheme into action.

5PM

Well, that was a massive waste of time. When I got to the gym, I put the weights machine on the highest setting and settled down for a gruelling workout. After a couple of fruitless attempts to move the bars I was ready to abandon my plan and go home. Unfortunately, an assistant who looked like the missing link between Neanderthal man and PE teacher stood behind the machine and offered to 'spot' me. He did this by decreasing the load one level at a time and shouting 'You can do it!'

He was wrong. I couldn't do it. Even when the machine was on the lowest setting, I couldn't do it. I thanked Missing Link for his help and made my shameful exit. Once again, I have my uncooperative body to blame for a humiliating day.

Monday 7th March

Today we had dental checks in the sports hall. I tried to get out of mine by showing the nurse how strong my teeth were, but she wasn't letting anyone off. I think they're trying to catch all the kids whose parents let them have fizzy drinks and sweets.

I was really fretting that my fangs would shame me by extending while the dentist was examining my teeth. To keep them under control, I took a long sniff of the bins they throw the lunch leftovers in, and made sure I was as far away as possible in the queue from Chloe.

In the end, it wasn't a problem. The dentist said

my teeth were the strongest and whitest he'd ever seen, although you could tell he was confused by how cold I was.

He then spent about half an hour looking at Wayne's mouth and tutting. I'm glad I don't have crisps and fizzy drinks every break like him. Say what you like about human blood, but at least it's natural. What comes out of the vein goes straight down my throat with no additives, colourings or preservatives. I'm quite a health buff when I think about it.

TUESDAY 8TH MARCH

12:20PM

Chloe is reading an anthology of Romantic poetry, which contains some by a vampire Dad used to be friends with called Lord Byron. If only she would put the book down and realize that there's someone every bit as brooding and dangerous as Byron right in front of her. And I can also write powerful poetry, just like him.

Why can't Chloe see that I'm just her type?

9PM

Craig has a pair of Nike trainers that are black with a black swoosh, so he can get away with wearing them as school shoes. Craig always gets loads of cool stuff because his parents are divorced.

Tonight I asked Dad if I could have a pair, and he said

no. I can't believe how tight he is considering his wealth. He always says that we'll draw too much attention to ourselves if we spend lots of money. What he fails to understand is that in this day and age, buying expensive trainers is normal. It's wearing scuffed old school shoes that's abnormal now. Social services would take me away if they saw the rags I'm forced to wear.

If he doesn't buy me some cooler clothes soon, I'll get teased for having fleas like Darren and nobody will ever sit next to me again.

Wednesday 9th March

Everyone was sniggering and looking at me in expectation as I sat down in Maths this morning. It took me a while to realize that Craig had put a drawing pin on my chair. I had to pretend it hurt just to get them to stop looking at me and move on to the next victim.

In the library at lunchtime, Chloe asked me what my political views were, but I couldn't think of any. I remember Mr Morris once saying that vampires are capitalists or capitalists are vampires or something, so I said I was a capitalist. Chloe didn't seem very impressed. I think I need to find a more interesting 'ist'.

On TV tonight there was a murder mystery set in the twenties, but they didn't get many details right. The vast majority of us didn't ponce around in country houses

Diary of a Wimpy Vampire

waiting to be murdered by butlers, we just got on with our lives. Although there was less technology, life wasn't that different really. Declaring your love to a girl is just as difficult whether you do it by hand-written letter or email, and my sister is just as annoying whether she's learning the Charleston or hip-hop dancing.

I've just had a strange thought. The twenties will be coming back round again soon! Mum and Dad must be used to this kind of thing now, but I'm not even 100 yet, so it's all still a novelty to me.

THURSDAY 10TH MARCH

8AM

Mum has washed my school shirt
with one of Dad's capes and
it's turned pink! I told her
that the red lining of his capes
would ruin everything, but she wouldn't listen.
She wanted me to wear one of Dad's shirts to
school, but they've all got ridiculous frilly bits.
I'm not going to school dressed as Duran Duran!

10AM

I made Mum drive me to the clothes shop to
get a shirt on the way to school, and we had to bang on

the door to make them open it early. Mum moaned the whole time, but this is what she gets for putting my school clothes in with Dad's outlandish garb.

9PM

I sat next to Chloe in Art today and she had a sniffle. It's weird, but if my sister had a sniffle it would drive me over the edge. Yet when Chloe has one it sounds like a gentle breeze blowing through rose petals. I am truly beginning to understand the power of love.

At lunchtime, Wayne was going round with a sponsorship form for a fun run he's doing for endangered species. I kept out of his way so I didn't have to pledge anything. Why should I? Vampires are an endangered species, but nobody ever runs for us. They run *from* us, but that's not the same.

4AM

They never put anything decent on TV at this time. It's really unfair on shift workers and the undead. I suppose I should be grateful that they show anything at all during the night. Believe it or not, it was only a few years ago that they used to play the national anthem and tell you to go to bed before midnight. And a few years before that, there was no TV at all. No wonder so many vampires got up to mischief in the old days. They had nothing else to do!

Diary of a Wimpy Vampire

FRIDAY 11TH MARCH

Craig was told off by the headmaster for wearing his cool trainers today. You should have heard him moaning about it. All they said was that he had to wear school shoes on Monday or he'd get detention.

In the old days, they used to whack you with a cane or leather strap if you did the slightest thing wrong. I was once hit with a slipper just for walking too fast in the corridor. Not that Dad had any sympathy when I told him. He just went on about the time he was tortured on a rack for whistling during longbow practice. Whatever I tell him, he always has to try and top it.

SATURDAY 12TH MARCH

I was bored tonight so I went for a walk in the graveyard. I realize that makes me sound like a vampire cliché, but it's the only place where I can go to be quiet and relax on a Saturday night. Everywhere else is full of people fighting and being sick on each other.

As I lurked moodily around the tombs, I heard human voices in the distance. I followed them and realized that John, Si and Brian had taken it upon themselves to come to the graveyard too. I thought I'd scare them for a joke, so I rushed out from behind a grave.

They let out shrieks of fear and dashed towards the exit, which was very cowardly for people who claim to be hardcore horror fanatics. I was surprised to see them fleeing so fast, especially Brian, who certainly never moves like that on sports day. They made such a speedy exit that I didn't get the chance to reveal that it was only me.

The weird thing was, as I raced after them to explain that it was all a prank, it sort of stopped being one. I really did feel like pouncing on them and drinking their blood.

I think the moral of this episode is that if you're going to pretend to be a blood-drinking supernatural being, make sure you're not actually a blood-drinking supernatural being, or you could get carried away.

SUNDAY 13TH MARCH

6PM

We all went out for a family hike again today. As usual,

87

Diary of a Wimpy Vampire

Dad drove his Volvo well over the speed limit. He says that his supernatural vampire speed makes it hard for him to drive as slowly as a human, but I think this is just an excuse. He needs to be careful. He could end up in prison for speeding and then I'd be from a broken home like Darren.

I've never understood why Dad buys Volvos. He says they've got strong frames which don't buckle in crashes, but why should we care? We could drive off the edge of a cliff and land in a fireball and we'd all be fine again after ten minutes. Still, at least it stops him from buying a sports car and becoming a complete embarrassment.

9PM

I've found out what 'ist' I am – an anarchist! I saw a politician on TV tonight saying that if we don't spend more on policing, society will break down into lawless anarchy and blood will run in the streets. Sounds brilliant!

MONDAY 14TH MARCH

Craig wore his normal school shoes again today, but as a protest he has written his persuasive writing essay for English about how we shouldn't have any school uniform at all. I suppose I should agree now that I'm an anarchist.

When I told Chloe, she said he'd been very mature to use his essay as a protest rather than simply writing it about capital punishment like the teacher suggested. I agreed with her wholeheartedly, and hid my capital punishment essay under my folder.

I was worried that John, Si and Brian might have started the rumour that there are vampires in town following my misjudged prank on Saturday night. I need to be very careful not to fuel this kind of gossip given my parents' reckless attack on the school caretaker. Fortunately, my goth friends are far too stupid to have understood what was going on, and they've been boasting about how they banished a spectre from the graveyard instead. Now everyone is chanting the *Ghostbusters* theme at them and I have no sympathy.

TUESDAY 15TH MARCH

The English teacher liked Craig's essay so much she showed it to the headmaster in the staffroom.

The headmaster said that Craig had been very assertive to write an argument against the rules rather than simply breaking them. He said that he couldn't go as far as to abolish school uniform, but that as a gesture of goodwill, he would let us have a No Uniform Day on Friday if we all give a pound to charity.

Diary of a Wimpy Vampire

Everyone is looking forward to it except for Darren, who only owns his uniform and PE kit, and is so poor that he should be receiving charity money rather than donating it. At first I was pleased about Craig's moral victory, but I soon began to worry that none of my clothes are cool enough.

When I got home I had to go on at Mum and Dad for ages to get some money for new clothes. Dad said I could wear something from his wardrobe if I wanted. I told him it was No Uniform Day, not Halloween.

I even threatened to run away from home, but I've been saying this for over eighty years, so it doesn't have much effect now. In the end, they coughed up a measly forty pounds, which is barely enough to buy some trousers and a top. When I mentioned to mum that I was going to spend it in the goth shop in the precinct, she even asked me to get her some candles out of the same money! They need to understand that prices have gone up since the nineteenth century.

Diary of a Wimpy Vampire

WEDNESDAY 16TH MARCH

Today I found out that my parents have attacked another person here in town! I was in the goth shop, and I heard one of the assistants talking about how he'd been ill for a couple of days and was still feeling 'seriously weak'. I went to the till and got a good look at his neck. Sure

enough, there were a couple of holes right over the jugular.

When I told Mum and Dad about it, they said I must have made a mistake and that the holes were probably just a novelty tattoo, but I know vampire bite marks when I see them. Either they're liars, or they're getting so overcome by their desires that they don't even know they're doing it any more.

If they must feed on someone in town, they could hardly pick a worse victim that the assistant from the goth store. If a normal human remembers something about the experience afterwards, they'll assume they're having flashbacks to a nightmare. But as goths believe in vampires, they'll have no problem accepting it and blabbing to their friends about how there's a coven in town. Before

Diary of a Wimpy Vampire

we know it, we'll have a huge queue of idiots in top hats, mesh shirts and winkle pickers banging on our front door and begging to be transformed.

Needless to say, we'd have to move to another town, and I'd be forced to leave my soulmate Chloe behind forever. It would be utterly unbearable.

I told Mum and Dad very firmly to stop snacking on local people willy-nilly, and slammed the door to emphasize my point.

THURSDAY 17TH MARCH

1PM

According to Craig, the kids from the toughest school in town are coming round after school to steal our phones and snog the best-looking girls. Everyone is really scared. I hope they don't take Chloe.

7PM

Nothing happened after school. Craig was just winding us all up. Everyone pretended that they didn't fall for it, but they did really. I have to admit, even I got swept along in the wave of hysteria.

Why am I so pathetic? I'm supposed to be an ancient and deadly creature of the night. Why was I getting worried about a bunch of kids who wear tracksuits and baseball caps?

Diary of a Wimpy Vampire

10PM

I am refusing to speak to Mum and Dad until they own up to
the attacks on the caretaker and the goth shop assistant.
How can they expect me to be open with them when they
string out such blatant lies?

The most infuriating thing about all of this is that I only
found out about these attacks by chance, so I dread to
think how many others they've carried out and kept hidden
from me. And if they find it so easy to deceive me on this
matter, what else are they keeping me in the dark about?

I know I sound paranoid, but this is what I've been
driven to.

2AM

Mum and Dad wouldn't let me have any blood unless I
started speaking to them again. I was thirsty, so I had
to give in to their demands, but I told them I will be
treating everything they say from now on with the
utmost suspicion.

FRIDAY 18TH MARCH

I wore my new black trousers and shirt from the goth shop
to No Uniform Day. I looked quite cool, but my scuffed old
shoes let my outfit down.

Chloe looked like a bit of a goth herself in a black t-shirt
and a long black skirt, which I took as further proof that

Diary of a Wimpy Vampire

I'm just her type, although she doesn't quite realize it yet.

Craig wore an expensive pair of white air-cushioned trainers rather than the ones that started the whole uniform controversy in the first place. Surprise of the day, though, was Darren, who wore a tracksuit bearing a proper brand name rather than the word 'sport'.

When I commented on this curious turn of events to Chloe, she confessed that the tracksuit actually belonged to her father, and that she'd secretly lent it to Darren so he wouldn't get teased. She is so caring and selfless. From now on I will try to think more about the needs of others rather than my own. That way she'll be more likely to let me drink her blood.

SATURDAY 19TH MARCH

This morning was rainy so I went for a walk in the park. I like going out in bad weather, because I don't feel the cold and I get the park to myself. I didn't quite get the relaxing stroll I was hoping for, though.

Diary of a Wimpy Vampire

As I entered the gates, I noticed several squirrels standing on their back legs and baring their teeth. I suppose it should have looked odd to me, but I'm used to this kind of thing. All animals hate me. Dogs growl at me, cats hiss and arch their backs, and I'm sure I've heard pigeons coo aggressively once or twice.

So I thought nothing when I saw a group of squirrels glaring at me as I went about my morning stroll. I wasn't really concentrating on them because I was thinking about Chloe, so I didn't notice when the nasty things surrounded me. They blocked the path ahead of me, and when I glanced behind me, I saw hundreds of them there too. Before I knew it, the vile creatures were jumping on me and scratching me with their tiny claws. As I ripped them off and threw them to the ground, more came forward. It was only when I ran out of the park that the foul vermin ceased their attack and returned to standing on their back legs and glaring.

I've heard of vampires being attacked by packs of wolves and snakes before, but never a load of mangy squirrels. Why does it always happen to me?

Diary of a Wimpy Vampire

SUNDAY 20TH MARCH

2PM

I didn't want to go outside again after yesterday's attack.
I don't know if I'm being paranoid, but I think word has
got round the animal kingdom that there's a vampire who
is too weak to fight back, and now they can all get their
revenge on my kind.

If you believe the stories, they've got plenty to get
revenge for. Dad once told me that a vampire sneaked on
to Noah's ark and chomped his way through hundreds of
now extinct species including the seven-headed snake and
the multicoloured panda. I used to believe Dad's stories but
now I think they're to be taken with a pinch of salt.

He also says that some vampires could mesmerize animals
such as dogs and cats and use them to attack enemies. I'm
not convinced that it ever really happened, but I know
that many dogs and cats were accused of consorting with
the undead and banished from towns in the great vampire
purges of the nineteenth century, so they've still got good
reason to hold a grudge.

9PM

My parents want me to play the piano for them but I don't
feel like doing anything for those liars. I used to quite enjoy
family music nights, but I don't often find myself in the

mood any more. And my dad always makes the same joke of saying, 'The children of the night, what music they make', in the style of Bela Lugosi from the old film of *Dracula*.

I'll stick to my PlayStation, thank you very much.

Monday 21st March

Craig lent me a new game today where you have to shoot zombies. It's rated '18' so Dad wouldn't let me buy it, even though I'm more than five times that age. It was quite a spooky game with atmospheric music, although it spoils the effect if you know that zombies couldn't do much harm to you even if they were real. I'd like to see one of that shambolic lot try and ram a stake through my heart.

I glanced in my sister's room this evening and caught her acting out a vampire scene with her Ken and Barbie dolls. She'd fashioned a cape for Ken out of a sweet wrapper and

97

Diary of a Wimpy Vampire

a couple of fangs using the ends of cocktail sticks, and she was making him chase after Barbie and feed on her neck. I watched her for ages before she spotted me. When she did, she got angry and slammed the door so hard it came off its hinges, so Mum and Dad made me fix it as a punishment.

I can't believe Mum and Dad punished me for something she did wrong! I would have complained if I felt I was dealing with rational and intelligent beings.

TUESDAY 22ND MARCH

We're having a Parents' Evening on Thursday and I'm dreading it. I know Mum and Dad will do something embarrassing. I think I'll ask them to sign the form to say they're staying away like Darren's mum does.

I gave Craig his zombie game back today as I've already completed it on hard mode. He was very impressed by how quickly I did it, and it made me wonder if I do have vampire powers after all, but only for computer games. I'm sure the extra eight hours' gaming time a night I get because I don't sleep has something to do with it, though.

We're supposed to analyse an article in a newspaper as our homework for Media Studies, but I forgot to buy one and the only papers I could find in Dad's study were ancient and yellow. I think it would confuse everyone if I did my homework about how *The Times* covered the sinking of the *Titanic*.

Diary of a Wimpy Vampire

WEDNESDAY 23RD MARCH

Luckily, the Media Studies teacher was off sick today, so it didn't matter that I hadn't done my homework. Even better, an old retired teacher called Mr Pilkington came in to cover, and he said that Media wasn't a proper subject and we were all wasting our time. He said that we didn't get taught properly these days and that he was going to give us an hour of real education for once. He then spent the lesson asking us about the British Empire. I was the only one who knew the answers, because we used to do all that stuff in school fifty years ago. Mr Pilkington said that I was the only true patriot in the class and I felt really proud. But then I got worried that I would get beaten up for being a swot, so I shut up.

I am totally dreading Parents' Evening tomorrow. I hope Chloe doesn't see us and realize what a family of freaks I'm from.

THURSDAY 24TH MARCH

Mum and Dad came to Parents' Evening wearing really embarrassing clothes. Dad wore a velvet suit and frilly shirt from the nineteenth century, and Mum wore a ballgown from pre-revolutionary France. For all the attempts at blending in they made, they might as well have turned up in a pumpkin carriage drawn by bats.

On the other hand, their supernatural allure did at least

Diary of a Wimpy Vampire

inspire my teachers to paper over some of the weaker aspects of my performance. Mr Wilson clearly took a shine to mum, and said that I applied myself very well in Maths, even though I got 11 out of 20 on the last test, and that was only because I'd done it before. Mr Morris said that my work in History was excellent, even if I sometimes embellished it with imaginary details about what life was like in the early twentieth century. Even Mrs Bowles said I was a joy to have around in cookery class. A joy to have around? I spend every lesson on the verge of throwing up into one of the bins as the food smells assault my nostrils. I couldn't be less of a joy to have around if I dragged my nails down the blackboard for the entire hour.

Diary of a Wimpy Vampire

I made a big effort to keep Mum and Dad away from
the gym where Mr Jenkins and the PE staff were grunting
through their meetings. The last thing I need is for Dad
to let it slip that I'm not really ill, and put me back at
the mercy of that torturer. As we were leaving, I saw Mr
Jenkins standing on the gym fire escape and staring at us
with great interest, so I herded them quickly away.

I'd forgotten about the hypnotic effect Mum and Dad
have on humans. Maybe I should introduce them to Chloe,
and see if their mesmeric attraction extends to me
by association.

FRIDAY 25TH MARCH

We were watching a DVD called *Life During Wartime* in
History today, and guess who turned up in it?

I did! And so did the rest of my family!

There was an archive
clip showing how children
had to go and live in the
countryside during the
Second World War, and
you could clearly make us
out in the corner of the
frame. We're usually good
at avoiding cameras, but we
must have missed that one.

Diary of a Wimpy Vampire

I hope nobody spots this and works out we're immortal. We'll end up getting driven out of our home by irate townsfolk. Plus, I still owe a considerable library fine in the last town we lived in, and I wouldn't want that to catch up with me.

It didn't look like anyone in the class noticed, though I couldn't help but wonder if I saw a slight look of confusion on Chloe's face. Is she beginning to suspect my true nature?

Step into my dark web of forbidden desire, Chloe darling...

Saturday 26th March

1 pm

I have bought a book called *The Secrets of Success with Women*. It must contain some very big secrets as the man on the cover has terrible hair and looks really sleazy. The techniques must be powerful indeed if they helped him get a girlfriend.

6 pm

I have finished the book now, but it didn't contain any secrets. It just said that you have to make eye contact, smile a lot and touch women's arms when you talk to them. I've heard this kind of advice bandied about for over eight decades now, and it's easier said than done. Also, the author made several stupid generalizations about dating in the past, a subject that he can't possibly know about. He said that it's harder to find girls now than it was in the sixties, the age of 'free love'. Well I lived through the sixties and, take it from me, it was just as impossible to approach girls back then. I wish someone had told me where all this free love was going on.

SUNDAY 27TH MARCH

My parents announced that we'd be going on a family hike today, and I foolishly agreed to join them. They took it upon themselves to dash up a rocky slope and I attempted to follow. I misplaced my footing, fell hundreds of feet down and broke my arm. It was really annoying and took almost five minutes to heal.

Obviously, as a vampire, I can't really be harmed unless someone chops my head off or rams a stake into my heart, but I can still get temporarily injured. I was hit by a car in the eighties, and I broke so many bones it took me almost twenty minutes to recover. I was inside an ambulance by then, and I had to wait until it stopped at the lights to run away. The whole situation was incredibly embarrassing, and it certainly made me think twice about crossing the road without looking.

At least I've never had a really serious accident, though. They say that Roderick of Colchester lost all his limbs in the

103

Diary of a Wimpy Vampire

Battle of Balaclava, and it took a week for his severed arms and legs to crawl their way across the battlefield and reattach themselves. It must have been a real hassle.

On the way back to the car we passed a group of ramblers who were really staring at us. I wish Dad wouldn't wear his cape when we go hiking.

MONDAY 28TH MARCH

10AM

In assembly today, the headmaster revealed the destination of our year's school trip next week. It isn't very good news for me, as we're all going to the zoo!

As animals hate me, a place filled with them is unlikely to be a suitable destination. Why do I have to get all the bad things about being a vampire, but none of the good things? I hate my life.

Pretty much any other school trip would have been better for me. Unless 'Chessington World of Garlic, Crucifixes and Vampire Slayers' exists. But I know that if I stay behind, another boy will sit next to Chloe on the coach and chat her up. I simply have to go, and the animals are just going to have to put up with it.

6PM

We had a Drama lesson this afternoon and I was in a group with Si and Brian the goths.

We had to devise a short piece to perform for the rest of the class, and Si suggested that we do it about vampires. He came up with a really corny idea about us emerging from coffins in a graveyard and boasting about the women we were going to bite. It was really inaccurate, and most of it was stolen from the vampire TV show they watch, but I couldn't be bothered arguing so I went along with it.

We performed our piece to the group, and Si and Brian put on hammy Eastern European accents. What is it with these Eastern European accents everyone does when they pretend to be vampires? We're deadly immortals, not plumbers! In the days before the vampire purges, there were covens in places as far apart as New Orleans, Paris, Alaska, Stockholm and Santa Carla. Admittedly, there was a coven in Transylvania, but it was by no means the only one.

After our piece, the Drama teacher Mrs Stokes said that it was good overall, but that I didn't put in as much effort as Si and Brian!

Diary of a Wimpy Vampire

This is so humiliating. I know I make a less convincing vampire than my parents, but I didn't expect to make a less convincing vampire than a pair of smelly goths!

TUESDAY 29TH MARCH

Today I hung around with the tough gang and won some street cred. Bet you weren't expecting that, were you?

Jay and Baz from the tough gang were making everyone play a game called 'Mercy' where you have to link fingers with someone else, and then press forward with your wrists until the other person says 'mercy'. Jay grabbed me as I was on my way to the library and said I had to play. He expected that I would give up and scream for mercy in seconds like everyone else he had been terrorizing, but I didn't even wince as he bent my palms back. Unfortunately, I didn't have the strength to mount a counter-attack either, so we just stood there for a couple of minutes like we were holding hands. Eventually, Jay gave up and put his hands down, and Baz said that under the rules of Mercy, I was the winner.

Jay said I was 'alright' and 'not as bad as the other weirdos' and I gratefully accepted his compliment. Word of my astonishing victory soon travelled around the school, and in some versions of the story, I even made him beg for mercy. The stories made me sound really heroic and I hope they reached Chloe's ears.

WEDNESDAY 30TH MARCH

4PM

Mr Jenkins is getting on my case about my continuing absence from PE. He came to the library at lunchtime and harassed me. He asked me if I was coming to his lesson today, and I said I wasn't. He really boomed the question out, probably because he's never been into a library before and doesn't know you're supposed to be quiet. He then touched his hand to my forehead and admitted that I felt cold and unwell. Thank you vampire temperature for getting me out of another miserable PE afternoon!

Diary of a Wimpy Vampire

Mr Jenkins walked away, but he kept shooting suspicious glances back at me. You can tell he really hates me. If I ever have to attend another one of his lessons, it's going to be hell. I must think of a better long-term strategy to escape him.

2AM

Craig has lent me a new PlayStation game, but I didn't realize until I started playing that's it's about vampires. I've been playing it for a few hours now and I'm really bored. I'm worse than those people who drive home from work and immediately start playing driving games.

THURSDAY 31ST MARCH

1PM

I intended to take my usual seat next to Chloe in Art today. However, when I arrived I noticed that Wayne was already sitting there.

To make things worse, the only seat left was next to Darren, and it's common knowledge that you'll get fleas if you sit next to him. In the end I had to construct a flea-proof barrier between us with an easel.

I started to get worried about Wayne as I watched him sitting next to Chloe. Craig once said he was a 'smooth operator', whatever that means. But I doubt Chloe would have been impressed by his artistic skills. All he ever does is draw pictures of the tattoos he wants.

6PM

Mum and Dad have been out hunting, and they've brought back some lovely type O- blood. Dad tried to tell me about the man he'd siphoned it from, but I didn't want to know. It always puts me off to find out about the people blood comes from. This is another reason why I don't want Mum and Dad to hunt in this town. Nothing is more likely to make me lose my appetite than finding out the blood I'm drinking came from the sweaty bloke who works in the all-night garage.

Diary of a Wimpy Vampire

Dad's very old-fashioned about who he feeds on and he still follows the hierarchy of victims laid out by the Vampire Council, which commands that you snack on people according to their status in society. So, for example, you can feed on a labourer whenever you feel like it, you can only feed on a merchant when you're ravenous, and you can never feed on a king.

It's a really silly and old-fashioned system, which lists 'apothecaries', 'costermongers' and 'falconers', but not computer programmers and call centre workers, and it's based on the sort of class system that our beardy History teacher Mr Morris gets angry about.

In fact, the whole thing is completely unjust, and if I think about for a moment longer it's going to put me off this lovely blood that I'm currently enjoying.

Friday 1st April

Today I asked Chloe to be my girlfriend and she agreed. I sank my teeth into her neck and drank from her jugular in the library at lunchtime. She's agreed to join me as a vampire and she's moving in next week.

April fool!

All joking aside, I expect to be referring to Chloe as my girlfriend in all seriousness soon, as I'm planning to make a move on her during the school trip.

Diary of a Wimpy Vampire

SATURDAY 2ND APRIL

I went out for a walk around town this afternoon and I ended up going past the old people's home. I know I sometimes complain about how boring immortality can get, but I'm glad I'm not going to get old. They all looked so bored staring out of the window and nodding off.

Perhaps I should stop moaning about my life and appreciate the good things about it. I'll never go bald, I'll never get fat and I'll never develop a taste for chunky knitwear. Plus, I'll have a girlfriend for the very first time as soon as I get round to asking Chloe out. All in all, things are looking up.

SUNDAY 3RD APRIL

I went downstairs to get some blood from the fridge this afternoon and I saw Mum and Dad snogging on the sofa. It was so disgusting I nearly lost my appetite. You'd think that after 200 years of marriage, the spark would have gone, but they're still all over each other.

Diary of a Wimpy Vampire

I think part of the reason why Dad appreciates Mum so much is that he had so many problems with vampire women in the past.

One of his ex-girlfriends was a psychic vampire who kept getting in bad moods with him over rows they hadn't even had yet, and she even locked him out of the house for forgetting their next anniversary. In the end, she came right out and told him that he was going to split up with her and that he didn't want to see her again.

Another of his ex-girlfriends was both telepathic and a constant nagger. If she wanted him to put up some shelves or clean the house she'd repeat the message in his brain for hours on end. Even when he went out he couldn't escape it.

But worst of all Dad's ex-girlfriends was the one who had

mind-control powers. Dad said that he would often come round in a daze and find himself buying her an expensive gift. He couldn't even relax in front of a game of wrestling, boxing or shin-kicking without being struck by the urge to go home and have a cosy night in.

After all that hassle it must have been a relief to go out with a normal vampire.

MONDAY 4TH APRIL

We've all got to be at school for half past eight tomorrow morning so we can get on the coach for the zoo trip. I'm going to wait there from eight to make sure no one else sits next to Chloe. The last thing I want is for Wayne to worm his way next to her and be a 'smooth operator'.

I will offer Chloe the window seat, to show to her how selfless and caring I am. I shall even buy some of those boiled sweets she likes.

Tomorrow's going to be good for me. I can sense it.

TUESDAY 5TH APRIL

Let's just say that the school trip wasn't a resounding success.

As we got on the coach, I made sure I was sitting next to Chloe. I could see Wayne wanted to barge in, but I didn't let him. Chloe and I had a good chat on the journey there and I demonstrated my maturity by resisting the temptation to

Diary of a Wimpy Vampire

laugh when the coach went past a tramp and Craig told
Darren to wave at his dad.

Anyway, we had a nice enough journey, but the zoo itself
was a disaster. As soon as I stepped through the turnstile,
I could hear yelps of panic coming from the cages. I asked
Chloe to hang back with me, so we could break away from
the other pupils.

The first animals we passed were the meerkats, who
all stood on their hind legs and nudged each other
disapprovingly. Next, we walked past a lion that retreated
to the back of its cage and roared obnoxiously at me. But
it was the monkeys that really drew attention to me. As
I passed them, they formed into a threatening rank and
howled at me. They threw rocks from their
enclosure with scary precision, hitting

my head a few times. I tried to pretend it wasn't happening, but it became harder to shrug off when the little monsters began to hurl themselves with great force against their cage. By this point frightened yelps and howls were coming from every direction and an angry zookeeper threw me out for provoking the animals. I hadn't even done anything!

I ended up waiting in the coach on my own while Chloe spent the day with Wayne! And they sat together on the way back! I can only hope that the smell of the cages put him off making a pass at her in the zoo.

Just when I thought things couldn't get any worse, I found that Craig had spread the rumour that the monkeys threw their poo at me and that I ran away in tears. Why couldn't we just have gone to the Science Museum like last year?

WEDNESDAY 6TH APRIL

It's amazing how quickly you can become a social outcast. Just a week ago, I was riding high in the popularity stakes following my Mercy victory over Jay from the tough gang. Now, everywhere I go, I'm greeted by mocking laugher and cruel jibes. Overnight, my very name has become an insult. I know this because I heard a pupil I've never spoken to saying 'Don't be such a Nigel' in the corridor this morning.

At break time, I saw that an obscene picture had been taped to my locker. It depicted me crying and covered

Diary of a Wimpy Vampire

in monkey excrement and the words 'Nigel has monkey bum disease' were written underneath it. The picture was unsigned, but from the crude style, I'd say the perpetrator was Wayne.

Chloe wasn't in the library at lunchtime, but I decided to sit there on my own rather than look for her. I have no desire to drag her into the scandal.

Resigned to my social failure, I deliberately chose to sit next to Darren in Maths this afternoon. But guess what? This time *he* built a barrier out of textbooks to block *me* out. Even that old fleabag considers me *persona non grata*.

Thursday 7th April

Today I tried to explain to everyone that the monkeys had thrown rocks and not faeces, but they wouldn't listen. I tried to tell Craig, but he made monkey noises every time I

Diary of a Wimpy Vampire

opened my mouth. I even tried to explain it to the girls from the popular gang but they ran away whenever I went near them in case they caught my monkey bum disease.

Once again Chloe was absent from the library at lunchtime. Perhaps she is also worried about contracting the disease.

FRIDAY 8TH APRIL

My life is over.

Yesterday lunchtime, Wayne asked Chloe out and she said yes. Unconfirmed reports suggest that they've already snogged.

As soon as I heard the news I went home. It is now approaching nightfall and I'm still too upset to write anything more. If these words are hard to read, it's probably because I've smudged them with bitter tears.

I have faced many challenges and setbacks in my time on this planet, but this latest blow is too much. I am simply too sensitive for this world.

117

Diary of a Wimpy Vampire

SATURDAY 9TH APRIL

It is now the Easter holidays. I have a couple of weeks off to try and process what has happened.

How am I going to get through the days?

How am I going to survive?

I know that great art can come from great heartbreak, so I will try and express my feelings in a poem when I have the strength to write more.

SUNDAY 10TH APRIL

I have now written my heartbreak poem. It is very deep and moving, and contains old-fashioned words like 'doth'. It was very difficult to put my pain into words, but at least it means that mankind will be able to look back and understand the true depth of my feelings.

MY LOVE HAS BEEN STOLEN

My love has been stolen
And I am in hell
Now in my heart
Nightmares doth dwell.
My love has been stolen
Am I am in grief
How could she forsake me
For a boy with bad teeth?

Diary of a Wimpy Vampire

MONDAY 11TH APRIL

I am too upset to drink blood. This lunchtime Dad noticed that I hadn't touched the flask he brought to my room yesterday and asked if anything was wrong. Like, duh! Earth to Dad! My life fell apart on Friday and it's taken him this long to work out that something is wrong.

Of course, I told him nothing. He wouldn't understand anyway. He's never had any problems attracting women.

God, I hate him. Sometimes I wish he'd never transformed me.

TUESDAY 12TH APRIL

I went for a walk in the countryside today and spent a couple of hours looking over the edge of a cliff. I wanted to end it all by jumping off, but then I remembered that it wouldn't really end anything.

No matter how many bones I broke, I'd only lie on the floor until my body mended and then I'd have to get up and continue my miserable existence.

The only thing I'd really be putting at risk would be my phone, which would get crushed, and then I'd have to go back to using my old one, which doesn't have a colour screen.

It wouldn't even hurt, as I don't feel pain. But I make up for this with the emotional pain I feel, which is the worst anyone has ever experienced in history.

Diary of a Wimpy Vampire

Wednesday 13th April

When you think about it, it's not very easy for a vampire to end it all. Even if you had the strength, it would be hard to drive a stake through your own heart, and beheading yourself would be tricky.

Dad once told me that the Archduchess of Austria managed to chop her own head off on a guillotine when Aldric of Lyons left her for a younger vampire during the French Revolution, but this is probably just another one of his tall stories.

I once saw a jar of garlic capsules in a health food shop, and wondered if I would die if I washed the lot down with holy water. I don't really want to try, though. I'll probably just get the worst migraine in vampire history. And my sister will choose that exact moment to blast out her teen pop at full volume.

No, I have no choice but to navigate this eternal river of loneliness in a boat of solitude.

Note to self: I must remember to include this powerful image in a poem.

Thursday 14th April

8am

There's only a month to go until I turn 100. I can't believe I'm nearly 100 and I haven't even fed on a girl's neck yet. Most vampires have done it loads of times when they reach that age.

12AM

My parents suggested that we go for a family hike today. Needless to say I refused. In the end, they went off without me, saying that I didn't know what I'm missing.

I do know what I'm missing – the point of existence.

2AM

I once read that a huge asteroid is going to destroy the world in a few hundred years. I'm willing it to hurry up, but I've got a suspicion that even the destruction of the world won't kill me. I'll just end up floating aimlessly around space for the rest of eternity. It won't be that different from my current life, when you think about it.

Friday 15th April

How could this cruel universe let me get so close to happiness and then snatch it from me?

It is like glimpsing a rainbow only to be condemned to darkness. It is like hearing beautiful music only to be condemned to silence. It is like smelling sweet rose petals before being condemned to Maths teacher breath.

I am truly at rock bottom.

Saturday 16th April

11AM

The hair I tape over my diary to make sure no one opens it has been broken!

I am so angry with my sister! I know she is the culprit because no one else has been in our house and my parents are too self-absorbed to care about what I'm going through. I am absolutely fuming. As soon as Mum and Dad go out hunting tonight, I intend to confront her.

11PM

I would like to make a correction. When I wrote yesterday

that I was at rock bottom, I got it wrong. I have just been beaten up by my little sister. *Now* I am at rock bottom.

When Mum and Dad went out, I dashed into her room and told her that I knew she'd been reading my diary. At first she denied it but when I told her about the hair, she had no choice but to confess. She said she'd only looked at it for a couple of minutes anyway because it was really boring.

I know that as a child, she can hardly be expected to understand the depth of emotion I deal with in these pages, but I must admit that this criticism sent me into a violent rage and I attempted to strike her.

As I've previously mentioned, my sister has all the mighty speed and strength expected of vampires, so she easily caught my hand, twisted it behind my back and slammed me into a headlock. She held me in this position until I promised not to lash out again and admitted that my real name was 'Mr Smellypants'.

You might have won this one, little fiend. But I shall never forget this mistreatment.

Diary of a Wimpy Vampire

SUNDAY 17TH APRIL

The only positive thing to come from my recent experiences is that I'm writing poetry of even greater intensity than before. My poems are now getting so profound they don't even rhyme.

THE HUNTER

If I am the biter why am I bitten?
If I am the attacker why am I attacked?
If I am the hunter why am I hunted
By despair?

In the future, scholars will look back on this period as a great time for my art. But that doesn't matter to me. I write poetry to express myself and I don't care what anyone else thinks about it.

Note to self: Look into possibility of getting poems published.

MONDAY 18TH APRIL

I ventured out of the house today to try and get some air, but I soon wished I hadn't when I saw Wayne and Chloe waiting together at the bus stop. They were getting the number 32 to the leisure mart, perhaps to go bowling, see a film or get a pizza.

And while they enjoy the taste of mozzarella, pepperoni and cheese-filled crusts, I shall taste only bitter despair. With an extra topping of depression.

(Note to self: Look into possibility of bequeathing diary to the British Library. These insights into heartbreak must not be lost.)

Perhaps I should leave town. Mum and Dad reckon we're the last vampires left, but I bet there are still some other undead families they don't know about in places like Sweden and Alaska.

Diary of a Wimpy Vampire

Or maybe I'll be killed by a vampire slayer, and then my poetry will be discovered and the world will realize what it's lost. Too late, world. You should have appreciated me when you had the chance.

TUESDAY 19TH APRIL

I popped out to buy the new issue of my computer games magazine this morning and I heard an old lady complaining about a recent illness in the newsagent. It sounded suspicious, so I took a close look at her neck, and sure enough there were a couple of bite marks right above the collar of her blouse.

I can't believe my parents have been up to their tricks yet again! They are insatiable! It's difficult enough coping with a broken heart without having to worry about an angry mob driving a stake through it because they've discovered my true identity. And all because my parents cannot be bothered to go further afield to hunt for me. They are so lazy.

As usual, they denied everything when I confronted them this evening, but who else could have done it?

WEDNESDAY 20TH APRIL

I was scared to go out today in case I saw Wayne and Chloe again. It would simply be more than I could stand to see that rotten-toothed fool parading around with the only girl I have ever loved. But I couldn't face another day of staring at my wall either, so I went to the shopping precinct and sat on a bench. An old man stood next to me and said he could see I was troubled. At least somebody noticed!

He asked me what the problem was, but when I started to tell him, it didn't take long for him to twist the conversation to the subject of Jesus. I looked up and saw that he was handing out flyers for the local church youth group. His crucifix pendant was dangling right in my face, so now I've got a horrible migraine as well as severe depression. I think I'll stay in tomorrow.

THURSDAY 21ST APRIL

Today was so pointless that when I tried to write about it a moment ago, my pen ran out because it couldn't take the

boredom. It took me ages to find a new one and after all that effort I can exclusively reveal that nothing interesting happened today.

I stayed in bed this morning, and this afternoon I went for a walk and kicked over a traffic cone in anger. A moment later I started feeling guilty and went back to put it upright again. How pathetic. I'm supposed to be a prince of darkness, and I can't even overturn a traffic cone.

Another brilliant day, then.

Note: I was being ironic in that last statement. Thought I might need to point that out in case my sister steals my diary and reads it again.

Friday 22nd April

I have written a new poem today. I will let it speak for itself.

THE PREDATOR

I am the predator
Who wants to suck your blood.
So how can it be that
You sucked the life from me
With rejection?
It sucks.

Saturday 23rd April

Today is St George's Day. There's an ancient superstition that vampires are most active on St George's Day. I was a pretty good argument against it today, as I did nothing but stare at my bedroom ceiling and reflect on how I've ruined my life.

Diary of a Wimpy Vampire

SUNDAY 24TH APRIL

Now it is Easter Sunday, where everyone makes a big deal about somebody who came back from the dead 2,000 years ago.

And what about me? I came back from the dead much more recently than that but nobody seems interested. Oh that's right, I forgot, no one ever cares about anything I do.

MONDAY 25TH APRIL

No school today, as it's Easter Monday. Not that I am looking forward to the torture of going back and seeing Wayne and Chloe holding hands.

Using my calculator, I've worked out that I've been awake for 30,717 days now. That's 737,208 hours without so much as a snooze. No wonder I'm getting tired.

TUESDAY 26TH APRIL

A ray of hope has entered my life! Chloe has dumped Wayne!

Diary of a Wimpy Vampire

At lunchtime, I provided her with a shoulder to cry on, and found out the details. Apparently, Chloe saw one of Wayne's sexist magazines in his bedroom, and said that she didn't approve of it. Instead of at least pretending to throw it away, Wayne defended it and said that girls only complain about these magazines because they're jealous. Chloe then dumped him for being a chauvinist.

If only I'd told Chloe that Wayne was a sexist a couple of weeks ago, I could have avoided all that heartache. According to Craig, Wayne's side of the story is that he dumped Chloe because she is 'frigid'. I looked this up in a dictionary and discovered that it means she has a cold temperature. Just like me! This proves we are destined to be together!

The playground was buzzing with the news of the break-up today, and Brian said to me that I should grab Chloe on the rebound. Although I'm reluctant to take romantic advice from someone whose girlfriend looks like an extra from *Lord of the Rings*, I think he might actually be on to something here.

WEDNESDAY 27TH APRIL

7 AM

Today is the day I'm going to finally ask Chloe to be my girlfriend. I can't risk losing her again. This time I'm really going to do it.

130

Diary of a Wimpy Vampire

The time of our dark union approaches, my beloved.

8 AM
Here I go! This is the last entry I shall write before finding true happiness.

10 AM
I waited outside the school gates for Chloe this morning, but when she arrived she was with two girls from the popular gang, who were grilling her for gossip about the split. When will these vultures let her move on with her life?

11 AM
I said hello to Chloe after Assembly, but she was late for Maths so I didn't feel it was the right moment to declare my love. Timing is everything in the eternal dance of seduction.

12 PM
I am now sitting in the library and waiting for Chloe to arrive. The girls from the popular gang never come here at lunchtime, so I'm certain she'll be alone this time. I'm so nervous I've chewed off my entire fingernail and I'm currently waiting for it to grow back.

Diary of a Wimpy Vampire

2PM

I did it! I asked Chloe to be my girlfriend! And – she said she'd think about it! Brilliant! I think.

In truth, at first she seemed rather embarrassed by my request, and said that she didn't want to jump into a relationship so soon after finishing with Wayne. I said I knew she was worried that Wayne would be upset to see her getting over him so quickly, but that she should put her bad experience behind her and follow her heart. She seemed swayed by my argument, and told me she'd consider it and let me know her answer tomorrow.

12PM

Tomorrow will either be the best or the worst day of my life. Ever since I got home, I've been lying in bed and wondering what Chloe will say. I wish I had vampire mind-reading skills like Dad's ex-girlfriend. At least that would get me out of the torture of waiting to discover my fate.

THURSDAY 28TH APRIL

Well, I have my answer now. Chloe has said that she likes me as a friend, but she doesn't want to go out with me. She was waiting outside the gates before school to drive these words into my heart. Needless to say, I went straight back to bed and I've been here ever since.

To the annals of vampire lore, please add the following:

132

Throughout the history of our species, it's been thought that the most effective ways to destroy a vampire are to behead them or drive a stake through their heart. However, I have now discovered that telling a vampire that you like them as a friend but don't want to go out with them is far more effective.

That is all.

133

Diary of a Wimpy Vampire

Friday 29th April

I somehow managed to muster the strength to get out of bed today and trudge through my weary life.

As I was about to enter the school gates, I noticed that Chloe was once again waiting for me. I wondered what further punishment life could have in store for me. Perhaps she had decided that she didn't even like me as a friend any more.

Chloe told me that she knew I'd been upset yesterday, and wanted to explain herself. She said that she wasn't ready to have another boyfriend so soon after dumping Wayne, and that she was afraid that I would also end up hating her if we split up too, and that I'm the only proper friend she's made since she moved to this town.

She asked me if I was fine with all this and I pretended that I was. But I think that there is hope. I think there's hope once again.

Saturday 30th April

I spent today looking through Dad's books for tips on how to get off with girls who only like you as a friend.

There was very little advice to be gleaned from them, which is hardly surprising when you consider that every other vampire in history was too beautiful to need advice on how to attract the opposite sex.

But I did find an interesting passage in a large book

called *Thomas of Arundel's Vampire Almanac for the Year 1739, Being the Third After Leap Year, Wherein Is Contained Lessons for the Undead Regarding Industry, Temperance and Frugality* (I'm guessing they weren't bothered about snappy book titles back then).

Inside, there was an account of a vampire from Devon who became infatuated with the only girl in his village who was immune to his powers of mesmerism. It says that in the end he got so impatient that he had to come right out and tell her he was a vampire to make her fall in love with him.

Diary of a Wimpy Vampire

It said that all human women find vampires irresistible, but sometimes you need to reveal your supernatural status to make them fall for your charms. This sounds like a rather biased claim, but it's got to be worth a try.

SUNDAY 1ST MAY

I have no idea how to tell Chloe I'm a vampire. Obviously, I can't ask my parents for advice, as they'd go mad if they knew I was telling a human about us.

It's a bit of a risk I suppose. For all I know, Chloe could be a vampire slayer posing as an ordinary schoolgirl with a secret undercover mission to destroy me and pick off my family one by one.

I must cease these paranoid thoughts! Everyone knows that vampire slayers don't even exist! They were just a scare story created by the vampire media hundreds of years ago to sell more pamphlets.

But it's possible she might be prejudiced against my kind. She might be opposed to blood-drinking on ethical grounds, like she is with foxhunting. I'm certainly not going to tell her about the hierarchy of victims outlined by the Vampire Council, as she is a liberal and would find it abhorrent.

MONDAY 2ND MAY

Wayne has accused me of stealing Chloe from him, even though I'm not actually going out with her yet. He told

136

Diary of a Wimpy Vampire

Craig to tell Paul to tell Si that he wants to fight me. Fearing that my reply would be deliberately misreported if I sent it back through these channels, I spoke to Wayne directly at lunchtime, letting him know that I'm not actually going out with Chloe, and that I don't want to fight him.

I hope I've straightened it out, as I really don't want to have to fight in front of everyone. Although Wayne couldn't do much to hurt me, I know nothing about combat.

Dad once tried to teach me vampire martial arts, but there's not much point in learning them if you don't have supernatural strength and speed in the first place.

Diary of a Wimpy Vampire

Whenever I tried to chop blocks of wood with my hand, I kept breaking my wrist, and we'd have to wait around for it to heal. In the end, he got impatient and told me it would be better if I just phoned him if I was ever in danger.

TUESDAY 3RD MAY

5PM

I tried to drop hints about my true nature to Chloe today, but she didn't pick up on them.

First I asked her if she's ever wondered why she's never seen me eating, but she thought I was trying to tell her I was anorexic, and said that I should tell the school nurse.

Next, I asked her if she's ever wondered why I'm so good at History. She pointed out that she beat me on the last test we had, so this clue didn't really work.

I then tried to change tack and told her that I don't sleep, but this only made her think I was saying I had insomnia. She said that I should consider buying a herbal remedy or a book of relaxation techniques.

In the end I decided to go for broke and show her my high pain threshold and healing powers. I got the compasses out of my geometry set and was about to dig the point into my hand when she reached out to stop me.

She told me that she could see I was disturbed and that I mustn't harm myself just to prove it to her. She said that

I should tell my doctor about the problems I'd revealed to her as they sounded serious.

Great. So now she thinks I'm a self-harming anorexic insomniac. That's hardly going to increase my sex appeal (except with goth girls). Revealing my true nature to Chloe might prove more difficult than I thought.

12PM

I've noticed that vampires in films make sly references to their nature when seducing human prey, so I've decided to slip these kinds of intriguing lines into conversation with Chloe. I've already come up with a few sophisticated ways to imply my nature:

'Music was so much better in the twenties.'

'I don't like *Dracula*. It's not very realistic.'

'Is that type O– I can smell?'

'Your heartbeat sounds fast today.'

'I apologize if I seem tetchy. I've been awake for the last 737,208 hours.'

WEDNESDAY 4TH MAY

The subtle and sophisticated approach turned out to be a waste of time. I even took to raising my eyebrows before making the vampire references, but the penny didn't drop. I think I'm going to have to be more direct.

Stupid Mr Jenkins is getting back on my case about PE

lessons now that I've been off for three months. When he passed me in the hall at lunchtime he said I was looking well. He was trying to catch me out, but I replied that my back still hurt.

That was a close shave. I don't have my kit with me, so I know that Mr Jenkins would make me do PE wearing something from the spare clothes box, which is covered in fleas. Just a small part of the humiliating revenge he has planned, no doubt.

I'm going to get Dad to say that I'm asthmatic and if Mr Jenkins makes me do PE, I'll have an attack and the school will get sued. That should be enough to keep the fiend away from me.

Diary of a Wimpy Vampire

THURSDAY 5TH MAY

Fate has handed a wonderful gift to me. There is a film about vampires showing at the cinema. I shall invite Chloe to come and see it, and it will create the perfect excuse to reveal my true nature to her.

It's all so simple! Chloe shall succumb to my forbidden passion in the leisure mart car park.

FRIDAY 6TH MAY

12PM

So far, my plan is going without a hitch. Chloe has agreed to come to the cinema with me. She has also agreed with my film choice, blissfully unaware that it shall mark her induction into the diabolical world of night.

Step into my trap, fragile prey.

4PM

My brilliant plan has hit a big fat obstacle. Chloe told Brian from the goths about our cinema trip, and he has rudely invited himself along. Now John and Brian's strange-looking girlfriend are coming along too, which doesn't even make the right amount of people for a double date. Perhaps if I make sure I'm sitting next to Chloe on the end of the row I can whisper the dark truth to her unheard by these surplus goths. But I'm sure the smell of them alone will be enough to kill the mood.

Diary of a Wimpy Vampire

SATURDAY 7TH MAY

Well that was a waste of eight pounds plus bus fare. I failed to sit next to Chloe, reveal my true nature or make her mine for the rest of eternity. And the film was rubbish!

Brian and John made a huge embarrassment of themselves on the way there by throwing boiled sweets at people from the bus window. If they're not mature enough to cope with travelling on their own, they shouldn't be allowed to. To make things worse, Brian's girlfriend was really egging them on.

Although I tried to position myself next to Chloe in the cinema, John barged in between us and I ended up wedged between him and Brian's girlfriend, who bought a trough of popcorn and a vat of Coke. She kept alternating between slurping the Coke, munching the popcorn and snogging Brian. From what I could hear between these disgusting noises (which wasn't much), the film was pretty appalling. It trotted out all the old vampirist tripe about us sleeping in coffins, turning into bats and crumbling into ash at the first sign of sunlight.

Still, Chloe said that she thought that the main vampire was 'gorgeous', so my plan might well have worked if those other idiots hadn't lumbered along.

I managed to sit next to Chloe on the bus back, but my efforts to chat her up were sabotaged by Brian and John repeatedly pressing the bell to annoy the bus driver. In the end, we were all thrown off and had to walk the rest of the way. Chloe was visibly irritated and I was forced to abandon any further seduction attempts.

Sunday 8th May

10am

Whenever I try to reveal my true nature to Chloe, I find it hard to put into words, so I've decided to set out the truth in a letter.

Diary of a Wimpy Vampire

Darling Chloe

I am writing to apologize for my behaviour over the last few days. You might think I have been acting strangely since I declared my love for you. But the fact is, I have been trying to unveil a dark secret.

The truth is that I'm a vampire, and I am almost 100 years old.

This might seem unbelievable or shocking to you. It might be a while before you are able to accept what I am saying. But if you consider the facts, you will come to accept it.

Have you ever wondered why I don't sleep? Why I don't eat? Why I feel no pain?

It is because I am one of the undead.

Do you feel drawn to me but overwhelmed by a mysterious sense of danger? Do I seem delicious but forbidden to you like a poisoned apple or some yoghurt that's been accidentally left out of the fridge?

Am I right to suppose that there was a look of suspicion on your face that time in History when we watched a DVD called Life During Wartime? Did you understand that one of the teenagers in the black-and-white footage was actually me?

Yours in eternal admiration,

Nigel

P.S. If you didn't recognize me in the DVD, you can get it out of the library. Pause it after 12 minutes and 35 seconds and look in the top right corner of the screen.

P.P.S. Don't tell anyone about this.

P.P.P.S. Don't ask me to prove it by turning into a bat. All that stuff is made up.

Diary of a Wimpy Vampire

1 PM

I have now posted the letter. I am prepared for the consequences.

3 PM

I am beginning to regret posting the letter. What if Chloe is repelled by my true nature? What if she shows it to her parents? What if my parents find out and abandon me for putting us all in danger?

6 PM

I am so stupid for writing our secrets down in a letter. What if the postman is a vampire slayer?

1 AM

Tonight I went out to retrieve the letter from the post box. At first I attempted to scoop it out with a coat hanger, but that didn't work, so I had to get my sister to use her vampire strength. I had to beg her for ages before she agreed. I ended up giving her thirty pounds from my savings to buy a new Magical Princess Fashion Doll to make her come down to the post box and rip it in half so I could remove the letter.

So now I've wasted thirty pounds, pleaded humiliatingly to my little sister and damaged council property, and all because I didn't have the guts to speak to Chloe directly.

No more excuses. Tomorrow I will tell Chloe the truth.

MONDAY 9TH MAY

Today went well for me. Or at least I think it did.

I stopped Chloe on the way back from school and told her I had something to reveal.

I tried again to tell her the truth, but my words kept coming out wrong. I said something about being 100, but she looked confused. I said something about how I don't have as much speed and strength as I should, but it didn't make things any clearer. Then I went off on a strange tangent about how I didn't really eat the sweets she gave me in the library.

But as I was stumbling through this nonsense, she started to look at me differently. Her face turned from impatience and confusion to that hazy look of desire I see on the faces of middle-aged women when Dad smiles at them. She reached towards me and the flow of blood in her wrists was so loud and fast that I couldn't hear what I was saying any more.

My incoherent wittering was silenced when she pressed her finger against one of my teeth. It turns out that I'd been concentrating so hard on trying to reveal my true nature I hadn't noticed that my fangs had extended and done the job for me.

Chloe ran her finger down one of them, as if to check they weren't from a joke shop. And then, still in a dreamlike haze, she leant forward and kissed me on the lips!

She looked at me for a second with that gorgeous type 0- blood filling her cheeks, and then dashed off. And that was the last I saw of her.

Tonight I shall do nothing except relive that brief, sweet moment over and over again!

TUESDAY 10TH MAY

Yesterday I wasn't quite sure if the day had gone well. Well I can confirm that today did as Chloe has now agreed to be my girlfriend!

When I arrived at the school gates this morning, she was waiting for me again, and this time she asked me loads of questions about vampires. I told her about everything – my age, my family, my blood-drinking. She found it hard to take in, but she was prepared to believe it now she'd seen my fangs.

Although she didn't admit it, I can tell she fancies me more now she knows I'm a vampire, just as the Almanac suggested. I just wish I'd revealed my supernatural nature sooner!

When I asked her if she'd be my girlfriend, she said yes! So now we are officially an item, although we've agreed to keep it secret from the rest of the school for the time being, as she doesn't want Wayne to get upset.

I don't care if he finds out! I don't care if he rams a stake through my heart! At least I would die happy!

WEDNESDAY 11TH MAY

I sat next to Chloe in History and I spent the entire lesson drawing love hearts with her name in the middle and showing them to her. Then I drew a more realistic picture of a human heart and I became intensely aware of the sound of blood spluttering through hers. I thought I might have gone too far with this drawing, so I kept it to myself.

I wonder when she'll let me drink her blood? Better take it one step at a time, though. We haven't even snogged yet!

THURSDAY 12TH MAY

I sat next to Chloe in Art this morning and we held hands all lesson. Let the school gossip, I'm not ashamed of our love.

An update on my ridiculous sibling: Tonight my sister tried to be controversial by putting a werewolf poster on her bedroom wall. She's seen a film in which an army of vampires battle an army of werewolves, and she's decided that wants to join 'Team Werewolf' rather than 'Team Vampire'. Needless to say, we've all chosen to ignore her pathetic gesture of rebellion. I even told her that I fully approved of her decision to join Team Werewolf, and offered to buy her a flea collar and a kennel to sleep in.

FRIDAY 13TH MAY

They say that Friday the 13th is unlucky. Not for me it wasn't. I had my first ever snog today!!!

Chloe let me walk her back from school, and when we were almost at her house, she let me give her a French kiss.

Diary of a Wimpy Vampire

It didn't last long, as my fangs began to extend, and I was worried they might impale her tongue.

I then walked her up to her door and went home. And since then I've just been lying here in bed and feeling happy about the way things have turned out. The whole world seems different now I've done a proper snog.

SATURDAY 14TH MAY

6PM

Happy birthday to me!!! Sweet 100 today!!! And now I've finally got a girlfriend, I don't even feel too bad about reaching this milestone.

My human birthday is always a time for quiet contemplation, rather than family celebration like my transformation day.

I spent today looking through the bags of old possessions I keep in my wardrobe: cigarette cards from the thirties, *Star Wars* figures from the seventies and obsolete console games from the nineties. I even had a look at my photograph of the orphanage in London where I lived when I was human.

I was falling into a state of wistful reflection when another shrill and hateful dose of teen pop came blasting through the wall and snapped me out of it. Trust my sister to ruin this special day.

Diary of a Wimpy Vampire

10PM

I just texted Chloe goodnight. I considered phoning her, but we've only been going out for four days and twelve hours and I didn't want to come across like an obsessive stalker.*

12PM

I have been going out with Chloe for four days and fourteen hours now.

*Apparently, it is an insult to call a human a stalker. This is a great compliment in the vampire world.

SUNDAY 15TH MAY

6PM

Today I harvested some human blood myself! Bet you weren't expecting that. I went out for a walk this afternoon, and I was crossing the road when I heard a cry for help coming from around a bend. I saw that a man had fallen off his bike as he was turning a corner, and what a stroke of luck – he was a courier delivering blood to the hospital!

The man was dazed, so I called an ambulance on his phone. But I couldn't resist opening up the back of his bike and making off with the blood. It was a bit naughty, but they must be aware of the temptation they're presenting

Diary of a Wimpy Vampire

when they write the word 'Blood' on the front of their vehicles as if they were vampire ice-cream vans.

When I got home, Mum and Dad were very impressed that I'd managed to bring home some blood, even if it was just boring old type A+.

10PM

I have been enjoying the blood I collected, but now I've started to feel slightly guilty. What if the person it was intended for is really ill? What if the courier gets the sack for losing it? What if the donor took the morning off work to give it?

I know I shouldn't worry about these things. Vampires are supposed to be able to glide around and glug human

152

blood as they fancy, but I can't help but feel guilty about the people I affect.

Perhaps I am too sensitive to be undead.

MONDAY 16TH MAY

This morning I told Chloe how much I'd missed her over the weekend. She said she'd missed me too and that she'd got a book about vampires out of the library to learn more about my culture. I told her that if she has any questions about the subject, she should ask my parents or myself rather than reading some work of propaganda that claims we can all turn into bats.

She got very excited at the prospect of meeting Mum and Dad, and I immediately wished I hadn't mentioned it. I can understand why she's so curious to meet some other vampires, but I know that they'll find some way to embarrass me if I bring her round. Wearing strange old-fashioned clothes, playing the harpsichord, biting her. That kind of thing.

But I will discuss the matter with them as I promised. Anything for my darling Chloe.

TUESDAY 17TH MAY

9PM

Tonight I asked Mum and Dad if I could bring my girlfriend

153

home to meet them, and I think it came as a shock. I don't know why it should – it's not like I'm twelve any more.

Mum said that she'd always imagined I'd settle down with a nice vampire girl. How am I supposed to do that when there aren't any left?

Dad said that he was happy for me, but that I should think very deeply about my decision to date someone from the mortal world.

Decision? Falling in love isn't a decision!

And think deeply? He hardly thought deeply when he was courting Mum in Paris 200 years ago. According to him, he fed on her neck within moments of meeting her, transformed her after just a week, and they'd had their vampire wedding before the month was out. He's hardly in a position to lecture anyone about restraint.

11 PM

Dad has given me a pamphlet called *So You're Thinking of Loving a Mortal?* It looks ancient and I'd be very surprised if it has anything relevant to say to a modern young vampire like me.

1 AM

Word has reached my sister that I have a girlfriend. Tonight she ran into my room and chanted the following:

Nigel and Chloe in a tree

K. I. S. S. I. N. G.

First comes love,

Then comes marriage,

Then comes Chloe with a baby carriage.

What my sister has failed to understand is that when you're in a mature and adult relationship, it's not something you're ashamed of, so this kind of teasing doesn't work. Also, given that I'm a vampire, the only way we could ever have a baby would be if I transformed a human one and spent the rest of eternity feeding it blood from a bottle every time it cried. And even the broodiest vampires have realized that's not a very clever idea.*

Though I was reluctant to sink to my sister's level, I soon realized that the only way I could get rid of her would be to accuse her of kissing a boy in her class called Kyle Brown. This had the desired effect of making her howl in shame and dash back to her room.

*The Vampire Council used to have a strict rule that you could only transform humans between the ages of seven and seventy. Anyone younger is likely to throw dangerous public tantrums, and anyone older just looks weird when they lift up huge rocks or run faster than cars.

WEDNESDAY 18TH MAY

6PM

This morning both Craig and John the goth asked if it was true that I was going out with Chloe. I said I had no comment on the matter, which they took as confirmation. I don't know why everyone is so surprised I have a girlfriend. Perhaps when they're more mature they'll understand love.

In the afternoon we had a Biology lesson on the human digestive system, which was about how they eat food and turn it into poo. Humans are pretty disgusting when you think about it (not Chloe, she is fragrant and lovely, but all other humans are nasty).

It made me wonder about the digestive system of vampires. It's clearly different, because we don't need to go to the toilet, but nobody has ever found out how it works. Perhaps I should donate my sister to science so they can find out.

Diary of a Wimpy Vampire

10PM

This evening I've been reading the pamphlet that Dad gave me. Needless to say, it's hopelessly outdated.

It's basically a work of propaganda produced by the Vampire Council, which claims that vampires should fall in love with their own kind because loving mortals is too risky.

It says that vampires will be unable to control their desire to drink human blood, and this will cause problems. The mortal could die if too much blood is drained from them, or they could get infected with vampire blood and transform.

Diary of a Wimpy Vampire

It says that many mortals will beg to be turned into vampires, but they won't understand what they're letting themselves in for. It's a really out-of-date leaflet because it says there's a danger of vampire overpopulation if too many humans transform, and every vampire will be fighting over the same scarce blood resources.

Overpopulation? According to Dad, we're the last vampires left. Surely extinction is a bigger danger than overpopulation.

1AM

I told Dad that the leaflet hasn't put me off having a mortal girlfriend and I think he's warming to the idea. I asked him if Chloe could come round for lunch on Sunday, and he agreed. He doesn't have any human friends, so I had to make it very clear to him that she is coming round to eat lunch rather than to be lunch. I think he understood.

THURSDAY 19TH MAY

1PM

Wayne has found out that Chloe and I are an item, and apparently I'm going to fight him in the playing fields after school. I'm dreading it, not because I'm scared of Wayne, but because I hate it when everyone stares at me.

Chloe said she was disappointed with me for agreeing to

the fight. I tried to explain to her that I hadn't agreed, and had simply been informed by Craig that I would be taking part. For all I know, Wayne might have found out in exactly the same way.

Chloe then said that she's refusing to attend the childish fight that's being held in her honour and doesn't care who wins.

3 PM

Craig passed me a note in Maths that said that Wayne is claiming to have snogged my mum. Wayne would be lucky to escape with his life if he ever tried!

I think Craig is stirring it up.

7 PM

I've had my first ever fight now, and I have to say I found the whole thing very awkward. I dutifully made my way to the playing fields this afternoon with an angry Wayne and an excited group of onlookers.

Once we were a good distance from the staff window, we dumped our bags on the floor, and waited for everyone to cluster round.

Craig lead the crowd in a rousing chant of 'Have a fight! See who's best!' Wayne then gave me a shove, but I couldn't really be bothered pushing him back, so I just stood there. He seemed really angry, so I can only guess what Craig claimed I'd done to his mum.

I tried to defuse the situation by explaining to Wayne that I had made no attempt to seduce Chloe until she dumped him. Rather than calming him down, this made him even angrier, and he threw a series of clumsy slaps at me. Feeling no pain, and unaware of what the appropriate thing to do was, I suggested that we forget the whole silly business. I thought my attempts to make peace had succeeded. However, I saw glint of true rage in his eyes and realized that he was preparing to throw a punch.

Unsure what else to do, I watched in curiosity as Wayne's fist hit me. I had a vague sense that I should pretend to be hurt when it made contact, but I felt too self-conscious to put on an act.

Diary of a Wimpy Vampire

It didn't matter anyway, as within a second of hitting me, Wayne was rolling around on the floor. It seems that when Wayne's hand crushed into my icy face, a bone in his index finger snapped.

Sensing that something serious had happened, most of the onlookers fled the scene. I offered to help Wayne, but he told me not to touch him so I skulked off home.

Friday 20th May

1pm

As soon as I got inside the school gates I was besieged by pupils asking me if it was true that I beat up Wayne so badly he had to go to hospital. Even members of the tough gang were looking at me with admiration. Where were these fair-weather friends when I was being accused of spreading monkey bum disease?

I didn't really care what they thought. I was more concerned that Chloe would be angry with me for being violent.

I caught her in the corridor on the way to Maths and she said that she'd heard about the fight. I was about to explain that I hadn't acted in aggression, when she gave me a big kiss! And after she'd said she was a pacifist!

After 100 years on this planet, I am still no closer to understanding girls.

7PM

For a while today I was almost starting to feel proud of my victory. But by the afternoon, word had reached the teachers that I beat up Wayne and the headmaster took me into his office for a completely unfair telling off.

To be honest, getting told off by the headmaster isn't the harsh experience it once was, when you'd join a row of wrongdoers and wait for a whack of the cane.

But the punishment you get now is worse in its own way. We had to have a chat about my 'aggressive tendencies', and I was forced to say that I now regretted my actions, which had made me less popular with my fellow pupils (the opposite is true), and that I'd learned that violence doesn't solve anything. The headmaster droned on about my 'anger issues' for a while, but he eventually let me go.

SATURDAY 21ST MAY

I saw Jay and Baz from the tough gang riding a shopping trolley around their estate this afternoon. They'd heard about the fight, and called me over to ask if I was a 'hard case'. I said I was and they told me to prove it by riding the trolley down a flight of steps. I was happy to rise to their challenge, even though I couldn't really see the point.

Diary of a Wimpy Vampire

The trolley tipped over at the bottom of the stairs, and I flew out and broke my wrist. I hid it in my jacket pocket while it healed, and Jay and Daz seemed impressed by my daring. I hope they don't ask me to become a full-time member of the tough gang, though. These sorts of hi-jinx would get very boring if you did them every day.

This evening I told Dad about the fight and Chloe's unexpected reaction, and he said that women always love it when men fight over them, even though they pretend they don't. Dad's views about women are often very outdated, but I think he might be on to something this time.

I phoned Chloe tonight, and she said she's looking forward to coming round to my house tomorrow. I warned her not to crack any jokes about turning into bats or sleeping in coffins, as these are offensive to my people.

SUNDAY 22ND MAY

Chloe came round today. I was worried that the visit might feel awkward, but I forgot about the mesmeric effect that my parents have on humans. Far from sitting in uncomfortable silence, Chloe instantly fell under their spell.

As they made small talk with Chloe, I could see her glancing from Dad to Mum, entranced by them. She didn't even mind when my sister barged rudely in for a stare.

After about an hour of chatting, we moved into the dining room and I was concerned to see that Mum and Dad had set places for all of us at the table. Mum microwaved a meal of chicken and vegetables for Chloe, and spooned it out onto the plate as if it were dog food.

Chloe thanked her and started eating. However, the atmosphere turned less cosy when Mum served glasses of blood for the rest of us. I think my parents just wanted to join in with Sunday lunch so Chloe wouldn't have to eat on her own, but it's easy to forget how disconcerting the sight of blood-drinking can be to a non-vampire. Especially if you let it run all down your chin like my messy sister did!

Diary of a Wimpy Vampire

Chloe lost her appetite and left the rest of her food. She kept on smiling politely, but you could tell she felt uncomfortable, and she left shortly afterwards. This is what happens with humans. They find the idea of vampires glamorous and romantic, but the reality less pleasant.

I can only hope that my parents' rash behaviour hasn't turned her against me.

MONDAY 23RD MAY

This morning I asked Chloe if seeing us drink blood had put her off me. She said that she'd found it a little disturbing, but she understood it was part of our culture. She is so tolerant and understanding!

I think she's right. I don't see any reason why I should be ashamed of my need to drink blood. It might look unpleasant, but so do hundreds of things that humans do all the time like wearing tight swimming trunks or combing their hair all the way across their heads when they go bald.

At any rate, human women are happy to let babies feed on their breasts, and that looks pretty disgusting to me. Is neckfeeding really so much worse than breastfeeding?

Of course, some would say that feeding on humans is unethical because it can weaken or kill them, but I don't think it's as bad as a lot of the things humans do. I bet if you added together all the injuries and deaths that have

166

Diary of a Wimpy Vampire

ever been caused by vampires, they wouldn't approach the damage mankind inflicts upon itself in the average war.

One of the best things about having a girlfriend is that it helps you to accept yourself and find confidence. For the first time in my life, I no longer feel ashamed of being a vampire.

TUESDAY 24TH MAY

9AM

I finally feel close enough to Chloe to share my poetry with her. I have written a new one, which I intend to show her today. I put lots of care into it, and even used a Thesaurus, which lists lots of words that mean the same thing, so you can write longer poems.

BLOOD SYMPHONY

As you sleep I watch
The moonlight on your neck
And listen to your blood.
It is a harmony of haemoglobin.
A symphony of sanguine fluid.
A prelude of plasma.
A concerto of claret.
A guitar solo of gore.
Play on, sweet music.

Diary of a Wimpy Vampire

3 PM

I gave Chloe a copy of the poem today and she said it
was very good. She covered up her neck when she read
it, though, so perhaps some of the imagery was a little
too explicit.

WEDNESDAY 25TH MAY

Dad was out tonight so I went to his study to look for
books on vampire-human relationships. The only ones I
could find were written by vampire supremacists who
regarded humans as little more than walking snacks, so
they weren't much use. One of Dad's bookmarks fell out,
and when I picked it up it turned out to be a letter from his
ex-girlfriend, the psychic vampire.

The letter was giving him all sorts of grief about things
he hadn't done yet, and I could understand why she would

have been so difficult to live with. But there was one part of the letter that I found intriguing. She mentioned some trouble that Dad would encounter this year! It wasn't very specific. I wonder if she was referring to the time in January when he drank the blood with a high level of alcohol in it and got ill.

I was going to ask Dad about it, but I thought he might be angry with me for going through his stuff, so I decided not to say anything. Plus, if she was such a good psychic she'd have been able to predict that she was going to get beheaded in the great vampire purge of 1878, so I doubt it's anything to worry about.

THURSDAY 26TH MAY

Someone farted in assembly today and everyone seemed to think it was the funniest thing that had ever happened. I didn't share their opinion. Perhaps it's because I don't have a human digestive system and can't pass wind myself that I don't find this bodily function especially funny. Or maybe I just have a more sophisticated sense of humour (I once laughed at an Oscar Wilde play).

Afterwards Chloe noted that we were the only two people in the hall who didn't laugh, and that includes Mr Jones, who was taking assembly. She said that we are much more mature than everyone else in our school.

I suppose I ought to be mature given that I'm 100

Diary of a Wimpy Vampire

years old. But I'll take compliments where I can get them, especially from my darling girlfriend!

Friday 27th May

Chloe has invited me round to her house for a meal on Sunday. Although I'm pleased that she's ready to take our relationship up to this level, I'm not sure how I'm going to get through it. Chloe has told her parents I'm allergic to garlic, but she needs to understand that my situation is more complicated than this. She thinks I can just swallow the food to be polite, but it doesn't work like that. Anything I try to force down will come right back up again. Which is hardly a good first impression to make.

I suppose I could pretend to have an upset stomach, but they'll wonder why I came round at all if I'm ill.

Perhaps if I sit next to the radiator I can slip the food down there discreetly. But this could cause an unpleasant stench, especially if they make tuna bake or macaroni cheese.

Saturday 28th May

I think I've come up with a good solution to the food problem. I've taken one of my dad's old jackets and sewn a couple of plastic bags inside the sleeves. Using sleight of hand, I'll pretend to put the food in my mouth while letting it fall into the bags. I've been practising, and I reckon I can do it quickly enough to avoid suspicion.

SUNDAY 29TH MAY

My food jacket was a success, at first.

I called round at Chloe's house on time, and waited to be invited inside by her parents.* I shook hands with them, complimenting them on their choice of furniture to distract from my cold temperature.

We sat down for lunch and Chloe's dad poured me a glass of fresh orange juice, which I pretended to sip. Chloe's mum then served the meal she had prepared, which was roast beef, boiled potatoes and carrots. I felt sorry for her when I saw the pride with which she dished it out. If only she'd left my cut of beef out of the oven I could at least have sucked the blood out of it.

I congratulated Chloe's mum on her cooking as I discreetly tucked it up my sleeves. When I had cleared my plate, I excused myself, locked myself in the bathroom and flushed the food down the toilet. The carrots kept floating up again and it took me five flushes to get rid of it all.

I took my place again at the table downstairs, but just when I was beginning to think I was out of the woods, Chloe's mum produced an enormous sponge pudding and

Diary of a Wimpy Vampire

jug of custard. Despite my protestation that I was full, she insisted on doling out a huge portion. I managed to get it into the plastic bags in my sleeves, but they got so full that I had to keep my arms held up at my sides to avoid custard seepage.

I just about managed to get away with it until it was time to leave and Chloe's dad held out his hand for me to shake. Not wanting to let the custard slide onto his hand, I was left with no choice but to shout 'High five!' He looked rather surprised but held his hand up and I slapped my palms against his.

As soon as I was out of sight, I poured the foul custard down the drain.

* I waited out of politeness, although I'm also rather superstitious about entering human residences. According to folklore, vampires experience intolerable pain if they enter a home without first being asked in.

As ever, the myth doesn't really stand up to scrutiny. Does everyone who lives there have to invite you in? Do you need permission from the landlord if they're renting? What are the rules for caravans?

Nonetheless, I don't feel it's worth the risk. 'Intolerable pain' doesn't sound much fun to me.

MONDAY 30TH MAY

The school holidays started again today, and for once they were welcome, as I got to spend some quality time with Chloe away from the attention of the school gossipers.

This morning we went down to the shopping centre. Chloe said that people who spend their lives looking around shops are shallow and materialistic, so we bought some serious newspapers and went for a coffee. Chloe had a frappuccino, and I got a cup of ice and poured some blood into it from my flask. I felt like a normal well-adjusted teenager, sipping a frappuccino in a coffee franchise with my girlfriend. Admittedly, it was a human blood frappuccino, but apart from that it was completely normal and well-adjusted.

I couldn't find much in the serious newspaper that interested me. There was a page of computer game reviews and a couple of cartoon strips, but that was about it. Chloe read all the news stories in her paper, though, even the ones about other countries! She is so mature!

Diary of a Wimpy Vampire

TUESDAY 31ST MAY

I went out for a romantic walk in the countryside with Chloe today. It was nice to walk at human pace instead of trying to keep up with my family.

Chloe said I should take my jacket off because it was hot, but I said I didn't want to in case I got a rash. She said that I shouldn't be ashamed of my rashes as they are part of who I am as a vampire. Let's hope she's this understanding about vampire culture when I ask to drink her blood!

I tied my jacket against my waist and felt a wonderful sense of abandon as I waved my bare arms around. When I got home, Mum saw my red arms and went mad at me for forgetting to put sunblock on. I told her I was in love and had no time for such trivial concerns.

WEDNESDAY 1ST JUNE

Chloe is going to Wolverhampton to see her aunt tomorrow. When I tried to persuade her to stay here with me, she said that she couldn't neglect her family duties, but because of the request I made in my poem she's decided to let me sit in the tree outside her bedroom window and watch her sleep.

I can't do many of the romantic things that vampires do for human women, like carrying them to Paris for the weekend, but I'm sure I can manage to sit in a tree for a few hours. I have arranged to be in the tree at half past twelve tonight, after her parents have fallen asleep, at which point Chloe will open her bedroom curtain.

Spoilt brat update:
My sister has announced that she wants learn to ride a pony. What a ridiculous idea! Imagine the fuss all the animals would make if she strolled into a pony trekking centre. I told her about my experience in the zoo but she took no notice.

Even if the ponies were stupid enough to let my sister near them, how long would she be able to resist sticking her teeth into one of their veiny necks?

When will my sister accept that she's not the princess of a magical rainbow kingdom, but a ruthless and bloodthirsty killer like the rest of us?

Spoilt brat newsflash: My parents told my sister she isn't allowed pony lessons. Anyone would think they were

Diary of a Wimpy Vampire

rational, fair and sensible. I don't know why they're acting so out of character.

THURSDAY 2ND JUNE

Chloe has gone to Wolverhampton now, and I'm resting at home in bed, feeling a little sore after my night in the tree.

I arrived at half past twelve as agreed, but I couldn't get up the tree at first. I ended up having to use the ladder from the back of their shed, which hardly enhanced the atmosphere of supernatural romance.

When Chloe saw me in the tree, she waved and then went to bed. It took her a while to go to sleep, because every time she opened her eyes to check I was still there, this made me laugh, and then she laughed too.

When she did get to sleep, I have to confess that I found the experience pretty dull. I stared at her and thought about my undying love for an hour or so, but then my mind began to wander. I was tempted to nip down to the all-night garage and buy a magazine, but I was worried that she might wake up and question the seriousness of my feelings.

Around 3am, I took my phone out of my pocket and played Snake until the batteries died. Chloe started snoring at round 4am, and it was so loud I could hear it through the glass. She woke up at 6.30am, waved goodbye through her window and then I left.

It was good to do some proper romantic vampire stuff, but I think I'll bring a crossword next time.

Friday 3rd June

12PM
I can't begin to express the heartache I feel upon being separated from my true love. This is probably how

Diary of a Wimpy Vampire

Sebastian of Lyons felt when his lover was imprisoned in the Bastille for twenty years. Except he didn't have the option to send texts like I do.

1AM

I went out for a walk in the graveyard again tonight to take my mind off my heartache, and guess who I saw there?

It was only Dad, lurking behind one of the graves!

Resisting the urge to let him know I'd caught him red-handed, I kept a good distance back and observed him. I couldn't believe that he'd denied responsibility for the attacks on the local townspeople, and yet here he was hanging around the graveyard at midnight waiting for the next victim to snack on. How dare he put my happiness at risk for the sake of his own greed?

In the far distance I could see a woman enter the

graveyard alone. Spotting his chance, Dad swooped. I tried to run after him and let him know he was caught, but I was unable to match his vampire speed, and could only watch from a distance as he sated his foul appetite on the innocent.

Eventually, I caught up with him and was just about to take him to task when I realized that the woman he was attacking wasn't a passing human at all, but Mum! And the worst thing is that they were kissing! It was so disgusting.

Looking very sheepish and embarrassed, they explained to me that it was the anniversary of the time they first met, and they were celebrating by recreating it.

I told them that I didn't want to know anything about their sordid activities, but they should at least tell me if they're going out at night, as my sister has been left at home on her own thanks to their irresponsible behaviour. What if a burglar came in?

To be fair, the burglar would be in more danger than my sister, but I was enjoying the moral high ground too much to concern myself with such minor points.

SATURDAY 4TH JUNE

I have written a poem to help me cope while Chloe is in Wolverhampton. I considered sending it to her, but I'm worried she might find it too graphic. Plus, it's slightly too long to fit on a text. When the time comes for my work to

Diary of a Wimpy Vampire

be published, Chloe cannot be shielded from the intensity of my feelings, but until then I'll keep them secret.

I WAIT IN ETERNAL PAIN

With your neck so long and blood so sweet

Life without you is incomplete

How I long to stick my fangs in your vein

Instead I wait in eternal pain.

SUNDAY 5TH JUNE

Chloe's dad will be driving her back from Wolverhampton now. I hope he's a safer driver than my dad, and that my love isn't stolen away from me by a fatal crash, dooming me to eternal grief. That would be just typical.

In just a few hours' time, we shall be reunited. Come swiftly, precious hour!

MONDAY 6TH JUNE

I went back to school today, and was reunited with my true love. I told her that the last four days had been the longest of my life, although from the sound of it, they would have felt even longer if I'd gone to Wolverhampton.

Wayne is going out with Sally Mulligan now. I think he's only doing it to get revenge on Chloe and me because he kept snogging her at the bus stop after school and looking over at us. Neither of us particularly cared.

We are in a proper, adult relationship now, and have no need to concern ourselves with the trivial lives of our immature classmates.

Plus, I know I'm a better snogger than him because Chloe said so.

TUESDAY 7TH JUNE

Today was so sunny that Chloe let me give her a hug. Because I'm cold, Chloe is usually reluctant to hug me unless she's wearing a jumper. But today she said she found my temperature soothing.

I'd better enjoy it while I can, because she's not going to want my freezing body anywhere near her when winter comes around again.

WEDNESDAY 8TH JUNE

A weird thing happened at lunchtime today. Chloe was looking at me in the library when a dreamy and distant look came into her eyes. I asked her if she was alright, but she just kept staring at me with strange contentment.

After a couple of minutes I alerted the librarian, who took Chloe to the school nurse. She needed to lie down, but was soon feeling fine again. The nurse interrogated her for a further twenty minutes about whether she'd taken any alcohol or drugs, and then she let her go. She was right as rain again in time for Business Studies.

Diary of a Wimpy Vampire

When I walked Chloe home later, she still seemed fine. I asked her about her experience at lunchtime, and she said that the room went swirly, she could hear a distant piano and smell rose petals, and she felt very safe and relaxed. The more I think about it, the more Chloe seems to have been showing the effects of vampire hypnosis.

But I don't have the vampire power of mesmerism, so I've no idea how that could have happened. How strange.

THURSDAY 9TH JUNE

We sneaked into the Music room at lunchtime so I could show Chloe my piano skills. I started with simple pieces like 'Chopsticks' and 'The Camptown Races', so she would be more impressed by what followed, then launched into Beethoven's 'Moonlight Sonata'. Chloe was overjoyed at my skills, but I didn't want to look directly at her in case I mesmerized her again and the nurse became convinced she was a drug addict.

I broke off and explained to Chloe that during eight and a half decades with no sleep, you get a lot of time to hone your skills. She asked what else I'd developed a talent for, but the only things I could think of were Connect Four and Tetris, so I turned back to the piano and continued playing.

Friday 10th June

Craig played an explicit rap song on his phone in Maths today. The rapper was being rude about a rival, and everyone was really impressed with all the swearing, but I didn't think it was a big deal.

It's nothing new, anyway. Dad told me that a vampire called Ludovico of Sienna once published an epic poem about how a love rival was ignorant, loathsome and tedious. He was found dead with a wooden stake through his heart two weeks later in what was thought to be a ride-by staking.

Mum and Dad are down in London again from tomorrow, so I'm going to invite Chloe round and play the piano for her. I might even light one of Mum's ancient candelabras and put on one of Dad's capes. I used to think all that stuff was really corny, but the more I vamp it up, the more Chloe seems to fancy me, so I'm happy to go along with it all now.

I don't mind playing up to stereotypes if it gets me some action!

SATURDAY 11TH JUNE

Chloe came round at six this evening, and said that she'd promised her parents she'd be back before nine. That didn't give me much time to establish the melodramatic mood and swoop in for a snog.

I had a quick check to make sure nobody was walking past, and then opened the door to show her my suit and cape. She stifled a laugh when she saw me but I could tell she thought it was really sexy.

I have to say, I don't quite understand why capes were so popular with vampires. I think it had something to do with shielding your skin from the sun, but I found it highly impractical. It kept swishing out behind me and knocking things off tables. Running around a candle-strewn castle with one of these things on sounds like a blatant fire hazard to me.

When Chloe was inside I sat at the piano and launched into Chopin's 'Funeral March' (no vampire cliche is too cheesy when seduction is on the cards).

Then I sat next to her and was just about to roll out some line about how I've searched through the endless fog of time for her when my annoying sister walked in and asked us what we were doing.

I told her that we were having a private conversation, but she failed to take the hint and plonked herself down on an armchair. Chloe politely chatted to her while I threw in a series of unsubtle suggestions about how she probably had something to get on with, all of which went right over her dense little head.

In the end I walked Chloe home, and got just one quick snog, which isn't much when you consider all the effort I put in.

Diary of a Wimpy Vampire

Sunday 12th June

Chloe has gone to church this morning, and there was no question of me tagging along. All those crucifixes would give me a splitting headache, and the rest of the day would be a write-off.

So now I've been on the PlayStation for seven hours straight. Craig once told me that computer games aren't as exciting once you get a girlfriend. I didn't believe him, but now I think it might actually be true.

Perhaps I'm becoming mature.

Monday 13th June

Chloe has several nicknames for me now because that's what happens in serious relationships. She calls me 'Fangy', 'Mr Freeze' and 'Nige of the Living Dead'. I thought these lacked gravitas, so I've suggested that she call me 'Nightwalker' instead. So far my suggestion has not been taken on board.

I had to see the careers advisor today. Over the years I've developed a strategy of pretending I want to work in a sector that I know they've got a leaflet on like healthcare or retail, so I can make the meeting as short as possible. Unfortunately this particular careers advisor insisted on grilling me about my interests. I played along, even though it doesn't matter what I want to do in the future, because I'll be a school pupil until society breaks down so much that schools no longer exist.

In the end she gave me a leaflet about IT and I binned it at the first opportunity. After her meeting, Chloe decided she wanted to help disadvantaged children in Africa. I admired her selflessness, but I tried to steer her away from the plan because Africa would be too hot for me.

TUESDAY 14TH JUNE

Mum and Dad are back from London with a new supply of delicious type AB+ blood.

I was happily tucking into some when Dad came into my room looking awkward. He sat down on the edge of the bed and explained that as I had a human girlfriend now, it was time that we had a talk about feeding. I told him that I didn't have any plans to feed on Chloe, but he went on with his prepared speech.

Diary of a Wimpy Vampire

He said that vampires need to be very careful when they feed in order to avoid accidentally transforming a human into one of us. He explained that unwanted transformation occurs when the blood of a vampire mixes with that of a human, so you should make sure that you don't have any cuts in your mouth before you feed.

We then sat in uncomfortable silence for a couple of minutes until he handed me another one of his old-fashioned pamphlets. I think if it were possible for vampires to blush, we'd have both been bright red!

WEDNESDAY 15TH JUNE

Chloe was engrossed in her homework this lunchtime so I went to the back of the gym to hang around with the goths instead.

I shouldn't have bothered. They kept asking if my girlfriend was busy and saying that they thought they weren't worthy of my attention any more. It was really immature and motivated by jealousy (admittedly, Brian does have a girlfriend, but mine is more attractive than his, so he has every reason to be envious).

I did my best to ignore it but I started to get riled when John said in a really sarcastic voice that I should go and check that my 'princess' was alright.

So I have officially broken friends with the goths now. Who needs friends when you have a girlfriend anyway?

188

Diary of a Wimpy Vampire

THURSDAY 16TH JUNE

The leaflet Dad has given me is called *Feeding on Humans Without Bleeding on Humans*. Although it had a serious message, I couldn't help laughing at the diagrams because they were so out of date. All the men were wearing huge velvet capes and the women were wearing gowns and corsets.

Nonetheless, I made an effort to take in all the safety advice in the leaflet. I just hope I can remember it if my desire for blood ever gets the better of me.

FRIDAY 17TH JUNE

Tomorrow I'm calling round at Chloe's house and then we're going out for a romantic walk in the park. Apparently it's going to be a hot day so I'm putting on extra sunblock. Should be good.

Diary of a Wimpy Vampire

SATURDAY 18TH JUNE

9AM

A strange start to the morning. Chloe has posted a note through our letterbox instructing me to meet her at the school gates rather than her house. It's definitely her writing, and nobody else knows she calls me 'Fangy', but I find it odd that she chose to write a note rather than ring the doorbell and tell me. It's not like she would have been waking anyone up.

The school isn't on the way to the park, so I think she has a surprise trip planned. I'm off to meet her now, though I'm a bit wary about going near school at weekends. There was an incident last October when a group of ex-pupils broke in on a Saturday and draped toilet paper around the corridors. I wouldn't like to be falsely associated with a weekend toilet paper attack if it happens again. I had enough trouble living down the monkey bum disease allegations.

6PM

Well, that was a stressful day to say the least. When I got to the gates of the school, I found another note in Chloe's handwriting telling me to go to the gym. I had no idea what she would be doing in there on a Saturday. The only thing I could think of was that she might be helping with the preparations for the summer fair.

Diary of a Wimpy Vampire

I saw that the fire doors to the gym were open, so I went in. As soon as I got inside, I felt like I was surrounded by bright flashing lights while the sound of metal scraping on metal was blasted directly into my brain. I fell down to the floor with my hands on my head trying to work out what was happening, and why Chloe thought that this would be a pleasant way for me to spend my Saturday.

The scene in front of me gradually came into focus, and I could see a barrier of bookshelves filled with crucifixes stretching across the width of the gym. All around me, the floor was covered in pungent cloves of garlic.

My first instinct was to run away, but as I forced myself to ignore the pounding in my head, it dawned on me that someone must know I'm a vampire, and I must be in trouble.

Was this an elaborate revenge planned by Wayne? Was it the goths' idea of a practical joke? Could it really be true that Chloe was a vampire slayer, as I had once speculated?

This last possibility was ruled out when I saw my darling girlfriend in a gap between two of the bookcases, tied to a chair and with a gag over her mouth. A figure was lurking behind her, and through the haze of my migraine I made out that it was Mr Jenkins, the PE teacher!

I told him I was sorry I had lied about having a bad back, but kidnapping my girlfriend and torturing me was surely an excessive punishment. He asked me if I was really stupid or just pretending, which I thought was a bit rich coming from a

PE teacher. He then bent down towards Chloe and took a good sniff of her neck. I wanted to get up and stop him, but I was still too weak from all the garlic and crucifixes.

Mr Jenkins looked at me and said that he loved the smell of type 0–. Then he smiled, exposing two elongated fangs! I couldn't believe it! My stupid PE teacher was one of us!

My head was spinning so much that it took a while for everything to fall into place, but at last I realized that it must have been Mr Jenkins who was responsible for the rogue vampire attacks in town, and not my parents after all. For a minute, I almost felt relieved, until I looked up again and saw his ugly face smirking at me.

Mr Jenkins told me that he knew all about my family, and that if I didn't find a way to bring my dad to the gym by nightfall, he would drain Chloe's veins so much that she'd never wake up again. Then he stooped down and pressed his fangs right up to her jugular. It was so unfair. She hasn't even let me do that yet!

I managed to extract a promise out of him that he would release Chloe if I brought Dad in. So I crawled out of the gym and stumbled back home, where I'm writing this and waiting for Dad to get back from his Saturday hike. As usual, he's not answering his phone.

I wish my stupid dad would hurry up and get here. He is putting my happiness at risk!

12AM

OK, I admit that if I'd thought about it, I would have realized that I was leading Dad into danger. But it's hard to think rationally when your PE teacher has just taken the love of your life captive.

So when Dad got home, I told him he had to come to the school gym as I'd be performing in a surprise talent evening. It wasn't a very good lie, and he was hardly

Diary of a Wimpy Vampire

falling over himself to get there, but I thought it was an invitation he couldn't really turn down.

I know it was wrong of me to deceive Dad, but I'd just found out that he'd been lying to me my whole life about us being the last remaining vampires. If even the PE teacher at my school was a vampire, then how many others were still around? Perhaps he didn't want to alarm me. Perhaps he was frightened that I'd run off and join another coven. Either way he should have told me the truth.

I ushered Dad through the door of the gym, telling him that the show was about to begin. The garlic and crucifixes floored us both when we got inside. I was prepared for it this time, but it was still really painful. I thought it might be easier for Dad to ignore the vampire repellents, but he seemed to be in just as much agony as me. By the time I managed to ignore my headache enough to see again, Dad was squinting at the gap between the bookshelves.

I heard him ask if it was 'Vaclav' he could see. I was about to tell him that it was just my stupid PE teacher who was causing all the trouble, when Mr Jenkins replied, 'Of course it is. You didn't think you could hide from me forever, did you?'

The weird thing was, my dad apologized to Mr Jenkins. I would have expected him to be angry rather than sorry. Mr Jenkins said there was no way he could be expected to show mercy when he had been shown none himself.

Mr Jenkins was good to his promise and released Chloe. She ran towards me and helped me to my feet. She was about to offer my dad a hand too when Mr Jenkins pulled out a Super Soaker water gun from behind one of the bookshelves. He told us that it was loaded with holy water and he'd cover my dad with it if we tried to rescue him. We

Diary of a Wimpy Vampire

were forced to leave Dad and Mr Jenkins alone in the gym as we made our escape.

Chloe helped me stagger out of the fire exit and across the playground. As I walked away from the gym and my headache faded, I began to think more clearly. We paused at the railings on the edge of the playground, and I stopped feeling frightened and started feeling angry. I thought about how Mr Jenkins had manipulated me to trap Dad, and how long he must have been planning his revenge. But the thing that really tipped me over the edge was remembering how he'd threatened to drink Chloe's blood when I haven't even done that yet. My dear sweet Chloe! The one mortal who understands and accepts me! How dare that vile fiend threaten her?

A look of alarm on Chloe's face snapped me out of my rage. I followed her gaze and saw that I'd somehow managed to bend back the iron railings I was holding on to. I tried bending the railing next to it and it gave like it was made of tinfoil. I bent another railing and then another. I could now feel a strength and power I had never known before flowing through my body.

I ran back to the gym in a matter of seconds and looked up at the high windows. I became aware that I was about to jump up high into the air and crash through one of them. Usually I would have been worried about doing this in case I landed in a funny way or got some glass in my eye, but I didn't consider any of this. I wasn't thinking rationally at all, to be honest. I was moving so fast by this point that I'm finding it hard to remember exactly what was going through my mind.

I know I jumped through the window, and landed on the

Diary of a Wimpy Vampire

floor beside Mr Jenkins. Now I was on the other side of the bookshelves, at a safe distance from the garlic and crucifixes and in a good position to attack. Mr Jenkins was ranting at my dad, but he turned his attention to me as I charged forwards.

I think Mr Jenkins was surprised at my newfound speed and strength, especially as I could hardly manage a press-up last time I'd been in one of his PE lessons. He tried attacking me with a flying kick, but I blocked it and forced him into a corner. He tried to punch me, but I caught his hand and pinned him against the wall. I would have said 'How's this for a press-up?' But I didn't think of it at the time.

Mr Jenkins wriggled free and jumped up to the top of the climbing frame on the gym wall. I leaped after him and ripped off one of the rungs of the frame to create a makeshift wooden stake. I tried desperately to ram it into his heart while he batted it away in terror.

I was getting the better of the struggle when I heard Dad calling from below. He said that we were vampires, and this was not how vampires do things.

He then started reeling off some ancient mumbo-jumbo I couldn't follow, but it must have meant something to Mr Jenkins because he climbed down and solemnly nodded his head. I did the same. It was only as we were walking Chloe home that Dad revealed I'd agreed to fight a duel with Mr Jenkins under the ancient rules of the Vampire Council.

Diary of a Wimpy Vampire

SUNDAY 19TH JUNE

In my anger last night, I forgot that killing Mr Jenkins would have meant permanent exclusion from vampire society. I would have had to leave Mum and Dad's house. And you can bet my sister would have moved straight into my room. She's always been jealous of me for having the biggest bedroom.

I am to fight the duel against Mr Jenkins at midnight next Saturday in the park. Neither of us will die, but one of us will eventually surrender, and go into exile for 100 years under terms dictated by the winner. I don't know exactly what Mr Jenkins has planned for me, but I bet it will involve press-ups.

If I win, I've decided to banish Mr Jenkins to a small town in Kenya called Nanyuki, because I saw on a map that it's right over the equator, so I'm guessing it gets loads of sunlight. Even if he worms his way into another PE teaching job, the sun will prevent him from torturing the pupils too much.

The annoying thing is that Mr Jenkins was in the middle of challenging my dad to a duel when I jumped in through the window, but because I attempted to kill him, I now have to take part in the duel instead. To be honest, I wish I'd left them to it.

Diary of a Wimpy Vampire

MONDAY 20TH JUNE

9AM

Dad has phoned school to say I'll be off sick this week as it's forbidden for me to see Mr Jenkins before the duel. I doubt he'll turn up at school either, as he'll be too busy honing his vampire kung fu. I'm not going to waste my time worrying what he's up to, though. I need to focus on my own preparation.

This afternoon I went to the park to test my vampire speed and I ended up circling the whole thing in a matter of seconds!

It's funny to think that I was so convinced I didn't have vampire powers, while they were in me all along, waiting to be set off. Perhaps the emergency situation I found myself in on Saturday forced me to unleash them. Or perhaps being in love has given me the confidence to access powers I've always had. I'd write a poem about it if I weren't so busy.

7 PM

Dad is supposed to be teaching me vampire martial arts today, but he's still angry with me for luring him to the school gym and putting him at the mercy of Mr Jenkins.

I've said sorry. He needs to get over it.

Anyway, I should be annoyed with him! He said we were the last four vampires on earth! Now it turns out there are hundreds of us still around, and some of them, like Mr Jenkins, have long-standing vendettas against Dad for transforming them. He says it only happened when he was young and reckless and he doesn't see why they still want revenge on him now he's settled down with a family.

I'm not allowed to tell my sister any of this, as Dad says she'll be happier not knowing, just as I would have been. The difference, though, is that I'm mature enough to cope with the truth. And rather than wasting my time accusing my parents of attacking the local townspeople, I could have been searching for the real culprit.

I have no doubt that I'd have used my powers of deduction to identify Mr Jenkins as the true perpetrator, and this whole unpleasant situation would have been avoided.

Diary of a Wimpy Vampire

TUESDAY 21ST JUNE

3PM

I went out to the countryside this morning to try and get some control over my vampire speed and strength. I think I'm getting there. All I have to do is stand at the bottom of a cliff and focus on the energy building up inside me and a few seconds later I find I've jumped right to the top.

It feels amazing to finally access my powers after eighty-five years of believing I didn't have them. I was having a great time splashing through streams, leaping up hills and uprooting trees, but I had to remind myself that I was here to train, not to mess around. It's brilliant to finally have these abilities, but they won't be much use if

Mr Jenkins commands me to spend the next 100 years on a desert island living off stinky fish blood.

7 PM

Chloe came round after school today. She's been grounded for staying out late on Saturday, and has chosen to take the punishment rather than reveal anything about us. I am deeply moved by her loyalty.

I ran down the street in just four seconds to impress her, but she told me I should preserve my energy for the duel. She said that she's very worried about it, especially as she won't even be allowed out to watch it. I told her I'd text her afterwards and that even if I was banished to somewhere horrible she was welcome to join me. I don't think I sold that idea very well, because she changed the subject.

She said she felt foolish for going into the school on Saturday with Mr Jenkins, but he told her that someone had daubed graffiti all over the gym and her sense of duty as a prefect took over from her common sense.

She gave me a quick kiss and rushed off home. I would have liked her to stay longer but in my current vampirey mood I didn't trust myself to hold back from sinking my fangs into her neck, so it was probably for the best.

WEDNESDAY 22ND JUNE

My sister couldn't believe it when I offered to play football

Diary of a Wimpy Vampire

with her today. Mum and Dad hadn't told her that I'd
finally got my vampire powers, and you could tell she was
looking forward to dishing out another humiliating defeat.

She took her penalties first and I let her score them all
like usual. But when she went into goal, I blasted the ball
at her with such force that it carried her through the back
of the net and into the fence at the bottom of the garden.
She tried to kick the ball back at my face, but I batted it
away with ease. She then charged towards
me at top speed, and couldn't believe
it when I ducked out of the
way. She ended up chasing
me around the garden at
such a pace that we
destroyed the lawn and
Mum sent both of us to
our rooms.

My sister's in a foul
mood now she's worked out I've got my speed
and strength. Anyone would think she'd be pleased for
me. She's probably worried that she might stop being the
centre of attention for once in her spoilt life.

Tonight I have been trying to learn vampire kung fu from
one of Dad's crusty old manuals, but it's very difficult to
hold onto a book when you're performing a forty-foot back
flip. I hope he stops fuming and agrees to teach me soon.

Diary of a Wimpy Vampire

THURSDAY 23RD JUNE

Dad has finally given in and agreed to train me. About time too. Anyone would think he wanted me to go into exile.

We drove to a field in the remote countryside to ensure that we couldn't be seen, and Dad demonstrated the basic moves of vampire kung fu. As I got more confident in my abilities, I could feel my strength increasing. It's like I feel more alive (or more undead, to be accurate).

By the end of the day I'd learned the vampire leap, the ghoul jab, the nightstalker punch and the undead roundhouse kick. I'm off to practise these again in the garden now.

FRIDAY 24TH JUNE

2PM

I must have looked worried this morning because Mum made a lovely warm bowl of type B+ to cheer me up. She seems more concerned than Dad at the prospect of losing me for a century. She said that all she ever wanted was to settle down to a quiet family life and didn't see why vampires like Vaclav (this is the name they use for Mr Jenkins) couldn't just forgive and forget.

Much as I hate Mr Jenkins, I wouldn't say his behaviour was entirely unjustified. From what I can gather, Dad transformed him over 200 years ago by accidentally

205

Diary of a Wimpy Vampire

infecting him with vampire blood while feeding on him. He
then refused to let Mr Jenkins join his coven and wouldn't
even train him in basic vampire survival, forcing him to
spend the next few decades drinking the blood of rats in the
sewers of Prague.

When I asked Mum why Dad behaved like this, she said
that he was a different vampire back then, and would
often drink too much blood and show off. She says that he's
changed now, and everyone should just leave us alone.

No wonder Dad was so embarrassed when he was giving
me that talk about safe feeding. It's clearly not advice he's
followed! I wonder how many other disgruntled vampires
are lurking around waiting to get revenge?

6PM

Chloe popped round again after school, courageously breaking the terms of her grounding once more. I asked her if she would join me in exile if I lost, and she said she'd have to find out about the local schools first to check she could still do Business Studies, English Literature and Psychology for A Level. At least this shows she's been thinking seriously about the possibility.

She looked upset as she said goodbye. But this is what happens when you date a dangerous supernatural being. If she wanted a mundane suburban life, she should have stuck with Wayne.

12AM

I must say I'm somewhat concerned by all this talk about Dad transforming humans by mistake in the past. I hope I wasn't an accident!

SATURDAY 25TH JUNE

I'm feeling nervous about tonight's duel now. Part of me just wants to surrender and take my exile, but 100 years is a long time. Imagine all the computer games I'll miss if Mr Jenkins sends me somewhere with no electricity. They'll be onto the PlayStation 40 by the time I'm back.

Dad has given me a leather holster with a solid gold stake in it. It feels unwieldy, but Dad says it's part of the vampire duel tradition. To make your opponent formally concede, you must pin him down and hold the stake over his heart. They used to give you genuine wooden ones, but they were outlawed by the Vampire Council's Health and Safety Division in 1881.

When I strapped on the holster it made me realize how serious all of this is. Mr Jenkins has had full control of his vampire powers for 200 years, while I've only had a week to get the hang of mine. Let's just say that if the Vampire Council's Gambling Division was still going, they wouldn't be offering very good odds on me.

SUNDAY 26TH JUNE

I went down to the park with Mum and Dad an hour early to warm up for the duel. Mr Jenkins turned up just before twelve, looking smug and confident.

I was ready to start straight away, but it turns out that vampire duels are stuffy and formal occasions. As I stood facing Mr Jenkins, my dad unfurled a large scroll and read out the 137 rules of vampire conflict set out by the Vampire Council in 1717. It was really boring and I stopped concentrating after a while, so I've no idea what exactly I agreed to.

By the time the duel itself started it was almost 1am, and I'd lost a lot of the energy I'd been building up. Mr Jenkins didn't waste any time, launching with a quick jab that broke my nose. Dad had taught me how to block these, but

I didn't remember in time. I backed away to give my nose a chance to mend, and Mr Jenkins came forward with a flying kick that knocked me to the floor and cracked two of my ribs.

Although I managed to get up pretty quickly, I found it hard to summon the same ferocity of attack as last week. I think this was partly because I'd started to feel sorry for Mr Jenkins since Mum had told me about Dad's mistreatment of him. I wish Mum had waited until after the duel to tell me there were two sides to the story.

Nonetheless, I landed a couple of solid blows on Mr Jenkins. He retaliated with a fast kick, but I swung out of his way. I was beginning to feel my strength and speed picking up now, and was able to match anything Mr Jenkins offered, but every time I made a move, he blocked it. Instead, I retreated, and Mr Jenkins did the same.

Diary of a Wimpy Vampire

We both waited, and then we both charged. I tried to strike Mr Jenkins with one of the roundhouse kicks I'd been practising, but I misjudged the move and he pulled me down to the floor. I struggled about, but couldn't get free of his grasp. He then pulled his ceremonial stake out of his backpack and ordered me to surrender.

Just as I was about to formally concede, though, I summoned my last ounce of energy and a strange image came into my mind. I saw a leaf, then an acorn and then the bark of a tree. I felt like I was running down a tree and then through huge blades of grass towards the silhouette of a man holding a large stake. I felt the weight lift from my body, and when my sight was clear again, Mr Jenkins was writhing around on the floor, covered in vicious squirrels!

I got to my feet and realized that my chance had come. I put my foot on Mr Jenkins' neck and held my stake over him. I asked him if he surrendered, and he said that I'd broken the rules by failing to declare my powers of animal mind control. I told him that I'd never done it before, so I could hardly be expected to declare it. After a few more grumbles he gave in. The squirrels scurried back up the trees.

When Mr Jenkins asked for the terms of his exile, I didn't have the heart to go through with my equator plan. I sent him to Alaska, which has always been a popular destination with vampires, and my only condition was that he didn't look for employment as a PE teacher. I saw no reason to make future generations endure what I've had to.

Mum said that I'd showed compassion worthy of the ancient vampire nobility and the best animal control she'd seen for decades. She hasn't been this proud of me since I passed Grade 8 Piano.

I rang Chloe to tell her that I had won, and she was overjoyed, although she had to whisper, because she isn't supposed to use her mobile after ten.

MONDAY 27TH JUNE

I went back to school today. In assembly the headmaster announced that Mr Jenkins had quit his job with immediate effect due to a 'family emergency'. I looked at Chloe and smiled, but we couldn't say a word about what's really happened over the last few days.

I feel really good after my victory. I no longer think of myself as boring old Nigel Mullet, but Nigel of Stockfield,

Diary of a Wimpy Vampire

master of vampire martial arts and animal mind control. And very tough to beat on Mario Kart.

TUESDAY 28TH JUNE

Sarah from the popular gang passed a note round in Maths today saying that she fancies me. At first I thought it was a wind-up, but when I glanced across at her, she blushed and looked away. Chloe ripped the note up when she saw it. I hope it made her realize what a catch she has!

This evening I looked at my face in the mirror to see if any vampire attractiveness has appeared. Something must have changed since the girls from the popular gang gave me four out of ten for looks, but I can't see what.

WEDNESDAY 29TH JUNE

Thanks to the exile of Mr Jenkins, we had a supply teacher called Mr Moss for PE today. I didn't bother with any excuses, as I actually want to do PE now I've got my vampire speed and strength. Obviously, I'd give myself away if I used them too much, but I can still switch them on just enough to be the best in the class.

In the gym, everyone was shocked at how easily I jumped over the vaulting horse and climbed up the ropes. I even went right to the top of the climbing frame and saw the gap where I ripped out the pole in my first conflict with Mr Jenkins. Nobody seems to have noticed it yet.

Diary of a Wimpy Vampire

At the end of the lesson, Mr Moss said that I should join a gymnastics club! After all the shocks I've suffered over the past few weeks, this has to be the biggest yet – a PE teacher I actually like.

THURSDAY 30TH JUNE

This morning Craig stuck a pound coin to the floor with superglue as a practical joke. He was waiting a few feet away and jeering at anyone who tried to pick it up. When I attempted to lift the coin, I uprooted the whole paving slab

Diary of a Wimpy Vampire

it was glued to. I must be more careful about keeping my vampire strength under wraps.

This afternoon I found out that two more girls from the popular gang fancy me! At first I was worried that someone might have told them I'm a vampire, but there's no way they can know. Perhaps I'm developing supernatural beauty. Or perhaps I'm just making more eye contact now. I don't know. It's all very confusing.

I remembered my vow to get revenge on the girls from the popular gang if they ever started fancying me, but I couldn't really be bothered. I have no interest in their shallow little world now.

Friday 1st July

I had fun playing around with my animal mind control power today. I looked at the neighbour's cat from my bedroom window and concentrated on it until I could see the world through its eyes. Cats must get so bored of looking at everything in black and white.

I made it jump up a tree, roll over on its back and then stroke its head with its paw before I let it go. It gave me a really dirty look and then dashed away before I could control it again.

Saturday 2nd July

Chloe's grounding has finished now, so we went to the

countryside to test out my powers. We found a nice deserted spot, and Chloe set me a series of challenges. First, I scaled a cliff face and jumped down again. Then I threw a huge rock across a river. My next challenge was to go through an entire forest without letting my feet touch the ground, but I fell down and broke my ankle, and we had to wait for it to heal.

When it was better, she set me a challenge to see how high in the air I could jump, but after a while I got worried that someone would see me from the road so I stopped.

SUNDAY 3RD JULY

7AM

Dad has agreed to drive me to the zoo today. I have some payback planned for all the animals that tried to ruin my life on the school trip.

6PM

I had fun on my trip to the zoo today, and I'd like to think I made the experience more enjoyable for all the other visitors.

As soon as the animals saw me they started to freak out, just as they did last time. They soon went quiet when they realized what I had in store for them, though. I stared right into the eyes of a meerkat that was standing guard on top of its enclosure. I got inside its mind and made it wobble from side to side as if it was drunk, and then fall flat on its back. Everyone around the cage started filming it on their phones so I made it do the same thing over and over again.

I left the meerkat and entered the mind of an orang-utan, which I made pull some funny expressions and fall off a tyre. As I stalked around the zoo, I made a baby elephant sneeze, a gorilla moonwalk and a giraffe pull a branch with its mouth so that it flew right back in its face.

This is what you get for messing with me, animal kingdom. I condemn you to the humiliation of becoming a cute Internet clip. Now you're the ones everyone is laughing at.

MONDAY 4TH JULY

I was feeling brave today so I came right out and asked Chloe if she was ready to take our relationship to the next level and let me drink her blood. She seemed quite shocked at first, but she became more open to the idea once I explained to her that if I drink just a little bit it won't do her any harm.

Obviously, if I get greedy and drink loads, she'll be ill for a couple of days, but I didn't tell her that because I'm sure I've got the willpower to hold back.

Chloe said that she trusts me, but she doesn't feel ready just yet.

TUESDAY 5TH JULY

I asked Dad for a thousand pounds to buy Chloe a diamond pendant, but he came out with the same old tripe about us drawing attention to ourselves if we spend too much. I don't know why he can't make an exception for something as important as this.

In the end he gave me twenty pounds and I bought Chloe a bat-shaped pendant from the goth shop. She was very pleased with it, and let me fasten it around her neck. I thought she might be so overwhelmed by my generosity that she would let me have a feed, but no such luck.

I don't mind, though. I can be patient.

Wednesday 6th July
We played football in PE today and I scored four goals. I

could have scored a fifth, but I was scared of revealing my powers, so I struck it wide.

THURSDAY 7TH JULY

I'm trying to find a new hobby to take my mind off the frustration of waiting for Chloe to let me drink her blood. So far I've attempted gardening, juggling and learning about dinosaurs, but none of them helped me stop thinking about how sweet it would be to dip my fangs into her neck. But I will be strong. Allowing a vampire to feed on you is a big step for any human to make, and I must be sensitive to that.

I'm sure Chloe will agree soon, but in the meantime I'll just have to suck it up. Or rather, not suck it up.

FRIDAY 8TH JULY

I went out for a run tonight. I only intended to go as far as the park, but I got really in the zone and when I stopped I was surprised to find myself at the seaside. I must be careful not to run past any speed cameras. The last thing I want is grainy footage of me dashing around at fifty miles an hour turning up on the Internet.

SATURDAY 9TH JULY

I tried to write a poem today, but I have to admit it's not up to my usual standard.

Diary of a Wimpy Vampire

LET US WANDER TOGETHER

Let us wander together
Through endless night
Surveying the world
By pale moonlight
Then you will let me
Sip your blood
It will be really nice
It will be really good

I'm especially disappointed by the ending, but I couldn't think of anything else. How strange that all the time I was in despair, great art was flowing from pen, but now that I've found contentment, this is the best I can do.

I don't really care, though. If misery is the price you have to pay for genius, count me out. Let someone else take on the responsibility of being the greatest poet of a generation.

SUNDAY 10TH JULY

Chloe came round today and I practised my mesmerism skills on her. It's quite tricky, but I think I'm getting the hang of it. I can now give Chloe just enough hypnosis so that she comes round again after a couple of minutes.

Now that I'm getting this skill under control, I'm pretty much ready to go with the blood-drinking.

Diary of a Wimpy Vampire

I won't put any pressure on Chloe to let me do it because I'm a gentleman. I really hope she lets me soon, though!

MONDAY 11TH JULY

Went to school today. Then went for walk with Chloe. Then came home and had type AB+ blood for dinner.

TUESDAY 12TH JULY

Quite sunny today. Chloe came round after school.

FRIDAY 22ND JULY

This is my first diary entry for a while, and I think it will also be my last.

The summer holidays start today and now I've finally got my vampire powers, I'd rather be outside enjoying myself than moping around in here.

Also, Chloe says she's ready to let me drink her blood, and I don't think it would be gentlemanly of me to write down anything about that, even in a secret diary.

I've had another look through Dad's leaflet about safe feeding, and I'm going to check myself thoroughly for cuts first, so there's no danger I'll accidentally transform Chloe.

She told me recently that she wouldn't mind if she did turn into a vampire. She said that I'm one and I seem to be enjoying myself. And she's right, I have been enjoying myself recently, I really have.

221

Diary of a Wimpy Vampire

But I still wouldn't recommend it to anyone. The first 100 years were terrible.

ALSO BY TIM COLLINS

Diary of a Wimpy Vampire
Prince of Dorkness

978-1-84317-524-7

£7.99

Adventures of a Wimpy Werewolf
Hairy but not scary

978-1-84317-856-9

£7.99

The Little Book of Twitter
Get Tweetwise!

978-1-84317-405-9

£3.99

WALKER'S
BRITAIN

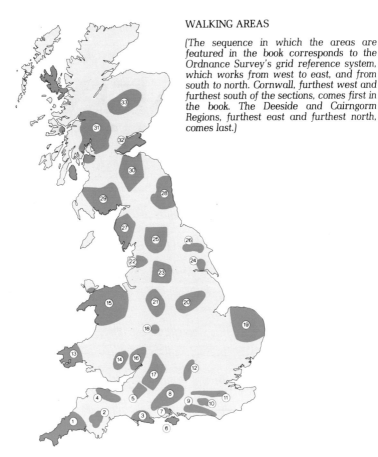

WALKING AREAS

(The sequence in which the areas are featured in the book corresponds to the Ordnance Survey's grid reference system, which works from west to east, and from south to north. Cornwall, furthest west and furthest south of the sections, comes first in the book. The Deeside and Cairngorm Regions, furthest east and furthest north, comes last.)

① Cornwall, page 14
② Dartmoor, page 24
③ Dorset, page 34
④ Exmoor and The Quantocks, page 42
⑤ Mendip Region, page 54
⑥ Isle of Wight, page 66
⑦ New Forest, page 72
⑧ The Wessex Downs, page 80
⑨ South Downs, page 92
⑩ Surrey, page 104
⑪ North Downs, page 112
⑫ Chilterns and Thames Valley, page 122
⑬ Pembrokeshire, page 132
⑭ Brecon Beacons and Black Mountains, page 140
⑮ North Wales, page 148
⑯ Welsh Marches, page 166

⑰ Cotswolds, page 172
⑱ Around Birmingham, page 182
⑲ Norfolk, page 188
⑳ East Midlands, page 196
㉑ Peak District, page 204
㉒ Lancashire, page 216
㉓ The South Pennines, page 222
㉔ Yorkshire Wolds, page 232
㉕ Yorkshire Dales, page 240
㉖ North York Moors, page 252
㉗ Cumbria and The Lakes, page 260
㉘ Northumberland, page 272
㉙ SW Scotland, page 282
㉚ South of the Forth, page 290
㉛ Highlands and Islands, page 298
㉜ Fife Region, page 310
㉝ Deeside and Cairngorm Regions, page 318

WALKER'S BRITAIN

The Complete Pocket Guide to over 240 Walks and Rambles

1992 edition

Re-walked and revised by George Toulmin

LONDON   NEW YORK   SYDNEY   TORONTO

This edition published 1994 by BCA by arrangement with Pan Books and Ordnance Survey.

Conceived, edited and designed by Duncan Associates, 78, Ramsden Road, London, SW12 8QZ with Mel Petersen & Associates, 54 Milson Road, London W14 0LB.

CN2930

Printed and bound in Great Britain by BPC Hazell Books Ltd
A member of
The British Printing Company Ltd

Sections introduced by	**Christopher Hall**
Illustrations	**Tony Graham**
Special contributor	**Marjorie Lampard**
Long Distance Section compiled by	**Jennifer Grafton**
Consultant	**John Trevelyan**
Design & artwork	**Nigel O'Gorman**
Researcher	**Trevor Dolby**
Assistant editor	**Joshua Dubin**
Editorial assistants	**Fred and Cathy Gill, David Arnold**
Picture research	**Linda Proud**
Art Editor	**Mel Petersen**
Editor	**Andrew Duncan**

Invaluable inspiration and advice was provided by Nigel Buxton.

THE WALKERS

Cornwall, **David Platten**; Dartmoor, **Liz Prince and staff of the Dartmoor National Park Office**; Dorset, Isle of Wight, New Forest, The Wessex Downs, **Anne-Marie Edwards**; Exmoor, **David Butler**; The Quantocks, **C. Trent Thomas**; Mendip Region, **E. M. Goold with G. Lane and S. Franklin of the Mendip Ramblers' Association**; Surrey, North Downs, **Janet Spayne, Audrey Krynski**; South Downs, **Ben Perkins**; Chilterns and Thames Valley, **Nick Moon**; Pembrokeshire, **Tom Goodall and members of the Pembrokeshire Ramblers' Association**; Brecon Beacons and Black Mountains, **Chris Barber**; North Wales, **James T. C. Knowles**; Welsh Marches, **Donna Baker**; Cotswolds, **Richard Sale, Nathan Sale and Mike Rogers**; Around Birmingham, **S. G. Wallsgrove, Denis N. Keyte, R. Pickard**; Norfolk, **Jeanne le Surf**; East Midlands, **Brett Collier**; Peak District, Northumberland, **Brian Spencer**; Lancashire, **Cyril Spiby**; The South Pennines, Yorkshire Dales, **Colin Speakman**; Yorkshire Wolds, **Geoff Eastwood**; North York Moors, **Walter Henderson**; Cumbria and the Lakes, **John Parker**; SW Scotland, **Ken Andrew**; South of the Forth, Fife Region, **Dave Forsyth**; Highlands and Islands, **Bill Brodie, Charles Target**; Deeside and Cairngorm Regions, **F. C. A. Gordon.**

For the original (1981) edition, another team of walkers strode hundreds of miles checking and testing the walks. Of these the late Anne Duncan, John Nolan, Fiona Duncan and John and Caroline Sharpe, Charles Target and Helen Alexander deserve special thanks. We are also grateful to Georgina Leyland, Hugo Charlton, Clare and Julian Whately, Louise Hallett, Paula Grant, Margaret Robertshaw, Lorne and Bill Cobb, Adrian and Diana Dent, Richard and Jane Clayton, Martin Mitchell, Bill Chester, the Preston C.H.A. Rambling Club, Alan MacPherson, Dr. and Mrs. Wynne Willson, Geoffrey Redmayne and Linda Abraham.

For the 1992 edition, check-walking was undertaken principally by George Toulmin, a retired civil servant, who lives in Cheltenham. George visted most of the book's walking areas in a marathon lasting more than 12 months in 1990–91. The editors and publishers acknowledge with gratitude his unique contribution not only to this edition, but also to the 11 reprints which preceded it. Thanks also to James Knowles for his work on the North Wales section.

CONTENTS

The book is divided into 33 sections representing the cream of Britain's walking. These are shown, with page numbers, on the map on the preceding, facing page. For ease of reference, the contents are also organized into six regional sections, with page numbers given below.

Using this book	page	6
Footwear and Clothes		8
The Walker, the Law and Safety		10
The South-West		12-63
South-east England		64-129
Wales		130-163
Middle England		164-213
Northern England		214-279
Scotland		280-327
Long Distance Walks: a briefing		328-334
Index of place names that are starting points, or near starting points of walks		335
Acknowledgements		336

All distances mentioned are approximate. Remember that the countryside changes frequently; landmarks disappear – especially stiles.

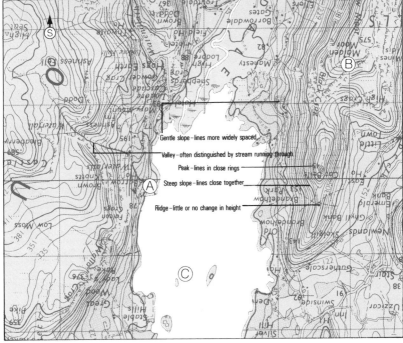

Gentle slope – lines more widely spaced

Valley – often distinguished by stream running through

Peak – lines in close rings

Steep slope – lines close together

Ridge – little or no change in height

You can do the routes in *Walker's Britain* just by following the directions linked to the numbers on the maps. However, some understanding of maps and map-reading will greatly add to your enjoyment.

The maps in this book were made by Ordnance Survey, the National Mapping Agency of Great Britain, usually referred to simply as O.S.

O.S. maps are the best available. They are based on detailed surveys: accurate measurements of the ground combined with aerial photography. No other maps are precision instruments in this sense.

The range of O.S. maps covers widely differing scales, for varying purposes. In this book are extracts from the 1:50,000 'Landranger' series.

To show the walking routes as clearly as possible, extracts from the monochrome versions of the 1:50,000 sheets have been used with the route marked by a green line which allows the mapping beneath to be read with reasonable ease.

1:50,000 maps are useful to walkers because, in colour, they show rights of way in England and Wales and are drawn to a scale giving enough detail for route-finding in most areas. For extra enjoyment of this book, use it with the relevant colour sheets. They open up limitless walking possibilities.

As a beginner, start by getting to know the meaning of the map's symbols (see inside front cover). Contour lines are the only complex ones. They are surveyed lines showing the height of the ground above sea level; with experience they enable you to 'see' the shape of the land–see the map opposite.

Before starting to walk, 'set' your map. If walking due north, have the top of the sheet pointing north; if walking south (see opposite), have the sheet upside down.

Next, identify two or three points on the ground and find them on the map (see A, B and C). This confirms your position.

Next, understand the full implications of the map's scale. On 1:50,000 maps, one unit on the map; represents 50,000 units on the ground. This is equivalent to 1¼ inches (3 cm) on the map for every mile (1.5 km) on the ground. An average walking pace is 3 mph (5 km/h) on the flat – a mile for every 20 minutes'. In hill country, add up to 50%.

Finally do not put the map away when you walk. Always know your position. Cross-check it by estimating distance against time, observing landmarks as they pass.

● The O.S. mapping used in this book does not show all rights of way, but the routes as marked are on rights of way or land with open access.
● The **sheet numbers** refer to the relevant O.S. Landranger sheet.
● The **six-figure number** following the sheet number is the grid reference of the walk's starting point on the Landranger sheet.
● **Mud after rain** means the route has a chance of drying out. **Mud** means suitable footwear must be worn.
● **The number of climbs** is a broad guide only. Remember **stiles** are of widely varying construction. **Path** usually means a narrow way – sometimes just beaten-down grass; **track** is usually broader and better defined.

crossroads   cairn

baseplate edge   magnifying glass   magnetic needle (red end)

travel arrow   dial   orienting lines

In poor visibility or on featureless ground, you need a compass. The 'Silva' type is the easiest to use with a map; here is one of several ways in which it works.

Imagine being on moorland when the cloud comes down. Your present position is a cairn. You want to make for a crossroads. Place the compass baseplate edge on the map so it connects cairn and crossroads. Turn the dial so that the orienting lines on the transparent bottom are parallel with grid lines running N-S on the map, the arrow pointing N. Then turn the whole compass, plus map, until the red end of the magnetic needle points to N.

Look up and distinguish a rock or clump of grass that lies along the line indicated by the travel arrow. Eyes on the landmark, walk to it. Repeat the procedure.

FOOTWEAR AND CLOTHES

You must have proper footwear for serious walking. Gum boots, gym shoes or kickers may be adequate for a stroll. Stout walking shoes will take you all day on country lanes. But if you walk regularly, and if you want to see the moorland and hill country – which means negotiating bogs and rough, stony ground, you need to protect your feet in leather walking boots.

Leather allows your feet to 'breathe' because it is porous. Ventilation is the key to comfortable feet because even if boots are sodden (as they will be – leather is no more than water-resistant), drying out can begin with the feet inside them. Rubber boots offer no such luxury: the feet are always slightly damp because the perspiration and condensation is trapped inside.

Only the stout construction of a walking boot can give the ankles the support they need to minimize risk of sprains. Only leather can mould itself to the feet, providing the fit that allows walking all day.

A genuine pair of walking boots costs as much as £100.00. Beware of other people's boots: they can never mould to your feet.

Wear in new boots on short walks – a total of about 30 miles (48 km) does the job. After walking, wash off the mud and let them dry naturally – direct heat distorts their shape. Wash them especially well after walking in boggy country: acids in marshy water can damage leather and stitching. While the boots are still wet, apply a dressing.

Clothes

When choosing walking clothes, remember that wind is potentially a serious problem. It reduces body temperature dramatically because of the heat loss in evaporation. A walk which starts in a light breeze in the valley can, on the hill-top, be a battle with a gale. Plan accordingly: have layers of clothing that can be shed, or added to. Remember, too, that significant body heat is lost from the head: so wear a hat.

Waterproofs need choosing carefully because of the condensation problem: your body warmth causes water droplets to form inside a waterproof garment if it is tightly closed against the rain. Some new materials claim to minimize the slight dampness so-caused, but ease of ventilation is still important. The waterproof anorak that opens up the front allows this, whereas one-piece, knee-length cagoules do not. Capes give excellent ventilation, but blow around violently in strong wind.

Buying boots

● Go to a specialist who will let you take time over fitting ● Try on boots before midday – later your feet may have swollen ● Your big toe ought not to press against the boot's toe ● When laced, the boot should hold the foot back, so that it does not slide forward when going downhill ● Sides of feet ought to be firmly held, but not squeezed when boots are laced ● The boot's heel should cup your own ● Your heel will move slightly in a new boot, but soon the boot's heel and yours should move together ● The back of the boot should be stiff enough to support your heel ● The uppers should be one piece of leather – no seams to leak ● A padded tongue and padded sides give extra comfort ● The sole must have some flexibility and be at least ½ inch (13 mm) thick. 'Vibram' or 'Commando' composition soles are reliable ● The welts should not stick out too far: this looks clumsy and if scrambling on the points of the toes long welts can lessen your contact with the ground, impairing balance. ● Boots should have a scree cuff for gripping the ankle and keeping out small stones. ● Hooks or 'D' rings are intended to be easiest to tie with cold fingers ● Two pairs of socks should be worn even with the perfectly fitting boot, a thin pair next to the skin, a thicker pair on top. The result is a cushioning effect and warmer feet. Most reputable dealers have thick socks at hand for fitting purposes.

Scree cuff

Padded tongue

'D' rings

Welts

Composition sole

Features of an efficient waterproof anorak

Zip can close to chin

Attached hood with drawcords

Elastic wrist bands in sleeves to keep out wind and rain

Large (map- or book-sized) button-down or press-studded pockets

Flap to protect zip from wet

Nylon gaiters to stop mud, stones and water from entering

Jeans, despite their popularity, are not ideal walking trousers. Wool or corduroy are warmer, and provide some protection against chilling wind even if wet through. The most comfortable combination for hill walking is knee-length breeches and socks.

The rucksack should contain waterproof over-trousers. The most practical type can be put on without taking the boots off. Increasingly popular are light, padded jackets to give body warmth with freedom of arm movement.

THE WALKER, THE LAW AND SAFETY

WALKERS' RIGHTS, AND DUTIES

Great Britain has more public footpaths than any nation on Earth. The network in England and Wales is more than 120,000 miles long; in Scotland, where the law is different, walkers theoretically enjoy even more open access to the countryside.

Moreover, in England and Wales, the right to wander in the countryside is supported by an interesting principle of law, itself an embodiment of many of the principles of social freedom we take for granted.

In law, public footpaths can be born at any time, on anyone's land, by the process known as dedication (but this may change). Dedication can be 'presumed', in which case, if a path is in use without a break for 20 years, it is presumed to be a right of way. Or it can be 'direct', in which case it is negotiated, or even compulsorily ordered. A landowner can prevent presumed dedication by closing the path just once during the 20-year period; but the principle, and the possibility, of creating new paths always exists.

A right of way is just what it says: a right of passage across someone's land. The landowner may rightly object if the walker does damage, or leaves litter. But he may not complain – legally – if the walker pauses on the path to enjoy the view, or to eat lunch.

Trespass

If a walker strays from the right of way, he is trespassing. In this case the landowner ought to insist that the trespasser returns to the right of way, or leaves the land. Should the trespasser refuse, the landowner may use the minimum possible force to make the trespasser do so.

It is not an offence, in itself, to trespass; if you are taken to court as a result of trespassing, the landowner will sue for damages. If you, the trespasser, are found guilty, you would pay these damages. They may or may not amount to much in terms of

cash; but you would also have to pay the landowner's legal fees: never cheap.

Maintenance

In British law, the landowner has a duty to maintain rights of way.

A minimum width must be kept clear and nothing may grow or fall over or onto the path. Paths running round the edges of fields must not be disturbed.

The line of a path must be apparent where it passes through crops. If it is not, the walker is entitled to walk the path, keeping to the right of way. Paths may be ploughed and left unrestored for 14 days, if the field has not been ploughed that year; or 24 hours otherwise.

Passing through crops can be a source of worry and confusion for walkers, who feel that it is better to trespass and thereby avoid damage, than to keep to the path. But in legal and practical terms, the best course is to keep to the right of way. The damage to a field under crops is minimal if the walker(s) keep in single file; the consequences of trespass may be worse.

The law allows walkers to make detours, making every effort to cause no damage, over or around obstructions when the path is blocked by machinery, wire or anything else.

The Ramblers' Association

All these privileges, which are all too often abused and neglected (especially where ploughing is concerned) are protected on our behalf by the Ramblers' Association.

This is a privately funded lobby group, and if you care about going on country walks, you should support it, too. It has many local branches, some of which helped to prepare this book. The address is on page 328.

Bulls

Do not let your country walk be spoilt either by being unnecessarily frightened, or foolhardy when there are bulls or cows around. Cows and bullocks (castrated bulls) may rush up to you in a field, but they are rarely being aggressive.

If you see a bull alone in a field where there is a public right of way, it is probably there illegally; if it is with cows, it is probably there legally. If you encounter a truly aggressive (ie, charging) bull in a field where there is a right of way, tell the police and the Ramblers' Association.

Stallions, boars and cows with calves should be treated with due caution.

The Landowner

Remember the landowner's point of view, whatever your feelings about private ownership of land. Farmers, rich or poor, provide employment. Possibly their chief objection to walkers centres on dogs, which can upset livestock and kill game. After that, damage to crops and property are the main causes of friction. Share the countryside: you have a right to be there, but it is not exclusive.

SAFETY ON THE HILLS

Britain's mountains and hills are not high, but they are dangerous. Because they are near the sea, their weather changes fast.

Much about modern life makes us especially vulnerable to their treachery. We are unfit, because we sit all day. We arrive at walks in the comfort of cars, from which it is doubly hard to imagine the potential nastiness of the serenely inviting hilltops. Once out of the valley, a perfect summer's day can turn, in minutes, to wintry ghastliness.

Almost all accidents, and tragedies, can be prevented by following these rules.
● Wear the right clothes (see pages 8-9) and footwear. Take spare clothing.
● Be equipped. The lunch box should contain some emergency rations – chocolate, dried fruit and biscuits. There should be a flask containing a hot drink. The prudent take a first aid kit, even on a day's outing. Learn first aid for frost bite, fractures, hypothermia and strains.

The same applies to a whistle, a torch and a spare battery. Know the distress signal: six blasts of the whistle, or shouts – in fact of anything – followed by a minute's silence, then repeated.

Take a map. The O.S. 1:50,000 sheet for the area (better, 1:25,000 sheets or the 1:25,000 Outdoor Leisure Map as well) and a compass.
● Say where you are going; or at least leave a note on the car windscreen. Report any changes of plan by telephone. When you are home, report in.

● Plan the route. Make sure it is within the capabilities of the weakest member of the party. Allow enough time to be home well before nightfall. Allow an extra hour for every 1,500 feet (457 m) to be climbed. Take a watch. Know what time sunset will be.
● Ring the pre-recorded 24-hour forecast, or the local met. office for a weather report.
● Do not go alone. Three is the minimum safe number. In an accident, one can go for help; the other stays with the injured.
● Move at the pace of the slowest. Never straggle. Never split up, unless to get help.
● If the cloud comes down, walk in single file with 20 yards (18 m) between each of you. The last man – or woman – uses the compass, directing the leaders.

If you are caught in poor visibility, and cannot find the way down, stop until the weather clears, find shelter or build a windbreak from branches or rocks. Put on spare, dry clothing. Sit on something dry. Eat part of the emergency rations and drink something hot. Build an emergency bivouac from anything suitable – a groundsheet, a plastic mack, a cape. If cold, keep the limbs moving. Stay awake. Loosen laces and cuffs; huddle close to companions.

THE COUNTRY CODE

Wherever you go, follow the country code.

Enjoy the countryside and respect its life and work.
Guard against all risk of fire.
Fasten all gates.
Keep your dogs under close control.
Keep to public paths across farmland.
Use gates and stiles to cross fences, hedges and walls.
Leave livestock, crops and machinery alone.
Take your litter home.
Help to keep all water clean.
Protect wildlife, plants and trees.
Take special care on country roads.
Make no unnecessary noise.

THE SOUTH-WEST

CORNWALL, DARTMOOR, DORSET, EXMOOR AND THE QUANTOCKS, MENDIP REGION

CORNWALL

If anywhere is Lyonesse, the lost land of Arthurian legend, it is Cornwall. However, the county has more real claims on our sense of the past. The narrow, illogically twisting lanes are a motorist's bane. But on foot one can see how, along with the sunken and often tunnel-like tracks which have never achieved tarmac, they are needed to link the scattered farms and hamlets. For this landscape was originally settled by the Celts. Here, the neatly centred villages of Anglo-Saxon England, and the relatively uncomplicated road pattern that goes with them, are rare.

It is an industrial landscape, too. All over the eastern part of the county are the crumbling engine-sheds and chimney-stacks of the once flourishing tin-mines. The waste of a newer industry, china clay, makes glistening white hills around St. Austell.

Inland, most of the county is a plateau. The exception is Bodmin Moor, a dome of carboniferous rock like its bigger brother, Dartmoor. Here are glimpses of a landscape little, if at all, changed since the Celts carved their scraps of fields from wilderness. Round all is an enchanting coast, nearly all of it walkable. But take your time: long indentations and steep cliffs make it surprisingly strenuous work.

Carn Brea
2 miles (3 km) Sheet 203 688413

Easy A panorama of industrial Cornwall, an Iron Age site and a castle-restaurant; comfortable strolling mainly on well-defined gravel paths. *Heath; one climb.*

Start From the A30 at Redruth turn on to the A3047. At hospital turn left and continue to crossroads. **Parking** up W arm of crossroads, on left just past garage; alternatively, on summit of Carn Brea (access via Carnkie) – start walk at ④.

Carn Brea's summit: the hill was fortified in the Iron Age.

① Turn sharp left at junction of tracks where path emerges on to open heath and continue round edge of Carn, leaving castle up to right. ② Follow the bridleway, keeping right at path junctions, to meet gravel-surfaced road; follow this to top of Carn. ③ Where path meets road, turn right up to the castle. ④ At castle turn left along ridge and follow any of the paths towards the monument. ⑤ From monument, follow track to right of rocks and along ridge to farthest rock outcrop. ⑥ From outcrop, follow the most obvious path straight down ridge towards houses in distance. ⑦ Where path reaches edge of heath, with iron gate on left, turn right along field wall down to lane, where turn right. ⑧ At junction of lanes, take right fork on to footpath, keeping to moor side of houses. ⑨ Follow any of the paths alongside Carn, keeping parallel to ridge. All converge at ①.

Carn Brea's 19th C. 'castle' houses a restaurant with good home cooking.

A former tin and copper mining area: 15 mine chimneys can be counted to the S.

The Dunstanville Monument, in honour of Francis, first member of the old Cornish family of Basset to be ennobled. They grew rich from mining.

15

CORNWALL

Advent Church
5 miles (8 km) Sheet 200 108839

Moderate Typical agricultural Cornwall –
mixed farmland with simultaneous views of
moorland, lush valleys and the distant coast;
and a church in a peculiarly remote setting.
*Water meadow, farmland, woods, moorland;
one climb; mud after rain.*

Start Camelford, on the A39 between Bude
and Wadebridge. **Parking** in Church Field
Car Park, on left just past traffic lights if
driving N.

① From Fore Street, turn left under arch
beside D.I.Y. shop. Plaque over arch reads
'River and Advent Church'. Follow river
bank, crossing and re-crossing on
footbridges. ② Where path emerges on to
road by granite bridge, turn right uphill
along road, to third gate on left with 'Public
Path' signpost. Follow the path, crossing
second field diagonally to mid-point of
opposite wall, beyond which are woods. ③
At edge of field, cross stone stile and take
path downhill through woods, and
diagonally across water meadow. ④ At far
corner of meadow, look for the footbridge
hidden among trees. Cross the bridge and
the stile in the wire fence, and leaving
bushes to left, climb bank. Follow field wall
up to road gate. ⑤ Just past Trethin Manor
Holiday Cottages (clearly labelled) look for
the stile leading off obliquely to the left.
Beware of the wide gaps in the granite cattle
grid in front of stile. Continue to ⑥ far edge
of first field, where Advent Church tower is
visible ahead. Head directly towards tower,
arriving at gate into churchyard. Leave by
small gate in E boundary, opening directly
on to field (E is the altar end of the church).
Continue ahead over stile and through a
gate, then look for a stile on the right.
Crossing this, continue directly away from
church to stile on to the road. Turn left and
continue to Watergate. ⑦ At Watergate, just
before stream, turn left at 'Public Path' sign,
and follow partly paved track through
rough meadows. ⑧ At edge of small
pinewood, cross three adjacent stiles. Cut
diagonally uphill, following line indicated
by the long, wooden step of the first stile
until you see a waymarked stile a little to the
left. Over it, continue past low cairns and
towards gap between trees around
Moorgate farm and large barn. ⑨ Join road
by barn. Ignore 'Public Footpath' sign and

steps in opposite wall; instead take rough
track which branches left off road 10 yards
(9 m) E of signpost. Follow track across path
of rough moorland, between field walls and
on across more rough moorland. ⑩ At metal
road gate, turn left along wall to a similar
gate. Follow the well-defined cart track
downhill to entrance of Aldermoor Farm.
Continue along lane to Treclago. ⑪ Just before reaching Treclago, turn right along lane.
This becomes a track and ends at a gate into
field. ⑫ Go through gate and follow hedge to
small gate in bottom right corner of field. ⑬
Cross footbridge to stile in middle of hedge
opposite and continue through next field to
stile leading to lane. Car park is opposite far
end of lane.

🏠 Camelford's North Cornwall Museum
features a mock-up of a typical, 19th C.
Cornish kitchen and many 19th C. farm
implements.

🌉 This is known as a clapper bridge – one
of the most ancient forms of bridge in the
country.

⛪ Advent Church gives visitors a feeling of
going back several centuries, indeed, its
congregation is mainly drawn from
the neighbourhood's farmers and
shepherds, a community relatively
unchanged by the 20th C. The tower with
8 pinnacles could be unique in Cornwall.

✕ Bridge Café; licence; take-away food.

The Rumps and Pentire Head

3½ miles (5.5 km) Sheet 200 936796

Moderate Some of the most accessible, yet dramatic, North Cornish coastal scenery; exceptional for viewing seabirds; a substantial Iron Age fort. *Cliff tops, pasture; mud after rain.*

Start From Wadebridge take the B3314 (just past school at top of hill when driving E) and continue to New Polzeath. **Car park** at end of road into New Polzeath.

① From car park entrance turn right and right again into Gulland Road, past public conveniences. ② At end of road, carry straight on down path to beach, across top of beach and up wooden steps on to path leading up left on to cliff top. After descending through gully ③ turn left at meeting of paths to visit Rumps Point. ④ After retracing steps from Rumps Point to path junction, keep right, along highest path, crossing stile into fields. ⑤ At third stile, follow path as it swings right for 10 yards (9 m) and then back on to top of Com Head. Leave top on side nearest fields to intercept well-defined path leading round back of Com Head. Later descend and climb gully and ⑥ immediately before low slate stile, climb stile consisting of 3 posts driven into wall on right; follow round edge of field to next stile and the quarry car park. ⑦ From car park turn left down lane to farm, and right at road

junction down to barns on left side of road. ⑧ By second gate on right past barns, turn right along public footpath, over stile; continue through 2 gates and fields. ⑨ Where path forks, take left branch up past houses and turn left into Gulland Road.

Polzeath, an undistinguished holiday village with a fine surfing beach.

Humble and prolific, thrift or sea pink is nonetheless pretty when, as here, it flowers *en masse* in April-Aug.

The tower (above Stepper Point) on the far side of the Camel estuary is The Daymark, a landmark for shipping.

The remains of the Iron Age fort on Rumps Point are not obvious, but 3 distinct ramparts can be made out. The views along the coast are famous; in a westerly gale, the sight of the seas breaking over Newland Rock and The Moules just as dramatic.

Several interesting seabird species breed on the cliffs, but the most captivating are the fulmars. They are grey-white, like gulls, but there the resemblance ends. They are supreme fliers, with long, narrow, stiffly held wings, perfect for gliding; watch them exploit the wind and cliff face for extraordinary feats of aerobatics.

CORNWALL

Roseland Peninsula

3½ miles (5.5 km) Sheet 204 868329

Easy Excellent views of St. Mawes waterfront, one of the south coast's great yacht anchorages, and a visit to Place Manor, open May to September. *Woods, cliff tops; one climb; mud after rain.'*

Start Porth Farm, near St. Anthony on the Roseland Peninsula – approach via Portscatho. **Car park** (National Trust) at Porth Farm; also a lay-by with limited space ¼ mile (0.5 km) up hill on left.

① From car park return to road and turn left downhill. ② Just before reaching head of creek, turn left off road and over footbridge by signpost reading 'Footpath to Place etc.' Turn right on other side of footbridge. ③ For uninterrupted views of creek, cross stile through hedge and continue to beach. To continue with walk, return to field. ④ Where concrete steps descend on right towards water, go through gate and along bottom edge of field to road. ⑤ At road, turn left if continuing walk or stopping at Place Manor Hotel. If visiting hotel, go through gate on to front lawn. ⑥ If visiting church only, walk past hotel along road. By iron gate and stile with signpost 'Coast Path and Public Footpath to St. Anthony Head' turn right for church. From church, retrace to road and continue. ⑦ At top of hill, by sign indicating right bend, climb stile and

continue on footpath across field. At steps on far side of field turn left. (There is a beach at bottom of cliff – access by steps and path.) ⑧ Having walked over Killigerran Head, drop down to beach past white marker post and turn left up path towards road. Car park is at opposite end of path.

🦶 The beach accessible from ③ gives the best views of the yachts in the Percuil River, and of St. Mawes, named after a Welsh prince of the 6th C. who became a monk.

🏚 Place Manor: sadly this formerly excellent hotel is now closed indefinitely.
The present building is Victorian, but there was a Tudor house here, and before that a monastery. Henry VIII and Anne Boleyn are reputed to have spent their honeymoon at Place, but its real fame is as the home of the naval family the Sprys, from whom the present owner is descended. Place means palace in Old Cornish.

⛪ The church butts right on to the house, giving rise to the claim that it is the only private church in England. Memorials to centuries of Sprys; the tower is 700 years old and there are some impressive Norman features.

🔤 'Roseland' evolved from the Old Cornish word ros, a spur or peninsula.

Brown Willy

5 miles (8 km) Sheets 200 and 201 138818

Energetic Cornwall's highest point, with views to the N and S coasts, and its nearest to hill walking. *Moorland, rocks, heather; 2 climbs; the heather and bracken can be extremely wet; the peat bogs, seen as dark brown patches, are easily avoided. Do not attempt in poor visibility.*

Start Take rough lane signposted 'Roughtor 2 miles' half-way up hill at N end of Camelford. **Car park** at end of lane.

① From bridge across stream below car park, follow faint, grassy path up to left end of ridge, where 3 giant boulders appear piled one above another. ② From the boulders (Showery Tor) bear slightly left along ridge to first rise (Little Rough Tor). ③ Approaching summit of Rough Tor, take any of the various paths winding between the rocks: all lead eventually to ruins of medieval chapel and memorial plaque on top. ④ From summit, identify stone wall on far side of moor below, leading off left from patch of trees. Scramble down over rocks and make for any point along wall. ⑤ Follow wall left, down to gate and bridge over stream, then up past ruins to trig. point just visible on summit of Brown Willy. ⑥ From the summit, it is safe to wander along the ridge, but do not pass the last rock outcrop. On return, retrace to gate and steps at ⑤. ⑦

Having re-crossed stream, follow wall round to track leading from Fernacre and turn right towards large, stone cricle. ⑧ From stone circle, regain track and follow past dead trees and ruined house to bridge over stream. ⑨ Leave track at bridge and, skirting left side of marshy area, head for far right end of ridge, where prominent boulder is perched on rocks (Logan Rock). ⑩ From Logan Rock, head for right end of stone wall ahead and follow stream back to car park. ⑪ After rain, area around stream can be marshy; bear right towards Rough Tor and intercept obvious grassy path from Rough Tor leading back to car park.

ⓘ Charlotte Dymond's memorial: this serving girl's fate still captures the imagination of local people, who believe she haunts the moor where she was brutally murdered. Doubt remains as to whether her cripple lover was guilty of the crime, for which he was hanged.

ⓘ A visitors' book hidden in a metal box near the summit commemorates the Queen's Silver Jubilee. The name Brown Willy is derived from the Old Cornish Bron Ewhela, meaning highest place.

ⓘ There are weirdly eroded granite formations near the summit of Rough Tor, pronounced Row-ter. A plaque on the summit, the site of a medieval chapel, remembers dead of the 43rd Wessex.

CORNWALL

Round the Lizard

5½ miles (9 km) Sheet 203 703126

Easy The British mainland's southernmost tip: geology and botany; crowded in high summer. *Cliff tops.*

Start Lizard village, reached by the A3083 from Helston. **Parking** at centre of village on green.

① From car park turn right past public conveniences along lane signposted 'Public Footpath to Kynance Cove', etc. ② By white chalet, fork right, up stone steps, on to footpath along top of wall. ③ Where path meets road junction by large National Trust notice-board, keep straight on past signpost for 'Kynance Cove and Car Park'. ④ From Kynance Cove, keep to seaward of buildings along grassy path at edge of cliffs. ⑤ At Polpeor Cove (by old lifeboat station) keep left above rocky beach, cross footbridge, go through hedge and climb steps alongside fence. ⑥ Where path meets track from Housel Bay beach up to village, turn left, then right after 50 yards (46 m), to follow coastline. ⑦ Where path joins lane back to village, keep right, along field side of hedge, towards Coastguard Look-out. ⑧ 100 yards past Bass Point House and Look-out, keep right at path junction by metal post. ⑨ From lifeboat station, continue on path round back of highest building, down first flight of steps and left past collection box. ⑩ At Church Cove, turn left past first house and up lane towards thatched cottage. Follow lane back to Lizard and car park.

🌱 The Lizard area harbours plants which thrive uniquely in the area's mild, sea-dominated climate, including large Lizard clover, sand quillwort and ciliate rupturewort.

🏝 Kynance Cove with its serpentine islets.

🔟 The cliff here is said to hold 700 unmarked graves of shipwreck victims.

🔟 Lizard Lighthouse, open to the public.

🍴 Housel Bay Hotel welcomes walkers.

⚓ Lifeboat station, open to the public.

🏭 In Church Cove is one of the many local establishments for cutting and polishing serpentine. The stone, seen everywhere in the cliffs and rocks, is a magnesium silicate formed by pressure and heat in the upheavals of the Earth's crust. The veins do look quite like serpent's skin.

⛪ Look for blocks of serpentine built into the tower of St. Wynalow's.

Looking E over Lizard Point (foreground) to the lighthouse and, beyond it, Housel Bay.

CORNWALL

Hensbarrow Downs
2 miles (3 km) Sheet 200 990590

Easy The route goes through Cornwall's china clay mining area, showing workings in detail. *Downland; one climb; mud after rain.*

Start Leave the A30 6 miles (10 km) SW of Bodmin, taking the B3274 for Roche. **Parking** in lay-by, on right side of road, just past chapel, when going S.

① From car park walk S nearly a mile (1.5 km) and turn right into wide new road (unmarked on map) signposted 'Nanpean and Whitemoor'; immediately turn left on to old minor road, leaving prominent spoil heap on right. Branch left on footpath just past farm gate. ② Where paths cross, continue forward, skirting right edge of wide, shallow hollow. ③ The path peters out; head for highest point of hill straight ahead across open grassland. (An RAF beacon will appear ahead and slightly to the right.) ④ From trig. point on prominent mound at summit, head for conspicuous radio mast in distance. On reaching wide, gravel-surfaced road, ⑤ turn right and follow road back towards ①.

🐦 Dense population of skylarks: do not tread on their nests.

⚒ A weird landscape of white and grey spoil heaps: the waste is quartz sand. The tips seen SW are working.

Mount Edgcumbe
1½ miles (10.5 km) Sheet 201 452533

Moderate All-round views of Plymouth Sound and the waters radiating from it. *Woods, farmland; 2 climbs; mud after rain.*

Start Cremyll, on the B3247; buses (with connecting ferry) from Plymouth. **Car park**: Country Park car park on B3247, 200 yards before ferry.

From car park, walk down road and turn left by telephone box next to Edgcumbe Arms, following public footpath signposted for Empacombe. Keep left past converted chapel and right at junction signposted 'Footpath'. ② Where field-edge path joins gravel drive, follow instructions on sign: straight on through gate and round edge of little harbour, across lawn and through wooden gate in far corner. ③ Where field-edge path meets road by iron gate and stone stile, cross road and go into field through gate opposite with signpost 'Public Footpath to Maker', etc. Follow the main cart track, roughly parallel to road. ④ Before gates and chainlink fence, turn right uphill and follow fence to second corner, where path leads off to left through woods. Cross stile into woods, turn sharp right, then left after 75 yards (69 m) by ruined gate. Follow waymarked posts up hill. ⑤ After crossing track, bear left up bank and past wall on right. Cross road and join path signposted 'Maker Church ¼ mile', etc. ⑥ From W entrance of church (same end as tower), follow hedge along car park field. ⑦ Half-way along field, cross stile in left wall and follow wall on left; again cross stile to continue with wall on right to stile and iron gate. ⑧ On opposite side of lane, cross stile and follow path through 2 fields, turn right at lane beyond and left at signpost for Kingsand. ⑨ Just after reaching open ground at Maker Heights, branch left along path signposted 'Kingsand ½ mile'. ⑩ At fork in 150 yards (135 m) keep right; approaching Kingsand fork left and continue through lanes of Kingsand to beach. ⑪ From E end of Kingsand, walk along rocks near high-water mark. ⑫ In about ¼ mile (400 m), at ruined building, turn left along path through bushes into field and turn right to gap in top corner of field, continuing to join broad track with benches. ⑬ Where path joins road at gate and stile, turn right and immediately left up path indicated by 'Coast

22

Path' sign (yellow arrow with acorn) ⑭ At fork in bridleway 100 yards (91 m) into wood, take left, upper, way and continue, following coast path signs between banks of rhododendrons. ⑬ Pass stone arch and in 55 yards (50 m) fork right to follow zigzag path down to lower level near water, emerging in clearing below half-timbered building (Lady Emma's Cottage) opposite Drake's Island. ⑯ Where path emerges again on to open parkland, with ruin to left, keep right and continue down to Barn Pool. Make way along coast through formal gardens to Country Park entrance.

🔖 A leaflet available in Maker church describes its remarkable history.

📖 Kingsand and Cawsand flourished because before the Plymouth breakwater
🍺 was built the bay was an anchorage for the Fleet – hence also the fine pubs.

♨ See the official guide book, or leaflet, for
❀ Mount Edgcumbe House and park.

Access to the SW Peninsula Coast Path is generally easy in Cornwall, and most parts can be walked in short sections. Tintagel to Boscastle is a famous stretch; the rocks of Bedruthan Steps, 6 miles (9.5 km) N of Newquay, should not be missed and from St. Ives towards Zennor there are some lovely coves visited by seals.

There is a disused railway line walk from Bodmin via Wadebridge to Padstow, through the picturesque Camel Valley.

Poltesco Cadgwith Nature Trail, near Helston, covers 3 miles (5 km) of woods, cliff tops and caves.

The circuit of Tresco, Scilly Isles, is an ambitious and rewarding project.

St. Agnes Beacon is also worth climbing.

VEHICLE FERRY FROM PLYMOUTH TO	
Roscoff	7 hrs
St Malo	9 hrs
Santander	24 hrs

DARTMOOR

There are two Dartmoors. First, the heart of the 300-square-mile (121 ha) plateau: apparently endless, rolling moorland and hills broken only by the grotesque tors – contortions of granite – on the summits. Here is the nearest thing to wilderness in southern Britain.

Second, around this central area, and still within the National Park, lie the wooded valleys (cleaves is the local word), twisting lanes and grey farmhouses where the green fields begin.

In its isolation, Dartmoor has preserved an enormous number of prehistoric remains. There are hut circles, standing stones, burial chambers, stone rows and crosses, dating from any time after 1800 B.C., all in settings of loneliness and power. Relatively modern are the spoil heaps and gullys made by the tin miners who flourished in the 12th to the 15th centuries, though they were there in the Bronze Age and did not finally depart until the 1920s.

Height and the nearby coast combine to produce wet and swiftly changing weather. Winds can be fierce, and the fogs descend in minutes, adding to the danger of bogs anything from a yard to a mile across. To avoid the latter, watch for the tell-tale vivid green Sphagnum moss and keep well clear of where it grows.

Hardly a year goes by without a well-publicized case of exposure on Dartmoor; often enough, victims find they have spent their chastening night out within yards of a road which was nonetheless hidden by fog or snow. Anyone walking the area, with or without a planned route, is urged to know and heed the advice given on page 9.

Princetown
4 miles (6.5 km) Sheet 191 587735

Moderate Much industrial interest, explaining why Princetown developed in such a remote, exposed position. *Moorland; one climb; do not attempt in poor visibility.*

Start Princetown, on the B3212 near centre of moor; infrequent, seasonal buses to Princetown from Plymouth, Yelverton, Tavistock and Moretonhampstead – special service – check times by ringing Plymouth 64014. **Public car park** at town centre.

① From car park almost immediately ② turn right passing prison officers' mess. ③ At road junction, turn right and follow main road to the toll houses (one each side of road) where ④ bear right; keeping wire fence to right, follow path to old railway line. ⑤ Turn left on to railway line and follow it 1½ miles (2.5 km). ⑥ Follow hard track leading off to right, in about ¼ mile (0.5 km) reaching Foggintor Quarry where ⑦ bear right, heading for North Hessary Tor, with mast on top. ⑧ At mast, turn downhill, keeping the wall on left. ⑨ Reach iron gate at end of track, turn left into lane and continue to Station Road; at end, turn right for town centre and car park.

🔟 Princetown Prison is part of a settlement founded in 1785 by Thomas Tyrwhitt and named in honour of the Prince Regent. It was first used in 1809 for French prisoners taken in the Napoleonic Wars. They were joined by prisoners taken in the 1812-14 war with the U.S. It became a convict prison in 1850.

In the old railway line to the Quarry there are granite sleepers.

Foggintor Quarry, now derelict and enclosing a quiet pool, produced granite for many local buildings, including the prison.

Dartmoor's rugged upland is a typical habitat for the buzzard, largest of the predators commonly seen in the SW. It is a bird with widely variable plumage, so much so that it is best identified on its size, and on its wheeling, soaring flight.

DARTMOOR

Widgery Cross
5 miles (8 km) Sheet 191 513848

Moderate *A pilgrimage to one of Dartmoor's most deservedly famous monuments. Lanes and moorland; 2 climbs; mud; do not attempt in poor visibility.*

Start Lydford, off the A386 S of Okehampton. **Public car park** in Lydford.

① From car park turn right along Lydford main street and at Y-junction bear right down Silver Street. ② At crossroads carry straight on, turn right at junction and continue to main road. ③ Cross main road with caution and take track opposite, then through gate on to open moor. Take upper track (faint and grassy), going over the shoulder of High Down and joining stony track leading diagonally down steep slope to remains of old tin mine by River Lyd. ④ It is normally easy to cross the river here, but after heavy rain a crossing can be found higher up. Go straight uphill, then make for Doe Tor (the tor without a cross), crossing the brook just above a small waterfall. ⑤ From Doe Tor cross to Brat Tor (NE), on which is Widgery Cross. ⑥ Take the grassy track down to river, where there is a choice of stepping stones or footbridge. Follow track over High Down to Dartmoor Inn on main road. Cross and follow road to Lydford.

Widgery Cross.

🏭 Wheal Mary Emma tin mine, worked for a short time about 1850, was named

after the young daughter of the then owner. ('Wheal' or 'weal' is the Cornish word for mine.)

🔟 Widgery Cross on Brat Tor was erected in 1887 by John William Widgery, a Dartmoor artist, to commemorate Queen Victoria's Golden Jubilee. The cross is unusual in that it is built of separate granite blocks: all the other stone crosses on Dartmoor – about 250 of them – were hewn out of single blocks. They were put up either to mark medieval boundaries or to guide travellers. Many marked paths linking monasteries.

Grimspound and Challacombe Valley
6 miles (9.5 km) Sheet 191 699835

Easy Shows the 2 fascinating human faces of Dartmoor – Bronze Age dwellings and centuries of tin mining. *Moorland; mud after rain. Do not attempt in poor visibility 1:25,000 map and compass recommended.*

Start Car park on B3212 6 miles SW of Moretonhampstead; infrequent, seasonal bus service between Plymouth and Moretonhampstead – special service – check times by ringing Plymouth 64014. **Car park** (gravel surface, fine views) on right just after reaching open moor if travelling in Princetown direction.

Tor comes from the Welsh word twr *meaning tower or heap.*

① From car park cross road and walk uphill past hut circles and through low heather to scattered stone blocks of Hookney Tor. ② From Tor, turn right, heading downhill to road. Cross, and continue down track towards Headland Warren Farm. ③ Just before farm turn left, passing it on upper side. Go through wicket gate, cross drive diagonally and go downhill through farm gate. Follow grassy track down valley. ④ Through gate in fence and continue in same direction to end of field, then past front of farmhouse and buildings. Follow track uphill, over top and into next valley. ⑤ Climb stile and continue up valley between conifer plantations. Where tracks divide, keep straight on. ⑥ At Y-junction, bear right. Track soon narrows, winding through mining area. Follow it uphill to Bennett's Cross beside B3212, where ⑦ turn right back to car park.

🔲 Grimspound's hut circles and village are thought to be Bronze Age structures. The hut walls are granite, which is why they have lasted so long. The roofs, in a wigwam shape, would have been of turf or thatch over poles laid up to a central point. The people who built these dwellings were both metal-workers and farmers, keeping livestock on the moors and protecting them in compounds.

⛏ Tin mining remnants; the gullies in the hillside above Headland Warren Farm date from the 16th C., when miners followed the rich seams of tin upward having exhausted the valley bottoms. The stone heaps are waste.

DARTMOOR

Becky Falls and the Bovey Valley
4 miles (6.5 km) Sheet 191 784794

Easy The comparatively lush, eastern fringe of Dartmoor; a fine waterfall, interesting plants and flowers. *Moorland, woods; 2 climbs; mud after rain.*

Start Parking areas on B3344 2½ miles (4 km) NW of Bovey Tracey. **Parking** 3 areas within 100 yards (91 m) of the cattle grid.

① From car park walk in direction of Manaton beside the B3344 to point where Yarner Wood ends (on left). Turn left and follow edge of wood up to higher road. ② Right along road to junction with B3344. Turn right. ③ Leave road after 120 yards (110 m). Cross bridge on left and follow path, keeping brook on right. To visit Becky Falls, take the railed steps; for the café, take the long footbridge. ④ Rejoin woodland path (waymarked by orange dots). Where well-defined path crosses, turn right. ⑤ Go steeply downhill and cross river by small stone bridge. Turn left along wide track. ⑥ Ignore next bridge. For views of Packhorse Bridge and Fairy Glen, go second left through gate. Rejoin track and climb to starting point.

Heath milkwort, unlike the other milkworts, has its lower oval leaves in opposite pairs. It usually flowers May-August.

✿ Trendlebeare Down is rich in plants, among them blue milkworts, yellow tormentil (its roots were used in tanning) and whortleberries (bilberries) with delicious blue-black fruits.

☀ Black Hill has prehistoric cairns.

〰 Becky (or Becka) Falls drop 80 feet (24 m) into the River Bovey.

🍺 Kestor Inn, Manaton (the name comes from *maen-y-dun*, Celtic for 'hill fort').

The blue-black fruits of the whortleberry (also called bilberry, huckleberry and whinberry) make excellent pies and jam.

Ditsworthy and Ringmoor Down
8 miles (13 km) Sheet 202 558666

Moderate Reveals the pretty Dartmoor, around the Plym. Downland, moorland, riverside. Do not attempt in poor visibility.

Start From the B3212 NE out of Yelverton, take road at Dowsland Cross signposted Sheepstor. In 2 miles (3 km), turn left on to road signposted Sheepstor and Burrator. ½ mile (0.8 km) past Sheepstor look for Ringmoor Cottage. **Car park** beside cottage.

① From cottage follow grassy track due W, climbing moor to Gutter Tor, at first out of sight behind horizon. Then drop to small slab bridge seen below at end of road. ② Cross bridge and take track past abandoned mine workings. Fork right after ruined buildings and follow narrow path down to River Plym. ③ Cross Plym at ford and go downstream to Plym Steps (stepping stones) keeping to ridge above river valley to avoid boggy patches. ④ Re-cross river at Plym Steps. Continue downstream past Bronze Age remains to Ditsworthy Warren House, where ⑤ continue in same direction, taking left branch of track to cross boggy patch. Cross moor to Legis Tor. ⑥ From Tor bear right, following path downhill to stepping stones near head of stream. Continue uphill over moor past stone circle until Ringmoor Cottage comes into sight.

The tin mine ruins are part of the Eylesbarrow complex.

Between Eastern Tor and Giants Hill are many Bronze Age relics.

Ditsworthy Warren House, mainly 16th C., was the centre of one of many warrens set up for breeding rabbits.

DARTMOOR

Highest Dartmoor
14 miles (22.5 km) Sheet 191 562917

Energetic Dartmoor at its most rugged and remote – the true wilderness; also has the spectacular Meldon Reservoir. *Moorland, woods; 3 climbs; mud; no definite path between ① and ②, but route easy to follow by landmarks except in poor visibility, in which case do not attempt. Compass and 1:25,000 map recommended. The route passes through Okehampton ranges and firing times must be checked; ring Plymouth 772312 or enquire at a local post office.*

Start Turn off the A30 about 3½ miles (5.5 km) W of Okehampton on lane signposted Meldon (not Meldon Quarry). **Parking** at Meldon Reservoir.

① Cross Meldon Dam. Climb directly to top of Longstone Hill, and on reaching level plateau bend right across to Black Tor. ② Spot the small, square army lookout hut perched on edge of Fordsland Ledge, and make for it with West Okement River in valley on right. ③ From hut look for top of High Willhays and make for it; from there bear left along army track to Yes Tor. ④ From the top of Yes Tor looking E look for 2 clumps of trees about 2 miles (3 km) distant. Aim for the right-hand side of the smaller clump, walking direct over open moorland, using grit tracks where useful. ⑤ Above clump of trees, cross East Okement River on track, then stay on track with river on left for 1¾ miles (3 km) to just beyond ruined cottage. Turn off track down steep hillside to

Okehampton Castle, the oldest parts of which date from late Norman times.

river. ⑥ Cross river on wooden footbridge, bear right on track up through woods, and cross 2 fields, continuing through Lower Halstock Farm to join metalled lane. Cross cattle grid and at T-junction turn right down larger road for about 200 yards (183 m) to waymarked gate. ⑦ Walk down middle of field, then take road to railway station, crossing by-pass. Turn left after bridge and continue along road with railway line on left. ⑧ At T-junction take footpath opposite which joins metalled road and leads to golf course. Just below clubhouse the path leads off across golf course. Follow it straight on for over one mile (1.5 km), through gate, fields, farm buildings, more fields to road. ⑨ Join road, re-cross by-pass and just past viaduct turn down grassy track on right. Keep near the river and cross it at small footbridge. Turn left up track and after row of beeches slant up across field, following hedge on right back to car park.

🛆 The water supply for all North Devon.

⁂ The cairn may be a Bronze Age burial place. Small stones from cairns were used for local road building in the 19th C.

🏔 High Willhays and Yes Tor, the highest points on Dartmoor; the ridge between them is called the 'roof of Devon'.

🏰 Okehampton Castle.

DARTMOOR

Cawsand and Taw Marsh
9 miles (14.5 km) Sheet 191 640942

Easy Introduces the bare, empty spaces of northern Dartmoor, and the impressive landscape of Taw Marsh valley. *Woods, moorland, river valley; one climb; mud; do not attempt in poor visibility.*

Start Sticklepath, on the A30 E of Okehampton; infrequent buses from Okehampton and Exeter. **Parking** The Devonshire Inn car park, opposite the Inn, using end farthest from road.

① Left out of car park and follow main road to bridge over River Taw. Walk upstream along footpath by river. ② Follow path into wood. It bears left uphill, then right and levels out. After gate, turn sharp left up field, keeping field edge on left; emerge on to moorland through gate in top left corner of field. ③ Walk up moor, aiming for the top (Cawsand Beacon)–a 1¼ mile (2 km) stretch. ④ From cairn on Cawsand Beacon continue on pony track in same direction downhill, then up the small rise of Little Hound Tor, from which make for the stone circle. ⑤ From stone circle retrace steps to slightly sunken track and continue in previous direction, bearing slightly right. Follow track along right side of next hill, Hound Tor. ⑥ Where track peters out, turn downhill, making for stream. Follow this downhill to where valley suddenly widens, where ⑦ curve left around base of Steeperton to meet River Taw. Cross river and continue downstream. Keep well left of river to avoid extremely boggy marsh. In 1¼ miles join ⑧ a stony track. Follow this to edge of moor where ⑨ continue on road to Belstone, ignoring left turns in village and following road downhill to A30 at Sticklepath; turn left to ①

🏠🚂 Sticklepath's Finch Foundry Museum has a working display of the machinery and the processes used by 19th C. blacksmiths and foundrymen. All the machinery is water-powered by the River Taw. Free car park; picnic area.

🔟 Behind the Museum is a former Quaker burial ground. Sticklepath was a Quaker stronghold in the 17th C. Friends from the village sailed to America with William Penn, the founder of Pennsylvania, in 1682.

🍴 Devonshire Inn, good food.

※ On Cawsand Beacon there is a good example of a Bronze Age burial cairn.

\↑/ The view W from the Beacon is to the peaks of East Mill Tor and Belstone Tor.

\↑/ Looking NE from Cawsand Beacon there is a clear view of the well-laid-out pattern of the strip fields of South Zeal–large fields sub-divided to grow different crops.

※ White Moor Stone Circle is another Bronze Age relic. Circles of stone marked points of assembly and enclosed burial grounds. The standing stone (*menhir*) 200 yards (183 m) distant is also a memorial.

Wandering Dartmoor at will is for the experienced and well equipped, but there is some safe, introductory walking.

The Forestry Commission has laid out 2 short walks from Bellever Forest Car Park, 1½ miles (2.5 km) from the B3212 at Postbridge.

The banks of the Plym can be walked from near Cadover Bridge, approached by unclassified lanes from the A374 at Plympton or the A386 (Plymouth to Yelverton).

Round Burrator Reservoir is a spectacular circuit: access from Norsworthy Bridge Car Park at NE end of reservoir; several waymarked trails nearby.

A beautifully wooded path runs about 3 miles (5 km) through the Teign Valley from Steps Bridge to near Clifford Bridge. Approach from Exeter along the B3212; find path by crossing river from car park and turning left into woods.

Dr. Blackall's Drive, a grassy track following a ridge above the Dart valley, is an exciting, 2-mile (3 km) stroll. Park at Bel Tor Corner, at top of hill on unclassified road between Poundsgate and Dartmeet. Reach track by following stone wall seen on left when facing SW (back to the road). At the corner, bear left, then right between stone walls. On reaching open moorland, take the right (upper) fork.

DORSET

Geologically there are five different Dorsets, which means that this small and astonishingly unspoiled county embraces a great variety of scenery. Right across the middle runs a belt of chalk hills, starting on the coast around Lulworth and ending (so far as Dorset is concerned) in Cranborne Chase. North of their escarpment is the clay Vale of Blackmoor. The western end of the county is limestone and clay; while in the east Purbeck (a mix of chalk, clay and limestone) and the heathlands are separate areas again.

The best walking companion is still Thomas Hardy. Often it is hard not to think the charming, false names of the novels more apt than the real ones – for instance, Mellstock rather than Stinsford for the village churchyard where his heart is buried. Individual lanes, farms and footpaths can be traced from the stories, though, alas, this is not a county that respects public paths as it should.

On the hilltops there are the ancient resonances. The county is rich in burial mounds from the Bronze and Neolithic Ages which have survived because until recently the hills were not intensively farmed. To the Iron Age belongs Maiden Castle, perhaps the most numinous earthwork in all Britain and several hours of exciting walking in itself. The South West Peninsula Coast Path follows the entire coast to its terminus at Poole Harbour.

Studland and Old Harry
4 miles (6.5 km) Sheet 195 043825

Easy Dorset's finest chalk cliff scenery, justly popular walking. *Farmland, cliff top, downland; one climb.*

Start In Studland (on B3351) turn right for Middle and South Beaches, then right in front of Manor Hotel; car ferry from Haven Hotel, Sandbanks. **Car park** (South Beach) on right after hotel.

From the cliffs above Old Harry – Studland Bay, Poole and Bournemouth.

① From car park turn right and follow minor road past Bankes Arms Hotel. ② As road curves right, turn left to follow sign 'To Swanage via Old Harry', this is the Coast Path; follow the blue flashes and acorn symbols nearly 2 miles (3 km). ③ Bear right, keeping to main track which climbs the down and follows top of ridge. ④ Through gate, past Nat. Trust sign and straight on, following blue arrow as for obelisk. ⑤ At cross-track turn right through small wooden gate by Nat. Trust sign; follow direction of blue arrow to Studland. ⑥ Cross stile and continue down surfaced lane towards Studland, ignoring left turns. ⑦ Cross minor road leaving cross on right and take lane ahead 'To the Church'. Take path on left of the church through churchyard. ⑧ At road turn right and continue a few yards to ⑨ T-junction where turn right to ①.

🐦 Well-established cormorant nest sites.

〽 Old Harry, his (smaller) 'wife' and 2 more oddities of erosion, the Haystack and Pinnacle – stumps of rock 'like a skeleton's lower jaw' wrote Hardy.

\↑/ The Needles and Isle of Wight.

🏠 A superb example of a small Norman church – massive arches, vaulted roofs.

DORSET

Littlebredy
8 miles (13 km) Sheet 194 591889

Moderate Littlebredy is the essence of timeless Dorset, a place to linger in. *Downland, parkland, woods; 2 climbs.*

Start From the A35 about one mile (1.5 km) W of Winterbourne Abbas take the road signposted Littlebredy. **Parking** close to village in lane to Littlebredy Farm.

① From parking walk a few yards away from village towards farm. ② Turn right at stile and gate (waymarked with blue arrow). Bridehead House is on the right, and cricket ground on left. ③ Go through gate and continue uphill following terraced path round hillside. ④ Walk round edge of wood, fence on left and ⑤ continue due S leaving barns behind. ⑥ Go straight on along well-defined path. ⑦ Take care here: track turns left to join a lane; turn right through a gate (blue arrow waymark) and follow path (hedge on left). Ignore the other right of way, leading from farther round the corner to Gorwell Farm. ⑧ Cross stile on left to see the long barrow 200 yards (183 m) on far side of hedge. Retrace to path and continue ahead following signs to Kingston Russell Stone Circle. ⑨ Straight ahead through gate to Stone Circle. ⑩ With Stone Circle on left and copse on right, walk over the field to the fence ahead, then a few yards left to a gate with blue arrow (no path). ⑪ Go through gate and with ditches and mounds of earthworks on left continue ahead down steep hillside (no path) to pick up well-defined track heading N at the corner of the wood seen below. ⑫ Follow track – trees on right – until shortly seeing gap in fence ahead, slightly to the left. ⑬ Go through gap, turn left and walk, cutting off corner, to gate in NW corner of the field (no path). ⑭ From gate follow track seen as a faint line leading down next field (boggy after rain), through gate in hedge to small bridge over stream. ⑮ Cross stream, go through gate ahead, then continue up field (hedge on right) to road. ⑯ Cross and follow bridleway through gates to right of Whatcombe House drive up the hillside opposite (house on left). ⑰ Continue slightly to left – path curves round hill, dips, then climbs to skyline. ⑱ Go through middle gate of three, then gate on right (signpost 'Bridleway to Littlebredy'). ⑲ Continue straight ahead over the field, following line of burial mounds (tumuli). The Hardy Memorial is seen ahead on skyline. ⑳ Continue along track to road by bridleway sign. ㉑ Turn right and follow road into Littlebredy. ㉒ At foot of hill bear right, then left through churchyard to church. Retrace to foot of hill and ①.

🏛 The 19th C. Bridehead House is named after the River Bride, which rises in the grounds. 'Brid' means roaring.

\†/ Possibly the best of the walk.

🔆 The Grey Mare is the prehistoric burial chamber, her Colts the standing stones.

🔆 Kingston Russell Stone Circle, a ritualistic monument, dates from about 1500 B.C. Some of the stones may have been moved.

🏛 Kingston Russell House (about 1730), birthplace of Nelson's Admiral Hardy.

Osmington and the Seaward Downs
7 Miles (11 km) Sheet 194 729831

Moderate An enchanting Dorset village, and the grassy cliffs characteristic of the area. *Village, downs, low cliff tops; one climb.*

Start Osmington, off the A353; buses. **Parking** for modest fee at St. Christopher's Garage, Osmington, on the A353 almost opposite signpost to Osmington Mills.

Partially waymarked. ① From garage turn right and follow A353 about 300 yards (274 m). ② Turn right down lane into Osmington village. ③ Facing 'Cosy Cottage' the road bends left; turn right uphill and follow track for almost a mile. (1.5 km). ④ Pass barn on left to go through iron gates. Leave the main track (which continues to Poxwell) and turn right towards another gate uphill. ⑤ Through gate, cross field ahead heading between highest electricity posts; continue along ridge to join sunken track leading to road. ⑥ Cross with great care and follow lane straight ahead downhill past farm buildings and through gate. ⑦ Continue straight on uphill to road. ⑧ Turn left along road and carry straight on (do not turn right for Ringstead). ⑨ Go through gate to keep on through Nat. Trust property for ⅓ mile (0.5 km). ⑩ At signpost turn right for 'Ringstead Beach' – narrow path. ⑪ The path divides; turn left to walk under 3-wire pylons. ⑫ Follow path slightly right to single-wire

pylons and turn right down steps, crossing stile and field to stony track. ⑬ Cross track and continue past another signpost to waymarked stile on the right. ⑭ After another signpost and stile, follow path past Rose Cottage to join Coast Path, where ⑮ turn right and continue. ⑯ When Path meets lane at Ringstead, turn left towards the sea. ⑰ Turn right, follow Coast Path a little over a mile (1.7 km) to Osmington Mills. ⑱ At road, turn right and continue 300 yards. ⑲ Turn left and follow path signposted 'Footpath Osmington Village'. ⑳ Cross stile on right and walk ahead, bearing a few yards to left of electricity post ahead; walk slightly uphill to signpost seen ahead; (beaten path heads slightly left at first). ㉑ Over stile just beyond signpost, bear slightly left down field to stile to left of gate, and slightly left again to stile with yellow marker. Turn right at road for ①.

🏛️📖 Village and church are full of interest – see the leaflet in church. Constable honeymooned and painted here.

📖 In *The Trumpet Major* Hardy describes 'forty navvies at work' on the chalk memorial to George III, visitor to nearby Weymouth. Locals were unimpressed: it shows him leaving.

🏚️ The site of a medieval village.

🍺 The Smugglers Inn.

DORSET

The Heart of Hardy's Wessex
5½ miles (9 km) Sheet 194 725921

Easy Much from the novelist's life and work. *Woods, town, downland; mud.*

Start From Dorchester take the A35 3 miles (5 km) towards Puddletown and turn right up lane signposted Higher Bockhampton. In about ½ mile (0.8 km) turn left for Hardy's Cottage. **Car park** signposted before Hardy's Cottage.

① From car park follow path signposted 'Hardy's Cottage via woodland path'. ② Turn left, as signposted, for Hardy's Cottage (note turnings for return journey). ③ Pass cottage on left and turn right to follow path into Forest. ④ Go straight over cross-track. ⑤ After a path joins from left, bear right a few yards, then continue previous line uphill. ⑥ About 250 yards (225 m) after top of hill turn along track half right, signposted 'Forest Walk'. ⑦ When path meets well-made track, continue along this. In about 180 yards (160 m) fork left on to smaller track through woods. ⑧ Track divides; continue, ignoring path to right. ⑨ Turn right, walk out of forest and down lane ahead towards Puddletown for nearly ¾ mile (1 km). ⑩ Turn left and follow path waymarked by yellow arrows over fields, and past school (stile and gate at corner of school grounds are concealed), nearly under power cables. Continue to A35. ⑪ Turn left along A35 a few yards and cross to group of buildings on right, just past bus stop. ⑫ In front of buildings take path on left signposted 'Bridleway Charminster'. ⑬ Where track turns left, follow blue arrows to gate ahead on to Ridgeway. ⑭ Leave Ridgeway almost immediately, turning left through gate to follow narrow track towards Yellowham Wood. ⑮ Path meets track; continue along this to A35. ⑯ Turn right along A35; continue about 60 yards (55 m) to lay-by on left where ⑰ turn left from its centre to enter narrow track just inside edge of wood. ⑱ At junction bear slightly left. ⑲ Path divides – bear right. ⑳ After descent, turn right to walk down to Hardy's Cottage.

🏠 See the board and leaflet describing
⍦ Thorncombe Wood Nature Reserve.

🏠 Hardy was born here in 1840; it is the home of the Dewys in *Under the Greenwood Tree* (view by appointment – 0305 262366). Few paths and villages in the area do not feature in the novels. Egdon Heath is at the end of the lane.

\!/ **Eustacia Vye** stood here and looked at the Quiet Woman Inn.

🏛 **St. Mary's** has fine Jacobean, wooden fittings. Puddletown is Weatherbury in *Far From the Madding Crowd*.

🏛 Medieval **Athelhampton House** opens at
♣ various times; walks in the grounds.

St. Aldhelm's (or St. Alban's) Head
5 miles (8 km) Sheet 195 974776

Moderate – but strenuous in parts. This is a sensationally beautiful walk, along one of the Dorset coast's most dramatically rugged stretches. *Farmland, cliff tops; short, tiring climbs and descents.*

Start Worth Matravers, off the B3069.
Public car park on right just before village when approaching from Kingston.

① From car park turn right towards Worth Matravers and continue along road a few yards. ② Turn right opposite Square and Compass along 'Footpath to Church and Hill Bottom'. ③ Cross stone stile on left and continue down field. ④ Turn left through small swing gate and cross churchyard to visit church. ⑤ Leave church by S porch and turn right, following the road right. ⑥ Turn left along 'Footpath to Winspit'. Continue about 1¼ miles (2 km); explore quarry. ⑦ Turn right to climb over top of quarry, following direction of sign 'To St. Aldhelm's Head'. ⑧ The path divides – bear right, away from cliff edge, fence close on right, to climb to coastguard station and St. Aldhelm's Chapel. ⑨ Walk behind coastguard station and continue along cliff path (sign to Chapman's Pool). ⑩ Just before the slipway and boat houses, turn right to climb hill and bear left round top of Chapman's Pool. ⑪ After the Coast Path enters the river valley, leave it and fork right beside the waymarked post. Walk uphill a little, then follow the river valley with river on left (hidden by trees). ⑫ Go through gate, over bridge, and follow minor road for 150 yards (137 m). ⑬ For a short-cut back to ①, follow this lane via the farm back to Worth. To continue, turn left where the road turns right uphill, following 'Bridleway to Afflington Farm' (mud). ⑭ Turn right along 'Footpath to Worth Village' (quarry overspill on left). ⑮ Climb stone stile and bear right over field (hedge and overhead cables close on right). At road turn left to village.

🏠 At the 12th C. St. Nicholas is buried Benjamin Jesty, a local man who pioneered cow pox vaccination 'and who from his great *strength of mind* made the Experiment from the *Cow* on his Wife and two Sons'.

🍴 The Square and Compass Inn is named after the local quarrymen's tools; cream teas at the tea shop.

📖 The furrows in this gorge, known as strip lynchets, were made by teams of oxen over 600 years ago, when strip farming supported a thriving Worth.

〰️ The huge galleries of the marble quarries are supported by columns of Purbeck Stone. The recesses harboured another local industry, smuggling. When the East Indiaman *Halsewell* was wrecked here in 1786, killing 168, some escaped by being swept into the caves.

🏠 The Norman chapel is dedicated to the man who brought Christianity to this area in the 8th C.

\↑/ W to Portland; E to the Isle of Wight.

\↑/ Chapman's Pool.

DORSET

The Giant of Cerne Abbas
6½ miles (10.5 km) Sheet 194 662017

Easy Dorset chalkland at its best; spectacular views for relatively little effort; great historical interest. *Village, hillside, ridge, downland, farmland; 2 climbs; mud after rain; slippery chalk after rain. Paths at ⑭, ⑯ and ㉑ may be ploughed out – follow directions carefully.*

Start From the A37 take the A352 and continue towards Cerne Abbas, which is off the road; frequent buses. **Parking** area just past village by a fork back to the village.

① From parking walk down road (giant on left) towards Cerne Abbas and soon ② turn left down lane. ③ Just before bridge turn right on to path along bank. ④ Turn left to cross stream and follow lane to Abbey Street. ⑤ Go down Abbey Street (church on left) to junction with road. ⑥ Turn left along road (Alton Lane). Continue about ¼ mile (0.5 km) after village. ⑦ Just past playing-field, turn left along track towards Giant Hill (unsignposted). ⑧ Main track bears right – carry straight on to follow bridleway as it curves up side of Giant Hill (2 iron gates). At top of hill carry straight on, fence/hedge on left. ⑨ At iron gate bear right, still with hedge on left. ⑩ Go through gate by bridleway sign, turn left and follow road about ¾ mile (one km). ⑪ Just past small wood on left, opposite bridleway on right, turn left through small wooden gate then right along top of field towards gate seen ahead. ⑫ Through gate, continue ahead, hedge on left. ⑬ At end of field turn left along ridge track. ⑭ After just over ¼ mile, watch very carefully for an iron gate, opposite a small gate, about 60 yards (55 m) past small wood on left. Turn left through gate, bear half right and walk slightly downhill to another gate (no path). ⑮ Through gate bear left down field to corner of small wood, where a double gate is seen. ⑯ Go through gates and straight over field ahead to gate. ⑰ From gate walk a few yards to join a well-defined track. Continue past Minterne House and the church to reach A352 by bridleway sign, and ⑱ turn left, continuing past right, then left bend, just after which ⑲ turn right through gate and go up track between trees. (Electric fence may obstruct gap at top – climb under.) ⑳ With low trees on left and hillside on right, turn left. The path is indistinct; after a few yards bear slightly right towards leftmost of two clumps of trees, until you can see gate in the

top left corner. ㉑ Through gate continue with fence on left up field to small wooden gate with waymarks in top left corner (not large iron gate on left). ㉒ Through gate, turn left and continue a few yards along bridleway, then follow bridleway as it bears right down East Hill. ㉓ At junction with lane, turn left – Up Cerne Manor ahead. ㉔ In front of Manor turn right and follow lane as it bears left to A352. ㉕ Continue to ①.

ⓘ Like most chalk figures, the giant is a mystery. He could be a Celtic fertility idol; and he could have been carved during the Roman occupation as a whim of the Emperor Commodus, who proclaimed himself a reincarnation of Hercules. Only this century was the grass removed from the phallus. Legends about him terrify local children.

※ The earthwork behind the giant, the 'Trendle' or 'Frying Pan', has produced evidence of Stone Age habitation.

The ruins of the Benedictine abbey which gave the village the second half of its name are in romantic riverside gardens.

 The glorious glass in St. Mary's E window may have come from the abbey.

On the right side of the churchyard is St. Augustine's Wishing Well. Its supremely clear water has, they say, never dried up. Drink it from a leaf, and wish.

Hardy knew this ridge walk well, and brought Tess along here on her wanderings. Below, in 'the loamy Vale of Blackmoor', he set *The Woodlanders*.

The gardens of Edwardian Minterne House are open in certain summer months.

Up Cerne Manor, with its honey-coloured front, was built around 1600.

Hardy's Dorset can be further explored with the help of the Hardy Trail, starting from Dorchester (leaflet from the Tourist Information Office).

A rightly popular cliff-top walk is from Lulworth Cove to Durdle Door.

The Dorset Coast Path can be walked in sections starting at several points; a particularly interesting and lovely stretch begins at Kimmeridge.

There is easy access for walkers to several large areas of Dorset owned by the National Trust, in particular Golden Cap, Portesham Hill and Brownsea Island in Poole Harbour.

The enormous earth ramparts of Maiden Castle are reached from the car park signposted off the A354.

The virile giant of Cerne Abbas stands 180 feet (55 m) from head to toe.

EXMOOR AND THE QUANTOCKS

Exmoor is moorland at its most benign. A few miles off, across an intervening vale, the Quantocks are a separate range of low hills, some 40 square miles (104 square km) in extent, gently rounded and bracken-covered. Together they comprise the cream of North Devon and Somerset's walking country.

During bad weather (rain drives in from the Bristol Channel), and with bad map-reading, it is possible to get lost on Exmoor, but the remaining areas of wide, open moor are now relatively small. Roads are frequent and one can park a car within 200 yards (183 m) of the highest point, Dunkery Beacon.

The three commanding attractions are the coast, the moors and the streams, and one can taste all three in a day's march. To the north there are the towering coastal cliffs which carry the South West Peninsula Coast Path on its marathon, switchback journey ending on the south coast at Poole. Inland, the main block of heather moorland extends South to Simonsbath in the heart of the former hunting forest. Between the moors, the enchanting streams tumble through deeply cut combes (hollows) with steeply wooded slopes.

Paths are plentiful. There is thorough signposting by the Exmoor National Park and a number of 'permissive' paths exist, opened by the owners as a special concession, to supplement rights of way.

Near Larkbarrow: a wistful, scarcely changing landscape.

Exmoor Forest

3½ miles (5.5 km) Sheet 181 835423

Easy Gives an impression of Exmoor's past appearance – modern farming methods make only a muffled intrusion. Once discovered, the tranquillity of Three Combes Foot is long remembered. *Moorland; one climb; mud; best appreciated in at least fair visibility.*

Start From the A39 at top of Porlock Hill, take the Exford road. In 2½ miles (4 km), at Lucott Cross, turn right and continue ¾ mile (one km) to cattle grid. **Parking** by roadside E of cattle grid.

① Go through gate in direction signposted for Doone Valley and continue straight on for 500 yards (457 m) to gate opening on to farm track. ② Turn right on to track through next gate to follow boundary bank on right. ③ As trees appear half left about ¼ mile (0.5 km) away, veer off towards them across open moorland, passing through gap in crumbling boundary bank and arriving at trees, part of the 'stell' at the foot of Three Combes. ④ Cross footbridge immediately below trees to right, then cross another bridge 50 yards (46 m) farther on, and another 30 yards (27 m) to left, which crosses Chalk Water. Climb track (re-passing stell down to left) and in 150 yards (137 m) fork right, climbing steeply. As path levels out, a small barrow and some standing stones are reached.

⑤ Veer left towards old boundary bank, avoiding boggy ground to left and heading for trees surrounding Larkbarrow ruins. Walk through ruins to farm track. ⑥ Turn left to follow track to gate at ②, and retrace steps across moor, heading for right end of trees on skyline.

ⓑ The route is through the former Exmoor Forest or royal hunting ground, sold in 1818 to the Knight family, who planted most of the mature trees seen today.

🚂 The remains of the unfinished 19th C. railway from Simonsbath to Porlock.

↑ The Bristol Channel and Wales beyond.

↑ Across the heart of Exmoor with Chains Barrow 6 miles (9.5 km) away.

☀ The stell, a round, stone-faced earthen bank surmounted by beeches, was built as a shelter for sheep.

↓ Red deer abound in this part of Exmoor.

🏚 Larkbarrow Farm is now a pile of stones because it was in the centre of a gunnery range in the 1939–45 war. The area was finally cleared of unexploded missiles only in 1981.

EXMOOR AND THE QUANTOCKS

Selworthy Beacon
5 miles (8 km) Sheet 181 897481

Energetic Shows some of Exmoor's spectacular coastal scenery, and gives access to some of the historic Acland family walks on the Holnicote Estate. *Hillside, coastal path, woods, riverside; one climb.*

Start From A39 one mile (1.5 km) E of Porlock, and continue to Bossington. **Car park** (Nat. Trust) at centre of Bossington.

① From car park cross bridge over Horner Water, then fork right on footpath signposted Selworthy. In 30 yards (27 m) fork left to go uphill, keeping straight on through narrow gate with stone wall on right. Turn left on reaching level, grassy path and continue 150 yards (137 m) to wooden seat. ② Turn right and climb steep, grassy path to another wide path at a higher level. Turn left on to this to skirt Bossington Hill, then keeping straight on to follow coast path towards Minehead, which is waymarked with an acorn symbol. ③ Where coast path forks left, carry straight on to Selworthy Beacon, there turning sharp right to follow path down to road. ④ Cross road and follow signposted footpath through woods to Selworthy. ⑤ Go through gate by church and turn right into Selworthy Green. Take path signposted to Bossington, skirting edge of woodland and crossing a wide track signposted to Allerford (passing 'Katherines Well') and forking left here to keep to edge of wood. One hundred yards (91 m) after fork, veer right under large, leaning pine trees and follow signs to Bossington until reaching a T-junction after the House of Lynch. ⑥ Turn left to follow lane across bridge to road, then right to follow road to car park.

🌳 Examples of holm (evergreen) oaks.

🏚 The paths in Selworthy Woods once totalled 40 miles, and were cleared of branches, even swept, by estate pensioners.

🏠 The cottages on Selworthy Green, built in 1828 for Holnicote Estate pensioners, are a picturesque monument to the old landowner's benign paternalism.

✗ Tea shop – cream teas a speciality.

⛪ One of the finest half-dozen on Exmoor.

The Barle and Exe Valleys
12½ miles (20 km) Sheet 181 874325

Moderate These beautiful, unspoilt valleys are the dominant feature of southern Exmoor; splendid views from the moorland between. *Woods, farmland, moorland, riverside; 3 climbs; mud after rain.*

Start From the B3223 (Dulverton-Exford) crossing Winsford Hill, follow signs to Tarr Steps. **Public car park** between Liscombe and Tarr Steps.

① From car park walk to Tarr Steps Bridge. Turn right to follow path with yellow waymarks along riverside to Withypool, passing wire debris trap and Bailey Bridge; after about 3 miles (5 km) pass the stepping stones below South Hill Farm. Continue to Withypool road. ② Turn left, and in 100 yards (91 m) right to follow path with red waymarks towards Exford. After stiff climb, 6 stiles and 4 gates, reach the Dulverton-Exford road. ③ Cross road and through gate on to Room Hill. Follow hedge on right, and as head of combe appears ahead, veer slightly left to descend the combe on wide, stony track to River Exe. Turn right to follow path with yellow waymarks to Nethercote Bridge. ④ Continue straight on along farm road for 50 yards (46 m), then fork sharp right uphill, following hedge on right. At top of hill, go through gate on right and carry on in same direction on boundary of grass and bracken. Go through next gate and carry straight on where wide track forks off left downhill. Follow the red waymarks until the path emerges on the Withypool-Winsford road. ⑤ Turn left and follow road into Winsford. Turn right after ford and follow road passing Royal Oak. ⑥ Turn left 150 yards (137 m) after 'Karslake' and follow path with yellow waymarks signposted Tarr Steps. Cross stream at Yellowcombe, and climb again through conifers to gate leading to grassland at Summerway. ⑦ From disused quarry continue in direction of sign to Tarr Steps, rejoining yellow waymarks in far corner. In 200 yards (183 m), path emerges on to open moorland of Draydon Knap. Follow it around boundary to the left arriving at the Exford-Dulverton road. ⑧ Cross road and follow Liscombe road to cattle grid. Here fork left to follow path with yellow waymarks across Varle Hill and Ashway Side back to Tarr Steps.

🛉 Tarr Steps, an ancient causeway over the Barle, may be prehistoric, but is more likely to be 500-600 years old. Reconstructed many times, it is protected by the wire hawser upstream.

꙳ The Barle is an excellent sporting river. Trout are seen in pools at many points. Otters, though rare, have been sighted downstream from South Hill Stepping Stones. Do not confuse otters with the smaller, more plentiful mink.

🦅 A heronry. The Exe upstream from Nethercote Bridge has dippers.

🍺 Both are excellent village inns; real ale.

⛪ Winsford church's list of vicars starts in 1280. Ernest Bevin was born opposite the Methodist chapel.

EXMOOR AND THE QUANTOCKS

Haddon Hill and Wimbleball
7 miles (11 km) Sheet 181 969285

Moderate Shows that man-made beauty can compensate for the loss of wilderness – something local people found hard to believe when the Wimbleball Reservoir was proposed. Offers fine views into the heart of Devon, with hundreds of square miles of rich pasture and few signs of human habitation. Best in May and June, when the greens of the woods and moorland are in strongest contrast, and the reservoir's blue most striking. *Moorland, woods; 2 climbs.*

Start Leave the B3190 at the right-angle bend 1½ miles (2.5 km) W of Upton. Cross cattle grid and follow signs to car park. **Public car park** (free) with lavatories.

① From car park make for Haddon Hill (signposted), following wide track passing trig. point at summit to where track ends under power cables. Carry straight on through heather to boundary fence. ② Turn right to follow track beside fence. Continue to follow fence line as track leaves woodland and narrows to path through rhododendrons. Pass under power cables again and keep straight on, diverging from fence. Fork left down a gulley and turn left to cross stile over fence and head downhill into trees. ③ After crossing another stile and descending steep stone steps, turn left on to the reservoir road and then right to cross wooden bridge over River Haddeo. ④ Turn

right at top of bridge approach to follow sunken track towards dam, turning sharp left, steeply upwards, just before dam. ⑤ At top of climb turn sharp right on to concrete road which crosses dam. Turn left at end of dam, and after climb fork left on to track signposted to Upton. Just after entering oak woods, join an old coach drive. ⑥ Turn half right to follow drive; turn right just before next gate, leaving drive. ⑦ After short climb, reach gate leading on to B3190. Turn right before gate to follow path inside the boundary towards start.

♨ Haddon Hill's fine heather moorland was threatened by agricultural 'improvement' until Exmoor National Park and the owner agreed to own and manage it jointly.

↖ Clockwise: the Quantocks; the Wellington Monument and Blackdown Hills; Yes Tor, Dartmoor's highest point; Winsford Hill and Dunkery Beacon.

⩔ A herd of pure-bred Exmoor ponies was founded here by Exmoor National Park in order to preserve the breed.

🏊 Wimbleball Reservoir and Dam, 🚢 landscaped to preserve the place's beauty and atmosphere.

🅱 The drive – 'Lady Harriet Acland's' – was constructed in the 18th C. for carriages.

Dunkery Beacon
6½ miles (10.5 km) Sheet 181 903438

Moderate Exmoor's highest point; views of some fine, coppiced oak woodland, most colourful in autumn. *Moorland, combe, woods; 2 climbs; mud after rain.*

Start From the A39 (Minehead to Porlock), take the Horner or Luccombe turning and follow signs for Dunkery until road forks at Webber's Post for Cloutsham and Wheddon Cross. **Car park** at Webber's Post.

① From car park walk along Cloutsham road to start of nature trail and follow trail to stone no. 2. ② Turn left to climb through carpet of whortleberry plants with stream below to right. At well-worn path turn right to cross stream. A quarter mile (0.5 km) after stony trail emerges from wooded combe on to open hilltop, it is crossed by a grassy path. ③ Turn left to climb through heather, veering right around head of another plunging combe, then forking left uphill to summit of Dunkery. ④ Turn right to follow ridge path to Rowbarrows (check direction with viewpoint indicator). Pass one barrow, then turn right to pass to left of the next. Take right fork to pass rainfall gauge and walk down to Cloutsham road. ⑤ Turn right to walk on, or parallel with, road to sign for Dicky's Path on right. Turn left and head for right corner of plantation and continue in same direction across heather to Stoke Pero road. At road turn left to church and

farmhouse. ⑥ Turn right to follow 'Priestway'. Continue on this path (signposted) into oak woodland, then follow signs to Webber's Post along boundary of wood with fence on right. As fence changes to wall and path emerges into open, the starting point at Webber's Post is seen half left. ⑦ Veer left away from wall and seat and nature trail stone no. 5, and fork left to follow track turning right at next sign to continue downhill to East Water. ⑧ Turn left to cross water, then take steep path on right up to Webber's Post; turn right through narrow gap in gorse near top to ①.

〰 The Horner and East Water valleys.

🌿 Parts of the walk coincide with the Cloutsham Nature Trail (guide published by Exmoor National Park) on the National Trust-owned Holnicote Estate.

🦌 Red deer may be seen all round the walk.

🦃 A likely stretch of heather for spotting grouse, a few of which remain.

⛪ At 1,013 feet (309 m) above sea level, this is one of the loneliest churches on Exmoor, and still lit by candles only; once used by couples who wanted quiet weddings.

🏠 Cloutsham Farm's 'Swiss' extension was built and used by the Acland family, owners of the Holnicote Estate.

EXMOOR AND THE QUANTOCKS

Hawk Coombe and Homebush Wood
4 miles (6.5 km) Sheet 181 885465

Moderate A route with several good examples of man conserving his immediate environment. *Streamside, woodland; 3 climbs; mud, especially in hunting season.*

Start At centre of Porlock, turn off by church. **Car park** in Parsons Street.

① From car park follow road with steam on right, passing disused mill and following signs indicating valley path and public bridleway to the head of Hawk Combe, passing 'Owls Barton' to end of surfaced road at 'The Stables'. ② Go straight on along woodland track, cross footbridge, take right-hand track at fork and cross another footbridge. Stay on the right side of the stream, passing dammed pond and tree nursery. ③ At ford, cross stream and follow main track to 4-way signpost and ④ turn right to follow path with red waymarks. Climb steeply and turn off right immediately before cattle grid. ⑤ Follow path with red waymarks along top edge of wood and through conifer plantation. ⑥ At end of plantation, leave waymarked path and turn half left through gate to follow hedge on right through 2 more gates to drive leading to house on right. ⑦ Cross drive and fork slightly left to follow sharply descending bridleway. Turn sharp right towards Hawk Combe. Veer left, then right downhill to path 'T' junction. Turn left and continue to ①

England's last substantial herds of red deer – largest of the deer – inhabit Exmoor.

🏛 An interesting Early English church, with a beautiful arcade of 5 bays, pieces of a Saxon cross and some outstanding monuments.

⩔ Red deer, seen frequently.

🍂 Many of the oaks have been coppiced: the heads lopped off, usually to provide winter feed or 'browsing' for the deer. The practice produces the many slim stems, with various uses, including charcoal burning.

⑂ Hawk Combe Head.

⑂ Porlock Bay, Hurlstone Point, Bossington Hill and Selworthy Beacon.

Nutscale Reservoir
5½ miles (9 km) Sheet 181 848419

Moderate Open spaces and superb moorland views; best from April to October – there is considerable bird activity in spring and, from summer onwards, the glory of the heather. *Streamside, hillside, farmland, moorland; 3 climbs; mud after rain.*

Start From the A39 at top of Porlock Hill take the Exford road, looking for car park in 3 miles (5 km). **Car parks** on the Exford side of the bridge over Chetsford Water.

① From car park cross bridge and turn right to follow Chetsford Water. ② Cross Chetsford Water at ford, where there are large rocks in midstream. Climb wide track immediately opposite, veer left and follow track uphill through heather. Go straight

across access road to reservoir, and join minor road for 200 yards (183 m) to edge of open moorland. ③ Turn left to follow farm track with wire fence on right descending through gorse and turning right through gate. In 100 yards (91 m) where road turns sharp left to descend to valley ④ go straight on through gate to join metalled track, which descends to an isolated cottage on right. Then follow the path down to Nutscale Water, cross the footbridge, turn right and then immediately left through a gate. Climb steep, stony track to Lucott Farm, turning left as the farm access road is reached. ⑤ At Lucott Farm turn left to take wide track which passes to the left of the farmhouse. This has yellow waymarks and climbs steadily with fields on both sides. ⑥ As the track goes through gate on to open moorland, go straight on, skirting the top of the deep combe which descends to Nutscale on left. Go through the next gate on to grassland and veer slightly right towards a marker in the middle of the field. Continue straight on through next gate to open moorland again and head for the right end of a row of trees on the skyline. The path becomes a grassy track through heather and reaches the Exford-Porlock road at Lucott Cross. ⑦ At Lucott Cross turn left and follow road to ①.

➤ The valley of Chetsford Water is the local quiet spot for bird-watching – relatively rare species seen include the merlin, smallest of the falcons, and the ring ouzel, resembling a blackbird with a white gorget (neck patch).

➤ Nutscale Reservoir, formed by damming Chetsford Water, is the water source for Minehead and District.

➤ Sympathetic conversions of old country dwellings for modern needs.

➤ Dunkery Beacon; North Hill and Selworthy Beacon; the Bristol Channel and Welsh Coast.

➤ Most of the route is on the delightful Holnicote Estate, now National Trust, which came into the Acland family in the 18th C. The 12,500 acres, mostly open to the public at all times, includes such landmarks as Selworthy Beacon and Dunkery Hill, and there is much of architectural interest. In the Aclands' day, the stag hunting was greatly prized.

EXMOOR AND THE QUANTOCKS

Wills Neck

5½ miles (9 km) Sheet 181 181338

Moderate An introduction to the woods and valleys of these hills, with a climb to their highest point for superb 360° views. *Hills, lanes, moorland; 2 climbs; mud.*

Start From Kingston St. Mary, N of Taunton, pass through village; where main road bears left at end continue straight on up Buncombe Hill. Turn left at café and shop at crossroads for Bishops Lydeard. In just over a mile (nearly 2 km) turn right at a house. In ½ mile (0.8 km) look for car park sign. **Car park** at foot of Lydeard Hill.

① From stile at NE end of car park take broad track along side of wood. ② Turn right through gate and woods. Turn left along unpaved lane, soon descending, and . in ½ mile becoming paved. After ½ mile (0.8 km) ③ at T-junction join road, passing old lime kiln on left. Continue ¼ mile to village and church of Aisholt. ④ Continue from church steeply downhill for 100 yards (91 m) to Old School House. Cross bridge over stream and go uphill for 200 yards (183 m) to ⑤ a sharp U-turn. Turn left at the 'No Through Road' sign and continue 300 yards (270 m). ⑥ Turn right before reaching farmhouse and continue up lane past cottage on right. Reach open moor and

take right fork to climb hill track for 300 yards (270 m) to track at edge of woods. Turn left along this track, continuing with woods on right for over 1½ miles (2.6 km). The track first climbs then descends slightly and bears right to car park at Triscombe Stone. ⑦ Retrace steps for 50 yards (46 m) and take broad track on right away from wood uphill over moor. In ⅓ mile (0.5 km) reach trig. point at Wills Neck. ⑧ Continue along ridge path (SE). In ¼ mile keep to left of wood. ⑨ Aisholt church comes into view below to the left. Continue alongside wood to stile and gate, cross, and continue with fence on right reaching car park in ½ mile.

🌱 Red deer may be seen all along route.

🦅 Buzzard country.

🏚 The lime kiln was last used in the 19th C.

🏠 Aisholt village (with a 15th C. church), where the poet Coleridge wanted to live – but his wife thought it too remote.

🏚 The poet Sir Henry Newbolt lived in the Old School House during the 1930s.

↗ Notably: E and SE, the Mendips; NW to Minehead; W, the Brendon Hills; SW, the length of Dartmoor; S, the Blackdown Hills and, SE, Pilsdon Pen.

Wordsworth's Quantocks
5½ miles (9 km) Sheet 181 155411

Moderate Reveals a variety of beautifully changeable scenery. *Wooded combe, moorland, ridge, woods, streamside; one climb; mud.*

Start In Holford on the A39 turn left immediately after the garage. In 0.3 mile (½ km) turn right (signposted Alfoxton and Hodder's Combe) and in 100 yards (91 m) find **car park** on left, just before Holford Green.

① From car park continue along road with green on left. In 200 yards (180 m), where road turns sharp right, continue between signpost and ancient dog pound up stony track for ¾ mile (one km) to open moor. Continue straight ahead on broad track uphill towards ridge; just past the first crest keep left and a little way over the next meet the ridge walk. Here ② turn left at crossways along ridge path. In ¼ mile (400 m) pass ③ Bicknoller Post on left (large stake in ground). Continue 180 yards (160 m) on main path and fork left, continuing along main path. In ¼ mile (0.5 km), pass through open, grassy area and keep to main path (on right) uphill. Continue along winding ridge path. In one mile (1.5 km), opposite the head of a combe on the right (between a post with fire-beaters and a fence-corner with a stile); ④ fork left along double track round side of

hill. Keep to this (passing 4 tracks on left) for ¾ mile (1.3 km). After passing solitary tree on left, go up steep rise to grassy, stony open space, where a path crosses. ⑤ Turn left, and descend wide, grassy path towards wooded area in valley below, changing direction from E to N. Continue downhill into woods (stony path) to reach stream. Continue left of stream on broad path for 100 yards (91 m), cross another stream by stepping stones and immediately turn right. In 100 yards, cross main stream by stepping stones, and continue along path on right side of river. In ¾ mile, reach picnic area. ⑥ Continue straight ahead on broad lane and in ¼ mile (0.5 km) pass cottage and Combe House Hotel on left. After more cottages, on outskirts of Holford, turn left past pillar box, then sharp left; Car park in 100 yards on left.

🏨 Alfoxton Park, an 18th C. manor house now a hotel and restaurant, where
✕ Wordsworth lived for a year in 1797 and produced poems about the Quantocks.

⚛ Hinckley Point Nuclear Power Station; the barrow on Thorncombe Hill, itself a vantage point worth a detour.

🦌 Red deer are seen regularly around Holford and in Alfoxton Park.

Doone Country
11 miles (17.5 km) Sheet 180 763433

Moderate Shows that Exmoor is a romantic moor, despite appearing less desolate and lonely than other moorland tracts. The *Lorna Doone* story is a true picture of these parts, and reading the book adds another dimension to the walk's enjoyment. *Moorland, streamsides, woods; 2 climbs; mud after rain.*

Start Brendon Two Gates, on the B3223 between Simonsbath and Lynton. **Parking** on wide verges immediately S of the cattle grid at Brendon Two Gates.

① Cross cattle grid. Turn right to follow track running parallel to Hoccombe Water, passing through one gate and eventually descending sharply to Badgworthy Water at footbridge below junction with Hoccombe Water. ② Turn left to follow path (yellow waymarks) towards Malmsmead, crossing bridge over Hoccombe Water and bridge over Lank Combe with Water Slide to left. Then make for Blackmore Memorial Stone, then Cloud Farm, where waymarked path veers left away from water. ③ At road turn sharp left to climb to brow of hill (over cattle grid, under power cables). ④ Turn left to follow gravel track, turning right across shallow stream after some isolated beech trees. As track peters out, fork left to make for head of next combe. ⑤ About 100 yards (91 m) after combe, leave track to fork left across 200 yards (183 m) of heather to join a distinct track from Malmsmead Hill. Turn right to follow this W, passing a 4-way and a 3-way signpost. ⑥ 350 yards (320 m) past 3-way sign, by tumulus (with Star of Bethlehem) fork right to dry bridge on the Lynton Road. Cross road to follow stream, criss-crossing at will, to stream's junction with Farley Water. ⑦ Turn left and continue upstream, again using either bank, passing large mounds of Holcombe Barrows after about 20 minutes' walking. ⑧ Where wide track descends to the valley from the right, veer left away from water to follow continuation of this track up combe. Go straight on from head of combe to hit road at ①.

🏚 Brendon Two Gates, a once-important entrance to Exmoor's royal hunting ground, had a combination of self-closing gates to prevent animals straying.

The grey wagtail – grey upperparts, bright yellow beneath – favours flowing water.

↑ Dunkery Beacon, 8 miles (13 km) distant.

🏚 Site of the medieval settlement which was probably R. D. Blackmore's model for the Doone stronghold in *Lorna Doone*. The novel features several Exmoor locations, in degrees of imaginative transformation.

🏚 Blackmore's probable model for the terrible Water Slide in *Lorna Doone*.

✕ Cloud Farm's café, and Malmsmead café, open seasonally, the latter licensed.

🦃 The occasional red grouse, and the last of Exmoor's black grouse may be seen.

🦃 Dippers and wagtails.

Exmoor is hospitable to the walker who wants to improvise; its bogs are harmless and the paths well signposted.

Porlock and Selworthy are useful starting points, the first for moorland routes, the second for the network of paths through Selworthy Woods, leading to Allerford, Bossington and beyond to Hurlstone Point.

There is nearly 20 miles (32 km) of the North Devon Coastal Path between Lynmouth and Minehead. Less ambitious coastal strolls can be devised using the paths on North Hill (access from Lynmouth) with spectacular cliff-top passages. (See pages 328-334.) Booklets describing the National Park's waymarked walks are available from Exmoor House, Dulverton (send S.A.E.).

MENDIP REGION

The Mendips (plain Mendip to the expert) are a modest range of hills, never higher than a thousand-odd feet 305 m), and running a mere 30 miles (48 km) from the Bristol Channel to Frome; but they are massive, constituting, for most of their length, a solid, unbroken wall rising abruptly from the willows and water of the Somerset Levels.

To explore the hills properly takes a little trouble: there are relatively few footpaths. On a fine weekend, the area's maze of lanes may be crowded, for this is Bristol's playground. On quieter days, the flat-topped Mendip plateau is extraordinarily lonely.

Some of the villages almost have a look of the industrial north in their grey limestone, and quarrying has taken ugly bites from the hills. To compensate, there are the natural wonders. The limestone here is soluble; rainwater gradually seeps downwards, eating away the rock, making great caves. Sometimes the roof falls in to produce a canyon like Cheddar Gorge.

North Wootton
2 or 5 miles (3 or 8 km) Sheet 182 564417

Easy Away from the main Mendip tourist area in the vineyard country, agreeably dominated by views of Glastonbury Tor. *Woods, farmland; one climb; mud.*

Start North Wootton, SE of Wells. **Parking** outside the church or in adjacent road.

① From church cross bridge and turn right to road along which turn left; take first left and follow lane to its junction with the Worminster road. ② Left on to road and continue to No Through Road sign. ③ At sign turn right, following lane past Mill House. Continue (later through wet section) to junction with Worminster – Pilton road. ④ Turn right, walking uphill to top. As road flattens, ⑤ turn sharp right (before reaching Y-junction). Take track (actually a bridleway) into wood, shortly keeping to main path close to edge of wood. ⑥ Continue ahead, pool to right, in a few yards leaving wood under wire on right. Continue in same direction (as through wood) using faint path along field edge. Continue through second field with hedge on right. Cross third field diagonally, leaving through gate into lane. ⑦ Follow lane downhill, looking for small brick building (pumping station) in field on right. Just past it, look for stile at top of bank on right. Cross into field, walking below pumping station, after it turning left, dropping to stile in field corner by shed with corrugated metal roof. Cross into road. ⑧

Left on to road, in 150 yards (137 m) meeting crossroads at Crossways Inn. Turn right back to church if not continuing. Otherwise straight over crossroads, leaving pub to right. Straight over next crossroads, ⑨ entering bridleway. Follow it to gate and overhead cables, continuing straight on along bank of stream to Redlake Farm. ⑩ Over bridge at farm and right along lane, following signposts back to North Wootton.

🏛 The church contains a Norman font. The pub at the crossroads – The Crossways Inn – was a cider press.

\↑/ Passing Mill House there is a clear view of some of the vineyards flourishing in the area. The centre of local wine-making is the nearby Pilton Manor Vineyard (The Manor House, Pilton), with an exhibition of wine-making and a wine bar with the local wine on sale.

\↑/ The harmonious scene looking back NE from Stoodly Hill is Worminster Sleight, Dungeon Farm and Church Hill.

\↑/ From the top of the hill, and frequently on the return to Wootton, Glastonbury Tor is in view. The tower itself is the remains of a 15 C. church; the town, with its ruined abbey and associated buildings, a formerly great religious centre and subject of legends going back to King Arthur. Beyond it spread the Somerset Levels, the low-lying area which was impenetrably marshy until drained for farmland.

MENDIP REGION

Flax Bourton Backwell and Bourton Combe
6½ miles (10.5 km) Sheet 182 507693

Easy Excellent vantage points and varied scenery close to Bristol; less used than the nearby Brockley and Goblin Combes. *Pasture, arable farmland, combes; 2 climbs; mud; path may be overgrown between* ⑭ *and* ②. Possible obstructions near ⑤ and ⑬.

Start Flax Bourton on the A370 SW of Bristol; buses from Bristol and Weston.
Parking in Station Road, from where find the start of the walk, the church in Flax Bourton main street.

① From Church walk E and turn up Bourton Combe. ② At top of lane continue on left of hedge towards Barrow church, crossing stile and iron kissing-gate, heading uphill and just to left of Barrow Court. Follow wall of Court, over stile in wire fence and out of drive leading to church. ③ Turn right on to road along estate wall and ④ at first stile on left at top of hill go through field adjoining Home Farm. Continue straight on over stile, downhill through gate; turn right before wood and continue to junction of short lane and minor road. (If right of way is obstructed by wire, follow hedge to left and round to junction.) ⑤ Continue straight across at end of lane into field (by Slade Lane sign) and uphill, through gate. Continuing in same direction, follow fence with wood on right and track, going through 3 gates. At gate immediately on left, ⑥ turn left and follow track along side of 'the Plantation'. Turn sharp right into field and then bear right across it, leaving Jubilee Stone on right. ⑦ Look carefully for gate leading out to lane where wall makes a right angle. Follow lane to crossroads. ⑧ Turn right, later first left, and in 100 yards (90 m) ⑨ take the narrow track on the right leading to Backwell Jubilee Stone. Continue past this downhill (left of stone) to a wooden stile on right. ⑩ Over stile and bear left across field looking down on to Backwell church, left. Take gate on right in corner and in a few yards turn right ⑪ where path bears to left. Walk up Farleigh Combe and exit to road over stile in left corner. Turn right along road for 90 yards (80 m). ⑫ Go through first gate on left, following well-defined, stony track and continuing along narrow path past derelict buildings into wood. Go straight ahead, slightly uphill, and continue to end of track past farm buildings. (If gate

across track at farm is impassable, walk 110 yards (100 m) to left through wood, then left on to track inside a gate.) ⑬ Turn sharp left and follow the buildings right round, almost doubling back behind farmhouse, to find a gate into wood. (This is the NW of the 3 gates.) Through it, continue about 700 yards (630 m), keeping on lip of combe. At a large clump of yews, bear left on minor track, climbing slightly to emerge on 'the Plateau' with a sheer drop on left. ⑭ Where open space narrows, about half-way along, take track to right through wood and downhill to lane which leads to Bourton Combe lane and point ①.

🏛 Barrow Court is a restored Elizabethan house on the site of a Benedictine nunnery built in 1211. The 12 statues ranged round the lawn represent the months of the year.

⑂ View of Long Ashton, the fruit research station run by Bristol University; beyond, Christchurch, Clifton and Bristol.

⛪ Backwell church has a Norman font, a medieval screen, a 15th C. chapel, and the tomb of Sir Walter Rodney.

⑂ View of Backwell church in the valley and the coast at Clevedon. Clevedon Court, built in 1320 with later additions, is a National Trust property within easy reach. Nailsea, noted for glass-making, is seen straight ahead across the valley.

🍺 Jubilee Inn.

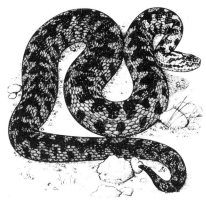

Adders (proper name, black adders) are brown with a black zigzag band on the back. Bites require hospital treatment.

Mendip Forest and Priddy Barrows
2 or 5 miles (3 or 8 km) Sheet 182 548513

Easy Enchanting coniferous plantation route, with a contrasting hillside section for the energetic. *Woods, pasture; one climb; mud.*

Start From A39 NE of Wells take unclassified road to Priddy, turning right at Hunters Lodge Inn. **Parking** at Forestry Commission cark park and picnic area, on right after big right and left bends.

① Head into wood on grassy path just past the first parking bay, between posts. Cross the car park circuit again; at a crosstrack about 200 yards (180 m) on, bear slightly left. ② In another 300 yards (270 m) turn left on to a metalled track, and continue, ignoring first left and bearing left where track joins from right. ③ Cross stile by gate to road; turn left and walk along road a little over ¼ mile (500 m) to next gate. ④ Re-enter wood and follow metalled track back to the road just north of car park. ⑤ If continuing, cross, taking track opposite to pool with lead mine workings ahead. ⑥ Continue to view mining remains, then retrace to pool and take path through trees on left. Follow it to road at farm. ⑦ Turn right along road passing Fairladywell Cottage, 80 yards (73 m) past which enter field on right over bars. Cross field past electricity post to stone stile, and continue across next field to gate into

lane. Exit on to lane, turning right. Follow this uphill, in ½ mile (0.8 km) continuing on deteriorating track. ⑧ Where path meets road, turn right through small gate and, bearing left, make for brow of hill. From brow, head for gate in gap between trees in far corner. ⑨ At gate turn right, aiming for barrows (mounds). Walk between barrows, continuing past two more barrows to fence gate by a stone wall. Walk over North Hill with wall on right, crossing stile, descending to the pool. At track retrace to ①.

The area is well known for adders, the only poisonous snake species in Britain.

St. Cuthbert's lead mines (closed; now Priddy Mineries Reserve) contain Roman remains. Records of mining here go back to the 12th C.

The gully contains the entrance to East Water Swallet, the deepest known cleft in the Mendips.

Priddy Nine Barrows and Ashen Hill Barrows are Bronze Age burial mounds.

To the E Mendips, and the Tower of Cranmore, above Cranmore Hall.

The Miners' Arms, once a lead miners' inn, is now a restaurant famed for Mendip snails; brews own ale.

Yarley and Hembury Hills
3½ miles (5.5 km) Sheet 182 514453

Easy Fine vantage points for viewing the Somerset Levels. *Farmland; one climb; mud; the District Surveyor has been asked to clear the obstruction at ⑦.*

Start The Pheasant Inn, near Worth on the B3139; buses from Wells and Burnham stop near the Pheasant. **Parking** behind the Pheasant Inn where the lane to Fenny Castle meets the B3139.

① Walk along the lane below Ben Knowle and fork right. ② Take first lane on right, following it uphill, then gradually downhill to T-junction by cottages. Turn right. Continue to next T-junction and ③ turn left uphill. Almost immediately turn right through gate of Keeping Cottage, continuing straight ahead through 2 gates along bridleway. Where bridleway stops, continue straight on uphill, across the field, through gate and straight on over brow of hill. Cross field to metal gate opposite. ④ Turn sharp left on to narrow track, becoming a bridleway, and follow to end. ⑤ Turn right towards Callow Hill, following the road round and turning left. ⑥ Where the road bends sharply left, go through gate on right and climb straight across the field, continuing in same direction through 2 gates on to ridge of Hembury Hill. Continue down the ridge (Glastonbury Tor ahead) and ⑦ near the hedge bear left to the end of the hill. Exit under wire near woodland unless obstruction at ⑦ has been cleared. Alternatively, make towards road to the right and continue along it into village. Past the hedge, bear right across the field to the gate near the cross and exit into lane where ⑧ turn left and continue to starting point.

\†/ Former peat cutting areas, of which the most significant were Meare and Shapwick Heath. The latter is now a nature reserve.

\†/ To the Abbot's Fish House at Meare (459418), quarters of the Abbot of Glastonbury's personal fisherman, who worked the substantial lake or mere before the Levels of which it was a part were drained for farmland.

⁂ The site of an ancient, wooden, possibly Anglo-Saxon fortification.

Across the Mendips above Wells
7 miles (11 km) Sheet 182 549463

Moderate An introduction to the Mendips, with Wookey Hole and the great cathedral town of Wells. *Arable farmland, pasture, grassy slopes; one climb; mud.*

Start Mountery Road, off New Street, Wells; frequent buses from Bristol and Street – alight at Walcombe Lane near point ①. **Public car park** in Union Street – reach point ① via Chamberlain and New Streets; parking in Mountery Road is limited.

① From junction of Mountery Road and New Street walk up the main road in the Bristol direction, and just beyond the crossroads ② turn left along Walcombe Lane. Continue to a small cluster of houses and ③ bear right past 2 garages along a short lane and take first gate on right by hydrant. Cross field to right-hand corner and enter public bridleway. Follow this (it narrows after gate on left and later becomes a metalled road) to its exit near the Pen Mast. ④ Walk past entrance to mast and cross 'Peggy Marriott' stile. Follow path bearing right away from mast, turn left at first gate and continue over waymarked stiles to the road above Rookham. ⑤ Turn left and walk down road to top of Rookham Hill. ⑥ Turn right along drove road and follow this nearly to Higher Pitts Farm. ⑦ Turn left into waymarked field and continue through 2 fields to crest of ridge. Then continue straight ahead downhill towards Wookey Hole, through 2 gates, then bearing diagonally left across next field to iron gate. Through this, continue straight ahead to the village school. ⑧ Downhill past old paper mill and straight ahead through Wookey Hole towards Wells. ⑨ Turn into field on left signposted 'West Mendip Way' and follow signs and waymarks whole way to its end at New Street, Wells. Turn right downhill to reach Union Street car park or walk a few yards uphill to Mountery Road.

❀ The garden and combe of Milton Lodge are open occasionally in spring/summer to raise money for charity.

🚃 The railway coach was converted about 1904 into a summer bungalow by H. E. Balch, distinguished local figure, pioneer of Mendip caving, and the first curator of Wells Museum.

↕ To Glastonbury Tor; Hinckley Point Nuclear Power Station; Brent Knoll, the National Trust property with earthworks and church, and, in clear conditions, the Quantock Hills about 12 miles (19 km) distant.

❧ Bee orchids flower in June and July on the slopes above Wookey Hole.

📷 Wookey Hole Cave, operated by Madame Tussaud's with a variety of additional attractions to the cave itself; a waxworks storeroom, Lady Bangor's fairground collection and the paper mill, with a demonstration of paper-making. All of them can be viewed in an inclusive tour.

🍺 Wookey Hole Inn.

MENDIP REGION

The West Mendip Way
14 miles (22.5 km) Sheet 182 385563

Energetic A section of the long-distance route from Weston-super-Mare to Wells, covering some of the finest Mendip scenery; passes above Cheddar Gorge. *Grassy uplands, drove road, farmland, woods; 4 climbs; mud.*

Start The West Mendip Way guide post by the quarry on the Barton road, close to the M5 SE of Weston; buses from Weston and Wells stop at Winscombe, 2 miles (3 km) from the start. **Parking** on the roadside a few yards S of the quarry.

The West Mendip Way is waymarked by fingerless oak posts, some (late 1991) due for overhaul or replacement.
① From lay-by go uphill along signposted bridleway. ② Turn steeply uphill at post labelled Shuta Shelve. Continue in same direction across Compton Hill and Wavering Down. (Divert from Compton Hill to summit of peak if desired.) Keeping to left of trig. point, go straight ahead and downhill through King's Wood to road. ③ Through gate and straight ahead to the A38. Turn left and in a few yards cross road to take drove road uphill. ④ Where tracks meet, take leftmost of several tracks (waymarked) and continue along drove road. ⑤ Turn left along lane to Winterhead Hill Farm. ⑥ Just before farm enter field on right and make straight for stone and wooden stile. Continue straight ahead, dropping steeply to track. Cross it, and descend steeply to small stream. Then uphill. ⑦ Bear left uphill

crossing stile at end, and continue to road. ⑧ Turn right, cross road and take track uphill following Cheddar sign. Straight ahead through gate. ⑨ Go along Hilltop Meadow drive, and at field gate take small gate adjoining it and follow track across mining area. ⑩ After two posts, bear left along track and through gate. ⑪ Turn left down lane and out to metalled bridleway. ⑫ Turn right along bridleway uphill. ⑬ Where bridleway turns left, go straight ahead down narrow (often muddy) track to Rowberrow Warren. Continue in same direction, crossing stream and climbing again to join track (labelled 'Public Bridleway to Blackdown'), through gate and on to Tyning's Farm. ⑭ Follow path out of farm and turn left along road to Charterhouse for about ½ mile (0.8 km). ⑮ Take metalled track on right to Charterhouse Farm and keep to right of farm buildings. Continue straight ahead across 2 cattle grids to top of field. ⑯ Turn left along top edge of field, follow wall and hedge downhill, over stile and down track beside Long Wood. ⑰ Cross stile opposite Long Wood entrance and continue along track to Cheddar Gorge. Go straight across road and steeply uphill. ⑱ About 100 yards (90 m) after top, turn left away from Gorge. (To visit Cheddar follow track running parallel with Gorge.) ⑲ Where paths meet take care to cross over junction and bear left uphill. Follow narrow path downhill looking towards Cheddar church. ⑳ Approaching wood on lower slopes, bear right on to track skirting it for ¼ mile (400 m). ㉑ Turn left along track into Nature Reserve and go straight ahead, continuing on track between market gardening fields. ㉒ Turn sharp right towards house, then left on to metalled road.

Just before junction with main road, ㉓ turn left along grassy track, through gate and up track. ㉔ In 220 yards (200 m) bear right and follow track round below hill, bearing left to follow track to gate – mud usually to be negotiated. ㉕ Through gate, follow stony (and often muddy) track to field. Continue across field to gate in right-hand corner. Cross to opposite gate ㉖ and make downhill across field. Pick up track and follow it to Batcombe Farm. Continue to road. ㉗ Turn left and continue to Wells-Cheddar road for buses back to starting point. Alight at Winscombe and walk along road to Barton (this distance included in the 14 miles).

The 30-mile West Mendip Way was devised to mark Queen Elizabeth's Silver Jubilee, and opened in May 1979.

The Miners' Arms, Shipham, and the Red Lion Inn, Draycott.

'Gruffy' grounds – remains of calamine mining. Calamine, a zinc ore, was mixed with copper to make brass, or mined for the zinc itself. The section of the vein excavated by each miner was his groove or 'gruff'. Its extent was defined by how far he could throw a tool called a law hack either way along the vein.

Gorsey Bigbury earthen circle—about 1800 BC.

Long Wood and Black Rock are nature reserves, the former with good examples of trees, such as whitebeam and ash, which thrive on the limestone that predominates in the Mendips. Both reserves have badger setts.

MENDIP REGION

Some N Mendip Villages
8½ miles (13.5 km) Sheet 172 633557

Easy Gentle scenery in an interesting and unvisited former mining area. *Pasture, arable farmland, woods; 2 climbs; mud.*

Start Church Lane, Farrington Gurney, at the junction of the A39 and A362; buses from Wells and Bristol. **Car park** in Church Lane.

① Left out of car park; follow road towards church. Through gate, leaving church to left, cross field, over old railway line and straight ahead. ② Half-way across, bear left over stile. Make diagonally across the next stile. Keep near left hedge to next stile; cross two fences and continue slightly uphill, bearing right to far end of field. ③ Through gate, bear left to stile in corner and in next field cross stone 'plank' and stile on left. Turn right, over 2 further stiles, then straight on to gate and on to road. ④ Turn left, then first right into cul-de-sac, then turn right across river. ⑤ In a few yards turn left along public footpath between houses. Cross stile into copse, over another stile and straight ahead into Greyfields Wood. ⑥ Bear left through wood, cross flat, stone bridge and continue uphill. Bear right over stile, cross field into wood again and follow uphill path in same direction to end of wood. ⑦ Turn right along lane, and ⑧ first left, continuing straight ahead to Maynard Terrace, Clutton. ⑨ At main road turn left over stile (Public Footpath sign), cross stream, cross field—recross stream by metal stiles and follow line of poles. Go through gate on right, across old railway line and straight ahead towards Clutton church. ⑩ Out through gate at Bendall's Bridge and turn right. ⑪ At church car park, turn left into field, go straight across through kissing gate and uphill through 2 further fields to reach the A37. ⑫ Turn right and shortly find footpath sign on left. Follow path through garden. ⑬ Uphill through 3 fields, making for top right-hand corner of third. (Ignore obvious stile in top hedge.) Cross stile near top of right-hand hedge, then across to gate on left. Turn right along edge of field and make for gate. Through it, bear slightly left across field uphill to the farthest corner. Find stile, bear left across corner of next field and keeping along ridge exit into lane at extreme end. ⑭ Turn left down lane. ⑮ At end of lane turn right uphill. ⑯ Left at Coley–Litton

How the colliery at Greyfield (near point ③) looked in its heyday: the area had several coal-mines, and some unsightly tips.

signpost and continue to Hinton Blewett green. ⑰ Take the Litton road from Hinton Blewett. ⑱ Take first lane on left and continue to its end. Into field, and straight ahead to footbridge. Straight ahead to stile into wood; cross, follow path through to field and turn right. ⑲ Exit into Pitway Lane and continue to the A37. Turn left, cross and continue along Church Lane to car park.

🏠 The Old Parsonage (about 1700), one of the Mendips' finest houses, now a hotel.

⛪ Clutton's church is 12th C. John Wesley, founder of Methodism, was refused permission to preach inside, so performed from a stone in the graveyard. It is unusual for the staircase leading to the gallery to be outside. The church has a connection with the famous actor Sir Henry Irving – his grandparents William and Elizabeth Brodripp are buried here..

\⫯/ To Cameley church and fish tanks, with Downside Abbey about 6 miles (9.5 km) beyond. Some of the monks of this Benedictine foundation are schoolmasters at Downside, the Roman Catholic public school associated with the Abbey. The community was started in 1793 by monks from the famous monastery at Douai in France..

🍺 The Ring of Bells – Wadsworth beer.

✗ The Farrington Inn – restaurant.

Cheddar Gorge's limestone cliffs winding 2 miles (3 km) through the Mendip plateau.

The banks of the Bradford-on-Avon to Bath Canal make an intriguing expedition, easy to navigate. The whole length is a substantial day's outing.

Three miles (5 km) N of Congresbury there is a waymarked trail in Brockley Combe, famed for its trees, including an outstanding avenue of limes; leaflet from the Brockley Combe Fruit Stall.

There are 2 waymarked walks in Ebbor Gorge, one through the gorge, one through the woods. Start from the picnic area just off the unclassified road between Easton and Wookey Hole, or from the entrance to Wookey Hole.

Starting on the road E out of Wells, to Dinder, there is a fine waymarked route via Dinder back to Wells.

SOUTH-EAST ENGLAND

ISLE OF WIGHT

First-time visitors to the Isle of Wight – locals call it 'the Island' – can be surprised at how well it has survived as a world apart; as a miniature, with cosier neater proportions, of the real-life England across the Solent.

Charles I was imprisoned at Carisbrooke, but the Island's royal connections did not begin in earnest until Queen Victoria bought Osborne. Lord Tennyson settled at Farringford, other Victorian notables followed, and the Isle of Wight became fashionable. The Victorian flavour still lingers, not only in the architecture of the seaside terraces, but in the tempo of life, which moves, even in holiday season, at the tempo of yachting ports and steam trains, against a background of farm- and woodland.

That is the Island's peaceful walking country, criss-crossed with well maintained, energetically signposted footpaths. Because the bus service is so good, it is terrain for the walker who likes improvising; no necessity for circular routes here.

For exhilaration, there is the chalk ridge which forms the Island's spine. Walking it has been compared to flying low over the whole landscape, only more exceptional, because of the wild flowers, birds and butterflies.

Godshill
4 miles (6.5 km) Sheet 196 527819

Easy The Island's gentler charms–a picture-book village and impressive 18th C. remains. *Woods, downland, farmland; 3 climbs (one optional); mud after rain.*

Start Godshill, beside the A3020, W of Shanklin; frequent buses. **Public car park** opposite Griffin Hotel.

① With Griffin Hotel on left, follow lane a few yards, then left at footpath sign. Cross

Godshill, probably the most charming and commercialized, of the Island's villages.

field and go along wooded valley. ② Just inside the wood, the path divides. Turn left and follow path uphill, keeping inside the wood. ③ Turn right along cross-track. Go through wood to gate opening into field. ④ Path is not clear, but make across field for farm buildings (Sainham Farm), leaving them to right; cross stile to join lane. Turn left following path signposted 'Gatcliff and Stenbury'. Continue on track across field, then through gate into wood. ⑤ To visit obelisk, go through gate and follow path (unsignposted) to right. To continue, go through wicket gate and take path signposted 'Wroxall and Godshill', following it along stone wall to Freemantle Gate. ⑥ Turn right if visiting Appuldurcombe House, which is about one mile (1.5 km) on. If not visiting house, turn left at gate.

🏠 The church has a rare wall painting of the Crucifixion.

⌂ Two museums – toys, natural history.

❀ Gardens to visit at Old Vicarage (with model village) and Old Smithy (aviary).

🏛 Ruin of Appuldurcombe House, with an elegant 18th C. exterior. Home of the Worsley family, one of whom publicly accused his wife of immorality. She denied taking 34 lovers, claiming it was only 27.

ISLE OF WIGHT

Yarmouth to Freshwater
4 miles (6.5 km) Sheet 196 355895

Easy A rewarding introduction to a considerable range of the Island's varied scenery with a happy contrast of bustling town and peaceful woods. *Seaside town, riverside, woods, farmland; mud after rain.*

Start Yarmouth; frequent car ferries from Lymington (on the mainland); frequent buses. **Public car park** at corner of Tennyson and River Roads. **Return** to start by bus – frequent services from Freshwater Bay.

① From car park into River Road, then first right into Mill Road, where there is shortly a footpath sign. Follow this path nearly 3 miles (5 km) ignoring all other signs until ② turn right on to the A3055, crossing bridge, then left into Stroud Road. About 150 yards (137 m) on, follow footpath sign pointing left. Path runs close to a cottage and appears to lead through garden. ③ Cross stile, join road and bear left. ④ Take Blackridge Road a few yards, then path signposted to right, which leads to bay.

📷 Yarmouth Castle, built in the 1540s by Henry VIII against French raids; grandstand views from the gun platform.

🦅 Wetland birds, including curlews.

🌼 Three fern species grow close to the Wilmingham signpost – hart's tongue, soft shield and broad buckler fern.

🌿 The cliffs are hung with samphire, the plant once popular for relish.

ISLE OF WIGHT

The Island's Roof
12 miles (19 km) Sheet 196 347857

Moderate An easily managed section of the Tennyson Trail, with views giving a superb overall impression of the Island; butterflies and plants at best in summer. *Downland, woods, farmland; 2 climbs.*

Start Freshwater Bay; frequent buses. **Public car park** on bay opposite beach or, if full, off A3055 on Afton Down. **Return** to starting point by bus – frequent service.

From road on top of East Afton Down the walk is waymarked by red flashes on posts and 'Tennyson Trail' signs. ① From car park follow beach towards East Afton Down. Climb wooded steps up cliff and take cliff-top path to road (A3055) where ② cross and take path signposted 'Bridleway'. ③ At gate bear right a few yards along road (B3399) to gate on right. Take path signposted 'Bridleway Newport'. ④ Go through gate into

woods and follow wide, grassy track. Keep straight on at next cross-track to gate on to Mottistone Down. ⑤ From car park, bear left along road, then left into lane rising to summit of Brightstone Down. ⑥ Turn left into Brightstone Forest. ⑦ Cross lane and follow path signposted 'Bridleway'.

🐝 Chalkland species including clustered bellflower, whose mauve flowers (May-Sept.) are in a distinct cluster.

👁 From Brightstone Down, views in clear conditions of whole island, from Culver Cliff (635854) to St. Catherine's Point (498754) to Freshwater Bay (347856).

🦋 At least 5 species of butterfly can be distinguished in this conserved area.

🏰 Carisbrooke Castle, probably dating from the late 11th C., and best known as Charles I's place of imprisonment in 1647 – 8 after defeat in the Civil War.

ISLE OF WIGHT

Tennyson Down and the Needles
7 miles (11 km) Sheet 196 347857

Easy The Island's chalk ridge at its most dramatic, with sweeping views of Solent and Channel. *Downland, cliffs, farmland; one climb; keep clear of cliff edge and do not attempt if misty.*

Start Freshwater Bay; frequent buses. **Public car park** in bay opposite beach.

① Leave car park facing sea and turn right along road. After 150 yards (137 m) take path signposted 'Tennyson Down'. Make for the monument, which soon comes into sight. ② Follow path straight on (due W) from monument. It bears slightly right, then through a gate. Continue about 1½ miles (2 km) to fenced areas. ③ Follow signs round fencing to Needles viewing platform. Last few hundred yards is along concrete road. ④ Retrace steps along concrete road to point by coastguards' cottages where road joins from left. Take path signposted 'Alum Bay', leaving road, crossing flagstones and climbing stile by sign. Path curves round grassy cliff, then downhill to road. Follow road to Alum Bay. ⑤ If not visiting bay, continue by path leading right, signposted 'Freshwater Bay' before road drops steeply. Freshwater is about 1½ miles (2 km) on. with Farringford signposted on way. For shorter version, frequent buses run in summer only from Alum Bay to Freshwater Bay.

\↑/ Freshwater Bay and St. Catherine's.

'Heads' and stems of the bee orchid (left) and autumn lady's tresses (right).

🐦 Tennyson Down to Alum Bay is a bird sanctuary. At dusk in summer, listen for the weird, dry trills of nightjars – strange birds with moth-like camouflage. Uncommon sea birds nest on the cliffs, including guillemots, razorbills, fulmars and (remarkable for southern England) puffins.

🌿 Orchids found on the chalk downland include bee orchid and lady's tresses.

🏖 Alum Bay's famous sands, coloured by minerals.

🏖 The Needles, chalk eroded by the sea.

🏨 Farringford, now a hotel, where the poet Tennyson lived 40 years from 1853. He wrote several of his most famous works there, including *Idylls of the King*, and loved walking the downs where, he said, 'the air was worth sixpence a pint'.

Havenstreet Steam Railway and Arreton

6 miles (9.5 km) Sheet 196 547919

Easy Takes in the Island's authentic steam railway and one of the several fine manor houses; best in May–Sept. – railway run-ning. *Wooded creek, farmland; one climb.*

Start Wootton Bridge, on the A3054 E of Newport; frequent buses. **Parking** in front of Sloop Inn, Wootton Bridge. **Return** to start-ing point by bus (not possible by steam railway)—frequent service from Arreton to Newport, changing for Wootton Bridge.

① Take the 'Bridle Road' signposted opposite Sloop Inn, with creek on left. Where track divides, bear right on to gravel track. Continue about 1¼ miles (2 km), crossing railway line and farmyard. ② About ¼ mile (0.5 km) past 'Keeper's Cottage' take care to turn left, ignoring track branching right. ③ Pass pond, continuing through gate ahead (not left through farmyard). ④ Turn left at road, continuing about 500 yards (457 m) to visit Steam Railway Centre. Retrace steps to ⑤ track signposted 'Public Bridleway Downend'. Follow this about 1½ miles (2.5 km). ⑥ At Combley Farm fork left leaving farmhouse to right. Track climbs Arreton Down. ⑦ Turn right on to road, then left at Hare and Hounds. ⑧ Take path signposted 'Public Footpath Arreton' on left after quarry. Path is unclear, but make for over-head cables, turning right beneath them. Drop steeply to stile (to right). Cross, go down steps, follow path towards manor.

🍺 The Sloop Inn.

🚉 Havenstreet Steam Railway Centre is a well-restored steam-age station with at least one train in running order. Round trips to Wootton take about 30 mins. Open Easter and Sundays, May–Sept., but check – times vary.

⚘ Robin Hill Country Park.

🍺 Hare and Hounds.

🏠🏠 Arreton Manor, early 1600s, with 3
🏠 ghosts (one a little girl in a blue dress),
✕ doll's house collection and National Wireless Museum. Tea room serves lunches. Country Craft Workshop.

⛪ St. George's, dating from pre-Norman Conquest, enlarged in the 12th C.

In addition to the Tennyson Trail, the Isle of Wight County Council has waymarked and signposted 6 other medium to long distance routes: the Worsley, Stenbury, Nunwell, Bembridge, Hamstead and Shepherds Trails. Leaflets describing them are available from local bookshops and stationers.

The Isle of Wight Tourist Board publishes a leaflet describing 6 interesting nature trails.

O.S. Sheet 196 covers whole island.

NEW FOREST

A 'forest', yet with wide-open views; dry, adder-haunted heaths and bogs juxtaposed; ancient common rights and the Court of Verderers coexisting with management by a public corporation, the Forestry Commission. The contradictions make this a singular and lovely place, of continually changing colours and shifting centres of interest.

'Forest' means a royal hunting ground, as opposed to a chase, which is a hunting ground, but owned by someone of lesser rank. The New Forest has served the Crown not only for recreation, but militarily: it was a vital source of oaks for the navy. There are plenty of beeches, too, and more recently, for quick profit, the Scots pines and sitka spruce. But the Forest is managed for amenity, rather than profit, and local conservationists are continually on guard against felling of the hardwoods.

Among and around the woodlands are the grassy Forest 'lawns' and the spreading, heather-clad heaths. There is much mud, too (it rarely dries out under the trees) and bogs occupy some 7,000 of the Forest's 92,000 acres (37 ha). They cannot dry out because they lie on top of impermeable geological deposits. The distinctive danger sign of these areas is cotton grass, which has whispy, white tufts in summer.

Under the trees, ones sense of direction departs rapidly; and because the Forest has been lived and worked in for so long, there is a labyrinth of tracks. Careful map-reading is essential.

Rufus Stone
3 miles (5 km) Sheet 195 271125

Easy Peaceful walking close to one of the
Forest's most well-known historic sites.
Woods, Forest lawns, heath: one climb; mud.

Start The Rufus Stone, signposted from the
A31 about 1¼ miles (2 km) W of the Cadnam
roundabout; frequent buses from Ringwood
or Southampton – stop is on A31 near Rufus
Stone turning. **Car park** at Stone.

① Leave car park by track marked 'access
to cottage'. ② At cottage and shed turn right
and make through woods (no obvious path),
keeping fence on bank in sight to left. In
about 500 yards (457 m), cross the stream
and make for houses shortly in view. ③ By
houses, bear left along gravel track. ④ Turn
left down grassy track, passing house named
'Woodpeckers'. Continue about ½ mile (0.8
km) to ⑤ T-junction, at which turn left along
road. At corner skirting garden of 'Walter
Tyrell Inn' look for ⑥ Car Free Area barrier
on right. Past this, make for track to left of
inclosure far right of open ground. Continue
straight ahead. ⑦ Path dips to cross stream.
Do not cross, instead turning left entering
wood where ⑧ just inside, turn left (away
from stream), following fringe of trees. After
crossing narrow stream and clearing, ⑨
turn right, following overhead cables uphill.
Where cables bear right, continue uphill
bearing slightly left, through gorse, in about
300 yards (274 m) meeting well-defined
track, on to which ⑩ turn left. ⑪ Where

*Forest ponies, the well-worn, but apt
symbol of these woods, heaths and 'lawns'.*

path divides, fork left. When it divides again,
bear half left downhill to Stone and car park,
at first hidden by trees.

🔟 The Rufus Stone.

🔟 The ancient hamlets of Canterton, which
means settlement of the Kentish folk.
They were in fact Jutes, the first Saxons
to settle the Forest in the mid-5th C.

🚩 The 'Walter Tyrell' contains a mural
depicting the killing of Rufus.

THE NEW FOREST

The Heart of the Forest
4 miles (6.5 km) Sheet 195 278081

Easy Reveals the extensive old woods at the Forest's centre; fine glades and a glorious streamside section; best if trees are in full leaf. *Heath, woods, streamside; mud.*

Start near Emery Down, off the A35 W of Lyndhurst. At New Forest Inn (conspicuous in village) take minor road signposted 'Bolderwood, Linwood, Fritham'; frequent buses to Emery Down. **Car park** White Moor Car Park, about ½ mile (0.8 km) from the turning by pub.

① Leave car park by barrier marked Car Free Area. Follow footpath ahead, ignoring all cross-tracks, for about ¾ mile (1 km). ② In sparse wood, path dips, becoming unclear. Continue about 100 yards (91 m) through muddy patches (may be flowing water), looking for ford through large stream. Cross, and make for gate at near right corner of fenced field. ③ Before gate, turn left, following fence to Hollidays Hill Keeper's Cottage. (Reptiliary other side of cottage.) ④ At barrier in front of cottage turn left on to gravel track. Continue through camp site to main road (A35). ⑤ Cross road and through stile by gate opposite, where ⑥ turn left and continue about 200 yards (183 m) to the large stream (Highland Water). Turn right, following bank until ⑦ two footbridges. Cross and bear left following

well-defined track which ⑧ shortly forks–bear left. ⑨ The track forks again–bear left. Continue on main track, which ⑩ turns left, crossrs a stream and meets the A35. ⑪. Cross, turn right and continue 50 yards (46 m) on verge to gate with cattle grid. ⑫ Through gate make for house, walking to left of it, then turning right with gravel track to skirt garden and 2 cottages, soon meeting a high wall. Continue to end of wall, then straight ahead for about ¼ mile (0.5 km). ⑬ About 30 yards (27 m) before bridge over small stream, take faint track on left up a wide, grassy ride. Path soon becomes clearer. ⑭ Where path divides, bear left. ⑮ Cross over intersection. ⑯ Keep left to cross White Moor to car park.

The tiny Dartford warbler, one of the Forest's relatively rare bird species. It has a long, dark tail and frequently perches on gorse, bouncing away erratically when disturbed.

⋎ Reptiliary; adders and other snakes.

⌑ The oak and beechwoods of Brinken and Gritnam are among the Forest's finest.

⬚ Until this century they supported several trades – charcoal-burning, woodcutting, swineherding and snakecatching. The most celebrated snakecatcher was Brusher Mills, at the height of his career in the 1890s. He was so-named because he swept snow from Brockenhurst Pond for skaters, but his real living was snakes, sold to zoos, and for medicine. He inhabited a hut in Gritnam Wood made of branches overlaid with turf, and died brokenhearted after finding it destroyed one night.

⊞ Allum House, typical of the pleasant houses built after the railway came.

The Queen Bower

6 miles (9.5 km) Sheets 195 and 196 298024

Easy Shows how lush the Forest can be; unforgettable oaks in the Queen Bower, which may be busy in summer. *Village, heath, woods, streamside; mud.*

Start Brockenhurst, on the A337; frequent buses; trains from Southampton and other stops on the London-Bournemouth line. **Public car parks** signposted at village centre.

① From car parks turn into village street, passing shops to reach footbridge and ford. Cross and turn left along the Burley-Ringwood road. ② Take gravel road right, signposted North Weirs. ③ At minor road, turn right for a few yards, then left over the car park at Beachern Wood. ④ Where the gravel track bends right, take path straight on through lightly wooded area. ⑤ Cross footbridge, ignore red waymarking and go through gate a few yards to right. After gate, follow path which bears right. ⑥ Go through gate by Aldridge Hill Cottage. Ignore obvious paths leading to camp site, turning left in front of cottage, crossing a small water course, then right over heath following a well-defined path with water course to right at first. At far side of heath, cross footbridge, climb track edged with shrubs, then cross 2 more bridges and a patch of heath. Go through woods to meet stream (Highland Water); follow it to Boldreford Bridge. Cross

and bear left on to open heath where ⑦ follow edge of wood, striking out across heath when the prominent white building (Cloud Hotel) is in sight on far side. ⑧ Follow minor road in front of hotel right, tracing way back to Brockenhurst centre and car parks.

〰 Oberwater, a typical stream of the central part of the Forest, its water tinged red-brown by the soil's iron content. This and other streams on the walk are typical kingfisher habitats.

〼 Fallow and roe deer may be sighted.

🏚 Rhinefield House, built 1885 in the then-popular pseudo-Gothic style – battle-ments, arched doors and mullioned windows. Open to the public; restaurant.

🔟 The Queen Bower owes its name to Queen Philippa, wife of Edward III (died 1377). She admired the oaks' fantastic shapes.

〼 The ponies graze this heath, as they do others all over the Forest, making the grass characteristically smooth, hence the term Forest 'lawns'. The ponies are descendants of a wild breed peculiar to the Forest and are owned by farmers, breeders and individuals with Common Rights. These are usually attached to houses, date from medieval times and permit grazing and fuel-gathering.

THE NEW FOREST

An attractive thatched New Forest cottage.

Burley
8 miles (13 km) Sheet 195 212031

Easy History and fine views on the Forest's SW fringe; follows part of a smugglers' way. *Heath, woods; 3 climbs; mud.*

Start Burley, off the A31; frequent buses. **Car park** by the Queen's Head.

① From car park turn right past Queen's Head, bearing right through village along road to Ringwood. ② At footpath sign pointing right join raised path beside road. When it meets road again, cross and continue a few yards. ③ Left over cattle grid and up lane following footpath sign. Near top, follow sign right into wood. ④ Leave wood by stile and turn right along lane. ⑤ Raised circular banks of Burley Hill Fort come into view. Just before it, *look carefully*

for *path running left downhill to right of a gully. Follow it, keeping gully to left.* ⑥ At cross-track turn right and follow this to road from Burley Street to Crow. ⑦ Left along road (crossing stream); in 50 yards (46 m) ⑧ leave road, turning on to first track leading right. ⑨ At choice of 3 ways, take the one bearing right. ⑩ Path divides. Turn left up the hill to a cross-track, where ⑪ turn right and continue to meet a wide grassy track. ⑫ Turn right along this and continue to minor road from Burley Street to Picket Post. ⑬ Cross road and straight on down track ahead. ⑭ At cross-tracks turn right. Follow path down to bridge, then uphill into Ridley Wood. ⑮ Entering wood, look for sunken track on right. Follow it ahead. When it rises to ground level, continue straight on through

Ridley Wood. ⑯ At edge of wood path divides; go straight on over small area of heath, through small wood and over bridge. ⑰ Path divides; keep straight on, then bear left with path to edge of Berry Wood. ⑱ At cross-tracks turn right and walk through edge of Berry Wood. ⑲ A jumble of paths. Follow the one bearing right over the heath towards Turf Croft Cottage, plainly visible ahead. Turn left past cottage and follow track to road over Burley Moor. Here bear right for Burley Street. ⑳ Over crossroads and right past post office. ㉑ A few yards on, turn left over green and walk up Randalls Road. ㉒ Turn left along wide crossing track on top of ridge. ㉓ Track divides; bear right to walk over banks of Burley Hill Fort; rejoin outward route.

In smuggling days, contraband, brought from the coast under Forest cover, was distributed at the Queen's Head.

16th C. Manor Tea Rooms – cream teas.

The hill fort is Iron Age. Views W to the Avon valley; NW to the Wiltshire Downs and SW (clear days) to Christchurch Priory (160925) and the sea.

The ridge was part of a smugglers' way.

Sunken track: a smugglers' rendez-vous?

Magnificent, pollarded beeches: pollarding is cutting off the tops, and produces the many sprouts.

THE NEW FOREST

Matley Heath and Wood
6 miles (9.5 km) Sheet 196 336104

Easy Many features of the Forest landscape in quite a short circuit. *Woods, heath, 'lawn', streamside; mud.*

Start Ashurst on the A35; frequent trains to Lyndhurst Road Station, by point ①. **Parking** area near Ashurst Hospital Gates.

① Leave parking area turning right; cross railway bridge. Left down the A35, in about 100 yards (91 m) turning left through gate. After 50 yards (46 m) ② turn right parallel to A35. Soon join poorly-defined track into wood on right. ③ Cross lane leading to Ashurst Lodge, go past Car Free Area barrier (no distinct path), then keep straight on. ④ At far side of heath, turn left. Continue parallel to road, in about ½ mile (0.8 km) joining gravel track at Forestry Commission 'Denny Wood Chemical Closets' etc. sign. ⑤ Enter wood past barrier, and continue along main track. Leave wood after ½ mile. In 400 yards (366 m) continue over crossing tracks. In 150 yards (137 m) turn left on to smaller crossing track. Continue with track until ⑥, turn left before bridge and follow path parallel to stream over footbridges. Continue 500 yards (457 m) over green, looking for footbridge in trees on right. ⑦ Cross bridge and go straight on with path for 400 yards

Deer can be sighted on most Forest walks, typically where woods or nearby cover meet open heath or grass. Most are fallow deer (left), but there are also roe deer (centre), and, S of the railway, Sika (right). A few red deer remain near Burley.

where ⑧ ignore crossing track. Continue 20 yards (18m) and bear right at Y junction. When track meets lawn, bear right to identify Ashurst Lodge lane barrier. Make for it; retrace to ①.

🍺 New Forest Inn; restaurant adjacent.

🏛 Blending of woodland, glades and heath is the essence of Forest scenery. A remarkable survival of medieval landscape into the 20th C.

The Valley of Dockens Water
8 Miles (13 km) Sheet 195 232142

Easy Reveals the northern Forest – hilly. *Woods, streamside, heath; one climb; mud.*

Start Fritham, N of the A31 – approach from Cadnam roundabout – other access from A31 blocked. **Car park** past Royal Oak.

① From parking return to Royal Oak and take lane on right leading past houses. ② Where track branches left and path right, carry straight on. ③ Cross green and footbridge, then take the right-hand of the 2 tracks into wood ahead. In about 50 yards (46 m) bear right. Continue about 250 yards (228 m) to locate gate into inclosure on left. ④ Turn right opposite gate and make way through trees, over clearing to stream. Cross and locate inclosure fence on left. Follow fence, bearing right, soon joining fairly well-defined wide path. Continue ¾ mile (1 km). ⑤ Be extra careful to halt in first sizeable clearing (after inclosure fence has borne away left, and passing 2 square posts on left). In clearing, path peters out. Cross bearing right to locate narrow, gravel path other side of trees, climbing a few yards. Follow it on to sparsely wooded hillside. Continue to Anses Wood, ahead. ⑥ Several paths in wood but continue with Dockens Water to right. Cross small stream, then

locate inclosure fence to left. Follow it, along grassy path, to Holly Hatch Keeper's Cottage. ⑦ Cross footbridge, follow track uphill and through Sloden Inclosure. ⑧ Leave inclosure to follow track over heath to car park. ⑨ For extension to Eyeworth Pond, left along road.

🌳 Gigantic beeches with ingrowths – branches growing back into the trunk or each other.

🖼 Evidence of a Roman Pottery.

🍺 A typical old Forest pub.

⚓ Eyeworth, once site of gunpowder works.

> O.S. 1:25,000 Tourist maps give helpful detail of this often confusing area.
> Waymarked by the Forestry Commission: 3 walks from Bolderwood Car Park; 3 from Rhinefield Ornamental Drive Car Park; one from Puttles Bridge; one from Wilverley Inclosure on the A35.
> Also try the Riverside Walk from Beaulieu to Bucklers Hard (leaflets from newsagent in village street); and walking beside the railway, leaving the car at a station, returning by train.

THE WESSEX DOWNS

Four chains of chalk hills are united in this section. From the east come the North and South Downs, from the south-west the chalk hills of Dorset and from the north-east the Chilterns. They all merge into, or closely adjoin, the chalk hills of either Hampshire, Berkshire or Wiltshire – the central chalkland of the country. In the physical sense, it is as close as anywhere to perfect walking. The turf is springy underfoot. The hills are not too high, but high enough to open spreading views. The slopes are not too steep, but steep enough for the walker to appreciate the good sense of the prehistoric folk whose tracks stick firmly to the tops and so provide mile on mile of ridge walking.

Of these tracks the Ridgeway is only the best known. It can be traced all the way to the Dorset coast in the south and to Norfolk in the opposite direction. Ridgeways were the usual routes of these old cultures, as is indicated by the monuments of Avebury, Stonehenge, the White Horse above Uffington and a mass of tumuli.

Then there are the valleys, whose chief charms are the chalk streams, admirably blending all the best qualities of rivers – hurrying sometimes, and at others slowing contemplatively.

The Nadder Valley
4 miles (6.5 km) Sheet 184 997296

Moderate A delightful village, with the chance to visit others; majestic ridge walk with grand views from Chiselbury Hill Camp; regimental badges carved in chalk hillside. *Farmland, downland; one climb; mud after rain.*

Start Fovant, signposted from the A30 W of Wilton; in village turn left at Y-junction and right along lane to church; frequent buses. **Parking** near church.

① Walk away from church following lane towards Fovant. ② Bear left through village towards A30. ③ Turn right to the A30. ④ Cross the A30 and follow the lane ahead, just to the right of the Cross Keys Hotel. ⑤ Walk a few yards down lane on right to see lake where the Fovant stream rises. Retrace to original route. ⑥ The lane curves left towards the grey stone house (East Farm); immediately past house turn right down short track to go through iron gate. The route ahead (to Chiselbury Hill Fort) can be seen clearly here – from ⑧ it is obscured. Continue straight ahead towards the down, hedge on the right, then left to side of Chalk Pit. ⑦ Bear left round the Chalk Pit. ⑧ Path peters out. Continue uphill a few yards to fence and embankment of Chiselbury Hill Fort beyond. ⑨ Get on top of embankment and follow it to the left. ⑩ Where embankment curves right, go straight on over grass to opening in fence. ⑪ Go through opening and turn right to walk along ridge track. In about ½ mile (0.8 km) ⑫ turn right to cross stile beside gate. Continue along path down grassy clearing, through a thicket to a steep grassy track which descends. ⑬ Cross stile and turn right along lane leading to A30. ⑭ Cross road and continue on track straight ahead. ⑮ Path divides – bear left. ⑯ Turn right to cross stile and walk down field to gate. ⑰ Through gate and continue along lane. Turn left to rejoin outward route and continue to ①.

🏠 Fovant's beautiful 15th C. church contains several delights, including a memorial brass recalling the building of the tower by Sir George Rede, rector in 1495. The priest's doorway is exquisitely carved.

🍺 The Cross Keys.

🎖 The famous military badges were carved by troops training in the area during the 1914-18 War; details on noticeboard in Fovant village.

Chiselbury Camp, a particularly fine example of an Iron Age Hill Fort, dates from about 800 B.C., but its site, the Ridgeway, is up to 2,000 years older. In early summer the embankments are golden with cowslips; views all round.

THE WESSEX DOWNS

Wherwell, the Test and the Anton
5 miles (8 km) Sheet 185 392408

Easy Access to the Hampshire chalk streams is not always straightforward, but this route takes in some characteristically lovely stretches: also some remote woods. *Stream- and riversides, downland.*

Start Wherwell, off the A303. From war memorial take lane to church; buses. **Parking** area near church entrance.

① From parking turn left through church gate to walk round church, church on right. ② Go through gate, turn right up lane, then next left. ③ Turn right under railway arch, following direction of bridleway sign. (Ignore footpath sign just before it on right.) ④ At top of field follow path left. ⑤ Follow path as it bears right between hedges – Anton valley on left. ⑥ Go through gate and continue over side of down (path indistinct), woods to the right, fence on left until reaching bridleway sign. Follow its direction downhill to gate leading to A3057. ⑦ Cross road and go through gate opposite. Follow direction of bridleway sign. Turn right at road, passing church. ⑧ Cross A3057 and take the straight track immediately ahead. Turn right at T-junction. ⑨ Take care, just before reaching wood, to leave the broad track and turn left along footpath running beside the wood

(wood on right). ⑩ Just past cottage on the right, join concrete track. ⑪ Where the concrete track turns left, follow path as it bears slightly right following direction of footpath sign along valley. ⑫ Just before the gate, turn right up the hill. ⑬ Leaving the wood, turn right, then follow path round the wood (wood on right). Continue to village.

🏠 The 17th C. house to the left of the churchyard stands on the site of Wherwell Priory, a Benedictine nunnery. It was founded in 986 by Queen Elfrida, widow (and second wife) of King Edgar, to amend for the murder of her stepson King Edward. Her motive, it is assumed, was to make way for her son by her previous marriage.

🚩 The White Lion.

🌳 Harewood Forest has spacious glades of
🌿 oak and beech where the scent of bluebells can be almost overwhelming in April-June. Nightingales nest here,
🦅 particularly in thickets at the fringes of the wood. They generally sing at night, but it is possible to hear them by day, too.

🗿 The obelisk records a connected murder, that of Earl Athelwold by King Edgar; Athelwold 'perfidiously' married Elfrida, Edgar's intended bride.

Burghclere

2½ or 4½ miles (4 or 7 km) Sheet 174 471611

Easy For little effort, an excellent introduction to much that is typical of the gentle, rolling Wessex countryside; also, a chance to see the Stanley Spencer murals in Sandham Memorial Chapel. *Woods, farmland; mud:* ⑫ – ⑬ *overgrown in summer.*

Start Burghclere, off the A34 5 miles (8 km) S of Newbury: frequent buses. **Parking** turn right at the war memorial and park on left in a few yards just before village hall.

① Walk away from village hall past war memorial to minor road ahead. ② Cross and follow path through trees, over stile and across field. Cross stile and turn left along track to minor road. ④ Turn left and continue to crossroads. ⑤ To see Memorial Chapel turn right, cross bridge and continue a few yards to brick building on right set back from road. Retrace to crossroads. ⑥ Continue down road signposted Ecchinswell. After ¼ mile (400 m) ⑦ at footpath sign cross stile. ⑧ Through gate turn left to walk along disused railway track. In about ½ mile (0.8 km) ⑨ where lane runs close to track, turn off track to lane, leaving a house to the left. ⑩ Turn right and follow lane to Y-junction where ⑪ bear left for a few yards crossing stream and going uphill (as for Ecchinswell). ⑫ Turn left along the track opposite road junction. ⑬ Turn left and follow the track as it approaches Earlstone Manor Farm. ⑭ Turn right through gate, leaving farm on left, cross field and go through gate to rejoin track; follow it one mile. ⑮ Cross road and follow road signposted Highclere back to ①. For a 2-mile (3 km) extension, do not leave railway track but follow it to Old Burghclere. Then follow bridleways to rejoin route at ⑪.

'Filling Waterbottles' – one of the 19 Stanley Spencer murals in the Sandham Memorial Chapel. They show the ordinary soldier's experience of war.

🏠 Stanley Spencer called on his experience as a private soldier in the 1914-18 War to conceive this moving and important wall painting sequence. Private generosity enabled the chapel to be purpose-built to house the work, which was completed in 1923-32. The canvas had to be woven in Belgium: no English loom was large enough. The name Sandham recalls the donor's brother, who died after serving in Macedonia, a landscape depicted in several of the murals. Keys are obtained from either of the almshouses.

THE WESSEX DOWNS

Inkpen
6 miles (9.5 km) Sheet 174 370620

Easy Apart from the obvious attractions–fine old houses and churches, spectacular views, ancient woods, the highest chalk hill in England–this area has a wealth of folklore. Best on clear days for long views. *Downland, farmland, woods, village, one climb; mud after rain.*

Start From Inkpen follow signs for Combe and Combe Gibbet. After climbing steep hill, the road divides (left for West Woodhay, straight on for Combe); frequent buses to Inkpen. **Parking** where road divides, by hill fort. If full, there is another parking area 50 yards (46 m) up track to Combe Gibbet. Alternatively, the landlord of The Swan Inn, Inkpen, allows walkers to use his car park if it is not full–'phone first. Inkpen 326.

Smooth, rolling Wessex chalkland, from the ridge path near Walbury Hill Fort.

① From car park follow direction of sign for 'Wayfarers' Walk' along gravel track. (It crosses the fort.) ② Where track meets metalled lane, keep straight on. ③ Turn left following lane signposted East Woodhay. ④ At cross-track turn left and follow path at first straight ahead down field, then curving right past farm. ⑤ At road turn left for West Woodhay. ⑥ At T-junction turn let for Inkpen and Combe. ⑦ Just after lane turns left round Great Farm, follow track on right. ⑧ Track meets road (Crown and Garter on left)—go straight across. ⑨ Follow path ahead as it bears slightly left. ⑩ In about 50 yards (46 m) path divides at a large stone. Continue leaving stone to left—keep straight ahead, crossing 2 streams. ⑪ Emerge from wood on to road. Cross. ⑫ Follow track straight ahead ⑬ Turn right along lane and walk past old school to meet road. ⑭ Turn left and follow road (Weaver's Lane) into Inkpen, turning left—Upper Inkpen/Combe Gibbet. ⑮ Turn right—Inkpen church. ⑯ Turn left

– sign for Ham. ⑰ Turn left at footpath sign towards the down and follow drover's road straight ahead. ⑱ At foot of down cross stile and bear slightly right uphill. ⑲ Meet ridged track and turn left to follow this to top of down. ⑳ Go through gate and turn left along track running along ridge top. Pass over Inkpen Hill (or Beacon) past Combe Gibbet to ①.

※ The magnificent Walbury Iron Age hill fort: 80 acres (32 ha) of hill top lie within its mile-round ramparts.

☘ Look for the corner of delicate white and silver plants in the charming memorial garden beside the church.

⛪ The gardens of the rectory beside the church garden were designed by Le Notre, who laid out the gardens of Versailles for Louis XIV. The terraces to the W are probably the site of the original Saxon settlement, Inga's Pen.

The rectory itself was built by Colwall Brickenden in 1695.

⛪ Inkpen's church was probably founded in the 13th C. by Roger de Ingpen, whose ancestors may well have received their lands from Hardicanute, son of the famous Canute. De Ingpen's tomb can be seen N of the high altar. Above the 13th C. font is a sculpture by the New Forest artist, Ron Lane.

🍺 The Swan – real ale.

※ Clear traces of Wansdyke, the great earth wall which ran 80 miles (129 km) from here to the Bristol Channel.

\↑/ On clear days 9 counties may be seen.

🔟 Combe Gibbet: the original was erected in 1676 to hang George Broomham and his mistress, who murdered Broomham's wife.

THE WESSEX DOWNS

The Ridgeway

6½ miles (10.5 km) Sheet 174 265851

Easy An introduction to the Ridgeway long-distance path and some of its most famous features. The Ridgeway is popular, so choose an off-peak time if possible. *Downland, farmland; one climb; the chalk is slippery after rain and sticks to footwear.*

Start Ashbury, on the B4000. In village turn on to the B4507 and look for Rose and Crown; frequent buses. **Parking** Rose and Crown car park.

① From car park turn right and walk along road to its junction with the B4000 (Lambourn Road) where ② turn right and continue a few yards. ③ Turn right at Ridgeway sign and follow the path through the gate up the hill. ④ At the double lines of quickset (small thorn trees) bordering the Ridgeway, turn left and follow the wide

track for just over 2 miles (3 km). ⑤ Pass the embankments of Uffington Castle on left, ignoring first footpath sign on left. Turn left at the second footpath sign towards the Castle. ⑥ Follow the embankment round (grassy area of Castle centre on left) but do not descend the hill. ⑦ When the embankments turn left, leave them and turn right (past 2 isolated thorn trees) and walk a few yards along the down for a magnificent view of The Manger and Dragon Hill; also portions of the White Horse. ⑧ Retrace steps along Ridgeway about one mile (1.5 km) until reaching the cross-lanes just before Wayland's Smithy. ⑨ Turn right along the metalled track. ⑩ Cross the B4057 (The Icknield Way) and carry straight on following the sign to 'Compton Beauchamp at foot of hill'. ⑪ Turn left along the lane to the right of Compton House leading to the church. ⑫ Go through wicket gate just to right of church gate and walk up field to farm gate ahead. ⑬ Go through gate, turn half right and cross next field, leaving corner of wood on right and clump of trees on hilltop well over to left. Continue on this line diagonally to cross 2 fences, looking ahead for small gate in corner of second field. (Path is indistinct.) ⑭ Go through gate, and with fence on left, follow field edge to cross stiles either side of a bridge. ⑮ Pass farm leaving it to left and continue through all gates, going straight ahead until line of power cables comes into view. ⑯ Bear left to follow line of power cables, crossing 2 stiles to fence on left. ⑰ Go straight on, fence and power cables on left; the path soon becomes a wide, fenced way. ⑱ Cross track by 2 stiles and continue round slightly left to go through a gate (marked with yellow arrow footpath sign) to join lane running through Kingstone Winslow. ⑲ From the gate turn left, then almost immediately right down small lane crossing a stream and rising to Ashbury. ⑳ After crossing B4000 take next left, then left again for the Rose and Crown.

🍺❌ Rose and Crown – try the home-made steak and kidney pie or mussels with shrimps and garlic.

✳ Wayland's Smithy, a Neolithic barrow or burial mound; legend told that Wayland, smith to the Saxon gods, would shoe a horse left with a coin by the tomb.

🔟 The Ridgeway (see pp. 328-34), possibly the oldest road in Europe, could date from before the last Ice Age – about 11,000 B.C.

✳ Uffington, a fine hill fort – 500 B.C.

↑ The early chapters of *Tom Brown's Schooldays* are set among these downs.

🔟 Where St. George killed the dragon.

The White Horse's date and manner of carving remain a mystery.

THE WESSEX DOWNS

The Avon Valley and Stonehenge
5 miles (8 km) Sheet 184 149411

Easy An exciting, unusual way to approach Stonehenge: the monument is directly ahead for more than a mile (1.5 km), growing in stature constantly. Visits other Neolithic remains, too, which add to the picture of this awe-inspiring centre of the great prehistoric culture of North Wessex. Best out of holiday season – fewest crowds. *Town, wooded riverside, downland; one climb; path may be overgrown between ⑦ and ⑨ – easily trodden down, but footwear to protect the ankles against nettles is advised. Stonehenge is open 15th March-15th October, 9.30-6.30; 16th October-14th March 9.30-4.00. Sundays vary. Closed Christmas Eve, Boxing Day, New Year's Day, May Day. Modest entry fee.*

Start Recreation Road, Amesbury, which is a lane leading from the corner of Church and Stonehenge Roads; frequent buses – from bus station turn left, left again past church and abbey, then cross river. First left is Recreation Road. **Car park** off Recreation Road in front of playground. *Optional return to start from Stonehenge by bus, last one leaving at 4.30 p.m.*

① From car park turn left and follow lane to cross Avon by 2 bridges. ② At cross-tracks keep straight on in direction of sign for Durnford. ③ Go through iron gate *but do not follow obvious track straight ahead.* Turn right and walk around edge of field, passing mound on left, reaching gate on right. ④ Turn left (back to the gate) and follow the valley (do not go uphill) with stream, then wider expanse of water, on right. ⑤ Straight on through small wood of willow trees. ⑥ Turn right over small wooden bridge. ⑦ From bridge follow path as it bears right for about 50 yards (46 m) (may be overgrown). ⑧ Follow path left to cross bridge over Avon. ⑨ Cross stile and follow path ahead a few yards then left to pass house. ⑩ Go through gate and turn right to follow lane to minor road. ⑪ Turn left and follow road for ¼ mile (0.5 km) until just before Wilsford church. ⑫ Turn right up well-defined track between 2 thatched cottages. ⑬ Follow track, passing Springbottom Farm on right. ⑭ Follow wide, grassy way which leads uphill between fences – Stonehenge directly ahead. ⑮ Turn right and follow A303 to junction with A344. ⑯ Turn left and continue to car park for entry to the monument. Either walk back to

Amesbury following footpath beside the A303, taking the first right which leads to Recreation Road; or take a bus.

The church is mainly Norman and Early English, with a well-carved roof.

There is nothing quite like Stonehenge anywhere else in the world. Exactly why these massive stones were transported, carved and set upright in these formations remains a matter for speculation. Some of the stones come from the Preseli Hills in S Wales – 135 miles (217 km) away. The place seems to have been devoted, at least partly, to sun worship. On midsummer's day the sun rises in line with the axis of the avenue leading into the monument. Recently experts have shown that the circle's positioning may have made it useful for certain astronomical observations. It was probably a burial place, too.

The majesty of Stonehenge now, and how it may have looked to those who used it as a cathedral, burial place, observatory and landmark up to 4,000 years ago. Its age is uncertain, but some authorities put its earliest form, a simple, circular, wooden building surrounded by a ditch and a few stone posts, as early as 2800 B.C. Around 800 years later, it could have looked more or less complete; but it seems that reconstruction and refinement took place over a further 900 years. The largest stone upright is 21 feet (6.5 m) high and sunk 8½ feet (2.5 m) below the ground. The larger blocks are sarsen sandstone, the smaller granite 'blue' stones.

THE WESSEX DOWNS

Cranborne Chase
9 miles (14.5 km) Sheet 184 944178

Moderate With its hanging woods, the Chase has a special charm. A historic village and some fine ridge walking; one magical path descending from the Ridgeway between arms of woodland. *Village, downland, woods; one climb; mud.*

Start Tollard Royal on the B3081; seasonal buses. **Parking** area just past left bend of B3081 (when approaching from Ringwood), on right.

① From parking area follow bridleway on right (no sign) uphill, wall at first on left, thatched cottage on right. ② Continue straight on to signpost at top of down, ignoring all side tracks – not quite 2 miles (3 km). ③ For optional extension to Win Green (highest point of Chase: fine views) follow direction of the sign along the grassy track ahead; retrace to this point, then continue straight on along minor road 25 yards (23 m) beyond sign on left. ④ If not visiting Win Green, turn right at signpost and follow road along top of down. ⑤ Where road turns left continue straight on in direction of sign for 'Rushmore only – past 'No Through Road' sign. ⑥ Where road bears right (slightly downhill) continue straight on along grassy track. ⑦ Straight on along Ridgeway for about 1½ miles (2.5 km). ⑧ Look for large, derelict building on right at head of a valley. Turn right and follow the track just past it, dipping towards woods. ⑨ At iron gate and joining track on left keep to main track as it bears slightly left at first. ⑩ Track divides – continue straight ahead along valley bottom. ⑪ Pass house on left and just before reaching road *turn right* to follow path uphill. ⑫ Path divides – bear slightly left along edge of wood. ⑬ Follow track into woods. Keep to main track, straight on over all cross-tracks. (Occasional waymarks – yellow blobs on trees.) ⑭ Cross beech avenue and follow track ahead (yellow dot on beech to left). ⑮ Cross over well-defined track and keep straight on. ⑯ A more open area to the left, wood on right. ⑰ Turn left at cross-tracks (not on map) – yellow blob on trees to left. ⑱ Cross over track, go through iron gate and go straight on over field – hedge close on right. ⑲ Leave gate into park on right and cross over track to walk along edge of field (trees on right) for a few yards. ⑳ Turn left at corner of field and follow edge of field (trees on right). ㉑ Where path bears left, look carefully for gate into wood on right (marked by yellow blob). Turn right through it. ㉒ Ignore first path on left and continue to cross-track. Turn left and follow path slightly downhill (yellow blobs). ㉓ At cross-track (not on map) bear left. ㉔ Cross metalled lane and go over stile into field ahead. (No path here.) Turn half right to cross avenue of beeches. Continue down field towards power cables (on right) to iron gate. ㉕ Go through gate and follow wide drive to B3081. ㉖ Turn right for ①.

🏛 Contains a startlingly detailed effigy of a crusader knight, Sir William Payne.

👁 Over Dorset and Hampshire.

Combe Hill, 5 miles (8 km) SE of Hungerford, is a focal point for several downland walks.

The prehistoric barrows on the downs just N of Lambourn are an easy and satisfying objective.

Some 5 miles N of Romsey on the A3057 the area around Horsebridge and Marsh Court gives some easy walking in the Test Valley.

Postern Hill, among the beech avenues of the Savernake Forest (off the A346), offers secluded paths and nature trails; and of course the whole of Savernake Forest is an honoured strolling ground.

There are several interesting trails around the prehistoric hill fort of Cadbury Castle. Approach via A303 7 miles (11 km) NE of Yeovil.

Cranbourne Chase was formerly a thickly wooded royal hunting ground of about 100 square miles (259 square km). The rights passed from James I to the Earls of Salisbury to the Earls of Shaftesbury and finally the Pitt-Rivers family, who lived at Rushmoor House.

An avenue of 500-year-old beeches. They are pollarded – meaning the heads were cut off to provide, among other things, feed for deer. The practice produced the many sprouting branches.

A museum of chimney pots at Chase Cottage opens on Saturdays and Sundays. Opposite is a 300-year-old well.

King John's Arms.

King John's House (13th C., restored 1889) was a hunting lodge and suggests why the village is 'Royal': King John frequently came here to take advantage of the hunting.

About a mile S of the village are the Larmer Tree Grounds, so-named because of the larmer tree or wych elm growing there which was a favoured meeting place for the hunt and for the administrative and judicial assemblies known as court leets. The tree blew down in a storm in 1894, to be replaced by an oak. More recently, the late General Pitt-Rivers turned the area into a public garden, with an entertaining collection of follies in the oriental style and an impressive little theatre.

SOUTH DOWNS

The dimpled, chalk hills of the South Downs stretch in a nearly unbroken chain a full 60 miles (97 km) from Old Winchester Hill in Hampshire to the sea at Beachy Head in East Sussex. Once they were mown short by sheep but today the ploughs creep far up the slopes and often right over the spine (carrying the South Downs Way) so that walkers are as likely to be threading a thin path through wheat as treading springy turf.

This is walking with wide views. To the south, the Channel, and the north, what Kipling called the 'wooded, dim, blue goodness of the Weald'. Walkers who find the downland chalk sticky in winter need only try the Wealden clay for something that really clings to the boots.

While the Weald was still waste, the Downs were being settled, as testified by the Neolithic flint mines (for example at Cissbury and Findon) and the earthworks of 'Beaker' and later folk. Millions of the flints are now embedded in the walls of the area's villages and churches. But note how very few of these settlements are on the downs. Nearly all lie crushed between the hills and the sea, or along the spring line to the north. The result is that, despite trains from London, these downs offer the loneliest walking in the south-east.

Eartham and Stane Street
5½ miles (9 km) Sheet 197 940106

Easy For a change with ancient sites, there is plenty to see on the ground. *Downland, woods; mud; path across field on Long Down between ③ and ④ may be ploughed out.*

Start About 4 miles (6.5 km) S of Duncton on the A285 take the minor road to Eartham, looking for car park on left within ¼ mile (400 m); buses along A285. **Car park** the Eartham Wood Forestry Commission car park.

①From car park turn left on to road and in 150 yards (137 m) turn right across stile at corner. Head SW along Stane Street. ②Turn left along A285. In 275 yards (251 m), turn back left along woodland track. ③At end of wood continue to stile just visible on brow of hill, then slightly right. ④Through swing gate. Follow line of conifers to Eartham. ⑤ Turn left, then right at George Inn. In 100 yards (91 m) fork left on downhill track. In 100 yards (91 m) fork left on downhill track. In ½ mile turn left, walking on inside edge of wood. In 150 yards (137 m) turn right. In another 150 yards turn right to join bridleway path. In 270 yards (240 m) turn left. Soon right on to farm track. ⑥Go over stile on left towards folly, immediately after farm track, and continue uphill, over stiles

Roman road construction: a typical width, as of Stane Street, was 25 feet (7.6 m).

to left of reservoir, following fence to ruined folly ⑦and trig. point. Continue along fence for 200 yards (180 m) then ⑧ bear left into wood and follow forest ride, ignoring side tracks. ⑨ Fork right downhill by massive tree stump. ⑩ Turn right. ⑪ Where woodland ends, turn left. ⑫ At meeting of 6 ways, turn left; follow Stane Street (signposted 'Halneker') to ①.

🅑 Stane ('Stone') Street was the Roman road running from Chichester to London in straight sections.

⛪ Eartham church has a memorial to William Huskisson, the famous M.P. for Chichester killed at the opening of the Liverpool-Manchester Railway – the first rail death.

SOUTH DOWNS

Clayton Mills and Wolstonbury Hill
5 miles (8 km) Sheet 198 300140

Moderate A pleasant variation of down and weald. *Downland, farmland; one climb; mud.*

Start Clayton, off the A273 N of Pyecombe. **Car park** at Clayton Green – entrance 150 yards (137 m) E of Clayton church.

① Go through farm gate opposite car park entrance. Follow boundary on left uphill, continuing in sunken track bearing left ② On emerging on to open downland, bear half left between clumps of trees, then follow sunken gully uphill to gate into Clayton Mills car park. ③ At far end of car park turn left on to rough track (bridleway) and at 2 forks keep right, continuing to top of rise beyond New Barn Farm. ④ Turn right following South Downs Way downhill to A273. ⑤ Cross road and turn left on to path behind hedge, then turn right on to road to Pyecombe church. ⑥ At road junction near church turn right on to rough track becoming enclosed bridleway and follow it to crest of hill. ⑦ Ignore crossing path, then turn left on to crossing track and, ignoring left fork, follow track to top of ridge. ⑧ Just over top, turn right on to signposted footpath to stile on to Wolstonbury Hill. ⑨ Bear half left through bushes to triangulation post then bear half right to join path descending steeply into wood towards Danny House. ⑩ In wood, bear half right then left to stile and gate, then go straight on, turning right in 100

yards (91 m), eventually reaching road and turning left. ⑪ After 320 yards (290 m) there is a Victorian post box on the left. (To inspect Danny House, turn left on to footpath through copse and go straight on across field to house.) To continue walk, retrace to road. A few yards further, turn right on to concrete drive. ⑫ At Hautboyes, over stiles to short enclosed path, small paddock, and field. Cross field and continue along edge of next to reach track. ⑬ Turn sharp right on to track, then immediately left to follow hedge to A273. ⑭ Turn right along A273, then left into Underhill Lane.

🏠 Clayton's church, listed in Domesday Book, has murals painted about 1150.

⚒ The mills – 'Jack and Jill' worked to 1908.

🌟 The earthwork is Iron Age.

🏛 The 1918 Armistice agreement was drawn up at Danny House.

Cissbury and Chanctonbury
9½ miles (15 km) Sheet 198 179112

Moderate Visits the South Downs' 2 most famous historic sites, and Steyning, well worth exploring. *Downland; one climb; mud.*

Start Steyning, on the A283; frequent buses. **Car Park** off Church St, opposite church.

① From White Horse at S end of Steyning's main shopping street, take Sheep Pen Lane, then Newham Lane straight on out of town. ② Leave road at Pepperscombe House and take path straight on into copse. Go straight on uphill ignoring all forks to right (including one near top of quarry); 220 yards (200 m) past top of quarry join bridleway bearing slightly right. ③ At seat, turn left, then, by clump of bushes, follow fence straight on to 5-way junction. ④ Turn right crossing South Downs Way on to fenced track and follow it to bottom of dip. ⑤ Turn left on to track down valley bottom and follow it for one mile (1.5 km) to T-junction. ⑥ Turn right on to rough track and follow it to car park at top of rise. ⑦ For the Ring, turn left and climb. ⑧ Retrace steps to car park, take track straight on through it and continue for ⅔ mile (one km) ignoring crossing bridleway. ⑨ At second crossways, turn left on to track and in 130 yards (120 m) fork right and follow enclosed bridleway straight on for ¾ mile (one km) passing house. ⑩ One hundred and fifty yards (137

m) past house go through gate and bear left, soon crossing road and continuing across field to join chalky lane. Follow this straight on to ridge-top crossways. ⑪ Turn right on to wide track and follow it straight on, later joining South Downs Way for 1¾ miles (3 km) to Chanctonbury Ring. ⑫ Continue straight on for over ½ mile (1 km) to track junction. ⑬ Bear half left and follow South Downs Way for ⅓ mile (0.5 km) to right bend. ⑭ Turn left on to signposted bridleway following fence on left to wood, then turning right to follow edge of wood. In about ¼ mile (400 m) ignore path descending through woods, but follow path into edge of wood, climbing slightly. After passing iron flagstaff and warning notice, you will see a path on left rising through the wood to meet you. ⑮ Double back down this, keeping right at fork in about 275 yards (250 m) and eventually emerging into avenue leading

Chanctonbury Ring, moth-eaten after storms, has been recently replanted.

straight to Steyning. After road bears right, a footpath on left leads through to High St.

※ Cissbury Ring is a massive Iron Age hill fort on the site of Neolithic flint mines.

🐾 The (restored) dew pond, made to water sheep and replenished by dew and mist.

SOUTH DOWNS

Ditchling Beacon and High Park Woods

5½ miles (9 km) Sheet 198 333130

Moderate An outstandingly beautiful and varied walk starting from one of the Downs' highest points. *Downland, 'bottoms', woods; one climb; mud; section between ③ and ④ often ploughed out - alternative route indicated.*

Start Ditchling Beacon: signposted from S of Ditchling on B2112. **Car park** on top of Ditchling Beacon.

① From car park, head E along ridge on South Downs Way. ② Cross road to Streathill Farm. In a few yards, turn right to follow track S past farm buildings. ③ Just after bungalow, go over stile and continue S on opposite side of fence. 220 yards (200 m) beyond last building, go through gate and bear half right SW across large field (may have crops, but right of way exists). Over brow of hill make for stile in fence to left of copse ahead. (Alternative route from ③: instead of going through gate by bungalow, bear slightly left, following track. In ½ mile (0.8 km) at end of plantation (by gate across track), turn right through plantation, cross stile and continue ahead beside plantation. Then follow hedge and fence to stile already mentioned.) Cross stile and small field to bridleway gate. ④ Through gate and follow track downhill to bottom; after two gates, track climbs through wood to crossroads under overhead cables. Turn right and follow track through former beechwoods. ⑤ Follow bridleway curving away from buildings on the right; as it approaches road a signpost indicates a right turn to 'Heathy Brow'. ⑥ Over the road, take signposted bridleway to 'Ditchling Beacon' downhill, through bridleway gate, turn right and follow line of fence on right to gate leading to enclosed track. Follow this ¾ mile (1 km) to meet South Downs Way, where turn right for Beacon and car park. The walk can be shortened by cutting from ④ back to the South Downs Way.

📗 Ditchling Beacon, at 813 feet (248 m) the
\|/ second highest point of the Downs, was where one of the great chain of fires was lit to signal the coming of the Spanish Armada. Views: N to the Surrey Hills and North Downs; SE to the chalk mass of Seaford Head beyond Newhaven

The harebell, left, flowers July-Oct; the aromatic, common wild thyme in June-Sept.

Harbour; W to Wolstonbury Hill and Pycombe; SW to Chanctonbury Ring and Devil's Dyke.

🔔 Westmeston church, attractively restored, has a 17th C. porch incorporating 14th C. timbers and a shingled bell turret.

🌿 Typical downland flowers include the blue harebell, small scabious, sweet-smelling wild thyme and various orchids.

Chilgrove and the Devil's Jumps
5½ miles (9 km) Sheet 197 828144

Easy The Devil's Jumps are particularly striking earthworks. A mostly sheltered route, suitable for poor weather. *Woods, farmland; mud.*

Start Chilgrove, on the B2141 N of Chichester, **Parking** across lane from The White Horse.
① Facing away from pub, walk along left edge of green, parallel to road. ② Thirty yards (27 m) short of the drive, go through gap on left and follow field edge. ③ At top of field bear slightly left, heading across field to right of nearest pylon. Continue on road bearing slightly right, passing cottage. Down and up hill. ④ At end of small green, turn left off road and pass flint cottages. Follow enclosed track. In 330 yards (300 m) ignore left fork. ⑤ Continue down to shed. At bottom, bear left, ignoring first stile but crossing another a few yards on. Climb gently with path along valley floor, later turning left and entering young woodland. In 50 yards (46 m) ⑥ stop at cross-tracks. To visit Devil's Jumps, turn right and in 360 yards (330 m) take path on left just before end of wood. Retrace to cross-tracks and continue downhill on principal track in

same direction. In about ¾ mile (one km) ⑦ turn left opposite Royal Oak and follow well-defined track along valley floor. ⑧ After 660 yards (600 m), fork left at signposted crosspaths. The track may be hard to see at first: follow the line signposted into the wood and look for another sign where a track is crossed in 100 yards (90 m). Continue on path, climbing gently. ⑨ Leave wood over stile and bear half right to cross second stile. Climb through strip of woodland and follow field edge under cables. Continue on enclosed track, soon bearing right and right again for Chilgrove.

🍺 The White Horse, Chilgrove, and The Royal Oak, Hooksway, serve real ale.

🏛 Old Monkton: abandoned medieval settlement; see the noticeboard by the stile near ⑤.

❋ The Devil's Jumps are Bronze Age barrows (burial mounds), reminders of the people whose 'period' began about 1800 B.C., and who used weapons and implements first of copper and later of bronze. Their way of life seems to have merged with that of the Neolithic people, the first farmers, who date from 3000 B.C.

SOUTH DOWNS

Alfriston, Jevington, The Long Man
9 miles (14.5 km) Shet 199 521033

Moderate An introduction to the E end of the Downs, with varied countryside. *River valley, woods, heath, downland; 4 climbs; mud.*

Start Alfriston, S of the A27 between Eastbourne and Lewes; buses from Eastbourne and Seaford. **Public car parks** at N end of Alfriston (free on west, paying on east).

① From either car-park exit, walk S to village cross. ② Turn left at cross then right following W bank of River Cuckmere to Litlington. ③ Cross bridge, follow macadam path to village street, then go left to church. ④ Just past church turn right then immediately left through farmyard. ⑤ By gated field entrance turn right into stony lane uphill and follow it straight on, ignoring all crossings or branching tracks, for more than 2 miles (3 km), crossing 2 ridges. ⑥ After passing through wood, fork right then left (signposts 'SDW') for Jevington church. ⑦ Turn left through churchyard to road, then straight on along it. ⑧ Opposite 'Old Post Office', turn left on to rough track. ⑨ Near foot of hill fork right (signpost 'Wealdway') into enclosed bridleway to Folkington. ⑩ At end, by Folkington church, bear half left on to cart track and continue straight on for more than ½ mile (0.8 km). ⑪ At far end of *second* wood where track descends, fork left up through gate and take defined path straight on, following contours of hill for one mile (1.5 km), passing Long Man to reach gate ⑫ Go

The Long Man of Wilmington, cut into Windover Hill, is 226 feet (69m) high.

through gate turning sharp left, uphill, and in 100 yards (91 m) turn right on to chalky track descending to road. ⑬ Cross road, take track straight on, then, after 100 yards (91 m) turn left over stile and bear half right across 2 fields heading for church. ⑭ Cross stile then turn right through gate and go straight on to road. ⑮ Cross road bearing slightly right and take path over 2 bridges back to Alfriston.

⛪ Alfriston church, the spacious late 14th C. 'cathedral of the South Downs'.

⌂ Alfriston Clergy House, 14th C., timber-framed and thatched, was the first building bought by the National Trust.

▦ Charleston Manor — 'a perfect hour in a perfect setting' — gracefully blends Norman, Tudor and Georgian elements.

❦ Lullingstone Heath is the finest chalk heath remaining in Britain.

⛪ Jevington church has a strange Saxon carving of Christ fighting a wild beast.

⛪ Wilmington church, 11th C., has a curious 'insect window', depicting St.
❧ Peter in the midst of bees, butterflies and moths. In the churchyard is a giant, twin-trunked yew, possibly 1,000 years old.

▣ The Long Man of Wilmington is a total mystery. No one knows when it was carved, or why.

SOUTH DOWNS

Bow Hill and the Mardens
15 miles (24 km) Sheet 197 787105

Energetic A substantial ramble with superb views, visiting 3 remote and beautiful churches. *Downland, woods; mud. Path between ② and ② may be faint, but is accurately signposted.*

Start Walderton, off the B2146 NW of Chichester. **Parking** just after turning off B2146, on open space beside stream.

① Follow stiled path SE from road junction climbing with fence to right in second field to edge of wood, then turn left into rough lane. ② Where lane turns left by Forestry Commission notice, turn right and follow woodland bridleway uphill to reach field. ③ Fork right and in 30 yards (27 m) turn right and follow path between fences to ruined barn, then left heading for far right corner of field. ④ Go through gate into woodland, then straight on. After about 150 yards (137 m), fork left and ignoring tracks to right go straight on to gate leaving wood. ⑤ Go straight on along edge of wood subsequently re-entering it. ⑥ 150 yards (135 m) after re-entering wood, turn sharp left, leaving wood again to climb with clearing on left. ⑦ At kink in track, turn right on to forest ride and go straight on for 1¾ miles (2.7 km) crossing Bow Hill, ignoring all crossing or branching tracks. Pass to right of Blackbush House, continuing with fence on left. ⑧ ½ mile (0.8 km) past house, at a sharp bend, fork left to continue N. ⑨ At edge of wood, turn right on to track to B2141, then left along it. ⑩ Just after right bend, turn right through iron gate, then immediately left to follow left side of tree line to stile, then straight on to stile on to farm road. ⑪ Cross farm road and another stile, then straight on left of second tree belt to reach track. ⑫ Turn right on to track and follow it through gates into wood. ⑬ At right bend, take lesser track straight on along edge of wood to road at 'Royal Oak', turn left on to it. ⑭ After far end of right-hand wood, turn right into rough lane. ⑮ Soon after sharp left bend, fork left on to enclosed path to B2141. ⑯ Cross road, go straight on to another road, then turn right. ⑰ At bend, turn left into rough lane, then fork right and, at farm gate, turn right along path to church. ⑱ Go through gate left of church, then resume direction to follow hedge on right downhill. ⑲ At bottom, cross stile; go left for 150 yards (135 m) then cross

valley to stile. Take path uphill beside hedge, later in belt of trees, to reach field. ⑳ Turn left and follow hedge to road junction. ㉑ Take Up Marden road straight on for 40 yards (35 m), then left over stile. Keep left of beech strip to next stile, then half right to cross stile in distant belt of trees, then continuing to far right corner of field. ㉒ Turn left on to track then, at road, go straight on into East Marden. ㉓ About 70 yards (63 m) before centre of village (thatched well), turn right over stile then half right across field to stile. ㉔ Cross stile and follow fence on left round 2 sides of field to belt of trees, then turn left and follow right side of tree belt into wood. ㉕ Climb steeply, ignoring crossing path, and at top, follow hedge, then lane straight on to road. ㉖ Turn left along road past farm, then right on to rough track. About 80 yards (73 m) beyond second black barn, turn left over stile and follow hedge on right. ㉗ By corner of wood, cross stile and follow edge of wood, zig zag downhill, then uphill as far as power line. Cross stile ㉘ into wood and in 50 yards (46 m) turn left on to track downhill and up again, ignoring branches to right. ㉙ At T-junction, turn right leaving wood and later re-entering it. ㉚ Ignore track to right, then at T-junction turn right following track veering left, then ignore crossing track and leave wood. ㉛ At right bend after cottages, bear half left into hedged lane, and follow it straight on into and through wood. ㉜ Where field becomes visible to right, turn right following outside edge of wood until it turns sharp left. ㉝ Turn right into wood, then immediately left, soon leaving wood and following track straight on, eventually reaching road. ㉞ Follow road straight on to junction, then take bridleway straight on. ㉟ By back of house turn left on to bridleway parallel to road. ㊱ Opposite house, bear right away from road and continue for ½ mile (0.8 km), then turn left and left again on to road to Walderton.

☀ On Bow Hill the 4 Bronze Age barrows (burial mounds) are a clear landmark. The area has a number of other prehistoric sites, including an Iron Age farmstead and Goose Hill Camp.

\↑/ Best views are not from the top of Bow Hill, but from the clearing a little to the W. The view N is to the Downs between Beacon Hills. The view S takes in Chichester and the coastal plain.

SOUTH DOWNS

Kingley Vale nature reserve and field centre is the oldest yew forest in Europe. Legend says the forest began in AD 900 with 60 trees, planted to mark the defeat of Viking marauders.

North Marden's Norman church, one of the smallest in Sussex, is little more than a room, simple and unspoiled.

East Marden's tiny 13th C. church has a chamber organ from St James's Palace in London and beehives in the churchyard.

In Up Marden, too, there is a small, remote 13th C. church. Its simple candlelit interior has been described as one of the loveliest in England.

SOUTH DOWNS

Chantry Hill, Michelgrove and Sullington

10 or 7½ miles (16 or 12 km) Sheets 197 and 198 087120

Moderate Has several of the Downs' best vantage points. *Downland, woods; one climb; mud; path between ⑧ and ⑨ may be* ploughed out.

Start From the A283 ¼ mile (0.5 km) E of Storrington's centre follow Chantry Lane to top of Downs. **Car park** on Downs ridge.

①From car park head E along South Downs Way. (For 7½-mile version, follow track W which begins shortly back down road, to join main route in about ¼ mile (0.4 km).) ② Fork left by barn and in 70 yards (64 m) turn left downhill and follow well-defined track to Sullington church. From church, turn W and continue to road (Chantry Lane), turning left uphill. Turn right along drive opposite ponds. Beyond belt of trees fork left uphill with trees to left (ignore stile on right). ③ Near top, fork left and follow fence to head of combe. Beyond gate turn back sharply right along top of ridge. Continue one mile (1.5 km) to meet South Downs Way at parking area. Cross, leaving ridge to bear left down slope. Follow bridleway to Wepham. In just over a mile turn right before gate into wood and make for gate across field. Through it, turn left. Continue ½ mile (0.8 km) to ④ where 30 yards (27 m) beyond double gate turn left and in 100 yards (91 m) right to climb Wepham Down. ⑤Beyond gate into field turn left, cross farm track and in 30 yards turn right through gate by telegraph pole. ⑥ At T-junction turn left between gateposts on woodland track. In 100 yards, at meeting of 4 ways, fork left. ⑦ At cross-track, turn left downhill joining road at bottom. Continue along road nearly ¾ mile (1.1 km), leaving road where it bends sharply left to join footpath over stile on right. Turn left and right, keeping fence on left. Where the ground dips away steeply into the combe, go down path to left. ⑧Turn right and cross floor of valley: the path runs a few yards right of the kink in the fence down the valley, and then straight up the other side, passing a drinking-trough, to a signpost on the skyline. ⑨ At this track junction turn left and climb shoulder of hill veering away from fence line on left. Head just E of N for barn seen intermittently on summit - path may be ploughed out. ⑩ Join track beside fence, running just W of N. ⑩ Go through gate and follow fence almost due

Skipper butterflies, typical of downland, are brownish, and aptly named.

N, later turning left and right, also following fences, for point ①.

🛋 Sullington's church has a Saxon tower, but was built mainly in the 13th C. The effigy of the knight inside may be the oldest of its kind in Sussex.

🏚 Parham House, begun in 1577 by Sir Thomas Palmer, who sailed with Drake to Cadiz.

\↑/ The view SW is of the valley of the River Arun, Arundel Castle and Park, with Chichester Cathedral beyond, and, on a clear day, the Isle of Wight.

🌾 On the NE slopes of Harrow Hill there are remains of Neolithic flint mines, one of which had a gallery 50 feet (15 m) long. The hill is also the site of an Iron Age fort or fortified cattle compound.

This area has 2 notable tracts of land with public access, ideal for improvised walking and rambling: the Seven Sisters Country Park, near Eastbourne, with the clifftops of Beachy Head; and the 183-acre (74 ha) Ditchling Common, N of Ditchling.

Off the Downs, the old railway line between Groombridge and East Grinstead is a country park.

The South Downs Way (see pages 328-334) is one of the most clearly waymarked and well-maintained of the long-distance footpaths, ideal for day trips because of easy access to short sections gained from the many roads cutting across it, principally the A286, A285, A24 and A23.

SURREY

A geological sandwich; historically insignificant;
architecturally and scenically undistinguished: that
would be an accurate but misleading description of
Surrey. It is a county of intense variety – cosy farmland,
heaths and woods – all within a half day of London.
Indeed, for a Londoner seeking a short winter day's walk
with the certainty of fast, frequent electric trains home,
it is ideal.

There are three principal landscape belts: the North
Downs, on chalk; to the south, a parallel line of hills, of
which Leith Hill, Hindhead and Holmbury Hills are the
chief, lying on greensand; and between and around the
rest, clay.

Two special pleasures are the commons, many in
public or National Trust ownership, and the woods. In
fact about 12 per cent of Surrey is covered with
trees – more than enough to offset suburbia.

Leatherhead and Fetcham Downs
4 miles (6.5 km) Sheet 187 163559

Easy A stretch of the Mole valley. *Farmland, parkland, riverside; mud after rain.*

Start Leatherhead, on the A24; frequent buses and trains – bus garage and railway station ½ mile (0.8 km) from point ①. **Public car park** at Leatherhead Leisure Centre, signposted from town centre – turn left just before railway bridge.

① Facing away from road, with Leisure Centre on right, make for kissing-gate. Turn right. Cross railway. Bear left. Cross stile and bear right. At top of hill turn left. ② At road, cross to drive of Bocketts Farm and continue in same direction with field on right. To avoid mud, take parallel path in trees on left. In ½ mile (0.8 km) ③ turn left on crossing track. Keep left at fork. Turn right at next fork to drive. ④ Turn right at Norbury Park drive. At end of fencing turn left. At corner of fence bear right to view-point seat. Retrace steps. Pass Norbury Park House. ⑤ One hundred yards (91 m) past end of fence on right, turn left downhill, later passing under bridge. ⑥ At cottage on right turn left on track. Follow river under road bridge back to Leisure Centre.

🔟 Local landowners long resisted the railway, but it hardly spoilt the scenery.

🏠 18th C. Bocketts Farm and Great Barn.

The view from Norbury Park of the Mole valley and village of Mickleham.

🦌 Deer may be sighted.

🏛 The house (1774) is noted for its painted room, with scenes dovetailing into views from windows. London is seen NE.

↖ E side of Mole valley; Mickleham.

🌊 The Mole is said to get its name from disappearing underground in drought.

SURREY

Friday Street and Broadmoor
3½ miles (5.5 km) Sheet 187 126458

Easy Friday Street is one of the most popular Surrey 'backwaters', but still serene; lovely views from earth bridge in Tillingbourne valley. *Wooded hills, plantations, farmland, river valleys; 3 climbs; mud after rain.*

Start Friday Street, S of A25, signposted from Wotton Hatch. In 1½ miles (2.5 km) turn left to **public car park** before lake at Friday Street.

① Turn right out of car park parallel with road. Pass lake on right. Bear right uphill. Continue over 2 roads. Carry straight on, later bearing right. Finally turn left downhill. ② Turn left through Broadmoor. Opposite last house fork right for 200 yards (183 m) to waterfall. Retrace to house. Go left a few yards to path on left, soon bearing left on to track. Pass house on right, carrying straight on uphill. After path flattens out continue over crossing path. Cross wide, sandy track. Forward, then downhill to junction of paths. Take second on left, still downhill. Turn left at crossing track, which later turns left. ③ As track bears right through farm maintain direction through gate on left. Cross stream. Through gate on right. Follow path to lane. ④ Turn left. After buildings, continue through gate uphill on bridleway for about 100 yards (91 m) taking first turning on left. Bear right uphill to stile. Cross field. ⑤ Over crossing track down to stile. At main track turn left. Shortly turn right over stile. Cross Tillingbourne. Go uphill through woods. ⑥ Cross road to footpath. As field on left ends, turn left on to path edging wood. Later bear left to cross stile. Right on to Kempslade Farm drive. Continue to car park.

🚩 Stephen Langton, born in Friday Street, was the Archbishop of Canterbury instrumental in Magna Carta.

📖 An intriguing but fanciful explanation of the name Friday Street is that it derives from Frig or Frigga, Norse goddess of Earth and Love, whose name is invoked in the day of the week.

The lake is one of many mill or hammer ponds in Surrey and north Sussex, a reminder that the area was rich in iron foundries or 'hammers'.

🦌 Deer may be seen all round the walk.

Winkworth Arboretum, Hascombe and Dunsfold
11 miles (17.5 km) Sheet 186 990411

Moderate A fine arboretum, 2 picturesque villages and a vineyard; arboretum at best in autumn or spring. *Parkland, farmland, woods, tree plantations; one climb; mud.*

Start Winkworth Arboretum, on the B2130 about 2 miles (3 km) SE of the A3100. **Car park** on road at Arboretum entrance.

① Leave car park with Nat. Trust collection box to right. When path starts downhill, soon turn right along contour for ½ mile (0.8 km), finally dropping to road. Continue in same direction for ½ mile. ② Turn left on to signposted bridleway. Shortly turn right on crossing track. When this turns right continue in same direction on path. Later bear left with path. At T-junction turn right through Hascombe. ③ Turn left beside inn. After ⅓ mile (0.5 km) continue on hedged bridleway for ½ mile. Go through gate and continue up sunken bridleway. ④ When bridleway ends turn right, skirting tennis court, later continuing in same direction across hillside for ½ mile. Turn left at drive. At gate in crossing lane take footpath diagonally right. Pass pond on left. Continue half right to stepped stile and road. ⑤ Cross to footpath opposite, making for free-standing tree. Continue across farm track. Go diagonally left, making for second set of bars in hedge. Turn right on to road through Dunsfold. ⑥ Immediately after Hawk and Harrier turn right on to footpath. At house entrance continue on path on right. At road turn left. Left again at signpost to 'Church

Green'. Facing away from church, take left lane to road. Turn left. ⑦ Opposite Hook House Farm, turn left on to signposted footpath. Diagonally right to stile. Continue with woods on right. Right over stile into woods. Just before field ahead, follow path forward until meeting track where turn left. Later, at junction, keep left on bridleway. ⑧ Turn right at road, continuing up Upper Vann Lane for over one mile. At Maple Bungalow turn right on to track. After ¼ mile (0.5 km) turn left at signpost, later bearing right with woods on left. ⑨ Turn left on to crossing path. Shortly keep right at fork, ignoring side turnings. Continue through plantation to road. ⑩ Cross to track opposite. After 80 yards (73 m) as path goes

downhill take small path on left. Finally drop to valley bottom. Forward through gate. ⑪ Soon fork right uphill, later going downhill. Follow track to T-junction. Turn right to road and car park.

🌳 The Arboretum is noted for its fine collection of maple and Pyrus species.

🍺 The White Horse and Hawk and Harrier.

⛪ Dunsfold church, described by William Morris as the 'most beautiful country church in all England'. A rarity, it was built entirely during the period 1260-1320: a masterpiece of medieval craftsmanship.

SURREY

Shalford and Chinthurst Hill
6 miles (9.5 km) Sheet 186 001471

Easy A good example of Surrey river walking, with fine views from Chinthurst Hill. *River- and canal-sides, farmland, wooded and open hill; one climb; mud.*

Start Shalford, at the junction of the A248 and A281 S of Guildford; frequent buses; frequent trains (Tonbridge-Reading line) – Shalford Station is adjacent to point ①. **Parking** near Shalford Station.

① From station right past the Queen Victoria for ¼ mile (0.5 km) to footpath on right signposted Shalford Mill. ② From visiting mill, retrace to main road, turn right, cross and almost immediately left on to signposted bridleway, soon bearing left. Cross railway. Bear right past cottages, continuing over green to main road. Bear right over River Wey. ③ Left on to towpath. In one mile (1.5 km) ④ turn left at road bridge. Left at T-junction. Shortly, after old barn and manor house, turn right and follow track, passing sewage works, continuing on narrowing footpath to road. ⑤ Cross diagonally to left and continue on marked footpath to Gosden Green. At end turn left and cross river and disused railway bridges. At T-junction straight across to signposted bridleway on left, at first with hedge on right, later between hedges. At next field bear right with hedge on right, later continuing on

hedged track to crossing path. ⑥ Turn right, soon up steps, following zigzag path to open hilltop. Retrace to steps. Continue on path to road. Turn left, passing road junction. ⑦ At postbox bear right to signposted footpath; Through gate, cross stream over stile, forward towards house and lane. Over second stile turn left. Continue in same direction over Shalford Common. ⑧ As common ends, bear right along Station Road, later turning right on to marked footpath between industrial buildings and over footbridge to station.

🏛 Shalford had an important fair in medieval times, possibly the model of Vanity Fair in *Pilgrim's Progress*. The stocks and whipping post remain outside the churchyard wall.

🏠 Shalford Mill, open to visitors, is early 18th C. It operated until 1914, and most of the machinery is intact.

�️ A section of the Wey Navigation Canal (opened 1754), built to avoid bends in the Wey between Guildford and Godalming.

🏢 Unsted Manor House and barn are listed buildings, the house part-14th C.

\↓/ Among views from Chinthurst Hill, with its folly, are NW, the Hog's Back, ♟ Guildford Cathedral on its hill and S, Hascombe Hill.

Blackheath and Farley Green

5 miles (8 km) Sheets 186 and 187 036462

Easy An example of Surrey's greensand heath walking; panoramic views; the heather is out in August, and the bluebells in May. *Sandy heath, forestry plantations; one climb.*

Start From the A248 at Chilworth Station turn off opposite Percy Arms and continue ¾ mile (one km) to crossroads where turn left continuing to end of road; frequent buses stop at Chilworth Station; frequent trains to Chilworth Station. **Car park** on Blackheath.

① Facing away from road, leave car park at far right corner; later downhill over crossing path to continue in same direction on wider track. ② Opposite first cottage on right, turn left, immediately taking 2 successive right forks. Pass cottage on left. Turn right on to crossing track. Left at next crossing track, immediately forking right. At hilltop maintain direction over crossing track, and take first turning on left. ③ At road turn left into Farley Green, turning right at green, touching road and forking right again. Pass barn and stile on right. ④ Shortly right, up to stile. Cross field and stile into woods. Continue straight ahead, keeping left at choices. Through holly hedgerow. Immediately turn right with plantation on left. Over crossing track. When path turns left, turn right avoiding right fork. ⑤ Cross road to track

forking left, soon at trees forking right. At T-junction turn right. At junction of paths take third on right, later down to lower path. ⑥ Turn left at crossing track. Soon left at lane; continue ½ mile (0.8 km). ⑦ Turn right on path, later between lakes to road. Turn right and continue 250 yards (230 m). ⑧ Take rising path on right, continuing over drive and several crossing paths. Maintain direction and at crest of hill bear left to pass cricket field on left. Continue past house on left. Turn right for car park.

Roaring heard in this valley sounds like, and is, a lion kept in a local garden.

To St. Martha's, the church thought, not quite correctly to be a popular stopping place for 'pilgrims' on the way to Canterbury.

By the path, at shoulder level, there is a wood ants' nest in the tree trunk growing out of the embankment.

Archaeologists think the temple which stood on this site consisted of a sanctuary 18 feet (5.4 m) square with an outer colonnade about 46 feet (14 m) square, standing in 10 acres (4 ha) of grounds. Both Roman and Celtic (ie native British) gods seem to have been worshipped, following the Roman policy of integrating their religion with that of their subjects.

SURREY

Reigate and Leigh
8 miles (13 km) Sheet 187 255499

Easy On the flatter land below the Surrey hills – a pleasant variation; rewarding in late winter – snowdrops in profusion along the stream near Wonham Mill. *Parkland, farmland, heath; mud.*

Start Reigate, on the A217; frequent buses – Reigate bus station is close to point 1; frequent trains – Reigate Station about ½ mile (0.8 km) from point ①. **Public car park** at entrance to Priory Park in Bell Street.

① From car park, Priory on right, cross grass to gap in trees ahead. Later fork right uphill. Continue along top of ridge. Downhill to steps. At road turn left. ② Soon turn right on to footpath. Continue with garden on left. At signpost forward diagonally over 2 fields. ③ Right on to road. Left at junction. Right beside house. After farm, bear left round field. Cross stile and turn right into lane. ④ At road turn left and continue ¼ mile (0.5 km). Opposite signpost on right turn left on to footpath. Cross bridge. Turn right. As field edge turns right, bear diagonally left to cross stile at end of line of trees. Over bars, making for stile near far right corner of second field. Turn right, and immediately right again to cross bridge. Bear left to churchyard path. ⑤ Bear right round church. Turn right on to road. Soon turn right on to footpath. Cross 2 stiles. Soon left over footbridge and field to road. ⑥ Cross to track opposite. After ⅓ mile (0.5 km) bear left past barn. Soon turn right over stile. Diagonally left to bridge. Bear right round field. ⑦ Right over stile. Cross River Mole. Left on to bridleway. Just before farm, turn left over stile. Turn right. Later cross stream. Later over stile and footbridge to road. ⑧ Turn right. Soon turn left on to footpath between pond and mill house. Turn right on to footpath. At gate to wood on right, turn left and shortly right to farm track. Turn right, follow track to heath. ⑨ Bear left to pass windmill on right. Bear right past house to downhill path. Cross road and green. Pass cottage on right. Continue to footpath (path avoiding mud higher on left). At lane turn left. ⑩ Left on to footpath. Cross road to footpath. Bear left round Priory Park lake. Continue in same direction to point ① and car park.

🗡 Skimmington Castle.

Reigate Heath's windmill, and the round house used as a chapel.

🏞 Reigate Castle grounds contain the remains of the moat, keep and excavations of a castle reputed to have belonged to William, Earl of Warren. It was surrendered to Louis, the Dauphin of France, in 1216 and French coins are said to have been found in the moat.

Under the court is the curious Barons' Cave, a long, curved crypt with a pointed roof cut from the hard sand. Tradition has it that the Barons conferred there prior to signing Magna Carta at Runnymede, in the Thames valley.

🏛 Reigate's Old Town Hall dates from 1728.

🏚 Reigate Priory, built in the 13th C., stood in these grounds until Henry VIII turned it into a house. Little of the Tudor building remains; the existing house is mainly late 18th C.

🏚 The Priest's House is actually a row of medieval, timbered buildings, with additions and renovations, and no overall theme; but nonetheless attractive.

❀ Snowdrops, flowering Jan.-March; they are uncommon in the wild.

⚒ The windmill dates from 1765 and the brick-built round house is a chapel, still
⛪ used for services on some Sundays.

The Priest's House: Horsham slate and large chimney stacks add to the charm.

Hindhead Common, Frensham Common, Witley Common – Surrey is the county of sandy heathland, the essence of convenient strolling. To vary the theme, try exploring the dramatic combes which occasionally puncture it, notably the Devil's Punchbowl on the A3. A nature trail is marked on the S rim.

The Forestry Commission have waymarked some trails from the Green Dene car park near Horsley.

A straight line route using the Pilgrim's Way: from Dorking station, go up Ashcombe Road and continue ahead when it ends, joining the Pilgrim's Way. Descend to Westcott and take the bus back to Dorking.

River walking: from Guildford, follow the River Wey to Godalming, taking a bus or train back, or vice versa.

NORTH DOWNS

Although the North Downs have a long-distance footpath of their own, The North Downs Way, this 140-mile (225 km) chain of chalk hills has never quite achieved the public identity of the South Downs or the Chilterns: a pity.

The Surrey end of the Downs comprises some of the most accessible walking in Britain, close to London and crossed at short intervals by train and bus routes. Here, local authorities, at their most enlightened, have built an estate of continuous public open spaces out of commons, land bought for green belt preservation and adjoining National Trust properties. Walkers have – for the Home Counties – the unusual experience of being free to wander, not confined to paths only, over many square miles of easy, wooded hills.

In Kent, as the Downs curve gradually towards Dover, there is greater restriction; but this is historic walking. Scholars dispute whether the Pilgrims' Way marked on the maps is any such thing, but there is no doubt that for centuries men and women went on foot and horse along these hills to Canterbury.

Gomshall and Hackhurst Downs
4 miles (6.5 km) Sheet 187 089479

Easy A pleasant way of climbing Hackhurst Downs, with some of the finest viewpoints between Dorking and Guildford. *Farmland, wooded and open hillsides; one climb.*

Start Gomshall, on the A25 between Dorking and Guildford; frequent buses; frequent trains stopping at Gomshall on the Tonbridge-Reading line. **Car park** at station.

① From station cross A25. Left under railway. Right on Wonham Way, later bearing left. As lane bears right, turn left beside house. Immediately right through gate. Continue in same direction over stream. After houses bear left to road. Turn left. ② Opposite Fish Farm turn right up lane. After about 200 yards (183 m), turn right up path bordering woods. Continue to lane. Turn left through farm. Cross railway. Continue uphill. Pass Blatchford Down sign on right. ③ Left over stile across cleared area to stile. Forward to seat. Turn right on crossing track. Follow main path, later through posts, to turn left on droveway, continuing ½ mile (0.8 km). ④ Twenty yards (18 m) before static water tank on right, turn left. As path bears left up to viewpoint seat, turn right to join main path downhill. Continue down Colekitchen Lane to A25. Turn left for station.

The North Downs in high summer – rich, rolling country, with Gomshall at the centre.

🐝 Gomshall village is famous for its beauty, its watercress beds and a tannery dating back at least to the 11th C.

∩ A 16th C. packhorse bridge.

⑲ The droveway on Hackhurst Downs – part of the North Downs Way – is an ancient track.

🐝 Bee and fly orchids.

NORTH DOWNS

Puttenham and Wanborough
3 miles (5 km) Sheet 186 932483

Easy Through 2 typical and charming villages on the N and S sides of The Hog's Back; shrub path at ④ best in spring. *Hillsides, golf course, farmland; 2 climbs.*

Start The Hog's Back, along which the A31 runs W from the Guildford by-pass. **Car park** ¼ mile (0.5 km) W of the B3000 turning.

① From car park entrance turn towards Guildford, continuing 250 yards (229 m). Turn right on to bridleway, continuing for ⅓ mile (0.5 km) to road. Turn left to Puttenham. Passing church, continue to main road. Turn right. ② Opposite Jolly Farmer turn left on to North Downs Way, continuing for almost one mile (1.5 km). ③ Immediately past Monksgrove Cottage and Farm House, turn left alongside garden. Continue, ignoring side turnings, to gate. After woods, cross field, bearing slightly left to gate into lane. Cross lane and grass area to gate. Cross field to another gate into another lane. Cross to stile and go up side of field to A31. ④ Cross to bridleway to Wanborough church. Turn left. Left at road. ⑤ At bend, turn right over stile. Go diagonally right uphill to A31. Cross to car park.

🏠 Puttenham's church of St. John the Baptist dates from about 1160, but was much restored in 1861. The well in the churchyard 'reappeared' in 1972 when a cypress tree subsided into it; it had been filled in more than 200 years earlier.

🏠 Puttenham village has many attractive tile-hung and timber-framed houses, some built in the 14th and 15th C.

🏛 Puttenham Priory (1762) is a fine Palladian mansion and the site of a much earlier house, part of the manor of Puttenham. This came into the Prior of Newark's possession in 1248, hence the house's name. There was never a monastic foundation here.

🏠 Wanborough, a beautiful hamlet which
🏛 seems to grow naturally from the hillside, has a tiny church (interior
🏛 measurements 44½ by 18 feet [13.5 by 5.4 m]); a manor house and an ancient tithe barn worth a visit.

Headley Heath, Brockham Hills, Juniper Top
7 miles (11 km) Sheet 187 205539

Moderate Little-used paths in an over-visited area of the North Downs; an incomparable path over Juniper Top, with magnificent views. A summer walk – especially troublesome mud in winter. *Heath, wooded hillside, chalk downland; one climb; exceptionally steep downhill path between ② and ③ best not attempted if wet.*

Start Headley, by the B2033 SE of Leatherhead. **Car park** (National Trust) on Headley Heath opposite the cricket pitch.

① Leave car park with Jubilee Plantation on left, walking parallel to road. As plantation ends, take third path on right. After continuing in same direction over crossing track, keep left at fork. At picnic area, bear left with pond on right. Cross bridleway to track doubling back on left. At crossing track go right for 150 yards (137 m). Take second of 2 paths forking off on left. Soon turn right on to crossing track. Over crossing track. Through gate ahead. Forward on path to road. Turn right. ② Turn left on to signposted path. Keep fenced field on left. At corner of fence continue downhill on track into trees. At lane, turn right, then left. ③ Soon turn right on to North Downs Way, continuing uphill and over bridge. After passing old chimney stack, turn left steeply downhill. Soon turn right on to track, keeping left at fork. Ignore side turnings and continue over ½ mile (0.8 km) on track at foot of Brockham Hills. Cross clearing, keeping buildings on left. After stile keep left at fork. Later ignore small right fork and when path divides into 2 parallel paths, the right one is preferable. ④ When paths rejoin at pillbox and pylon on left, turn right uphill. Turn left up steps at North Downs Way sign; forward right on track. Later left downhill on North Downs Way, soon turning right. Later, at crossing track, turn right to road. ⑤ Cross to track opposite with fenced caravans on right. Turn right with fence. Take first path on left. Continue over crossing track. Later emerge on open hillside of Juniper Top. Continue downhill. ⑥ Near bottom of slope turn right on path doubling back into scrub. Later keep left at fork. Over stile and

right on enclosed path. Continue in same direction over 3 more stiles, with fence on left. After next stile go downhill and cross drive to maintain direction up surfaced track. ⑦ After passing through brick gate posts, turn sharply left down to main bridleway. Turn left. Soon, at junction of paths, forward through fence on left to path going diagonally uphill. After passing seats, rejoin bridleway on right. Go straight ahead over junction of paths to ①.

🏠 Brockham Museum Trust area has a collection of old railway rolling stock.

↑ Views from Juniper Top are magnificent. One takes in Norbury Park House, an 18th C. mansion, once the home of Dr. Marie Stopes, feminist and reformer.

☘ Wild orchids in early summer.

☘ The profuse heather on Headley Heath is at its best in late summer. Sweeping views in most directions.

NORTH DOWNS

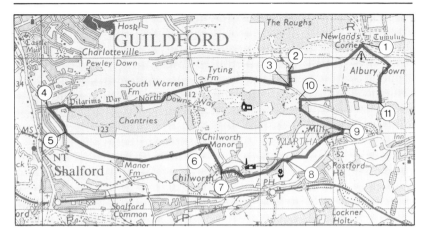

Newlands Corner and Albury Downs
7 miles (11 km) Sheet 186 044492

Moderate Varied walking with superb views from one of the Downs' key points. *Hillsides, farmland, woods, lakesides; 2 climbs.*

Start Newlands Corner on the A25 W of Guildford. **Public car park** at Newlands Corner.

① From car park go S downhill. Turn right on path keeping trees on right. After ½ mile (0.8 km), fork left downhill. Soon enter woods. Bear left to road. ② Cross to steps. Turn left on to roadside path, continuing for ¼ mile (0.5 km). ③ At lodge turn right, continuing for ¾ mile (one km). After Tyting Farm, cross road to track. Keep on main track as it bears left, then right. ④ Turn left round Chantry Cottage on track. Continue for a few yards on road before turning left over stile. ⑤ Straight ahead on footpath with upward slope of Chantries on left. After ½ mile (0.8 km) bear right opposite farm and immediately left, continuing in same direction on track for ¾ mile. ⑥ At road turn right. In a few yards turn right on to path. At road turn right. ⑦ Soon turn left through gate beside West Lodge. Follow main path through woods for ½ mile. Through high bank of earth, and follow river to lane. Turn right and continue for a few yards. ⑧ Left over stile. Cross field diagonally to stile. Go along edge of 2 fields with ditch on right. Continue along garden boundary to lane. Turn left, with lake on

right. Bear left with next lake on right. ⑨ Turn left beside Millstream Cottage. Follow path for ½ mile to heath. Bear right towards pine trees, going through posts, then left to road. ⑩ Cross to footpath opposite. Later cross track and right round field edge. Turn left at corner. Later through gate. Continue to lane. ⑪ Turn left, continuing for ⅓ mile (0.5 km). Bear right with lane. At pillbox on right turn left on track rising over Albury Downs. Ignore side turnings. Through posts to car park.

↑ The rightly popular view from the crest of the Downs at Newlands Corner.

⌂ St. Martha's Chapel, near the walk route and on the 'Pilgrims' Way' to Canterbury, dates from Saxon times. Damaged by a gunpowder explosion in the 18th C., it was left derelict for a long time, but rebuilt in 1848.

⌘ Chilworth, being a good site for a water-wheel, was a centre of industry for centuries. In 1625 the East India Company set up mills making gunpowder and cordite; in Queen Anne's reign they manufactured bank notes, too. By the end of the 17th C. there were 16 mills at work and they were still in use until the end of the 1914-18 War.

♣ Jewel-weed – orange balsam – grows in the river. It was first found growing wild in England on the River Wey in 1822, by John Stuart Mill.

Woldingham, Marden Park and Tandridge Hill
5 miles (8 km) Sheet 187 360563

Easy Rewarding views for comparatively little effort. *Parkland, farmland, woods; mud.*

Start Woldingham, off the A22 E of Caterham; frequent buses; frequent trains to Woldingham. **Car park** at Woldingham Station.

① Through door on upside platform of station to drive. At lodge turn left, continuing for nearly one mile (1.5 km). ② Opposite S end of school buildings turn right on to signposted footpath up steps. After ½ mile (0.8 km), at open field, pass to left of line of trees. Soon pass waymarked stile on right. Cross next stile and go steeply downhill to lane—part of North Downs Way. ③ Turn left. Follow North Downs Way waymarks to T-junction at top of Tandridge Hill. Turn right. ④ At signpost on right, turn left into woods. Soon take middle of 3 paths, later passing large hollow. Several paths here, but continue ahead soon leaving wood. After stile, go downhill to drive. ⑤ Turn right, soon bearing left uphill. After ¾ mile (one km), pass Marden Park Farm. ⑥ Turn right over railway and left on track to station.

🏰 Marden Park, now the Convent School of the Sacred Heart, is reputed to stand on the site of several earlier houses. One was a feudal manor, left derelict after the Black Death wiped out the village of Marden. But the first reliably documented building here was the mansion built by Sir Robert Clayton, wealthy 17th C. Lord Mayor of London. The present Tudor-style buildings date from 1880. The modern buildings erected for the purposes of the school have fortunately done little to damage the scenery.

🌺 The rare leopardsbane flowers here from late March into April. A member of the great Compositae (daisy) family it has a bright yellow, daisy-shaped flower, similar to that of the celandine.

🌱 The broad-leaved helleborine, another uncommon plant, grows in the woods. It is a member of the orchid family and its flowers – reddish mauve – appear from July to September.

Broad-leaved helleborine (left) is native to the British Isles. Leopardsbane (right) was introduced from elsewhere.

Chevening
5 miles (8 km) Sheet 188 489578

Easy Fine views over the Weald of Kent; a well-known house in a gracious setting. At the end of February, the snowdrops could be mistaken for snowdrifts. *Farmland, parkland, woods; one climb; mud after rain.*

Start Chevening, N of Sevenoaks. **Parking** on grass verge near church.

① From church turn right and go through churchyard. Continue straight ahead on hedged path. At road turn left. In a few yards ② turn left uphill on North Downs Way. Follow the waymarks, later crossing drive by house and eventually reaching a minor road. ③ Turn left and continue for ⅓ mile (0.5 km). ④ At Keeper's Cottage turn left. At end of woods bear left downhill with fence on left. ⑤ Through kissing-gate, then left following waymarks across estate to where path crosses, forming T-junction. ⑥ Turn right to Chevening church.

🏛 Chevening House, mid-17th C., was probably designed by Inigo Jones. It was the birthplace of Lady Hester Stanhope (1776-1839), the famous eccentric and traveller. Her father, the 3rd Earl, an amateur inventor, launched the first small boat to be powered by steam on the lake in the park. The family bequeathed the house to the nation in 1959, and it is now used for official entertaining.

🏠 This, and several walks in the section, use a length of the North Downs Way, an offical long-distance path. See pp.328-334.

Lullingstone Park and Shoreham
7½ miles (12 km) Sheet 188 506646

Moderate The attractive village of Shoreham and fine views from the hills, despite the proximity of the M25. *Parkland, farmland, forestry plantations; one climb.*

Start Lullingstone Park, signposted from Well Hill, off the A21 N of Sevenoaks; frequent trains to Shoreham, where the walk can be joined in ½ mile (0.8 km) between ⑤ and ⑥. **Public car park** at entrance to Lullingstone Park.

① Bear right out of car park on track. Soon turn right by trees to cross green into woods. Continue over green and uphill. Turn right over ladder stile to road. ② Turn left. Soon turn right on to signposted footpath. Right over stile. Later, diagonally left downhill. Turn left at road. ③ Right at T-junction, continuing for just over ½ mile (0.8 km), ignoring left turning. ④ Opposite Timberden Farm Cottage, turn left on signposted footpath. Uphill into woods. Over crossing track. Continue downhill out of woods. Cross stile. Downhill to road. ⑤ Turn right, and shortly left. Cross bridge. Left at riverside path. ⑥ Left over bridge. Bear right beside river. Cross stile and continue in same direction along field. At next field bear slightly left. Maintain direction between cultivations. ⑦ Right on road for ¾ mile (one km) to main road. Cross, turn left on to path above embankment. (Easier access to embankment about 30 yards [27 m] to right.) ⑧ When path drops to road, cross to track opposite. At Roman villa turn left along private road. ⑨ Just past gate towers of

Lullingstone Castle, turn right on to track into Lullingstone Park. Avoid left fork. Follow track for 1½ miles (2.5 km) back to ①.

🔟 Shoreham's 1914-18 War memorial is a white cross cut in the turf of the chalk hillside to the W of the village.

🏠 At Water House, Samuel Palmer, the visionary painter, lived for some years. He used the village as a background in his strange and touching pastoral paintings. William Blake often came to visit him here.

⛪ Shoreham's parish church of St. Peter

and St. Paul, dating back to the 15th C. but much restored in 1864, has one of the best examples of a medieval carved rood screen in England.

🏛 At Lullingstone Castle – in fact, an 18th C. house – the first game of lawn tennis was played in 1873. In the grounds are a herb garden and a 14th C. church.

🏛 Lullingstone Roman villa is one of the finest in the country. In about AD 370 the owner and his family became Christians and built a chapel in the house above a room which was probably used for pagan rites. No other Roman house in Britain is so-equipped.

NORTH DOWNS

Otford, Knatts Valley and Romney Street
11½ miles (18.5 km) Sheet 188 524594

Moderate Knatts Valley offers the impression, at least, of remoteness, surrounded by over-populated Kent. *Open and wooded downland, farmland, open valleys, wooded hilltops; one climb; mud after rain.*

Start Otford, on the A225 N of Sevenoaks; frequent trains to Otford station. **Car park** at Otford station.

① From station turn right uphill. Right at T-junction. Soon turn left up North Downs Way path. Later continue in same direction with fence on right. ② At road junction, forward on road. Shortly right over stile. Go diagonally to corner of wood. Continue with woods on right. Cross drive and forward through gates of Hildenborough Hall. ③ Left over stile, continuing in same direction. Later bear left over 2 fields, through woods and diagonally left over field. Continue with woods on right. ④ Turn right at road, later turning right. Left on North Downs Way track. Continue in same direction, later with fence on left. Cross stile on left into woods to path on extreme right. Continue along field with fence on left. ⑤ Left through gate and up track. Left between barns. Go diagonally down field, keeping fence on left. Maintain direction over next field. Continue with woods on left. At farm, bear left to road. ⑥ Turn left for a few yards. Right over stile. Follow track past buildings to road. Turn left. Soon turn right on footpath. Keep hedge on right. Continue over stiles. Turn left on crossing path. Shortly go steeply downhill. Right at road. ⑦ Right at T-junction for 1½ miles (2.5 km) through Knatts Valley. ⑧ At road junction on right turn left up track. Turn left with track. At gate at top of track turn left on path. Ignore left turning. After ½ mile (0.8 km) straight on over clearing through gate with house on left. Continue in same direction for ½ mile. ⑨ Turn right over stile. Continue half right over 2 fields to stile into woods. Continue straight ahead to road junction. Turn right with house on right. ⑩ Opposite Fox and Hounds turn left over stile, bearing right to stile. Turn left over another stile. Keep trees on left until field ends. Over stile beside telegraph pole and down to road. ⑪ Left for a few yards. Right over stile. Follow garden fence to

Otford's Tudor remains, a pleasant end of walk stopping and picnic place with seats and a stream close by.

second corner, then ahead to stile in trees. Downhill and up to stile. Follow to road. ⑫ Turn right, continuing 300 yards (274 m). Left over stile and forward on track. Pass pylon. Downhill to open hillside. Turn right. Re-enter woods. Over stile and downhill initially with fence on left. ⑬ At road, left. Shortly right on footpath crossing railway. Forward, then diagonally left over field. Left on track. Left at road. Pass pond. Cross to church on left. (Diversion on path signposted Sevenoaks to visit Tudor palace.) Retrace to churchyard path signposted Kemsing. Pass wall on left. Continue to car park and station.

▱ Otford has the remnants of a 16th C. palace, one of the residences of the Archbishops of Canterbury. It had been rebuilt from a manor house belonging to Archbishop Warham (1518), who also owned Knole, and was acquired in 1537 by Henry VIII.
Brickwork from the old palace has been incorporated in the row of cottages between the tower and the gatehouse. The latter was used as a dovecot in the 19th C.

⛪ In Otford church, by the green, there is a 17th C. timbered porch and an 11th C. nave. One of the monuments in the church is in remembrance of Elizabeth Polhill, granddaughter of Oliver Cromwell and daughter of General Ireton. The Church Hall was designed by

Edward Lutyens, whose brother was vicar of Otford.

🏠 In Otford's main street there are 16th and 17th C. houses, including the attractive 'Pickmoss'.

🍺 In the Bull Inn there is panelling which may have come from the old palace.

🏛 Broughton Manor has a medieval hall and a 16th C. gable.

🌿 Flowers of the area include common milkwort, with its delicate blue, pink or white blooms, rich yellow rock rose and salad burnet, with its cucumber scent and petalless flowers.

Colley Hill, Box Hill and Newlands Corner are the North Downs' time-honoured contribution to Sunday afternoon strolling. Remember there is a road to the summit of Box Hill, and miles of heath behind it.

A delightful, waymarked 'greenway' starts from Hollingbourne on the B6213 one mile (1.5 km) N of the junction of the M20 and A20 E of Maidstone. The route goes to Harrietsham, turns left at the church there and climbs to the Pilgrims' Way, along which one can return to Hollingbourne.

The Alice Holt Forest, 4 miles (6.5 km) S of Farnham has trails.

CHILTERNS AND THAMES VALLEY

For the walker, the Chiltern Hills and the eastern end of the Thames Valley have two great plusses: accessibility and scenery.

Train and bus services crossing the hills at intervals along their 50-mile (80-km) length enable Londoners to travel out by one route, tramp across country and return by another. At their disposal is a dense network of public footpaths – more than four miles (6.5 km) to every square mile (2.5 square km) – twice the national average. What is more, the paths are kept in excellent shape by the Chiltern Society. Signposting, waymarking and even restoration after ploughing are all above the norm.

The Chilterns are classic chalk country, hung with beechwoods, under which there is relatively firm going all the year round. In this terrain a typical route means slipping in and out of the woods and across the small intervening fields of the valleys.

Modestly dramatic country with wide views of the south midland plain can be enjoyed on the hills' escarpment, to the west. The ancient green road, the Icknield Way, runs along the scarp-foot, and behind, the hills drop gradually to the Thames in a series of winding valleys. Those marked on the map as having few roads can seem amazingly remote in atmosphere from London, less than 40 miles (64 km) away.

Ivinghoe Hills

6 miles (9.5 km) Sheet 165 963160

Moderate The spectacular north Chilterns downs – wide views and prehistoric sites. *Downland, farmland, woods; 3 climbs; mud after rain; between ⑮ and ⑯ the path, although a public right of way, may be ploughed out or under crops; route is ill-defined and prone to bramble growth between ⑦ and ⑧ .*

Start Ivinghoe Beacon, signposted from the B489 SW of Dunstable; infrequent buses (Luton to Aylesbury service) stop at foot of Ivinghoe Beacon, from where take path uphill to join route between ⑯ and ⑰. **Car park** signposted on Ivinghoe Hills road.

① Turn left out of car park on to road. ② Take first gravel entrance on right and go straight on past military warning sign referring to former use through scrub to fence at top of steep slope. ③ Left on to Ridgeway Path, soon crossing stile and continuing downhill to stile at next fence. ④ Just before stile, left along fence line to cross stile into scrub rising to wood. ⑤ At crossways, straight on, then at T-junction turn right for top of Clipper Down. ⑥ At fork, go left, leaving cottage to left and fields on right. ⑦ About 200 yards (183 m) beyond end of last field, left into slightly sunken track, then, by double-trunked tree on right, half right to road. Then right to entrance of Ward's Hurst Farm. ⑧ Turn left up farm

drive. ⑨ At farm, left then right through yard, emerging by silos. Then straight on along track downhill, keeping right of fence. ⑩ Follow right side of tree belt straight on downhill, crossing fence through scrub at bottom end of wood, then left passing Hog Hall. ⑪ Join drive, then straight on to A4146 at Dagnall. ⑫ Left along road to corner of radio station fence. ⑬ Left into hedged bridleway beside fence, continuing around back of radio station, turning right, left and right again until emerging through bridle gate into field. ⑭ Right, then left, still following radio station fence line to far right corner of field. ⑮ Through hedge gap and bear half left through field (which may be under crops) to top of Gallows Hill. ⑯ Half left over top of next hill to summit of Beacon ⑰ Left, heading for bend in road left of small hillock. ⑱ Just before bend, slightly left on to worn path parallel to road back to car park.

〽 Incombe Hole, 250 feet (76 m) deep, possibly the most spectacular combe in the Chilterns; it was cleared of scrub by volunteers organized by the Chiltern Society, famed for its footpath work.

🎋 Pitstone windmill (1627) is the oldest of its kind in Britain.

🌟 The Beacon is topped by traces of an Iron Age fort, probable date 600 BC. Views include Mentmore (902197), the Rosebery house now a meditation school of the Maharishi Yogi.

CHILTERNS AND THAMES VALLEY

Turville Valley
5½ miles (9 km) Sheet 175 747910

Moderate *Turville Valley is popular but comparatively unspoilt, the village a beautifully harmonious collection of buildings. Heath, woods, farmland; 3 climbs; mud after rain.*

Start Turville Heath, off the B480 between Henley and Watlington. In village take cul-de-sac to Turville Grange. **Parking** within 15 feet (4.5 m) of road edge.

① Facing Grange gates, turn right through scrub along back of heath. ② Left on to road, then half right at junction on to path, keeping left of tree. ③ After 150 yards (137 m), fork right, then, after another 100 yards (91 m), fork left of hawthorn tree, go straight on to edge of wood, and follow left-hand waymarked path to stile at its far side. ④ Half right across field, then half right past tree to stile at Southend. ⑤ Cross stile and turn left along concrete lane to farm, then straight on down hill to crossroads at Dolesden. ⑥ Straight on across field towards windmill, then take bridle lane into Turville. ⑦ Turn left passing church, then, opposite black barn with turret, right up 'Barn Cottage' path. At stile, half left uphill across field, through corner of copse, then hillside scrub to hilltop wood. ⑧ Along edge of wood, then at T-junction, left on to track to a road. ⑨ Uphill along road, bearing right. ⑩ At second road junction, left on to path across field into wood. ⑪ About 30 yards (27 m) into woodland, turn right, following path straight on to road at Gray's Barn. ⑫ Left on road. At its end, take woodland bridleway straight on downhill. ⑬ At left bend, go straight on over stile, then half left downhill. ⑭ Straight on across next field to road. ⑮ Straight on along bridleway, climbing to Turville Heath. ⑯ Turn left along back of heath to Grange.

🌲 The avenue is of old lime trees.

🏠 18th C. Turville Grange.

Turville Court and estate belonged to Bysshe Shelley, grandfather of the poet. The house was built in 1847.

🍺 Both pubs serve real ale.

The church is Norman, its tower 16th C.

In warmer weather, Turville's Bull and Butcher is popular for lunch in the garden. The pub is one of the village's several timber-framed cottages and houses, mainly dating from the 16th to the 18th C.

🌾 Cobstone Windmill is an 18th C. smock mill, i.e. with a revolving top to bring its sails in line with the wind.

Great Kimble and Whiteleaf
4½ miles (7 km) Sheet 165 826060

Moderate The central Chiltern escarpment, with its wooded slopes, patches of downland and picturesque villages below. *Woods, farmland, downland; 2 climbs; mud after rain; may need clearing between ⑰ and ⑱.*

Start Great Kimble, on the A4010 S of Aylesbury; frequent buses. **Parking** in unsignposted lay-by S of church.

① From church take lane into village. ② Just past thatched cottage, left over stile and straight on to gate, then slightly right to stile by pylon. ③ Straight on, crossing drive, then half right across field to stile. ④ Beyond stile, left, then straight on, keeping right of hedge, to Askett. ⑤ Right, then left along Askett Lane to stile. ⑥ Right to stile in corner of field. ⑦ Straight on, after marsh turning half left to footbridge, then on to road at Monks Risborough. ⑧ Straight on to church tower, then left to village side street. ⑨ Left, then right to A4010. ⑩ Take path left of school to road, then right to T-junction in Whiteleaf. ⑪ Left, then right on to path

climbing past thatched cottage. ⑫ Right at fork, climbing steeply. At crossing path, straight on uphill through wood to clearing above Whiteleaf Cross. ⑬ From looking at view over plain, turn round and go straight on downhill to the Plough, Cadsden. ⑭ Straight ahead between pub garden and car park, right on to path, left at fork 300 yards (270 m) from the Plough (ignore waymarked path up hill). ⑮ In 170 yards (150 m) turn right up gully; after 80 yards (73 m) left up slope, follow fence on left (down in parts) to far side of wood. ⑯ Left along bridleway, crossing road to track behind lay-by car park. ⑰ By second noticeboard for riders, fork right on to narrow, terraced path to old fence on far side of scrub. ⑱ After stile, half right across field to stile right of far corner, then left down bridleway to Great Kimble.

🔟 'Kimble' derives from Cunobelinus or Cymbeline, the ancient British king.

🏛 Hampden signed his refusal to pay Ship Money in this church.

🍺 All 3 pubs marked serve real ale.

🔟 Experts cannot agree the age of Whiteleaf Cross, or its purpose; but it may be a marker on the Icknield Way.

CHILTERNS AND THAMES VALLEY

The timber-framed buildings characteristic of the Chilterns area (and elsewhere) were built by several methods; the most 'woody' appearance being given by the box-frame construction (top). The wooden frame carries the whole load of the roof, with the walling material acting simply as weather-proof filling for the gaps. As such, it was originally made of the simplest material, typically wattle and daub (below). This was flexible strips of wood woven around stiffer uprights, and coated with suitable 'daub', often mud mixed with clay. When it deteriorated, it was almost always replaced by brick panels, properly called brick nogging.

The Lee and Little Hampden
8, 4½ or 3½ miles (13, 7 or 5.5 km)
Sheet 165 900043 and 85040

Moderate (8-mile route) or **easy** (4- and 3½-mile routes). Typical of the best central Chiltern countryside. *Farmland, ridges and 'bottoms'; three climbs on 3½-mile route, four on 8-mile route; mud after rain.*

Start (of 8- and 4½-mile routes) The Lee, E of the A413 between Amersham and Wendover; (of the 3½-mile route) Little Hampden, W of the A413. **Parking** along S side of The Lee green – do not block entrances or use pub car park without landlord's permission. At Little Hampden, on common land opposite the Rising Sun (this is not pub car park). If full, return to foot of hill, then left and left again to Cobblers Hill Road. In 1¼ miles (2 km) stop at Cockshoots Wood Picnic Area, beginning walk from there.

For 8-mile route, walk ①-㉗; for 4½-mile route, walk ①-⑫, then ㉔-①; for 3½-mile route, walk ⑲-㉓, returning by ⑬-⑲.

① Leaving green by memorial, take road to crossing power line. ② Turn left, crossing stile. Pass to left of black barn, cross second stile then follow hedge on left until entering wood. ③ At far side of wood, left along track to road. ④ Cross road and follow hedge on right, passing straight through copse. ⑤

Beyond copse, slightly left to stile, then straight ahead along drive to bend, then through gap in trees into pub car park. ⑥ At far side left up track to stile in hedge on right, then straight on to second stile. ⑦ After stile, half left, heading just right of right-hand of 2 distant cottages. ⑧ Straight on through garden, then half left towards left end of wood on horizon, arriving at stile in hedge at bottom of field. ⑨ Straight on over 2 fields to stile just right of Durham Farm. ⑩ Cross road, then half right to stile right of old farm, then straight on along road to A413. ⑪ Turn left, then, crossing road at lay-by, right on to signposted path across 2 fields. ⑫ If doing 4½-mile route, sharp left along signposted path to A413; if continuing, straight on over railway bridge, then right. ⑬ Follow fence on right for 190 yards (170 m), then diagonally left to pick up corner of another fence, keeping right of this fence to road. ⑭ Cross road, then uphill to gate under tree, then slightly left, following hedge on right, leaving field through gate. ⑮ Right through second gateway on right, soon entering lane. ⑯ At edge of wood, through gate and right for Dunsmore crossroads. ⑰ Left passing pond, then left over stile and half right downhill over four stiles to bridleway. ⑱ Left into bridleway, then in wood half right uphill to Little Hampden. ⑲ If starting 3½-mile route, head down road. Otherwise left on to road. ⑳

Opposite church, left on to bridleway across valley, then uphill through wood and farm to road. ㉑ Take bridleway left of post box, then, just beyond house, left into wood and follow waymarks. ㉒ At first fork, left; at second fork, right; at third, right. At cross-tracks, bear left down sunken path to gateway. (If starting 3½-mile route here, take waymarked path from rear of picnic area, then at fork left to old gate out of wood.) ㉓ Straight on to railway bridge. If doing 3½-mile route, left just before railway. Otherwise over bridge, through gate, over stile, half right on to right-hand signposted path to A413. ㉔ Turn left, cross road; in a few yards turn right, following hedge on left. Continue uphill to gate. ㉕ Just before gate, turn right, walking parallel to road to join it at road junction. ㉖ Left, then right over stile; follow hedge on right to far side of field. ㉗ Right, then keeping left of churchyard over several stiles to road, where turn right for green.

🏠 Church Farm is partly 13th C., and with the village's 2 churches stands inside the remains of a prehistoric fort.

🏦 The Lee green was created by Sir Arthur Liberty, founder of the Regent St. store, and owner of the Manor House.

🏫 18th C. Mayortorne Manor (spellings vary), once the home of the local writer, H. J. Massingham.

Little Hampden, and Great Hampden across the valley, bear the name of the family that produced Buckinghamshire's most honourable politician. The Hampdens had been the most influential landowners in the county since before the Norman Conquest, when in 1635 the 'reigning' squire and M.P. for Wendover, John Hampden, refused to pay the arbitrarily levied tax called Ship Money. As much a gesture in defence of democracy as a deliberate challenge to the king's authority, it remains one of the most famous incidents of the years leading to the Civil War. Hampden died of wounds early in the war. His great-grandson lost much of the family fortune in speculation, but retained Hampden House, now a girl's school. It contains some interesting Hampden associations, but the nearby parish church has more: a relief of Hampden falling wounded from his horse at the Battle of Chalgrove Field, portraits and inscriptions.

🏠 The church is 13th C. with a 15th C. porch and some good medieval murals.

🏠 Manor Farm is 16th-17th C.

🍺 All 5 pubs marked serve real ale. The Rising Sun, Little Hampden, does not welcome muddy boots.

CHILTERNS AND THAMES VALLEY

Henley, Hambleden and Stonor
13 miles (21 km) Sheet 175 763826

Energetic The Thames Valley Chilterns, with the beautiful Hambleden Valley and superb Stonor Park. *Farmland, hills; 6 climbs; mud after rain; path between ③ and ④ may be overgrown.*

Start Henley, on the A423; frequent buses from High Wycombe and Reading, infrequent services from London and Oxford; by rail, the London–Reading line, changing at Twyford. **Public car park** near station.

① From Henley church, cross bridge and turn left through silver gates to path on right to meadow. ② Turn right, cross road to stile right of iron railings, then half left through meadow, golf practice area and up through scrub. ③ By corner of fence on left, half right to stile, then straight on through wood (ignoring right turn). ④ Half right across field to hedge gap near single tree. ⑤ Left along road, then, before copse, right on to farm track. Continue to far end of copse on left. ⑥ Straight on through hedge gap and downhill to road, then left. ⑦ At 'Flower Pot' turn left, then right on to track to Hambleden Lock. ⑧ Cross lock, weir and A4155, then take Hambleden road. ⑨ At Rotten Row Turn, go through kissing-gate and follow path parallel to Hambledon road. ⑩ Right into village, then left by post office into back lane. ⑪ After bridge, fork right over stile to far corner of field, then continue along road to left bend. ⑫ Left into lane, then at corner of wood slightly right up inside edge of wood, then along track into second wood. ⑬ At crossways turn right, then left at track junction, ignoring right forks. Continue downhill to valley bottom. ⑭ Cross track bearing half right. Following waymarks, leave wood and take fenced track to farm. ⑮ Join concrete track, forking right through farm, then right along road to junction. ⑯ Take path straight on downhill (bearing left on entering wood), then up again. ⑰ Slightly left across field to right of fence to tree clump on horizon, then to gate into lane to Southend. ⑱ Cross road and take track straight on downhill through wood. ⑲ By first of row of pines on right keep left and in 330 yards (300 m) look out for a fork (the waymark on a tree may be obscured), left on to path through plantation and Stonor Park to road. ⑳ Turn left and continue to far end of Stonor village. ㉑ Just past farm, left over stile and straight on uphill into wood. ㉒ Near hilltop, straight on along farm track. At crossways, on to Coxlease Farm. ㉓ Just past second barn, sharp right through double gates on to track past farmhouse and along ridge-top. ㉔ At end of track, over stile, then right, shortly entering wood. ㉕ Straight on across field to road, then left. ㉖ Just past 'Rainbow', left on to Fawley road, then right on to track (Oxfordshire Way) uphill to field. ㉗ Slightly left to rails and gap in trees at corner of field. ㉘ Half right across fields to stile hidden in bushes left of cottage. ㉙ Cross road and take track opposite. ㉚ At sharp left bend, through kissing-gate. Cross park, downhill to A423, left into Henley.

⌒ Henley's elegant bridge was built in 1786. The famous regatta is in July.

🏠 Hambleden Mill, a 17th C. water mill.

🎏 15th-16th C. Yewden Manor.

🍺 The Stag and Huntsman, real ale.

🏠 Hambleden's charmingly clustered cottages date from the 16th C. The manor
🎏 house is 17th C.

🎏 Stonor Park, famous for its Roman Catholic connections: Edmund Campion, the Jesuit martyr, sheltered here during the Tudor religious persecutions. Mass has been celebrated in the chapel for 8 centuries.

🍺 The 18th C. Stonor Arms, real ale.

🎏 Henley Park dates from the 18th C.

For more beechwood walking, try Burnham Beeches, off the A355 N of Burnham, or the beechwoods of Ashridge, approached across Berkhamsted Common. On the Ashridge Estate (Nat. Trust) there is a marked walk starting from the Information Centre at the Bridgewater Monument, outside Aldbury.

The Chess Valley near Chenies competes with those of Turville and Hambleden for wholly delightful walking.

The Thames towpaths are the basis for many easy routes. An attractive stretch can be reached from Cookham.

Walking the escarpment W from Wendover over Coombe Hill is rightly popular.

WALES

PEMBROKESHIRE

The county of Pembrokeshire that was – now but a corner of Dyfed – is a distinct walking entity. It sits on the oldest rocks in Wales. The coastline is correspondingly fretted, indented and studded with bays. It is the only one in Britain to be made a National Park, and the path which follows its cliffs and headlands is truly one of the walking wonders of the world. Its beauty catches the breath despite the gross interruption of Milford Haven, now a major oil terminal, and a pox of caravan sites which cluster as thick as the puffins and guillemots.

Go waterproof, for this is Wales. On the weather maps, the coast shows up as a thin strip of relative dryness – less than 40 inches (102 cm) a year. Locals say the precipitation rises by an inch (2.5 cm) a year for every mile (1.5 km) travelled inland. On top of the Preseli Hills, 70 inches (178 cm) is not uncommon. Inland Pembrokeshire – if you can call it that, for nowhere is more than ten miles (16 km) from salt water – is not always a distinguished landscape. Early daffodils and potatoes flourishing in a warm, moist climate, together with the small farms, remind many of Cornwall. Perhaps the best echoes come from the Preseli Hills, and the line of Norman castles which marks what was formerly the English south from the Welsh north.

Ramsey Sound

6 miles (9.5 km) Sheet 157 735254

Moderate A magnificent, and comparatively trouble-free, section of the Pembrokeshire Coast Path; chance to view the rip tide sweeping through Ramsey Sound, making white water at The Bitches Rocks. From late April to late summer there is a succession of wild flowers. *Sunken lanes, cliff tops, beach, coastal scrub; several short, steep climbs; mud after rain.*

Start From St. David's take the unclassified road signposted 'Lifeboat Station/St. Justinian's. **Parking** on hard shoulder of left verge past T-junction.

Partially waymarked. ① Walk S along the unclassified road, Treffeiddan Moor on the right, continuing straight ahead at crossroads to Porth-clais Harbour. ② Climb the Coast Path, signposted behind the hut, and follow it for about 4½ miles (7 km). ③ Follow the road to ①.

\↑/ Carn Lidi has a Stone Age burial chamber on its N slopes.

🏚 Boia's Rock, the base of Boia, an Irish pirate who operated in St. David's time.

🏚 Porth-clais was the harbour for St. David's, up the River Alun. There are

The black and white razorbill, among the most handsome of this coastline's sea birds; the sharp beak can hold several fish for the young.

some well-reconstructed lime kilns at the harbour head.

\↑/ Skomer Island, a nature reserve noted for its puffins; beyond, out of sight, is Skokholm, famous for its huge Manx shearwater colony.

\↑/ The treacherous Bitches Rocks.

🏚 The ruins of St. Justinian's Chapel, reputedly the 6th C. saint's burial place after his murder on Ramsey Island. Friend and confessor of St. David, he retired there, by tradition because mainland monastery life became too lax.

PEMBROKESHIRE

Scotsborough Woods
4 or 6½ miles (6.5 or 10.5 km)
Sheet 158 118009

Moderate A rewarding woodland walk, much of it using a sound earth track under trees – ideal for dull or wet weather. *Woods, farmland; 2 climbs; mud.*

Start From Tenby take the B4318 and continue ½ mile (0.8 km) to lay-by at Causeway Mill. **Parking** in lay-by; if full, use car park at swimming pool complex at junction of A4319 and B4318, ¼ mile (0.5 km) from ①.

Yellow waymarks. ① Enter Scotsborough Woods by waymarked stone stile or gate and continue on track. ② After ruins of Scotsborough House, turn left (waymarked) into poorly drained area. The track is distinguished by small banks and mature trees. ③ Follow the 3-foot (one km) wide earth track for ¾ mile (one km) through trees to the railway viaduct. ④ For 4-mile route, turn sharp left and follow ⑧ to ⑩. Otherwise pass under railway and go right, following uphill track to A478, passing Woodville Cottage. At road turn left and continue to ⑤ road signposted to Waterwynch Bay: sandy beach at low water, ideal for a picnic. To continue, walk as far as ⑥ caravan site entrances, where take lane leading to Knightston Farm. ⑦

Enter woods on left immediately before farm buildings. ⑧ Pass under bridge again and take track on right, continuing to brook by folly ruins. Cross stile and continue left uphill, joining track (wire gates) to Astridge Farm. ⑨ Turn left downhill on stony track beyond farm buildings. ⑩ Go through metal gate and cross middle of first and second field, using waymarked stiles. After second, continue along wood edge over 3 stiles to join B4318 200 yards (183 m) from ①.

⊳ The ruins date from the Middle Ages; the former owners, the Ap Rhys family, have a memorial in St. Mary's Church, Tenby. The house was once approachable from the sea by a creek.

⚘ The colony of flowers like white bluebells are triangular-stalked garlic flowering May-June. The sloes can be prolific.

⇞ Lundy Island, 30 miles (48 km) out in the Bristol Channel, appears as a low, dark rectangular shape on the horizon.

⇞ The skyline of Tenby, formed mainly in the 19th C. when the town was developed into a seaside resort. Augustus John, the painter, was born there.

⛪ The primitive, but interesting church at Gumfreston can be visited by going through the metal gate and continuing via Gumfreston Farm.

Preseli Top
5 miles (8 km) Sheet 145 075289

Easy A quick route to the roof of the Preseli Hills, with astonishing views; heather, gorse and whortle-berries, at their best in late summer, early autumn. *Heather hillside, woods; one climb; soft peat.*

Start Rosebush, on the B4313. **Parking** in lay-by SW of village.

① Take track signposted 'Unsuitable for Motor Vehicles' on right side of cottage. ② Use detour towards plantation to avoid marshes. ③ Go through metal gate and stock fence. ④ From cairn and trig. point strike out for the small 'cairns' (tumulus). ⑤ Aim NW towards the plantation corner and turn left to follow edge of plantation for ¾ mile (one km). ⑥ Turn left into plantation through the gate and follow signposts for Rosebush back to ①.

⚒ The Preseli Hills are well known as the source for some of the smaller stones at Stonehenge, some 140 miles (225 km) away on Salisbury Plain. Experts think that 2 different types – dolerite and rhyolite – came from 3 separate sites. Among the most ingenious theories on how they were transported such a distance involves the glaciers of the successive ice ages. They could have penetrated far into England, providing a surface on which to haul sledges.

🔟 This is a section of the ancient route to and from Ireland used by the prehistoric peoples centred on Salisbury Plain. The objective was the Wicklow Hills, with their gold and copper. Preseli, a sacred area (as the many cairns, hut circles and burial mounds suggest), must have been an important 'staging post' before the embarkation at Whitesand Bay.

▮ The pub clad in corrugated metal is the sad reminder of attempts to give Rosebush a tourist trade in the late 19th C. Because of the slate mining, the village was already connected with the outside world by railway. To attract visitors, the metal building was erected as a hotel. Two lakes were dug, and advertised as spa waters. The public was not convinced of their curative powers, and the mines failed to prosper.

Three commonly planted conifers seen in Pantmaenog Forest: Norway spruce, left; Japanese larch, centre, and Sitka spruce.

Afon Angof Valley
4 miles (6.5 km) Sheet 145 031316

Moderate Ideal for the solitary walker, mostly on hard surfaces, but with virtually no traffic. *Farmland, valley; one climb.*

Start From Fishguard or Narberth take the B4313 and continue to its junction with the unclassified road signposted Puncheston. **Parking** on verge by road junction.

① From parking walk downhill in direction of Puncheston and take the access track to Penymynydd Mawr Farm. ② From the farmyard go through gate between house and buildings; this leads to a track, which should be followed, hedge on left, past barn to reach metal gate into field. Go through and follow footpath round edge of fields to arrive at stream. In absence of bridge and stile, cross the wire. ③ Take the sunken access track left of the buildings to cross concrete cattle pound. At farm access drive, cross and continue 150 yards (137 m) by track to field gate. Through it, turn right (uphill) and continue to where gate gives on to grassy track. Continue on this past field intersections (3 gates) to junction with wider grassy track. ④ Turn left downhill and continue on lane to village. (There is a short cut to ① through the cemetery.) At junction of Green Lane and metalled road, turn left

Common buzzard attitudes: gliding (top), gaining height (left) and soaring (right).

and continue on road to Glyn Helyg Farm. ⑤ Turn right on to track and go through gate leading to bridge over river. Cross and ⑥ take track along valley. After starting to climb hillside, at sharp left bend go through gate on right to follow track across 2 fields and reach farm. Continue on surfaced track leading uphill to road at metal gate. ⑦ Turn left and continue on road to ①.

🍷 Drover's Arms; bar food.

🦅 Buzzards likely to be seen: habitual soarers, as many as 20 may wheel together in great circles.

🔟 The graveyard of the neglected Morvil church contains an early Christian stone with a cross and circle symbol.

Cych Valley
6 miles (9.5 km) Sheet 145 240360

Moderate Comparatively sheltered in contrast to other walks in this section but still with a feeling of space. *Farmland, plantations, woods, hillside; one climb.*

Start From the A478 at Crymmych or the B4332 at Boncath, take the road to Bwlch-y-groes. **Parking** on verge by village sign 150 yards (137 m) E of crossroads.

① From crossroads go through ornamental gate-posts and follow track downhill towards Blaenpistyll Farm. Continue past farm access by grassy track to road. ② Enter Economic Forestry Group plantation by small gate. After ¾ mile (one km) take right fork to reach lake. ③ Continue round to lakeside cottage. Walk behind house to see waterfall; continue by house access track to road. ④ Turn right downhill on to minor road, taking left fork to Cych Valley. Turn right and continue ¾ mile to reach Bridge Cottage, under trees. ⑤ Go through metal gate by side of house, and at rear of house cross bar stile to follow track through woods. Turn right at metal gate to farm. ⑥ Go through farmyard (may be temporary gates) to sunken lane; continue by road to Clydey church. Turn right and ⑦ go through farmyard to the centre of 3 gates and

continue uphill, following left side of hedge through 2 fields. ⑧ Pass ruined cottage on left and bear slightly right across field to fence. Then cross gate stile to join road by village school. Turn left for ①.

Ffynone House is an example of the early work of John Nash, one of a few houses he designed in Pembrokeshire. It was built in the early 1790s for the banker Sir Benjamin Hammett, some 20 years before Nash reached the height of his fame working for the Prince Regent on Brighton Pavilion and, among other famous London landmarks, creating the palatial terraces of Regent's Park.

Ffynone is not obviously the architect's work: the S front was redesigned in the early 19th C., and there was extensive remodelling in 1904. But his characteristic elegance is preserved in the hall and vestibule ceilings, the staircase and the drawing room. (House not open to the public.)

The Afon (River) Dulas joins the Afon Cych downstream, which later flows into the Teifi, which, with the Tywi, is the Pembrokeshire area's main river.

The tower of Clydey's church is Norman; there is a splendid font and a stone carved with a very early script.

137

PEMBROKESHIRE

Gwaun Valley

4 or 8½ miles (6.5 or 13.5 km)
Sheet 145 035350

Moderate Dramatic changes of mood as the route changes sides of the valley. *Plantations, moorland, woods; 2 climbs; mud; soft peat.*

Start Take the unclassified road running through the Gwaun valley. **Car park** (Forestry Commission) at Sychbant.

Partially waymarked. ① From rear of picnic site follow path uphill along right side of stream. After ½ mile (0.8 km) enter plantation by waymarked stile. ② Turn right immediately; continue on path with fence on right, ignoring left-hand track after 100 yards (91 m), by Forestry Commission signpost, to stile at limit of plantation – about ½ mile. Then follow grassy track to

fence and metal gate at roadside. ③ Continue E along rear of Bedd Morris Stone Car Park, with fence on right. Follow fence across Carningli Common, turning left at waymarked post, then right. At second small metal gate, with Carnedward Rocks on right, locate ④ poorly defined animal track immediately to left of rocks. Continue on this downhill through 5 fields and gates to bridleway at Pen-rhiw, where ⑤ turn right through waymarked gate downhill, with stream – likely to be wet. Exit on to road. For shorter version, turn right back to ①. To continue ⑥ enter wood by waymarked metal gate and follow well-defined path. ⑦ Climb steeply by cascades to metal gate and continue straight ahead along right edge of field. Turn right along road, crossing bridge over stream. Immediately after bridge ⑧ turn on to access track to Gernor and cross river by ford or footbridge, uphill. ⑨ Skirt farm anti-clockwise, cross stream and go

PEMBROKESHIRE

through gate (waymarked on reverse side of tree). Continue straight up sunken lane and cross waymarked gate. Turn right immediately; after ½ mile cross gate and continue on farm track. Go through farm; bear slightly left on to moor to corner of field. Continue 100 yards (91 m) with fence on left and ⑩ cross fence at junction with second fence leading up from valley and ruins. Follow this fence downhill. At ruins, join well-defined grassy track downhill to road. ⑪ Turn left and continue to ⑫.

⁂ Bedd Morris, a ritual standing stone.

⁂ The hut circles date from about 200 B.C.

⩗ Carnedward Rocks, raised volcanically.

\↑/ The slopes of Carningli feature a stone hill fort and hut circles.

Below, the hill fort on Carningli.

The rocky promontory of Dinas Head, 4 miles (6.5 km) E of Fishguard, has some fine coastal paths and a wildlife trail. Access via village of Rhos Dinas.

West of Fishguard there is walking over the Pen-caer Peninsula to Mathry, where buses run back to Fishguard.

A few miles SW of Tenby there are trails at Penally and Lydstep, the latter with caverns to visit.

A trail for industrial enthusiasts showing wool manufacture up to the 1930s is at Dres-Fach Felindre off the A484 E of Newcastle Emlyn.

There are 3 forest trails round the Hafod Estate, 2 miles (3 km) SE of Devil's Bridge.

Bosherton's tranquil ponds, 5 miles (8 km) S of Pembroke off the B4319, are the start of several routes.

BRECON BEACONS
AND
BLACK MOUNTAINS

There is no finer mountain profile in all Britain than the firm but gentle tilt of the Brecon Beacons' three chief peaks, Pen y Fan and its slightly lower neighbours, Corn Dû and Cribin. As crows, or rather buzzards, fly, little more than a mile separates the three summits. They thus provide a classic ridge walk, but a tough one with hundreds of feet dropping and climbing between the high points. Don't try it in bad weather. The north face of these mountains is scooped out into great *cwms*; the one between Pen y Fan and Corn Dû is called King Arthur's Chair. To the south the slopes of these red sandstone mountains decline more gently towards the coal valleys of South Wales.

The Black Mountains are separated from the Beacons proper by the valley of the Usk. They face north-west on to the deep and winding valley of the Wye. Lovely as that river is, many find the little streams that hurry down the slip slope of these hills even more attractive. All this is set within the protection of the Brecon Beacons National Park, which also embraces mountains stretching west into what used to be Carmarthenshire and the easy strolling of the towpath beside the Monmouthshire and Brecon Canal.

Ysgyryd Fawr – the Holy Mountain
2½ miles (4 km) Sheet 161 329164

Moderate An isolated hill – one of the 3 dominant peaks of Abergavenny – with an unusual shape, fine views and strange legends. Offers a splendid ridge walk, over a mile (1.5 km) long, leading gently to the summit. *Farmland, woods, ridge, rocky valley; 2 climbs; mud.*

Start From Abergavenny take the B4521 NE. Continue 3 miles (5 km). **Car park** (small) on road.

① From car park cross stile and follow side of field to reach a stile. ② Follow path via steps through plantation to reach stile. ③ Turn right to reach waymarked path leading to ridge above. Follow crest of ridge to reach trig. point. ④ Descend the steep N slope with care to reach valley below. ⑤ Turn left and follow path through valley and woods to join outward route at ③.

🏚 On the W side of Ysgyryd Fawr there are steep cliffs where a massive landslip left a deep cutting. Local legend has it that this was made by Noah's Ark passing over the mountain, or by an earthquake at the time of the Crucifixion.

※ To the S of the summit there are traces of the defensive ramparts of an Iron Age hill fort.

The Holy Mountain, its S ridge leading off to the right.

↑ The Black Mountains, through the Vale of Usk towards Herefordshire and across Gwent to the Bristol Channel.

🏛 The site of the medieval Chapel of St. Michael, with 2 upright stones marking the entrance. It was used until the 17th C., and is the most likely explanation of why the mountain is called Holy.

141

BRECON BEACONS AND BLACK MOUNTAINS

Crib y Garth – the Cat's Back
5 miles (8 km) Sheet 161 288328

Moderate An easy walk with a big mountain feel and superb views for little effort; an interesting section where the ridge narrows, becoming a series of rocky steps. *Ridge, plateau, valley; one climb; mud.*

Start From Longtown take the road to Llanveynoe and then up the Olcho Valley. **Car park** at foot of Cat's Back.

① From car park cross stile and head up slope. Soon reach the ridge. ② Continue along ridge, where the gradient is easier. It becomes rocky and narrow for a few hundred yards, then broadens into Black Hill, marked by a trig. point, where ③ follow well-worn path NW and descend to the head of the Olcho Valley. ④ Turn SE and descend the valley to reach road. ⑤ Follow road to ①.

This short E ridge of the Black Mountains is known locally as the Cat's Back, and from a certain angle it does vaguely resemble a sleeping cat. The narrow ridge is similar to that of Ysgyryd Fawr (see page 141).

The Black Mountains are so-called because from the Hereford side they almost always seem black. Like the Beacons they are made of Old Red Sandstone; it can be glimpsed through the screen of gorse and heather.

To the W is the long Hatterrall Ridge which carries Offa's Dyke Long Distance Path over 160 miles (257 km) from Sedbury to Prestatyn in N Wales (see pages 328-334). E are the plains of Herefordshire and NE, in the far distance, the Clent Hills, near Birmingham.

BRECON BEACONS AND BLACK MOUNTAINS

Waun Fâch and Pen y Gader-Fawr
9½ miles (15 km) Sheet 161 251286

Moderate Right into the heart of the Black Mountains, with quite a gradual ascent to their 2 highest peaks; pick a clear day – dramatic views. *Farmland, reservoir, mountain paths, high plateau, streamside; 3 climbs; mud. If inexperienced in hill walking, do not attempt in poor visibility.*

Start From Abergavenny follow minor road to hamlet of Fforest Coal Pit, then continue straight on to enter Grwyne Fawr Valley. Follow road to **parking** at picnic site about 6½ miles (10.5 km) from Fforest Coal Pit, just after road crosses to right of stream.

① From near the picnic site follow a wide track leading up to the Grwyne Fawr Reservoir. ② Continue past the reservoir following a path near the Grwyne Fawr stream to reach the N escarpment of the Black Mountains. ③ Turn left to follow track leading over Pen y Manllwyn and on to the summit plateau of Waun Fâch. ④ Continue about one mile (1.5 km) along well-worn path to the hump of Pen y Gader-Fawr, where the summit is marked by a cairn. ⑤ Descend to the edge of a forestry plantation on the left and follow track down beside a stream to the valley below. Follow the Grwyne Fawr river to the right and ⑥ ford shallow stream near picnic site to return to ① .

⚑ Foundations of a village built to house those who constructed the Grwyne Fawr Reservoir, started 1912.

⊷ The reservoir, with its graceful dam, holds 376m. gallons (1,709m. litres).

⩟ Waun Fâch – meaning small bog – is the highest point of the Black Mountains.

BRECON BEACONS AND
BLACK MOUNTAINS

The Llanthony Circuit
12 miles (19 km) Sheet 161 312222

Energetic Varied walking with fine views taking in 2 ridges of the Black Mountains and some historic ruins. *Mountain ridges; mountain valley; 2 climbs; mud.*

Start From the A465 at Llanfihangel Crucorney take the B4423 for Llanthony. In 2 miles (3 km) stop at the Queen's Head Inn. **Parking** near Queen's Head.

① From the Inn take lane leading uphill to reach a metal gate giving access to open hillside. ② Continue along track to reach Dialgorreg stone. ③ Follow crest of ridge to reach the tall cairn of Garn-wen. ④ Continue on this track until reaching another cairn at Bal-bach. ⑤ Turn right and shortly ⑥ take the right-hand track leading down into Cwm Bwchel. On reaching stile ⑦ follow waymarked path past farmhouse and down through a dingle to reach a metal footbridge. Cross and continue into Llanthony village. ⑧ Follow lane up to Llanthony Priory and cross stile by Abbey Farm. Continue around rear of Priory beside long, stone wall to reach a stile. Go diagonally up through field to reach stile near right corner. Continue uphill through woods to stile. Go straight up field to another stile. ⑨ Turn right to follow well-worn track, soon gently climbing the hillside. On reaching crest of ridge ⑩ turn right and follow Offa's Dyke over Hatterrall Hill, past

Llanthony: the South Tower and the Prior's House contain a hotel.

a trig. point and down to the embankments of Pentwyn fort. On reaching metal gate take road downhill to ⑪ cottage on left, from which take track on right leading down through trees. At road turn right. At next junction ⑫ turn left and follow road back to ①.

🍺 The Queens Head, some 300 years old.

📷 The tall, beautifully symmetrical cairn is craftsman made.

🏛 Llanthony Priory, an Augustinian house, was founded in the early 12th C. In the 15th C. the monks tired of the harsh local weather and built a second Llanthony in Gloucester. The poet Walter Savage Landor bought the ruin in 1802 with romantic dreams of restoring it – but did not succeed.

📷 This path was christened *rhin crw* – beer track – because monks may have used it to transport beer between the Priory and Longtown.

📷 A section of Offa's Dyke long distance path (see pages 328-334); here, it does not follow the earthwork built in the 6th C. by King Offa of Mercia.

🌿 Iron Age Pentwyn Fort; fine views.

BRECON BEACONS AND BLACK MOUNTAINS

The Brecon Beacons Horseshoe

8 miles (13 km) Sheet 160 032179

Energetic A satisfying day's walking, particularly for those visiting the area for the first time: it takes in the Beacons' highest and most shapely summits. By any standards this is dramatic walking with an impressive traverse of Corn Dû, Pen y Fan and Cribin. Possibly best in autumn, when the route is less crowded and the colouring highly attractive. *Ancient way, mountain ridges, plateau, escarpment; 3 climbs; mud. Do not attempt in poor visibility without a 1:25,000 map and compass.*

Start From the A465 at Cein-coed-y-cymmer take the minor road via Pontsticill to the Neuadd Reservoirs. **Parking** near Taf Fechan Water Board buildings.

① From parking area follow fence to right to reach a track. Turn left, cross stile and follow path beside fence. By metal gate head upwards to join Roman road. ② Turn left and follow this ancient way to its highest point, known as The Gap. ③ Climb path on the left leading to summit of Cribin. ④ Descend the W slopes to a col and then climb steeply to the summit of Pen y Fan following well-worn path. Cross the summit plateau to reach the trig. point. ⑤ Follow path to the SW, descending at first, then climbing to the summit of Corn Dû. ⑥ Descend on the SW side of Corn Dû to Bwlch Duwynt and follow escarpment via Craig Gwaun-taf and Craig Fan-ddu to the trig. point at Twyn Mwyalchod. ⑦ Retrace steps and follow track steeply downhill to left edge of plantation. Follow side of plantation to more gentle ground below. Head across to a wooden gate giving access to right of way across the dam. Follow path up to metal gate and return to ①.

🚉 The twin reservoirs are fed by Taf Fechan.

📖 This ancient route crossing the Beacons may be of Roman origin.

🗻 Cribin is a shapely peak, sometimes called the Welsh Matterhorn – a title shared with Cricht in Snowdonia. The steep N ridge is known as The Snout.

↕️ Pen y Fan: see opposite page. (Take care on the edge of the NE face.)

↕️ Corn Dû: see opposite page. A Bronze Age burial mound was excavated here some years ago.

🗻 The long and beautiful valley passed on the W side of the 'Horseshoe' is Cwm Crew. Notice the moraine – glacial debris – near its top end.

Pen y Fan from Cwm-llwch
6 miles (9.5 km) Sheet 160 007245

Energetic One of the most interesting ways of climbing this famous mountain – the highest in S Wales. The beautiful lake of Llyn-cwm-llwch comes as a pleasant surprise for those who have not been this way before. *Wooded valley, open mountainside and ridges; 4 climbs; mud. See warnings on page 11.*

Start Take the Ffrwdgrech road opposite the Drovers' Arms on the W side of Brecon. At fork take the middle road of the 3 and after crossing stream bear left off road; go straight over the crossroad and on to the track. **Parking** in clearing after gate.

① Follow track to reach a stile near Cwm-llwch Cottage. ② Continue on track uphill, forking left at second cairn, to reach lake. ③ Ascend track on right to gain ridge and obelisk. ④ Follow ridge to summit of Corn Du. ⑤ Continue NE to reach summit of Pen y Fan. From trig. point follow path on left. ⑥ Continue about one mile (1.5 km) along ridge and ⑦ descend from crest of ridge over open country to reach outward route near Cwm-llwch Cottage.

〰️ Llyn-cwm-llwch, created by glaciation, is reputed to be bottomless: in fact it is 60 feet (18 m) deep at the centre.

📖 The Tommy Jones Obelisk tells a tragic and mystifying tale.

↕️ Corn Dû and Pen y Fan are the highest peaks of the Beacons, and of S Wales. Views range from the nearby Black Mountains to the Preseli Hills in the W to Cader Idris (NW) and Exmoor (S) – but conditions have to be near-perfect.

🐦 Dozens of ravens frequent the summit. Distinguish them from crows by their massive size and slightly pointed tails.

Hay-on-Wye is a starting point for walks S into the Black Mountains and N into Radnor Forest.

At Ystradfellte, 6 miles NE of the A465 at Glynneath, a popular walk starts from the car park; waterfalls.

The Brecon-Abergavenny Canal is beautiful walking.

NORTH WALES

This is no mere region, but a nation in miniature. For here is the stronghold of the Welsh language; a coastline which arguably includes the finest estuary in Europe (the Mawddach); fertile farmland (Anglesey and the Vale of Clwyd) and, above all, range upon range of mountains. It is pointless to name them all, but there is one for everybody.

There is Snowdon itself, whose summit is the highest slum in England and Wales; however, work has been done in recent years aimed at tidying it up. For the inexperienced, the railway climbs almost to the top and there are five paths to walk up. At the other extreme of difficulty are the tough, rough Rhinogs, running south towards Dollgellau. Beyond them is Cader Idris, and running north-east from that lovely mountain are the Arans and the Berwyns, also held in highest regard by connoisseurs of upland beauty.

Next to Snowdon across the Llanberis Pass are the Glyders and fierce Tryfan, and then beyond Llyn Ogwen are the Garneddau, a superlative range extending almost to the north coast, unbroken by pass or road and thus the preserve of those on foot. Carnedd Llywelyn is only 80 feet (24 m) lower than Snowdon. From it survey the country eastwards beyond the Conwy Valley, the Denbighshire Moors, and the Clwyd Hills, nearly in England.

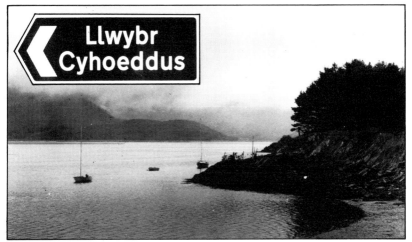

Mawddach Estuary
3 miles (5 km) Sheet 124 636142

Moderate A short but fairly energetic walk with views of the Mawddach Estuary and Barmouth, also the Rhinog mountains. A short detour takes in Llynnau Cregennen, 2 small lakes held by the National Trust. Best views are obtained when the trees are bare. *Woods, farmland; one climb.*

Start On A493 Dolgellau to Twywn road, about ½ mile (0.8 km) outside the village of Arthog on Twywn side. Buses. **Parking** in large lay-by below village school.

① The route is signposted by school. Follow the very steep track up through woods, passing some remote cottages and eventually reaching ② a single-track lane. To extend the walk, bear right and follow the lane past the farm. Just beyond farm a track leads down to the left; follow this to Llynnau Cregennen. To continue, turn left at the lane and go steeply downhill. ③ At the main road turn left and after ¼ mile (0.4 km) take the marked footpath to the right. Follow it ½ mile (0.8 km) across the Arthog bog. At edge of estuary, go left along driveway and then old railway trackbed to A493. Return to the car park.

\t/ From the railway and footbridge there is a sweeping view of the estuary which William Wordsworth called 'sublime'.

The Mawddach Estuary and, inset, a reminder of the Welsh for public footpath.

\\ The woods above Arthog are a home for many warblers, including the little chiffchaff, which gets its name from its song; the green and yellow wood warbler; and the black cap, often called the northern nightingale.

\t/ Inland from Llynnau Cregennen the heights of Cader Idris are seen: Cader means Chair of; Idris was a legendary warrior-bard.

NORTH WALES

Nant-y-Gamar Woods

3½ miles (5.5 km) Sheets 115 and 116 795821

Easy A rich and varied section of countryside, still unspoilt though close to Llandudno. Fine views of coast, town, mountains and of Anglesey. Much interest – the old tracks are largely 15th C. or earlier; there are rare limestone flowers, butterflies in profusion and plenty of birdlife. *Farmland, woods, heath; one climb; mud.*

Start Walk or drive along the Llandudno promenade to Craig-y-Don; frequent buses. **Parking** on seafront close to County Hotel.

① Walk down Queen's Road, past shops and a small park. ② Past entrance to North Wales Medical Centre turn left up stony track. ③ Turn right then left along track at bottom of wood. ④ Go through gate on to limestone pasture, and walk up hill to next gate ⑤. Go through gate and follow track through oak woods past Gloddaeth Hall. ⑥ Bear left along path up through Nant-y-Gamar woods. ⑦ Emerge on to Nant-y-Gamar hill. Turn right along wall. ⑧ At end of wall go through gate and turn left past small farm. Walk down farm road. ⑨ Take path leading down through woods down to Bodafon Road, then follow road to seafront.

♣ The woody plants in the hedge show that the track is from 400 to 500 years old. Since each species takes about a hundred years to become established .

⑲ In 1980, silver coins, minted in Chester and dated 1034, in Canute's reign, were found by the path and valued at £20,000.

✖ Many butterfly species (spring, early summer) including speckled woods, gatekeepers and meadow browns.

♤ The trees beside the track are holm oaks, the evergreen variety, with small, dark green leaves, bright green acorns and tassels of tiny yellow flowers.

▦ Gloddaeth Hall, a 15th C. building, was once the home of the Mostyn family, still large landowners in the area.

↘ Birds in the open country include ravens, buzzards and the stonechat, whose alarm call sounds like pebbles knocking together.

Conwy Mountain and the Sychnant Pass

10½ miles (17 km) Sheet 115 783774

Moderate Magnificent views, prehistoric interest, birdlife, plants and marvellous air – a unique blend of sea breezes and mountain winds. Best in spring to autumn – the upland areas really are bleak in winter. *Town, moorland, farmland; 2 climbs; mud after rain.*

Start Conwy, on the A55; frequent buses; trains to Llandudno Junction, about one mile (1.5 km) across river. **Car parks** in Conwy.

① Take the A55 (Bangor road) out of Conwy, passing through arch in town walls. After 150 yards (137 m) cross narrow railway bridge and turn right. Around left hand bend, turn right into Mountain Road on the right. ② At end of terrace of cottages take the footpath uphill. ③ Follow the path on the inland side of the ridge. At end of ridge follow path round small hill, then inland. ④ With farm on right, head downhill and keep straight on until the Sychnant Pass road is reached. ⑤ Cross road and take signposted footpath. Shortly after lake a stony track is reached. Follow this round to the right, and continue on it as it wanders uphill and across open country, tending to bear right, eventually ⑥ reaching point where wooded ravine can be seen ahead, together with small farm at edge of wood. Keeping farm to the right, follow track to left up a small valley. ⑦ This track meets another from the left; turn right. Follow the grassy track beside a stone wall across the hills. After ¾ mile (one km) ⑧ go through a couple of gates on to metalled, single-track lane. Continue downhill. ⑨ At telephone box, turn left downhill. ⑩ Turn right at T-junction and walk to Henrydd. ⑪ In the village turn left. In ½ mile (0.8 km) ⑫ take the lane to the left. ⑬ At Groesffordd turn right. ⑭ After ½ mile (0.8 km) take track to left, just before a row of cottages, and marked 'Unsuitable for Motor Vehicles'. ⑮ Having climbed steep hill this track eventually crosses the Conwy-Penmaenmawr road. Cross and go down the track opposite which runs into the valley. ⑯ Bear right along the bottom of the valley until reaching Mountain Road.

Castell Caer Seion, covering 10½ acres (4 ha), is one of the many Iron Age forts in the area.

⌇ The view encompasses Anglesey and Conwy Bay.

🗡 On the wilder sections of the route there is a chance of seeing peregrines, a fine falcon which now nests on the cliffs and hills of North Wales. Most notable of its characteristics is the dramatic 'stoop' after prey, a near-vertical dive during which it reaches speeds of as high as 200 mph (320 km/h). Choughs, a rare crow with curved red bill and red legs, can also be seen on this walk.

Bronze Age stone circles, standing stones and burial chambers are seen close to the route.

🚩 The castle, now a splendid ruin, was built in 1283-6 by Edward I, part of a chain intended to pacify the Welsh.

NORTH WALES

Gwydyr Forest
3½ miles (5.5 km) Sheet 115 792568

Easy Fine views of Snowdonia; woodland with a variety of interest from rare birds to disused lead mines. *Riverside, woods, meadow; 2 climbs; mud. If inexperienced in hill walking, avoid in poor visibility.*

Start from the A5 turn on to the B5106 (Betws-y-Coed to Llanrwst road); trains to Betws-y-Coed, ¼ mile (0.4 km) away from start. **Public car park** past bridge on left, very shortly after turning on to B5106.

①From car park take path beside river. ②At massive rock, just before end of wood, bear away from river and follow path diagonally uphill through fir wood. Continue to bungalow seen ahead. ③At metalled forest road turn left and carry on past farm. In about ½ mile (0.8 km), at bend in road, take path running to right. (If you reach Forestry Commission parking notices you have gone too far.) ④ Cross stile into meadow and follow painted footpath markers. Follow path across 2 stiles. ⑤At Forestry road turn right. ⑥ At T-junction go straight on. ⑦ At next T-junction bear left and cross metalled road. ⑧ At Y-junction go left and keep straight on, passing end of Llyn Park lake. ⑨ Very shortly after turn right at next T-junction, then bear right down path after 25 yards (23 m). Follow stream into ravine, past Aberllyn lead mine workings. ⑩ Take lower path, with Conwy valley on left. ⑪ Return to car park.

🐦 In the thickest parts of the Forest lives the goldcrest, 3½ inches (9 cm) long, the smallest Bird, with willow-green plumage and a gold crown bounded by black stripes. Redpolls, siskins and crossbills are all pine forest finches now often to be seen in Gwydyr Forest.

↓ The Forest has a rare inhabitant, the pine marten, distinguishable from the squirrel by its slim build, bushy tail and light under-parts. Other mammals include the polecat, much commoner, not such a climber and looking like a short-legged black cat.

🪨 Aberllyn mine, worked for much-needed lead ore in the Napoleonic Wars, is now disused. It is possible to find small quantities of the ore – cubic in shape and silvery in colour – in the spoil heaps.

Porth Ysgo and Hell's Mouth
9½ miles (15.3 km) Sheet 123 207267

Moderate A walk for viewing coastal scenery, some of it wild. Goes through an area covered with an ancient pattern of small, well-enclosed fields. Particularly spectacular with a westerly gale blowing, driving the sea into Hell's Mouth. *Cliffs, shore, farmland, common; one climb.*

Start From Aberdaron take the steep road signposted Rhiw. At crossroads with telephone kiosk turn right and drive down lane to deserted Ysgo Farm. **Car park** marked at Ysgo Farm.

①From car park take path marked to Porth Ysgo. From beach retrace to Y-junction and take ②path running straight inland through kissing-gate. This joins the lane at a T-junction. Turn right. ③At next junction turn right and follow the road up to Y Rhiw village. ④Turn left at the crossroads. Take the next left, then ⑤ turn right up the metalled track leading past transmitting station. ⑥ At cattle grid go straight on through field gateway and follow the track to the summit of Mynydd Rhiw. From the summit follow the track down to the lane and ⑦turn left. ⑧At the T-junction turn left and continue to bear left. After 1¾ miles (2.6 km) ⑨turn right then after a few yards left and immediately after right. Continue along this lane and ⑩ turn left at the next T-junction. Follow this lane down to ⑪ the road junction with the telephone kiosk, cross the lane and return to the car park.

〣 Hell's Mouth has been the scene of many wrecks during SW gales.

↑ From Mynydd Rhiw there is a fine view of the bay of Hell's Mouth and the whole Lleyn Peninsula, with Bardsey Island at its tip, reached by boat from Aberdaron. Bardsey is called the Island of a Thousand Saints: it was a place of pilgrimage from about the 5th C., when St. Cadfan founded its first monastery. It is a bird sanctuary (rare migrants) and nature reserve – good views of seals.

↓ Many hares, stoats and weasels.

🍺 At Aberdaron there are 2 agreeable pubs, the Ship and Ty Newydd Hotels.

Turf-covered stone walls of the Lleyn Peninsula create a landscape unlike any other in North Wales.

NORTH WALES

Vale of Llangollen
5 miles (8 km) Sheet 117 215423

Moderate Aspects of Wales not covered by the other routes in this section: part of the Telford Canal towpath, and glimpses of early Welsh history. *Canal-side, hillside; 2 climbs.*

Start Llangollen, on the A5; frequent buses.
Parking in the centre of Llangollen, preferably near the bridge.

① At the N end of the bridge walk up to the Canal Museum, then walk E along the towpath, past stone bridge and pass under road bridge. ② Walk up beside next stone bridge and cross canal. ③ Cross road and follow lane up beside Sun Trevor Hotel. A few yards on take signposted public footpath to left. At junction of paths go right, up to the lane and ④ turn left following lane uphill, along edge of Creigiau Eglwyseg escarpment. ⑤ After about 300 yards (274 m) from Y-junction turn down lane to left, over cattle grid. Cross stile ⑥ and follow path as it crosses meadow and rises very steeply to Castell Dinas Bran. ⑦ On far side of ruins follow zigzag path downhill to end of wooded lane. ⑧ Follow path down to Llangollen.

⌂ Canal Exhibition Centre, with horse-drawn canal trips.

Thomas Telford and one of his greatest civil engineering feats, Pont Cysyllte aqueduct.

🔟 The Shropshire Union Canal was one of Thomas Telford's greatest engineering feats. The famous aqueduct carrying it over the Dee 3½ miles (5.5 km) to the E is more than 1,000 feet (305 m) long.

🦅 Kingfishers are seen around the canal.

〽 Eglwyseg Rocks – limestone terraces.

🦅 The woods are notable for pied fly-catchers, redstarts and woodpeckers.

🏛 Castell Dinas Bran was first an Iron Age hill fort, then a wooden castle, in the 13th
↑/ C. a stone building, and a ruin by the late 1500s. The view is of Valle Crucis Abbey.

Aberdovey

7½ miles (12 km) Sheet 135 613959

Moderate Covers one of North Wales' most beautiful estuaries, with terrain akin to downland that contrasts to other routes in this section. Spectacular on fine days with the shadows of clouds sweeping across the hills; grand views of the coast towards Aberystwyth with the sea rolling in. *Hillsides, lakeside, farmland, woods, upland grazing; 2 climbs; mud after rain.*

Start Aberdovey on the A493; frequent buses; trains – Aberdovey is on the Cambrian coastline. **Car park** on the front.

① From car park walk up Copper Walk Street ②. The route runs steeply uphill, inland, first through a modern housing estate, then up a narrow lane ③near to brow of hill. Turn right, follow track across hills. In about 2 miles (3 km) go through gate and continue on well-defined track about one mile (1.5 km) to Lyn Barfog. ④ Going down to the lake take the track which runs to the left. ⑤ Follow the path down to lane in valley, past farmhouse dated 1741. Turn left along the lane and continue to group of houses on left, where ⑥go down drive past houses and through gate. ⑦Cross footbridge and turn right, following cart track up through woods on to open country (track

very muddy after wet weather). ⑧ Keep to cart track, passing several gates. Near top of hill, pass through gate and follow indistinct course of track diagonally right across field ⑨ to where gate can be seen on skyline. ⑩ Passing through 3 gates, a sunken lane is reached. ⑪ Contine down lane to reach outward route and return to ①.

🏚 Aberdovey, popula'r today for small boat sailing, was a ship-building centre in the days of the sailing ships. These are recalled in the Outward Bound Sailing Museum on the waterfront.

↑/ From the hills there is a splendid view of the Dovey Estuary, one of the most beautiful in Wales, and of the long sweep of the coast towards Aberystwyth.

🦅 Birds conspicuous in the area during summer include skylarks, wheatears and redstarts. The skylark is often no more than a speck in the sky, pouring out song, but when it is at close range, starting up suddenly from the ground, it shows its white outer tail feathers and even its crest, though this is often flat. Grey-brown wheatears catch the eye by flirting their black and white tails. Their colours are much more subdued than those of the beautiful male redstart, with his blue-grey back, black throat and russet-orange breast and tail.

NORTH WALES

Bala Lake and Glyn Gower
5½ miles (9 km) Sheet 125 903322

Moderate Provides a picture of the country round Bala, the largest natural lake in Wales. *Valley, hillsides, plantations, lakeside; one climb; parts of the forest are wet; keep to the public footpaths.*

Start From Bala take the B4391, turning right on to the B4403. Continue about 3 miles (5 km) to Llangower; lake train to Llangower from Bala, summer only. **Public car park** at Llangower.

① From car park turn left along road; 200 yards (182 m) past the church ② turn right and follow the lane and track all the way up the valley, finally reaching a remote farm. ③ Walk directly across front of farmhouse and take the path which swings around uphill immediately behind the house. ④ Follow marked path on to top of hill. Ruined cottages will be seen. Cross to them, with ruins on left, follow old wall and fence uphill, keeping wall on left. ⑤ The entrance to plantation is reached. Follow path straight ahead through trees. ⑥ Climb stile and follow path alongside wire fence. ⑦ Cross stile on right, taking path through dense trees. ⑧ A firebreak is reached (wide gap in trees). Walk downhill along this firebreak, ignoring path to left. ⑨ A forest road is reached. Turn left. Walk downhill, eventually reaching the original route up Glyn Gower, and, in about ½ mile (0.8 km) the B4403. Cross the road and follow the track ⑩ to the lakeside and car park.

〰 Bala Lake is the largest natural lake in Wales 3¾ miles (6 km) long and ½ mile (0.8 km) wide. It is located in glacier-cut basin Llyn Tregid. The surrounding hill country has fine walking: the many gates across the roads mark the boundaries of the various sheep walks. The River Dee flows out of it, giving it–and the town nearby–their name, for *bala* is Welsh for 'outlet'.

🖽 The Lake railway (opened 1972) follows the course of the old line from Ruabon to Barmouth, which closed in 1965.

Ⅴ The lake contains its own, distinct fish species, the gwyniad. Its ancestors are likely to have been sea-freshwater

Though a distinct species, the Bala gwyniad is one of the whitefish family, with 7 other roughly similar members in various U.K. lakes and lochs. It is rarely caught.

migrants of the salmon family, land-locked by ice during the glacial eras. The lake is also rich in perch, pike, roach, grayling and brown trout.

Ⅴ There are sweeping views from the top of the Glyn Gower hills.

Newborough Warren and Llanddwyn Island

6½ miles (10.5 km) Sheet 114 423656

Easy A stretch of remote coastline on Anglesey with magnificent views of Snowdonia; geology and natural history. *Village, forest, shore, dunes; short stretches among the dunes may be boggy.*

Start Newborough, off the A5, along the A4080 at the S corner of Anglesey; buses. **Parking** in Newborough village.

① From crossroads at centre of village take the road marked to 'Beach and Llanddwyn Island'. ② Immediately before the church take the path to the right, then passing behind the church, cross the meadow, bearing right. ③ Follow the path through the forest out on to the beach. ④ If tide permits, walk across the beach to Llanddwyn Island. If water is high, it drops after about one hour sufficiently to cross. Follow the path to the lighthouse and point. ⑤ Retrace steps to ④, then turn right to walk along the beach until level with the end of the forest. (Do not go up to the car park area half-way along this stretch.) ⑥ Walk along the edge of the Forest with the warren on the right; follow the path until it reaches a narrow lane running down from the higher ground on the left. ⑦ Walk up this to ⑧ the road. Return to village.

🏛 Newborough's charter and its English name were conferred by Edward I.

⚒ The island's rocks are some of the oldest in Britain – Precambrian, formed about 600 million years ago.

🦅 Shags and cormorants nest on the island, and terns and gulls are plentiful. Ringed plovers nest on the beach – if not disturbed. In the Warren are harriers and short-eared owls.

🌸 The Warren and Island are parts of a nature reserve famous for its flora. There is a tremendous variety of plant life to be found all along the route - meadow, forest, dune and sea cliff species abound.

NORTH WALES

The Roman Steps and Llyn Cwm Bychan

12 miles (19 km) Sheet 124 622299

Energetic Crosses the Rhinogs, whose rocky, shattered terrain is unique in Snowdonia. *Wooded lane, lakesides, rocky mountain terrain, forest, moorland, farmland, riverside; one climb; some sections are extremely boggy – strong waterproof footwear essential at all times; dress well – passes through exposed country.*

Start In Harlech turn into the steep, narrow road beside Barclay's Bank. Continue ¾ mile (one km) to crossroads (telephone box). Go straight across and continue 2 miles (3 km). Turn left and continue to marked **car park** and picnic place.

① From car park turn right and follow lane uphill. ② Take the signposted path to the right. ③ Follow track, first through oak woods, then across open country. ④ After climbing Roman Steps, a rocky cairn is reached at the summit of the path. Ahead a forest can be seen. Climb down from the cairn to clearly defined path in gully to left and follow this path to a stile into the forest. ⑤ Climb the stile and follow path, initially through dense trees, then down firebreak (avenue in trees). Keep to the path and firebreak until a forestry road is reached. ⑥ Turn right and continue along it, ⑦ taking left fork at next junction. Turn right downhill at next T-junction and on sharp left hand bend ⑧ follow the path leading uphill straight ahead. The path is clearly defined and leads to forest gate on to moor. Follow the path which runs across the hills and through a pass. ⑨ Arrive at a farm at Nantcol. Take the road down into the valley, going right at the fork. ⑩ At the hamlet, cross the river and turn right. Continue back up the single-track lane for the 4 miles to the lake and car park ①.

🌱 Among unusual plants in the area are sundews, which trap their insect food on the sticky hairs on their spoon-shaped leaves, and twayblades, their stems of greenish yellow flowers rising from 2 opposite stem leaves.

🦅 Beside the lake and the rivers, sandpipers perch on banks and stones, bobbing their rounded white-edged tails up and down.

🦋 Marsh fritillaries may be seen.

🏛 The Roman Steps may have been laid by Roman, British or medieval builders. They are broken flights of 'stairs', formed of flat slabs of unhewn rock, buttressed at the sides by upright blocks, and were once part of a trade route between Bala and the coast.

⚠ The heather conceals rocks and fissures – keep to the path.

🏛 Harlech Castle, about 3 miles (5 km) along this road, was built by Edward I between 1283 and 1289. It was besieged by the Welsh in 1294-5 and held by a garrison of only 37 men. It was the last stronghold to fall in the Wars of the Roses, and among the survivors was a boy of 12, who was to become Henry VII, founder of the Tudor dynasty.

Two Lakes Walk
13 miles (21 km) Sheet 115 783630

Energetic Excellent hill walking across some safer slopes of Snowdonia, covering a wide variety of terrain typical of northern Snowdonia. Some exposed upland country: dress appropriately in winter. *Rough pasture, heather hillside, woods; 3 climbs; some sections boggy at all times. Do not attempt in poor visibility.*

Start Trefriw on the B5106; buses; Llanrwst Station is about one mile (1.5 km) from Trefriw across the river. **Public car park** at Trefriw opposite the Woollen Mill.

① From car park cross road and go over bridge to right. Turn left up first road on left and climb steeply to signpost ② pointing right to Cowlyd. Follow this road uphill past small village cemetery. It climbs steeply for 2 miles (3 km) – ignore all side turnings. On top of moors follow road as it drops down to deserted farms. ③ Take path to the left and walk to Llyn Cowlyd. At the dam turn right and ④ follow the edge of the lake for 1¾ miles (3 km). Climb track at far end of lake and ⑤ cross the second of the 2 footbridges. ⑥ Follow the wide, grassy and boggy track, bearing left downhill, down to the stile and past cottage in trees. ⑦ At A5 walk down to Capel Curig. ⑧ Take signposted footpath beside the church (opposite the couple of shops). Follow path - clearly marked - 2½ miles (4 km) to Crafnant. As the path reaches the road beside the lake, ⑨ bear left

Water from Llyn Cowlyd supplies Colwyn Bay and a power station at Dolgarrog.

along a stony track. Pass cottages in the woods and before reaching house called 'Hendre' take marked footpath which runs off right across meadow. On reaching Forestry Commission road turn right and follow the road to the far side of the lake. ⑩ Turn left at end of lake and take lane down through woods to ①.

🪡 Trefriw Woollen Mills have made Welsh cloth since the early 19th C., when they were powered by water from the River Crafnant. They are open to the public, and have a shop attached to them.

🪶 The area abounds in birds: buzzards, ravens and grouse in the open country, dippers, grey wagtails and sandpipers on the rivers; pied flycatchers, redstarts, wood warblers in the woods in summer.

🏞 Llyn Cowlyd, a man-made lake in a flooded valley, provides local people with water. When a dam burst below the lake in 1925, there was a serious flood. In winter wild swans may be seen here, otherwise the lake lacks wildlife.

🏞✕ Capel Curig is a notable climbing centre, and E down the A5 there are several cafés.

🪶 On Llyn Crafnant, another reservoir, there is good trout fishing. The lake is a habitat, too, for wild duck and heron.

161

NORTH WALES

Llyn Dinas and Aberglaslyn Pass
9 miles (14.5 km) Sheet 115 588483

Moderate This is one of the most beautiful parts of Snowdonia: south-facing, it is always warmer and lusher than the N, and it has rugged mountain scenery. Superb variety – mountains, woods, rivers. In May and June the hills are covered with wild rhododendrons in flower. *Riverside, meadows, lanes, hillsides, mountain pass; one climb; some wet meadows – waterproof footwear is essential.*

Start Beddgelert, on the junction of the A498 and the A4085; frequent buses. **Car Park** at the Porthmadog end of the village.

① From car park walk down village street away from Royal Goat Hotel. ② Before road bridge over river turn right along road beside river. Cross footbridge at end of this road and bear left beside river. ③ Follow path alongside river, climb stile, and walk down lane and track following the course of the river. Pass copper mine. Llyn Dinas is reached. ④ Follow clearly defined path alongside lake, over the hill, and then beside wood. Cross meadows and go past farm ⑤. At end of driveway ⑥ turn right on to single track lane. Follow the lane for about 3 miles (5 km) passing an old quarry and then a farmhouse on an S bend. Shortly after, a wooden footbridge is seen on the right. ⑦ Pass through a gap in the low stone wall and walk across the meadow to this bridge. ⑧ Cross and walk to the left end of the barn seen ahead. Follow the track up through the oak woods. ⑨ At the top of the hill keep to the wall, go through gate and follow the old cart track. ⑩ Passing ruined farm buildings follow the stony track up the hill. At brow of hill a gate is seen to the left across the meadow. Make for this, go through and follow the paving stones up the hill. ⑪ Go through the farmyard and join the farm road running downhill. (If the llamas are here, ignore them: they are harmless if left alone.) ⑫ Where the farm road meets the lane turn right. Go through village of Nantmor and ⑬ walk along main road for a short distance, turning into car park with information point and toilets. Climb old railway embankment and walk through tunnel ⑭, which is very dark. The ground is even, but the tunnel can be avoided by diverting left at entrance along

The River Glaslyn roars beside the road through the Aberglaslyn Pass.

a path which rejoins the route at far end after some scrambling. ⑮ Cross the footbridge and turn right. Follow the marker posts across the water meadows to Beddgelert.

⑯ Beddgelert means 'grave of Gelert'. Gelert was the hound of Prince Llewellyn, who one day left the dog to guard his baby son. When he returned the child was missing and the dog horribly bloodstained. Llewellyn killed the dog on the spot, only to find his son asleep, hidden by bedding, and beside him the huge body of a dead wolf. Gelert had saved the child's life, and in remorse for killing his faithful dog, the Prince built a memorial to him. This is in a meadow on the S side of the village.

🛉 A Celtic priory was founded in Beddgelert in the 6th C., followed, in the 12th or 13th C., by a small Augustinian (i.e. following the rule of St. Augustine) priory. All that remains of it is the village church, once the priory chapel.

⛏ Mine workings remain from the time when Beddgelert was the centre of a thriving copper mining industry

☘ There are uncommon plants and flowers in the meadows and lanes: it is worth taking an identification guide.

🦙 The Llamas sometimes seen grazing here are kept for their wool.

🚶 From detour around tunnel go to bridge for fine view of gorge.

🚂 A section of the former Welsh Highland Railway.

A nature walk through oak woods begins at the car park on the B4410 2 miles (3 km) W of Maentwrog.

The market town of Corwen on the Dee is a starting point for paths along the river and into the Berwyn Mts.

Llangollen is another departure point for Dee-side walks. The aqueduct at Pont Cysyllte is to be found 3½ miles (5.5 km) to the E off the A5 or A539.

The Lleyn Peninsula's coastal paths offer considerable scope.

About ¾ mile (one km) N of Llanallgo on Anglesey there is a peaceful, historical trail with a Bronze Age tomb.

MIDDLE ENGLAND

WELSH MARCHES

Borderlands are places of mystery and anomalies, and it is these qualities which make the area where England and Wales meet a paradise for walkers. In the south, the Forest of Dean is an ancient woodland sitting on top of a coalfield, with Foresters exercising unique and ancient rights. Through it flows the River Wye, having left Wales by the flank of the Black Mountains: a river of great beauty, and not only at the over-visited Symonds Yat.

Herefordshire (now joined with Worcestershire), is one of the last remaining great farmscapes of England, far less damaged by contemporary agriculture than most; but you must pick your paths with care as few are well-walked and obstructions are frequent.

On the eastern side of Herefordshire the Malvern Hills rise to nearly 1,400 feet (427 m) – a miniature mountain range. From end to end it is an easy 9-mile (14.5 km) walk with spectacular views. A truly clear day may produce almost unbelievable sightings: Plynlimmon in the north-west, the Mendips in the south and the Wrekin in the north.

The Southern Malverns
3 miles (5 km) Sheet 150 758368

Easy A comparatively unpopulated and unknown area of the Malvern Hills, but characteristically beautiful. *Hillside, woodland; one climb; mud.*

Start From Ledbury take the A438 in direction of Tewkesbury and continue 5 miles (8 km). **Parking** on left of A438 (going from Ledbury) at the road's highest point – the foot of Midsummer Hill, near cottages.

① Walk down to crossroads and turn right on to minor road. ② Leave road at lodge (small toll payable at times) and walk along the estate track, entering beechwoods and continuing one mile (1.5 km). ③ Leave wood by iron gate and continue straight on with track for 200 yards (183 m); turn right through gate and cross field, keeping right of wood, to gate and road. Turn right along road to Whiteleaved Oak. ④ Immediately after postbox, where road bends right, take track to left. In 100 yards (91 m) bear right on to grass track, through gate, and follow path along side of hill back to road at ①.

Midsummer Hill's twin peaks are the site of an ancient hill fortress.

Between Midsummer Hill and Swinyard, 2 of the South Malvern Hills, lies the lovely wooded valley unpoetically named the Gullet.

Midsummer Hill, at the least conserved, some say prettiest end of the Malverns.

Raggedstone Hill, S of Midsummer Hill, looks bare and bleak. Local legend says it is haunted, and that its shadow carries a curse. To the S of it is the beautifully named Valley of the Whiteleaved Oak.

The Black Mountains, in Wales.

Wye Meadows
5 miles (8 km) Sheets 1449 and 162 557268

Easy Typical, lesser-known Herefordshire countryside – a pleasant walk for an evening or half-day finishing at Lough Pool Inn. *Meadows, woods, riverside; one climb; mud after rain.*

Start From Ross-on-Wye take the A49 in direction of Hereford, going second right after the roundabout, left at T-junction and right at fork. **Parking** at Lough Pool Inn.

① Cross stile opposite Lough Pool Inn and walk down valley. Enter wood by stile to right of pool, then cross second meadow to road near Sellack church. ② Take track to right immediately after church. and almost at once through left-hand gate, passing to left of pool and bearing left to river bank. ③ Continue on river bank for ½ mile (0.8 km) past second wood, then turn left through field gate to road. ④ Turn right and follow road for one mile (1.5 km) (sign-posted 'Hoarwithy/Little Dewchurch'). Take signposted public footpath into second field after river turns off to right. Return to river bank and follow this over stiles to bridge at Hoarwithy. ⑤ Cross bridge, take path on right, leading to lane into King's Caple. ⑥ Turn right at crossroads, leaving road to cross suspension bridge at Sellack Boat, and follow path back to church. ⑦ Retrace to ①: be careful to take right fork after entering wood.

🐦 Game birds are bred in the woodlands here – keep dogs on leads.

〣 The River Wye (in Welsh *Gwy*) rises on Plynlimon in the Cambrian Mountains of central Wales. Five rivers have their source on that one mountain: the Severn, the Wye, the Dulas, the Llyfnant and the Rheidol. The Lower Wye, winding from Ross, takes in some of the most peaceful and beautiful country in Britain. (Parts of this stretch can be explored by boat.)

🐦 The Wye is a notable salmon-fishing river and the home of many water-birds, including kingfishers, wagtails and redshank. The latter are recognized in flight by the white triangular patches on the rump and the trailing edge of each wing.

⛪ Hoarwithy church, of an unusual Italianate design, contains a number of mosaics.

⌒ Over this stretch of the river there are two bridges: an iron one at Hoarwithy and the suspension footbridge at Sellack Boat.

🍴 The Lough Pool Inn, an old timbered building, serves an imaginative range of snacks and meals. Its bright log fire in winter is a welcoming sight at the end of the walk.

Tintern Abbey and the Devil's Pulpit
7 miles (11 km) Sheet 162 539012

Moderate A section of Offa's Dyke long-distance path; visit Tintern Abbey (short detour); particularly fine views; atmospheric in autumn and winter. *Riverside, crags, farmland; 2 climbs; mud after rain.*

Start From Chepstow take the A466 in direction of Monmouth and stop ½ mile (0.8 km) N of Tintern Parva. **Parking** in lay-bys on A466 just N of bridge; or at Old Station, Tintern, ¼ mile (400 m) S, from which you can walk along old railway to the bridge.

Waymarked except for forest road from ④ *to* ⑤. ① Cross bridge and turn right by the Brockweir Country Inn then right along footpath past Moravian Church. Follow yellow arrows across meadow. ② Turn right on to track, climbing above river, and ③ where path begins to descend, opposite a wall, turn sharp left, signposted 'Devil's Pulpit'. Continue to follow yellow arrows, climbing steeply till you turn right into a broad track. ④Ignore the next arrow, keeping right along the track, continuing slightly downhill and passing below Shorn Cliff. Follow track 1¾ miles (3 km) round loop to meet Offa's Dyke Path, marked with yellow arrows and an acorn sign. ⑤ Turn left along Offa's Dyke, following acorn signs, to Devil's Pulpit. Continue downhill through meadows; at signpost take branch 'via River Wye' to Brockweir and ①.

🚩 Brockweir has a pottery.

🍺 The Anchor Inn at Tintern, part 13th C.,
✗ serves good food and real ale.

🍺 Brockweir Country Inn.

🏠 Tintern Abbey, now a venerable ruin, was a Cistercian house, founded in 1131 by Walter FitzRichard, Lord of Chepstow, although what remains belongs to buildings of a later date.

📕 The Devil's Pulpit acquired its name
\↑/ from the story that Satan preached from it to the Abbey monks to entice them from their work.

※ Traces of Offa's Dyke, constructed in about 784 by the Mercian king Offa to mark the frontier between Celt and Saxon. The great earth rampart stretched 100 miles (161 km), from near Prestatyn to the mouth of the Wye. For long-distance path see pages 328–334.

The otter, rare in England now, but still occasionally spotted on the quieter stretches of the Wye. It should not be confused with the (smaller) mink.

WELSH MARCHES

British Camp and Eastnor Park
6 miles (9.5 km) Sheet 150 764404

Easy Views E and W over the Cotswolds and over Herefordshire into Wales. *Ridge, parkland; one climb; mud after rain.*

Start From Great Malvern take the A449 S and continue 5 miles (8 km). **Car park** (for British Camp) at foot of Herefordshire Beacon.

①Climb path signposted at front of car park to British Camp. Continue S along ridge path taking path to 'Hangman's Hill' at first stone marker. ② At second marker, just over the top of Swinyard Hill, take path to 'Obelisk', soon joining a track leading to the gate of Eastnor Park. ③Go through kissing-gate and follow slightly rising path to obelisk, continue on track (occasionally marked with white-topped stakes); then between two lakes and slanting up to the left to the metalled Ridgeway. ④ Turn right on to the Ridgeway and continue 2 miles (3 km) to A449. Ignore right turn to Netherton, also

later right turn. ⑤Return right along A449 to car park.

Herefordshire Beacon is chiefly famous as the site of the huge British Camp, one of the best examples of an ancient hill fort in Britain. It commanded the only existing pass through the Malvern Hills, and perhaps held 20,000 men. According to tradition, Caractacus was captured here in A.D. 75.

On the S side of the Beacon is a recess known locally as the Giant's Cave, but marked on the map as Clutter's Cave. It is man-made, but for what purpose no one knows.

The grounds of Eastnor Park, skilfully laid out, contain some exotic trees, and also shelter a herd of deer. The obelisk is a memorial to the Somers family, owners of Eastnor Castle, built in 1810-17, in the elaborate 'Gothick' style, by Robert Smirke.

Arthur's Cave
6 miles (9.5 km) Sheet 162 564158

Moderate A popular but unspoilt walk with exceptional views over the Wye and Forest of Dean; archaeological interest. The punt ferry used between ① and ② does not operate some winter months. Check at Forestry Commission Hut, point ①. *Woods; 2 climbs; mud.*

Start From the A40 5 miles (8 km) N of Monmouth, take the B4229 for Symonds Yat and turn right after one mile (1.5 km). **Parking** at Symonds Yat Rock.

From log cabin at top of car park take waymarked path 'Wye Valley Walk'. Follow this to river and cross by punt ferry. ②At top of steps turn left into road; ignore waymark for riverside path and follow road through hairpin past hotel. Soon take rocky steps to left up behind hotel. Follow path to join wider track and continue about ¼ mile (0.5 km) to a (waymarked) right fork leading to a forest road; in another 150 yards (135 m) ③ fork right to follow a narrow path through coniferous plantation. Follow waymarked path, joining a forest road for about 100 yards (90 m), to Arthur's Cave. ④ From cave, follow waymarked path above Seven Sisters Rocks (each rock is off the path), then descend following waymarks steeply to river bank, turning left to walk beside river to suspension bridge. ⑤ After crossing turn left to continue beside river. At rapids, opposite island, double back up wide track, and sharp left in about 100 yards (90 m). Rejoin path out just before reaching road.

⑩ Symonds Yat Rock, over 500 feet (152 m) above sea-level, took its name from
\↑/ Robert Symonds, a 17th C. High Sheriff of Herefordshire. ('Yat' or 'yacht', in the Forest of Dean, mean 'gate' or 'pass'.) Magnificent views of the Wye Valley and Forest of Dean.

🔦 In Arthur's Cave — according to legend a refuge of the hero-king — there were fossil remains of hyena, mammoth, rhinoceros and flint tools.

\↑/ More fine views of the Wye and the Forest of Dean from Seven Sisters Rocks.

∩ At the Biblins there is a swing bridge
🚩 over the Wye and a picnic area.

✕ Refreshment hut at Symonds Yat.

The Forest of Dean is widely regarded as this area's centrepiece. Many of its paths are waymarked (yellow arrows), and it is easy to improvise routes taking in the great rocks. One starting point is the lay-by near Staunton on the A4136 just over 3 miles (5 km) out of Monmouth. Walk along the road towards Staunton, take the forestry track on the left, forking right to reach Suck Stone. From there climb the path to the top of Near Hearkening Rock – unforgettable at sunset.

Paths from Great Malvern, 7 miles (11 km) SW of Worcester on the A449, find their way easily to the tops of the Malvern Hills.

Signposted 5 miles (8 km) SE of Hereford on the Mordiford Woolhope road, a car park and picnic site give access to woodland walks with fine views of Hereford and the Welsh mountains.

From New Radnor (on the B4362 from Presteigne at the foot of the Radnor Forest Hills) there are walks around the town's Norman ruins and paths into the surrounding hills.

Knighton, in the Teme valley, is a centre for walks into the nearby border country, and along Offa's Dyke.

COTSWOLDS

Here – perhaps more than in any other part of Britain – beauty depends on the built environment. The towns and villages, despite all the mistakes and horrors of recent decades, reflect the earth itself by the uniformity of their building stone. That stone is, of course, the limestone of the Cotswolds and it comes in a score of subtly varying shades of grey and gold. Out in the countryside the uplands of the wolds are, however, somewhat bleak, not least because the fields are separated by stone walls which, though once joys of skilled craftsmanship, are now mostly crumbling and in ruin.

The wolds, today almost all arable, were once vast sheep-walks which provided the wealth for the gracious town houses and churches of the area. The rivers of this region are all quite exquisite and their meanders link strings of little settlements. On the western side of the hills is the escarpment, bold and in places cliff-like. In geological time it has retreated, leaving behind outliers of the same limestone such as Bredon Hill. The 100-mile long (160.9 km) Cotswold Way – a walk of great views – runs along this escarpment from Chipping Camden to Bath.

Ozleworth Bottom
2 miles (3 km) Sheet 162 794928

Easy Ozleworth is the most delightful of the bottoms–the valleys cut back into the escarpment–that are so distinctive of the Cotswolds around Wootton-under-Edge. *Woodland, farmland; one climb.*

Start From Wootton-under-Edge take the road for Alderley, Hillesley and Hawkesbury. In about one mile (1.5 km) turn left at the Ozleworth signpost. Continue about 2 miles (3 km) to the obvious sharp left bend with house opposite. **Parking** with care in vicinity of left bend, or turn right to bottom of hill, stopping on rough road past cottages.

① From bend walk down to cottages and ② locate gate on left. Climb to the right across the field, aiming for gate to woodland ③; go through and follow track, ignoring side turnings, about ⅓ mile (0.5 km), soon continuing along edge of wood and across open field where track is indistinct. In about 150 yards (137 m) turn right on to track veering right. Continue to ④–the bridge. It has been wired off because it could be a danger to animals. Use felled trees to cross wire. Turn right and continue, keeping to open, following path parallel to stream. In ½ mile, at fence, cross, bear right and soon sight gate below. ⑤ Through it, cross stream and in 100 yards (91 m) join outward path. At ③ bear right, ignoring outward route. ⑥ Turn left at track and follow it to ①.

St. Nicholas's tower may have been part of a local landowner's hunting lodge.

⚏ These cottages are all that remain of a woollen-mill village of several hundred people.

⚒ Likely country for green woodpeckers, an unmistakable bright green.

⛪ St. Nicholas's Church, built before 1131, has an unusual six-sided tower and round-headed windows, that give it an Italianate look.

COTSWOLDS

Edgeworth Manor
4 miles (6.5 km) Sheet 163 948059

Moderate Edgeworth, set in the high wolds at the head of a valley, is a beautiful and typical Cotswold hamlet. Not recommended in autumn or winter – mostly exposed. *Farmland, parkland; 2 climbs.*

Start Edgeworth, best approached via Sapperton, signposted from the A419, Stroud-Cirencester road. **Parking** on main road.

The stately Edgeworth Manor is said to have been built on the site of a Roman villa.

① Go down hill between houses opposite the church and into open fields. In fields climb to the right to a wide track. Follow this. ② Where the track meets the road cross to the track opposite and continue. ③ Where the track exits from the triangular section of woodland, turn sharp right on to another track. ④ At road, follow the road opposite. ⑤ After crossing the bridge, the road rises steeply. Take the first obvious track right (through gate) leading into woodland, continuing to ①.

🏚 Edgeworth lies close to the grass-covered Ridgeway, an ancient British track. From Roman times it was used to carry salt south from Droitwich, where the springs still rise from beds of rock salt. It was also a route for the drovers bringing sheep and cattle in great numbers to Cirencester and even to Smithfield in London, to the Christmas market.

The hamlet stands at the head of the valley from the Frome, also called Stroud's Golden Valley.

⛪ In St. Mary's the remains of an earlier Saxon church can still be seen in the W part of the nave.

🏛 Edgeworth Manor, a 17th C. building, was enlarged in the late 19th C.

Northleach's Wool Church
8 miles (13 km) Sheet 163 115145

Moderate Wool was the Cotswold's wealth, and it paid for some superb churches and houses; the church at Northleach is certainly among the finest, and arguably the most remarkable because the village itself is so small. Yanworth is especially delightful in spring. *Farmland; one climb.*

Start Northleach, on the A40 between Cheltenham and Witney. **Parking** in Northleach.

① Leave Northleach with the church to the right and turn right into lane. Follow this over the A429 and on into Yanworth. ② From Yanworth church follow lane between buildings and downhill into a valley. After the lane starts to rise, go through gate on left, continuing to small wood, left. Just beyond wood, go through gate into fields. Keep field boundaries to right and head towards the power cables. Pass beneath them and continue to lane. Turn right and continue to road. ③ At small District Council building take the bridleway left and continue to the A40. Follow track opposite downhill towards Hampnett, turning right at the track junction. ④ Turn left along track next to 3 large barns, and follow the fence to the A429. ⑤ Follow the lane to Folly Farm, but carry straight on where the farm lane bends right. At the road turn right for Northleach.

🏛 Northleach was one of the centres of the Cotswold wool trade, thriving from the mid-14th C. to the mid-17th C. The church is a 15th C. building with a tower and a noble porch in the Perpendicular style. Inside are the memorial brasses to many of the merchants of Northleach, their feet resting on the sheep and the woolsacks which gave them their wealth; the brasses are engraved, too, with their marks, which were stamped on the bales of wool. One brass is in memory of Thomas Fortey, a merchant who died in 1447. His epitaph speaks of him as a 'renovator of roads and churches' and he rests in the beautiful church which he did much to rebuild.

🍺 The Union Hotel.

🏛 In Yanworth, a Saxon wool village, the church has some Norman remains.
🏚 Facing the church is a fine old barn with an entrance for the packhorses and carts which carried the fleeces.

🏛 Hampnett church, a neat Norman building, was oddly decorated inside with bright stencils late last century. Over 100 years earlier, the church got a name for having a rector who would marry couples without asking awkward questions.

↑ An excellent view of Northleach church.

Bourton-on-the-Hill
5 miles (8 km) Sheet 151 175325

Moderate A route through 2 fine examples of large Cotswold village; a wealth of pleasing stone houses and cottages. *Parkland, farmland; 2 climbs.*

Start Bourton-on-the-Hill, on the A44 W of Moreton-in-Marsh. **Parking** in village.

① Leave the A44 towards Batsford Aboretum. ② At the lodge go left through a gate and cross field to blue gate. Go right for 10 yards (9 m), then left on to track. ③ At obvious sharp left bend in track go right a few yards to park wall and follow wall to road. ④ Across road to path opposite through copse. ⑤ Cross 2 fields, keeping boundary to left. Go through gate on far side of second field and turn left on to track. In 200 yards (183 m) go right through iron gate and downhill through large field. Keeping fence to the right, make for gate. Through gate. Keep farm buildings to right. Cross field, keeping pond to left. Over stile and follow right edge of field to grass track. Follow track to road at Blockley. Continue through village. ⑥ Leave Blockley by B4479 (i.e. same road) and make for Bourton. ⑦ Take second lane on left (the last turn before the A44). Along it take the first obvious track to the right. Follow it, ignoring track on right just after old quarries, to A44 just above Bourton.

Smooth Japanese maple, seen among the Arboretum's superb oriental collection.

⊞ Batsford Park, late 19th C., was once the family home of Lord Redesdale, whose daughters were the famous Mitfords. Its Arboretum and Garden Centre are open each day, 10 a.m. to 5 p.m., April–November.

⑲ This is an ancient fish pond.

⑲ Blockley has an astonishing industrial history. The Domesday Book recorded 12 mill wheels on the Blockley Brook, which is fed by a number of unfailing springs. These later powered silk mills, an iron foundry, piano, soap and collar factories, and made the village one of the first to be lit by electricity. Now this quiet place has no silk mills, and the mill buildings have become pleasant houses with an imposing old church at their centre.

St. Catherine's Brook
1½ or 3 miles (2.5 or 5 km) Sheet 172 778703

Easy Typical of the relatively unwooded, low valleys that are found in the Southwolds, the Cotswold area between Bath and the M4; reveals a straightforwardly excellent example of the Cotswold, and the English, country lane. *Farmland; in wet weather 150 yards (137 m) between ④ and ① is likely to be waterlogged.*

Start From the A46 between Cold Ashton and Swainswick take the road signposted St. Catherine. **Parking** near St. Catherine's Court.

①From the Court go downhill along the lane. 180 yards (160 m) after Orchard Farm drive, take the path to the left signposted (inconspicuously) Public Footpath. At bottom, cross a drive to gate waymarked with yellow arrow and dot on black background. ②After crossing the field, join a farm road, turning left before reaching buildings. Continue at same level through gate and to a stile. Beyond this, waymarks on two electricity poles take you to a second stile by the brook. ③For a short-cut back to the start, cross the footbridge on the left, cross end of garden to half-stile in the hedge and continue up the field. If continuing for longer walk, follow yellow arrows. ④Continue on hedged track (water-logged after rain) to meet a lane. Turn left, and left again when the lane from ① is reached.

The 13th C. church is reached through the walled garden of the house.

🏛 St. Catherine's Court, originally a 15th C. monastery, was rebuilt in the 16th C. into 🏠 a Tudor mansion with a magnificent porch.

🌲 Some exceptionally fine larches.

⚑ The Rocks, a 19th C. castellated mansion with 'Gothic' features.

COTSWOLDS

The Coln Valley

6 or 8 miles (9.5 or 13 km) Sheet 163 145052

Easy Follows a beautiful river from one lovely Cotswold village to another; some of the best walking in the area. *River meadows, farmland, parkland.*

Start From the A433 at Bibury, follow signs to Coln St. Aldwyns. **Parking** in Coln St. Aldwyns; alternatively Quenington or Bibury.

① Across the bridge, take the signposted bridleway/footpath and then the signposted footpath to the right. Make for the tree ahead and continue to the wood. Take the obvious track in the wood. After emerging, follow the well-defined track close to the river. ② After two gates, cross stone stile and ascend through a strip of woodland. Continue with wall on right; the track becomes a bridleway and then a lane, leading to the road beyond Bibury Court. Turn left, and left at the main road. Follow this into Bibury. ③ Cross the footbridge to Arlington Row, continue past cottages and uphill to Y-junction. Turn left between houses, on to path signposted to Ready Token. Continue to post with 5 footpath arrows. Go straight ahead through 2 fields. At the far corner of the second turn left on to a broad track and continue to road. ④ After two houses take the signposted bridleway to left across the middle of the field and in front of a house. After crossing two more fields, continue on left of stone wall, shortly descending to return to the bridge. For the 8 mile (13 km) version, continue from ④ to crossroads. Turn right (the Fairford road), then bear left for the village centre. Before crossing the river, turn left again. After leaving the village, turn right at junction (signposted Southrop, Lechlade) and in 60 yards (55 m) go through kissing-gate on left. Follow path across 3 fields to a bridge to road. Turn left for Coln St. Aldwyns.

▮✕ The New Inn, Coln St. Aldwyns, has a courtyard bar, a magnificent dovecote, and serves excellent food; a free house.

✕ Bibury Trout Farm has fish for sale.

⌂ Arlington Mill Museum has many relics of a mill mentioned in the Domesday Book. The millrace, in which are rainbow trout, is lit by underwater floodlights. Open daily, 10.30 a.m. to 7 p.m., March-October.

⌘ Bibury Court, now a hotel, is a lovely building, dating in part from Tudor times, but mainly from the mid-17th C.

♦ Arlington Row, originally a 14th C. sheep-house, was converted into weavers' cottages in the 17th C.

The River Coln winding through the water meadow at Bibury, described by William Morris as 'the prettiest village in England'.

COTSWOLDS

Cleeve Common
10½ miles (17 km) Sheet 163 023282

Energetic Includes the highest point of the Cotswolds, almost the last unenclosed section of high wold and a stretch of the Cotswold Way. The Common is open and bleak - dress warmly in cold weather. *Farmland, common; 2 climbs.*

Start Winchcombe, on the A46, Cheltenham-Stratford road; frequent buses from Cheltenham. **Parking** in Winchcombe, or the large lay-by near point ⑧.

① Leave Winchcombe along Vineyard St. following signs to Sudeley Castle. After Castle entrance, follow Cotswold Way waymarks to Cleeve Common. The route is waymarked by arrows, mostly yellow with white dots, and occasional signposts. 140 yards (125 m) after reaching the Common, where the Way turns right, continue towards the radio masts. ② From the masts you can visit the trig. point. Retrace to the masts and continue by turning right along wall, leaving masts to left. ③ At the end of wall, ignore arrows of the Cotswold Way and follow track steeply down under hill fort, and then skirting the cliff of Cleeve Cloud. Follow the track and road to the head of Rising Sun Lane, and continue at the same level (later climbing slowly) to the clubhouse of the golf course on Cleeve Hill. Alternatively, follow Cotswold Way marks from ③ across hill-fort and past view-indicator, continuing 100 yards (90 m) to clubhouse after Way turns off to the right. ④ At clubhouse take the well-signposted and well-worn track. ⑤ After passing through 2 gates, bear right to follow the wall of Postlip Hall. Keep the wall to the left and continue sharply round to a stile with waymarks. Ignore the Cotswold Way and follow plain yellow arrows over stile, through farmyard, and down valley. ⑥ Nearly ½ mile (700 m) after crossing a private drive, at the far corner of a long field, cross the stone-slab bridge and take the track leading towards Postlip House. (If doing the walk in the reverse direction take care to continue to the stone slab bridge.) ⑦ Go through the mills by making towards 'Reception', then turn right past fire station and follow covered way. Ignore waymark on right in the middle of the mills, continuing along the road past two cottages. Follow lane until it bends sharp left. Cross the stile ahead and continue across 3 fields to road. At road, continue ahead for a

The church in the grounds of Sudeley Castle.

short walk back to town centre. Alternatively go right (signposted Belas Knap) for 200 yards (183 m) to two gates on left with two stiles between them. ⑧ Cross the left-hand (stone) stile, go down to river, following it to exit from sports ground. Turn left at road for town centre.

🍺 The George was once a pilgrim inn for ✕ Winchcombe Abbey, long since gone. It serves excellent food.

🏭 Winchcombe Pottery ⅔ mile (1 km), open shop hours.

🏰 Sudeley Castle has strong Tudor links, especially with Katherine Parr, Henry VIII's widow. The castle is open every day, 12 noon to 5 p.m., March–October; the grounds an hour earlier.

🏛 Wadfield Farm is an elegant 17th C. building in a splendid position.

🗝 Remains of Wadfield Roman villa, including part of a mosaic pavement.

❊ Belas Knap is a huge Neolithic long barrow (burial chamber). The dry stone walling at the lower part of the false entrance is original–some 6,000 years old. The barrow was first opened in 1863, and since then, excavations have produced 38 human skeletons.

𑜱 The trig. point marks the highest point in the Cotswolds, 1083 feet (330 m) above sea level.

𑜱 Cleeve Cloud – the name comes from *clif*, a cliff, and *clud*, a rock or rock mass – is an exposed edge which shows the structure of the local limestone, the golden-coloured hallmark of Cotswold building for centuries.

\/ The Panorama Dial points out some interesting views.

🏛 Postlip Hall is 16th C.

🏭 The two paper mills at Postlip, which date from the 18th C., are still at work, making air and oil filter paper for cars.

The old Severn to Thames Canal is good walking. Take the Tarlton road from Coates to find the canal just past the railway bridge. Walk as far as the tunnel, where there is a pub.

Cooper's Hill – scene of cheese rolling – provides a climb (one part nearly vertical) that could be combined with some of the Cotswold Way.

A walk along the Thames runs from the A417 at 225 981. Follow the path to the pub at 247 986.

Cotswold Farm park, signposted from the B4077 at the A436, provides either short strolling to view its rare animals, or a longer walk along the River Windrush up to its head near the village of Ford.

AROUND BIRMINGHAM

The Birmingham conurbation spreads and spreads, but at least its suburbs are infiltrated by countryside. The walks in this section all begin within 30 minutes' drive of the city's centre, some much sooner.

Indeed, one can walk right round Birmingham on the 162-mile (260 km) West Midland Way, which ingeniously links public footpaths and bridleways at an average distance of 12 miles (19 km) from the conurbation's outer edge. And a pleasant walk it is too, for this, to quote the novelist Henry James on Warwickshire, is 'midmost England', perhaps the purest expression of Englishness in landscape anywhere. Ambridge, the Archers' village, is supposed to lie somewhere between Warwickshire and Worcestershire.

To get the most from walking here requires some openmindedness. Industry is woven into the fabric of many parts, and it must be embraced. The canals are absorbing, gentle strolling; while some localities, considered industrial, or built-up beyond recall, offer pleasant surprises.

Tanworth-in-Arden
5 miles (8 km) Sheet 139 113705

Moderate Typical Warwickshire village and country; a spectacular, mile-long, tree-lined avenue, at its best in May. *Pasture and arable farmland; 3 climbs; mud after rain.*

Start Tanworth, off the A4023; weekday trains from Birmingham Moor St. to Danzey, near point ⑦. **Parking** at the Green, Tanworth.

① From the green, pass Ivy Stores into Vicarage Hill. ② Enter field on right immediately after Bellfield housing estate. Aim for lower end of estate. Cross road to join 'mile walk' (marked 'Private Road') to Umberslade Park. ③ At road, turn right. ④ Opposite lodge, follow 'Public Footpath' sign. After gate into second field, follow hedge on left round to fence in corner, then keep long hedge on left. ⑤ From gate at corner, keep same course across 3 fields, aiming for gate near electricity pole at hill top. Follow hedge on left to pass to left of Bickers Court Farm and join farm drive. ⑥ Turn right at road. ⑦ Cross Henley-Tanworth road and take track over railway. Where track turns left, continue with hedge on right. After gate, follow path as it curves around field boundary. At corner, turn left at farther gate and head for Forde Hall, passing to right of farm buildings. ⑧ Go right up lane, over crest of hill. ⑨ After slight right bend, go over fence on right. Following mature hedge on right, continue straight towards church,

The balsam poplar's leaves and buds smell delightfully aromatic, notably in spring.

over 2 bridges and up hill. After fence at top, turn left along beaten track and road to ①.

🏛 Tanworth's church is part 13th C. The village's name recalls that the area was thickly wooded by the Forest of Arden.

🍺 The Bell Inn is modernized, but retains some country pub atmosphere.

⌒ The landowner insisted the bridge was built to a special design, of grey stone – more to his taste than blue brick, like the other 63 on the line.

🌲 The mile-long avenue is of balsam poplars and chestnuts.

\↑/ The Avon Valley, with the town of Broadway and the Cotswolds beyond.

🏛 18th C. Umberslade Hall, now flats.

🏛 Forde Hall dates from the 17th C.

183

AROUND BIRMINGHAM

Hartshill
3½ miles (5.5 km) Sheet 140 317944

Easy Reputedly an industrial area, but there is varied walking. *Hillside, woods, farmland, village; one climb; mud after rain.*

Start From B4114 in Hartshill follow signs to Country Park. **Parking** in Country Park.

Leave car park following foot of mound and continue across field to ① gateway into wood. Follow main path down hillside to gateway into field, then walk round right side of field. ② Go through gate half-way along field, then follow round left side of field to top corner. Go through gate and follow hedge on left. ③ Just over crest fork downhill with hedge on right. ④ Go through farmyard and on to road. Turn right and continue over railway to T-junction. Turn right and in ½ mile (0.8 km) ⑤ follow the drive towards Spring Farm. ⑥ In field on left after railway, cross diagonally right to angle of fence then continue along boundary. From field corner head straight for canal bridge visible ahead, diverging from hedge on left, crossing farm road 80 yards (72 m) from sharp bend, and crossing another field. (Footpath over these two fields may be ploughed out.) Cross bridge and continue over next field. ⑦ Cross track, climb bank, then across to estate entrance and continue up road for about ¼ mile (400 m). ⑧ At road junction go down path to right of several blocks of flats, and into wood. ⑨ At T-junction go left, and in 15 yards (14 m) right. Climb twisting through woods to ①.

🚇 The quarries produce red granite and manganese ore, abundant in the area.

🏛 The Manor House, part 14th C., was the
🏠 home of Robert Glover, put to death for his religious beliefs in 1555. The alms-
⛪ houses S of the churchyard date from 1728. The church has some fine 14th C. stained glass.

🏚 Birthplace of poet Michael Drayton.

✳ A skeleton thought to date from Anglo-Saxon times was excavated here in 1824 – with a shield and spear.

🌲 The Country Park's woodland is a
🦅 mixture of broad-leaved and coniferous trees, a classic habitat for great tits, blue
🐦 tits and coal tits.

Fradley Junction
8 miles (13 km) Sheet 128 116114

Easy Satisfying walking country N of the conurbation, not in the much-used Cannock Chase; absorbing canal activity, especially in summer. *Farmland, woods, canal-side; mud after rain.*

Start Curborough Road, off Eastern Avenue which is off the A51 at lights (signposted Trent Valley and Streethay); frequent buses stop near end of Curborough Road. **Parking** in Curborough Road.

① Cross Eastern Avenue and walk up path at foot of embankment, diverging from road at an underpass. ② On joining a drive, turn right and continue along the path straight ahead, crossing stream and passing through a wood. ③ Straight through the village and turn right at the post box in wall. ④ Where lane swings right, go left through first gate into field. Walk up field and cross railway by stiles. Continue half left on slightly raised path, aiming well to left of farm. Continue ahead along left edges of several fields to reach road by bungalow. ⑤ Turn left, then immediately right up a farm track. ⑥ At T-junction, turn left over bridge, then right, taking the track skirting the wood. ⑦ At road turn right, cross canal and follow canal towpath to Fradley Junction. ⑧ Walk back along towpath as far as first bridge. Cross, and go through gate on right into field. Follow this bank of canal to second woodland area, where bear left to road. ⑨ Cross road and across field to gate (route marked by orange arrows). Go round end of dispersal bay of old Fradley airfield. ⑩ In 150 yards (135 m) cross stream by plank bridge and continue left along fence. At end of fence, cross stile and follow power lines; then continue to corner of fence and half right to gate. ⑪ Follow drive round to right. Cross road, follow edges of fields, crossing final one to cross railway again at stiles. ⑫ Cross field towards house, joining drive and then track to left of house, to join made-up path. ⑬ Left down path, through gap in hedge and cross field to start.

🚩 Fradley is the junction of 2 canals. One, the Trent and Mersey, was brought through Fradley in 1770. The other, the Fradley to Whittington Brook section of the Coventry Canal, was completed in 1782. Josiah Wedgwood, the famous potter, was hon. treasurer of the company that built both canals, and one of their main cargoes in the 19th C. was fine clay for the potteries at Stoke, including Wedgwood's own Etruria Works. The Trent and Mersey is linked, by a section of the Coventry Canal, with the Oxford Canal, and this in turn leads to London via the Thames.

The Trent and Mersey Canal Society is restoring the Trent and Mersey, and its ancillary workings, including the old mile posts. Some of the buildings at Fradley Junction are owned by the British Waterways Board, and some privately.

🍺 The Swan overlooks the canal.

🏠 There is a former boatmen's chapel at the canal junction, one of the few ever built, and now used as a garage. Bargemen were generally regarded as lawless outsiders, and had fewer welfare benefits.

AROUND BIRMINGHAM

Frankley Beeches
9 miles (14.5 km) Sheet 139 972782

Moderate Pleasant walking, through almost encircled by conurbation; notable views of Birmingham. *Farmland, parkland, woods; 3 climbs; paths frequently ploughed out between* ⑧ *and* ⑨, ⑫ *and* ⑬, ⑭ *and* ⑮.

Start Waseley Country Park; from Birmingham centre take A38, turning right on to Frankley Beeches road. Bear left at unmarked mini-roundabout to Country Park. **Parking** at N end of Country Park.

① Leave car park and turn left along lane. Turn left at top of hill into field. Follow its left edge. ② Cross stile, turning right then left, climbing to top of hill. Continue along well-used track and path downhill to farm. ③ Turn right at farm track and in about 40 yards (36 m) follow field edge, hedge on left. Through gate, and follow second field edge, boundary on right. Through gate and continue with plantation on left, over stile, through gate and downhill, farm coming into view. ④ Turn right along lane, crossing motorway to road. ⑤ Turn right along road and after 100 yards (91 m) right again on to road towards Frankley and Country Park. ⑥ Turn left just before M5, then left at first gate into field. Follow right edges of 3 fields, cross next diagonally, follow right edges of 2 fields (crossing wire each time); right immediately on to path; left after 50 yards (46 m) on to track. ⑦ At cross-tracks, continue slightly right of ahead, along left edge of field. At embankment through gate into woods and left downhill. ⑧ Diagonally right over mid-field to stile (overgrown) at end of row of trees. Continue straight up hill past oak, then along left sides of 2 fields. ⑨ Turn right over fence after crossing third fence, then cross field to track, in sight from about 15 yards (14 m). Follow this past 'Gun Range' to farm; at farm, left up track on to road by pub in Illey. ⑩ Turn left along road, cross M5, right again, then left. ⑪ Through gate into field. Cross to edge of housing estate. Follow path crossing 2 metal stiles downhill towards reservoir. ⑫ Over stile, cross field over hill, to gate on to road. Left along road to church, where turn right up track to hilltop with Frankley Beeches. ⑬ Downhill to road, then along road passing farm on left. ⑭ Turn right along road to pass farm buildings, then left over stile. Down field to stile, then cross next field to bridge over disused railway. Cross. ⑮ Straight on with bank on left.

Foxes are an established feature of suburban areas – proof of the animal's adaptability and scavenging habits.

Where estate path crosses stream, bear right (through wire) to outside of estate and continue across mound, bearing right to join track to farm. ⑯ Along track to farm, then on to road turning right back to car park.

↑ Windmill Hill, 940 feet (286 m), has contrasting views – Birmingham and the Black Country to the NE, the Severn Valley and hills beyond to the SW.

↟ Foxes are seen occasionally.

▣ Unlike the nearby Clent Hills, Wasely, made a Country Park in 1971, has reasonable visitor numbers. In Anglo-Saxon, 'waer' means sheep, 'ley' pasture.

⌁ Part of Birmingham's water supply.

❧ Frankley Beeches were given to the National Trust by Cadbury Bros. Ltd.

> The bridleways and footpaths of the Clent and Lickey Hills have long been the staple walking areas S of the conurbation. To relieve the pressure on them, try Hartlebury Common, ½ mile (0.8 km) SE of Stourport-on-Severn; Kingsford, one mile (1.5 km) NW of Wolverley or Nunnery Wood, 1½ miles (2.5 km) E of Worcester – more distant, but still accessible Country Parks.
>
> Canal walking: the Trent and Mersey; the Stratford Canal; the Coventry Canal and the Grand Union.

NORFOLK

This is a county for artists, including, of course, all the great names of the Norwich School. Many people think, wrongly, that the landscape is featureless and flat; certainly the painters were not drawn to it for that. In any Norfolk view, the biggest single element is the sky, and it was the brilliant light which entranced Crome, Cotman and the rest, and still inspires the walker.

Choose where you go with care. Public paths are none too many. The coastline can be walked more or less continuously, and the mixture of long dunes, beaches, red-roofed villages, twisted pines and low cliffs is rewarding. Inland, the countryside rolls gently, but never quite enough to be described as hilly, although in Norfolk the merest bump is *called* a hill.

The walker sees more of the Broads than anyone in the nose-to-tail boats, for on land there are the wide vistas of the surrounding marshes. Breckland may disappoint those who find dense forestry plantations dull going. The best of inland Norfolk may well be the middle and eastern parts. Here are a mass of twisting lanes, churches, farms and hamlets – an ancient landscape compared with that to the west, which was much more strongly influenced by the dead straight divisions of parliamentary enclosure.

Burnham Market Town and Sea Marshes

5 miles (8 km) Sheet 132 832421

Easy A route with much of interest on it, or nearby: pleasant market town with Georgian houses, interesting churches, Scolt Head Nature Reserve, Holkham Hall and Burnham Thorpe, birthplace of Nelson. *Town, farmland, sea marsh; paths between ③ and ④ and ⑤ and ⑥ may be ploughed out.*

Start Burnham Market, off the A149. **Parking** in the market square.

① Opposite the war memorial take Herrings Lane uphill past track leading to church. After third electricity pole ② turn left through gap to field corner. ③ Follow left edge of field to track; turn right to road. Cross and continue through Burnham Norton to sharp left bend. ④ Turn right and bend left to double gates. Go through and follow track ahead to stile and more gates. Turn along left edge of meadow to brick building. Continue up to sea wall. ⑤ Turn right to end of bank. Cross field, making for windmill. ⑥ At road turn left, then right and follow track ¼ mile (0.5 km) to another road. Turn right to Burnham Overy church. ⑦ Follow B1155 back to Burnham Market.

✕ Fishes' Restaurant offers such delights as Pacific oysters, *scallops au gratin* and salmon fishcakes with crab sauce.

Low horizons, vast skies and the windmill – unchanging elements of Norfolk landscape.

🦅 Waders and marshland birds.

🏚 Remains of Creake Abbey.

🏛 Holkham Hall, the great 18th C. Palladian house of white brick, seat of the Earls of Leicester.

NORFOLK

Stalham
2 miles (3 km) Sheet 133 373247

Easy Typical town and landscape of the Norfolk Broads, where the peak of boating activity is in spring and summer. *Broads, farmland, town; some paths may be ploughed out in early spring.*

Start Stalham on the A149; fairly frequent buses in summer. **Car park** (free) in Stalham.

① Facing away from Yacht Station, opposite the green, turn left and left again round dyke head to sharp right bend opposite track. Turn right to swing gate. ② Through gate, aim half left across field to road, where turn right to farm. ③ Turn right and follow lane for ¼ mile (0.5 km) to swing-gate. By it ④ turn left through wide gap and continue to road. ⑤ Cross into Stalham. ⑥ Turn right towards church, where turn right to main road and return to yacht station.

⥮ An excellent coarse fishing area: plenty of roach in the dykes; the reach past Wayford Bridge is noted for bream.

The Maid's Head dates from the 15th C.

⛪ St. Mary's (late 15th C.) possesses, by accident, an extremely fine 16th C. font. During the last century it was found, covered in plaster, beneath the floor. Local historians assume it was hidden there to escape damage in the Civil War.

Great Yarmouth
9 miles (14.5 km) Sheet 134 522075

Moderate Stirring views of Burgh Castle, impressive remains of a Roman fort and, in season, the spectacle of migrating birds on Breydon Water. *Town, farmland, villages, banks of Breydon Water. Path between ⑥ and ⑦ may be ploughed out.*

Start Great Yarmouth; frequent buses and trains. **Car park** near the Two Bears inn.

① From pub cross Southtown Bridge and continue on A12 ¾ mile (one km) to Boundary Road into which ② turn right, cross footbridge over by-pass and continue through industrial estate to Coopers. ③ Continue along footpath on Coopers' northern boundary to Gapton Hall Road. Turn left for 80 yards (75 m); ④ cross road and continue along footpath to track. Turn left to farm road; ⑤ turn right and continue straight ahead to a kissing gate ⑥ in front of white cottages. Through gate continue over field to wooden rails, where ⑦ continue ahead to kissing gate then take farm track to road. Turn right, and continue to church where turn left to Fort. Take path on left of fort to edge of bank to stile. ⑧ Continue 3 miles (5 km) along Breydon Water, then on rough road to broken bridge. ⑨ Keep to river bank then take path to road. ⑩ Turn left, past transformer, and continue to ①.

🏰 Burgh Castle was a Roman fortress – Gariannonum – built in about A.D. 300. The marsh that now surrounds the ruins and the sand bank on which Great Yarmouth stands were then under the sea.

Around the mid-6th C. St. Fursey founded a monastery on the castle site, but wisely removed to France when the Viking invasions began.

🌱 Breydon Water is either a large lake or
🏹 mud flats, depending on the state of the tide. Its banks, covered with yellow flags – irises – are a blaze of colour in May-July. Iris is the Greek word for rainbow.

In late summer and autumn waders arrive on passage to winter quarters. Winter brings various seabirds, particularly cormorants, sheltering from the North Sea weather. In March there is the booming call of the bittern.

The occasional Norfolk wherry may sail past. On narrower parts, where sailing is difficult, they are punted along with a pole called a 'quant' or 'spreet'.

NORFOLK

Holt and Letheringsett
6 miles (9.5 km) Sheet 133 082378

Easy Undulating countryside – to disprove the all-too-common belief that Norfolk is flat. In fact the route shows a fair cross-section of Norfolk landscape from attractive heathland to sheltered woodland rides; a walk for all seasons. *Heath, town, villages, farmland, woods.*

Start Holt Country Park, signposted from the B1149. **Car Park** (free) in Country Park.

① From car park turn left into grassy ride. Go over crossing track then bend right on track to a pond. Go left to cross ② a stile and join track, turning left and continuing ¼ mile (0.5 km), then left again into lane. Follow this as it bends right to road. ③ Turn left and continue ½ mile (0.8 km) into Holt. Continue through main street and curve right down Letheringsett Hill to ④ car park, where continue straight ahead to the dell. Keep to the higher ground, but then go downhill and turn right through ferns to road. Turn left, continue about one mile (1.5 km), the whole way on pavement. ⑤ ·Just past church turn left into lane and follow this. Just past cottages in Thornage turn left to ford. ⑥ Cross, turn left and immediately right on to track beside brick shed. Continue uphill, turning sharply right with track. Continue ¼ mile (0.5 km), then left at top to ⑦ iron gate.

Cross wooden rails, turn left and continue straight on ¼ mile to wooden gate, then road. ⑧ Turn left then in a few yards right on to track. Follow this to road, where turn right and continue ¼ mile on main road to ①.

🍺 The Feathers Hotel, fronting the market
✗ place, is a 17th C. coaching inn; food and real ale.

🏫 Gresham's School, Holt, the public school, was founded in 1555 by Sir John Gresham, one of the 4 brothers who became Lord Mayors of London. Among its pupils this century have been the poet W. H. Auden and composer Benjamin Britten. On a site close to the school was born a less enlightened celebrity, Alice Perrers, the hideous and calculating mistress of Edward III.

🏫 A humble, but remarkable local man is buried near the churchyard entrance. Johnson Jex, a blacksmith by trade, became obsessed with making clocks and watches, and developed into a master of the craft, but without gaining more than local recognition. His epitaph recalls this, describing him as a 'scientific anchorite' or hermit. Examples of his work are in the Bridwell and Castle Museums, Norwich.

🏛 The Hall is a Palladian manor house.

Peddars Way

4 miles (6.5 km) Sheet 144 934871

Easy Part of Norfolk's most ambitious unofficial long-distance path (see page 328-334) and an outstanding nature reserve. *Heath, woods.*

Start at Peddars Way sign on the A11, 5 miles (8 km) from Thetford and 23 miles (37 km) from Norwich. **Parking** on heath.

① Follow direction of Peddars Way sign ¼ mile (0.5 km) to level crossing. Cross and continue on Peddars Way to road. ② Turn left to second crossroads. ③ Turn left through army camp and continue ½ mile (0.8 km) to road junction, where ④ cross to track into forest and ⑤ go straight ahead for ¼ mile (0.5 km) to crossing of rides with field gate on right. ⑥ If visiting reserve, enter through gate. Otherwise continue left one mile (1.5 km) to level crossing and ①.

East Wretham Nature Reserve lies within the Norfolk area known as Brecklands. In contrast with the Broads, this is a landscape of pine forest, heath and boggy meres or lakes. It covers some 300 square miles (121 ha). The varied habitats are a haven for several notable species of birds and wild flowers:

The stone curlew is a rare visitor in March-Oct., identifiable in the air by its white wing bands and, at night, by its sharp 'coolee' call. Crossbills may be seen, or more likely detected, among the pines: they feed by extracting the seeds from pine cones with their sharp, 'crossed' bills, leaving a pile of debris on the ground below. They are not native to this area, but periodically, when the crop of pine cones fails in Scandinavia, they flock here across the North Sea in search of new supplies – a phenomenon known as irruption and an interesting contrast to conventional migration.

The meres used to puzzle observers because they seemed to fill and empty at whim, regardless of rainfall. It is now clear that their level is governed by the water table in the underlying chalk and not the height of the devil's sense of humour as local old wives have claimed. Rare plants include: Spanish catchfly (flowering June-Aug.); field wormwood (Aug.-Sept.); spiked speedwell (July-Oct.); and sickle medic (June-July).

Fly agaric, with its distinctive scarlet cap speckled with white is prolific in the East Wretham Nature Reserve area.

NORFOLK

Sheringham and Weybourne Cliffs

10 miles (16 km) Sheet 133 158431

Moderate Along some typical Norfolk sand cliffs. Crosses high ground with good views, but sheltered enough to be an all-weather route. *Farmland, heath, shore, cliffs, woods; may be overgrown along railway between ⑥ and ⑦ – use field edge instead.*

Start Sheringham Station; frequent trains.
Car park Station Road Car Park.

① From Station Road Car Park turn right past roundabout into Holway Road. Continue uphill and opposite Beech Avenue turn right into grassy lane. ② Continue into Upper Sheringham, pass church and turn left for Holt. At crossroads ③ turn right for King's Lynn. In ¼ mile (0.5 km) ④ turn right into drive bordered by white rails. Follow drive, then perimeter track of camp, bending sharply left near end, but at next left bend continue few yards to stile and ⑤ into wood. Turn left to follow paths then track, continuing ½ mile (0.8 km) to road. ⑥ Turn right towards railway and before bridge left on to track, passing prefabs by left edge of rough ground then continuing on well-defined path. When close to railway get on to disused track and turn left to continue to cutting, where ⑦ turn right and descend bank. At bottom turn left into bracken, later

bearing right to road. ⑧ Turn right, then in a few yards left on to path between hill and field. At road turn right to church, where turn left to the beach. ⑨ Turn right and continue round cottages along beach or cliff top past lifeboat station, where turn right and continue to Sheringham. Continue through town to ①.

🏵 Sheringham flourished with the Edwardian vogue for seaside holidays.

🏵 The Poppy Line steam railway, restored voluntarily by enthusiasts, provides trips between Sheringham and Weybourne from Easter to October.

〰 The deep water off Weybourne, unique to this coastline, has long been regarded as the prime place for a foreign invasion to land. No one has taken advantage of this, however, since the Angles came ashore here in the 7th C.

🌱 Samphire, the plant with fleshy, tubular shoots which grows wild on the cliffs and shingle near the sea, is sometimes available in the local shops. The fleshy parts can be boiled and eaten with butter or pickled in vinegar for a relish. Some say it tastes like asparagus; to go with it, fresh crabs and lobster are on sale in the shops on the sea front.

NORFOLK

Blickling

6 miles (9.5 km) Sheet 133 192270

Easy One of the most interesting of Norfolk's great houses makes a splendid centrepiece for the route. *Farmland, parkland.*

Start Aylsham on the A140; frequent buses.
Car parks in Aylsham.

① From the church walk N over the railway, past Burebank School to double gate. ② Through gate, go half right towards corner of wood, then follow high hedge to road. ③ Turn left and continue to junction. Turn right and use parallel path on left, continuing to church. Continue past Hall and turn right past Buckinghamshire Arms to park gates. Go through and ④ continue to gate, then across to lake. Go round end of lake (lake on right), then left to ⑤ the road, where turn left and continue ½ mile (0.8 km). Pass farm and in 100 yards (91 m) turn left on to a well-defined path to a wood where ⑥ turn right, then bend left to mausoleum. Fork left to crossing track, where ⑦ turn left, continue a few yards then turn right to a wood and an iron gate. ⑧ Over gate, turn left to road, where turn left. Continue ¼ mile (0.5 km), where fork right downhill past cottages to road. ⑨ Turn right to Silvergate. Turn left then right into Weavers Way, where ⑩ follow signposts to 'Avenue', and follow this

to road. Turn right, continue to crossroads, then left, past school, to ①.

🏠 In a manor house on the site of the present Jacobean house Anne Boleyn spent her childhood. She was the second of Henry VIII's wives, beheaded in 1536. Not only does she 'walk the Bloody Tower with her head tucked beneath her arm', but is said to commute to haunt Blickling.

From Holme-next-the-Sea, 2½ miles (4 km) NE of Hunstanton along the A149, there are excellent seaside walks with superb flocks of seabirds, especially in winter.

The wildlife centre at Blakeney Point can be approached by a path from Cley off the A149.

Several marked walks go from Cromer W along the coast to East Runton and inland to Beacon Hill Roman Camp.

Hoverton Great Broad Trail starts a short boat ride from Wroxham (just off the A1151) at the top of Salhouse Broad.

Near the sea at Bacton Wood, 2½ miles NE of North Walsham, are forest trails starting from a car park and picnic sites.

195

EAST MIDLANDS

Intensively cultivated, Lincolnshire has few public footpaths, and these often vanish beneath the plough, or barley, or potatoes. Moreover, the fields are long and rolling; daunting even to those most confident they know the line of the right of way. Leicestershire and Nottinghamshire have rather more paths. Often, they cut intriguingly across the neat, planned pattern of fields left by the Parliamentary enclosures, still the major influence on this landscape. The paths, of course, pre-date the enclosures.

The Lincolnshire Wolds (chalk) and Lincoln Heath (limestone), two modest features of the area, are part of the twin belts of chalk and limestone which swing right across England from Dorset to Yorkshire. Slightly elevated above the surrounding flatlands, they give surprisingly dramatic views.

To the north-east and the south lie the wistful immensities of the Lincolnshire marsh country and the Fens. West of the Trent, Charnwood and Sherwood Forests have lost most of their trees, but still muster echoes of medieval wilderness.

Lincoln Heath

7 miles (11 km) Sheet 121 025517

Easy Gentle walking, much of it with a peaceful air though close to the A15: wide horizons, a Roman road, 'lost' villages. *Farmland, woods; mud after rain.*

Start Brauncewell, ¾ mile (one km) off the A15 (Lincoln-Sleaford road). **Parking** on road verge in front of farm buildings just beyond limestone quarry.

① Cross road and follow signposted track alongside stone wall on left. Turn right on to the path on far side of tree belt. Continue with trees on right for 330 yards (300 m). At gap in tree belt turn left beside stone wall, changing sides in mid-field. At end of field, turn right to join lane. ② Continue 250 yards (229 m) to main road. Turn right and in 100 yards (91 m) left down lane signposted B1191. Continue for 660 yards (600 m). ③ Where road bends left enter strip of woodland on right following well-used path. Keep straight on across track towards Mount Farm, cross stone bridge and bear right along edge of Ten Acre Plantation, the Oaks and Spruce Covert. ④ Keep straight on along well-surfaced track where road to Hill Farm joins on right. At lane leading into Bloxholm ⑤ turn right and continue for 600 yards (549 m). Turn right over grass-surfaced bridge about 20 yards (18 m) past gate on left. Continue straight ahead, keeping dyke on right. Cross wooden bridge and stile by reservoir and

continue with dyke on left to next stile and footbridge. Turn left on to farm road, and in about 100 yards (90 m) right, again with dyke on the left. At bend in dyke bear right for 20 yards and cross ditch to follow dyke on left up to stile in wire fence. ⑥ Go over stile and walk across paddock aiming for corner of stone building. Continue to stile at end of paddock. ⑦ Turn left after stile, left again at the by-way, and right before reaching farmyard. Continue up the hill past stone house. ⑧ Turn right at lane and continue ¾ mile (one km) to A15. ⑨ Cross A15 and join signposted footpath, keeping hedge on right. Turn right at farm track. In 250 yards (a little way past gateposts) turn left off track along grassy path to pass along top edge of Hillside Plantation. ⑩ Turn right at cottage to lane, and ①.

🏠 The A15 here follows the course of the Roman road King Street.

🏠 Site of a medieval village.

🏠 The site of the vanished medieval village of Dunsby: in the great house lived the Death family, one of whom was christened Welcome Death.

🏰 Bloxholm Hall and estate are much reduced in splendour from the time of one distinguished owner, the General Manners who served at Waterloo.

EAST MIDLANDS

Braunston and Launde Abbey

7½ miles (12 km) Sheet 141 832065

Moderate None of England's grandest
scenery, but this countryside has its own
quiet charm and some fine views. *Wooded
hills, lush valleys, village; mud after rain.*

Start Braunston, 2 miles (3 km) SW of
Oakham. **Parking** – with care – on church
green, Braunston.

① From Green walk along Wood Lane. ②
Near top of hill where the road to Ridlington
bears left, continue straight on up road,
which soon becomes a stony track, then a
grassy lane. Ignore footpath to Lissington. ③
At end of grassy lane bear left to well-
defined track around edge of field. Go
through bridleway gate and follow track on
right towards top of hill. At reservoir on
hilltop turn right through gate. ④ Where
track bears left in field go straight on for 200

yards (183 m) to signposts showing
Braunston, Launde and Withcote. Continue
left (hedge on left) towards Launde. Just before
end of field turn left through gate and
immediately right over causeway. Continue
down left bank of little valley to join another
bridleway. ⑤ By ruins of Cole's Lodge and
signpost follow bridleway over gully and
through gate. Continue by the hedge (river on
left) and cross bridge at other end of field. Go
through gate ahead and slightly right. Bear
half left into next field and make for top left
corner and edge of Launde Park Wood. ⑥ At
corner go through gap in hedge (not gate on
left). Follow faint track, keeping railings on
left. Pass Launde Abbey. Go straight ahead
through wire fence and gate to climb
shoulder of hill. Follow track through gate
up to road. ⑦ At road turn left. In 60 yards
(55 m), before cattle grid, double back
across field, passing to left of cable post.
Continue over rise and down far side of
gully to meet river again. Cross plank with

handrail. ⑧ The right of way continues straight on uphill to a large barn, not in sight at first. Just past barn turn right down avenue. Go through gate by cottages to the Launde road. ⑨ Cross road, keeping Dowry Cottage on left. In 300 yards (274 m) turn left off track by bridleway signpost. Follow hedge past horse jumps, go through gate on left and walk up field, keeping hedge on right. ⑩ At top right corner go through gate, turn left and continue 30 yards (27 m). Turn left through gate and continue along grassy lane. Go through gate at end of lane and turn right downhill on another grassy lane. ⑪ In 25 yards (23 m) turn right through hedge, over railings at foot of oak tree. ⑫ Braunston church can be seen 1½ miles (2.5 km) down the valley and this is the general direction for the next 13 fields. Follow dyke on left until the third field and cross stout bridge. Keep dyke and stream on right and after crossing stile and bridge keep hedge on left until stile; cross paddock to church.

By the belfry door of the church is a stone carving, more or less recognizable as a woman. It is probably a Saxon fertility idol. In the early days of Christianity, churches were often built on sites of pagan worship. For hundreds of years the carving served as a doorstep, until one day during the 19th C. it was turned over to reveal the carving and suggest the possibility that the earliest Christian converts hereabouts entered the church by trampling on the image of their former deity.

Launde Abbey is a house built on the site of a Norman Priory founded in 1125. Thomas Cromwell, the Tudor statesman who executed the Dissolution of the Monasteries came upon Launde in the course of his work and liked it so much he appropriated it for himself.

Launde Abbey.

Kirklington to Laxton

4, 6½ or 9 miles (6.5, 10.5 or 14.5 km)
Sheet 120 682576

Easy A walk of contrasts through quiet
woodland, grassy lanes and over Mansey
Common. *Farmland, woods; mud; some
paths under crops and ploughed over before
and after Eakring. Point ⑱ to the end is
simple to follow without map.*

Start Kirklington on the A617. **Parking** off
the main road on the side road leading to
Hall Farm – at foot of hill on Newark side of
village; alternatively the Normanton lane, 50
yards (46 m) away. **Return** to start possible
by car only from Eakring, Kneesall or
Laxton.
① From parking continue up road in
direction of Hall Farm for 170 yards (155 m).
Turn right over cattle grid (waymark) and
follow well-defined track around shoulder of
hill. ② At hilltop cross cattle grid (waymark)
and go straight on towards prominent barn.
Continue on main track for 50 yards (46 m).
③ Turn right off track, keeping hedge to left.
On entering strip of woodland turn right and
follow meandering track to end of trees. ④
Turn left across ditch (waymarks) and go
straight on, keeping Roe Wood on right for
full length of wood. Turn right through wire
crossing ditch and continue along edge of
Roe Wood to end. ⑤ Twenty yards (18 m)
beyond end of wood turn right over bridge
and immediately left on to well-defined
track. Where track bears left continue on
footpath straight across field to hedge just
left of barn. (It is permissible to keep on
track round edge of field to point where
footpath crosses.) ⑥ Turn left off track by
end of hedge and aim just left of Orchard
Wood Farmhouse, crossing hedge into
another field on the way. ⑦ Turn right
behind house and buildings on to farm road.
At end of Orchard Wood farm buildings turn
left across field to electricity pole 50 yards
(46 m) distant. Go straight on towards
Dilliner Wood, keeping hedge on right. ⑧ Go
down slope and enter next field by tree. Go
straight ahead across corner of field to
bridge with 2 stiles. Cross and bear half left
to 2 old telegraph marker posts and bridge to
Dilliner Wood entrance. ⑨ Continue straight
on ignoring cross-tracks. ⑩ Leaving wood
turn left and follow horse-tracks across
Mansey Common for about 120 yards
(110 m). Turn half right off horse trail and
follow meandering track through scrub. Go

down steep bank to cross footbridge. Climb
bank to field. ⑪ Strike across field aiming
for third electricity post from left. Keep line
of wire about 80 yards (73 m) to left. Go over
farm track to footbridge over dyke. ⑫ Cross
and aim for electricity post on far edge of
field. Cross rubble-covered bridge and aim
for end of hedge just to left of double
electricity post. ⑬ At end of hedge turn left
then through or over gate. Walk down field,
hedge on right. Turn right through hedge at
bottom and follow remnant of grassy lane
straight on. ⑭ Follow grassy lane along edge
of field to 2 double electricity posts. Turn left
through hedge and continue straight on
along side of field. For Eakring (4-mile walk)
turn left in a few yards and follow track to
playing fields and Triumph Road, where
there is access by car. ⑮ To continue, go
straight ahead keeping hedge, later stream,
on left. Continue to Church Hill, then road. ⑯
At road turn right. In 200 yards (183 m)
where road bends right go straight on along
grassy lane for 170 yards (155 m). At
beginning of second field on right turn right
through opening. Walk uphill diagonally left
across this and the next field, aiming just to
the right of the electricity pylon. From the hill
crest aim just to the right of the 2 trees
below the church tower. Cross concrete
bridge and bear left up farm track for 250
yards (229 m). ⑰ Turn right over fence
(waymark) and continue diagonally left
through 3 fields, going through gaps in
hedges. At left corner of third field enter the
grassy lane and turn right. Cross the field
and continue straight ahead at the
waymarked bridleway gate. Do not take the
track to the right but go straight on along the
line of poplar trees, up the hill to cross the
A616. Continue straight on with Kneesall
village triangle on right. ⑱ Pass post office
and go straight up Ossington Road for 550
yards (503 m). Turn left up well-defined
track through waymarked double gates.
Follow grassy lane, ignoring all side
turnings, for 1¾ miles (3 km) to the road.
Turn right to Laxton.

🏛 Stone Cross marking site of Pulpit Ash.

⛪ St. Michael's Church, Laxton, once an
🏛 exceptional medieval building, was spoilt
by Victorian rebuilding. A leaflet
describing Laxton's fascinating project
to preserve the medieval open field
farming system, and other features, is
available at the church.

EAST MIDLANDS

Tennyson Valley
9 miles (14.5 km) Sheet 122 334748

Moderate Fine views, lovely contoured dry valleys, remoteness and scattered communities unknown to many people who have lived in the area all their lives. *Farmland; section between* ⑧ *and* ⑨ *may be ploughed out – follow directions carefully.*

Start Tetford, signposted from the A16 S of Louth. **Parking** by the church.

① From parking walk away from church, past post office and village hall. By sharp left bend turn right through kissing-gate on to signposted footpath and cross field to white footbridge. Cross and turn right along track and road by mill house. Turn right over road bridge at main road and continue past chapel and school. ② Where road turns right up Tetford Hill go straight ahead on well-marked bridleway and Roman road. Ignore farm track on left. After about 700 yards (640 m) ignore uphill track on right and continue along Roman road to white bridleway gate and bridge. ③ Cross bridge and turn right. Follow the *diverted* bridleway along edge of stream for 400 yards (366 m), turning left along signposted, stony track by earth bridge. Keep straight on at cross-tracks, continuing 300 yards (274 m). At end of trees turn right to follow headland and small dyke on right. Just past wood, by gate on left, turn left along old road. Turn right along concrete track and continue to road where ④ turn right up Belchford Hill. At T-junction turn left along Bluestone Heath Road. Just past abandoned quarry track on opposite side turn right through sparse hedge and fence. Go diagonally across field to gate by left edge of spinney. Turn right down tree-lined lane to Oxcombe. ⑤ Opposite postbox in house wall turn left down track immediately beyond cart shed. Aiming for Farforth, keep to track, with fence on left. Cross earth bridge over stream and keep straight on with fence on right. Turn right into stackyard and left to church. ⑥ At end of churchyard turn right along broad track behind church. Continue on well-defined track round valley edge by wood, through gate and across field to left of spinney. Ignore bridge into wood on right, leaving track and walking to the left to a broken gate in corner of field. Follow headland forward, keeping ravine and Jericho Plantation just below and to right.

Harvest mice, the most delightful occupants of the agricultural E Midlands' great corn-fields, at a typical nest site.

Cross stile to left of cattle trough and continue straight on along edge of field until possible to descend to drive of the Old Rectory. Continue to road and Ruckland. ⑦ Continue down road and about 150 yards (137 m) beyond bridge turn left along signposted track. In nearly one mile (1.5 km) cross cattle grid and follow track into Worlaby. Turn right at side of church and continue uphill, keeping dry valley on right. Climb stile at roadside. Continue uphill a few yards and ⑧ turn left up well-defined track marked by footpath signpost. In 300 yards (274 m) turn right to climb bank and stile by signpost. Over stile bear left through gap in hedge, over rise in hedgehill and across field to line of trees. Aim for fifth or sixth tree, where there is a waymark. Go straight on over shoulder of hill, keeping just to right of remnant of hedge line. At bottom of hedge go straight ahead into corner of field. Cross barbed wire and make for left side of cottage ahead. Cross track and go straight ahead along lane towards church.

🏠 The 14th C. church contains a conspicuous memorial to Captain Edward Dymoke. The Dymokes, who lived locally until the end of the 19th C., are champions of the crown: the head of the family used to attend all coronations 'well armed for war, upon a good horse'.

🍺 The White Hart Inn at Tetford boasts 2
✗ literary connections, centring on its oak
settle – the long, wooden bench. It
supported Dr. Johnson when he
addressed the Tetford Club in 1764; and
Tennyson, who was born and raised at
nearby Somersby, rested on it between
bouts of skittles. Real ale; dining-room.

📖 The cabinet-maker's workshop behind
the pub is worth exploring.

↖ Extensive views.

⛪ A few yards along the track is the
county's smallest church, whose vicar
runs no less than 15 scattered and
isolated communities. Dedication to St.
Olave reflects Viking influence.

↖ To the coast.

The Lincolnshire County Council has
created a series of first-class walks in
the E Midlands area. All have efficient
waymarking – arrow symbols on posts,
stiles, gateposts and existing public
footpath signs. They are described in a
series of modestly priced leaflets.

One, on Lincoln Heath, takes in the
Preceptory of the Knights Templar at
Temple Bruer. Another, in the Vale of
Belvoir, follows part Grantham Canal.

There is a fenland walk starting at
Heckington, giving insight into the
landscape's development, and another
at Fishtoft, with a splendid section on
top of the bank of Hobhole Drain.

The Grimsthorpe Estate walk is of
interest to naturalists and a route at
Bardney gives a glimpse of undisturbed
remains of medieval strip farming.

PEAK DISTRICT

There are few peaks: the name derives from that of an English tribe. The highest land, over 2,000 feet (610 m) around Bleaklow and Kinder Scout, is more or less flat-topped, though rough heather, peat and bogs make this true mountain terrain – dangerous to the unwary, especially when the weather comes down.

Here, at the southern tip of the Pennines, the Pennine Way starts its trail north, and here, too, in 1932, there were fisticuffs between ramblers and gamekeepers. Today there is free access to the moors under one of the Peak National Park agreements covering 70 square miles (28 ha). The Park also provides benevolent wardens, first-class information centres and gentle strolling on disused railway tracks.

South of Edale, the millstone grit of the Dark Peak gives way to a 20-mile (32-km) wide limestone dome, the White Peak. This is not such harsh country, decorated by stone walls and small beechwoods. Its rivers have worn the limestone into small chasms (notably Dovedale) as romantically picturesque as the Dark Peak is romantically wild. Both are beautiful.

Ilam, Thorpe and Dove Dale
4 miles (6.5 km) Sheet 119 136508

Moderate Takes in not only the popular Dove Dale with its Stepping Stones but also escapes the crowded places, exploring the lovely lower reaches of the Dove and its sister river the Manifold. *Riverside, village, limestone country; mud after rain.*

Start Ilam, off the A515; buses stop at the Ilam crossroads 2¾ miles (4.5 km) from ①. **Parking** in the grounds of Ilam Hall, signposted at village centre.

① From Ilam centre cross the bridge, turn left over stile and follow the river downstream past series of waterfalls. ② Cross bridge and continue up lane to Thorpe village. ③ Cross the Ilam road and continue in direction of signpost to Lin Dale. ④ Enter Dove Dale at the Stepping Stones. Either cross over these and follow the road, or stay on same side using the path, crossing by footbridge lower down river. ⑤ At car park turn right and cross series of fields behind the Izaak Walton Hotel back to Ilam.

🏠 Ilam Hall, built in Victorian times by Jesse Watts Russell, a local manufacturer, now contains a youth hostel.

🏘 Ilam, a model village built by Watts Russell, is in a style with echoes of

Ilam Hall, Dove Dale; the beautiful grounds are worth exploring.

London and the Home Counties – a curiosity in these parts.

🗓 The River Dove's virtues were praised by Isaak Walton in *The Compleat Angler.* He stayed nearby with his friend Charles Cotton. Dove Dale is 'Eagle Dale' in George Eliot's *Adam Bede.*

🚩 Peveril of the Peak and Isaak Walton Hotels.

THE PEAK DISTRICT

Padley Gorge
5 miles (8 km) Sheets 110 and 119 251788

Easy A delightful woodland walk which leads easily to the gritstone edges above the Derwent Valley. *Gorge, woods, meadows, gritstone edges; one climb; mud after rain; in the early stages of the walk several alternative paths climb through the gorge; all join higher up – but if the stream is kept in sight or hearing route-finding is simple.*

Start Grindleford Station off the B6521; buses to Fox House Inn, from where walk can be joined at Longshaw Lodge, near point ③; trains to Grindleford. **Car parking** at station is limited; motorists may prefer to use the National Trust car park entered from B6521 by a track a little way south of the Grouse Inn. (If starting from NT car park, climb 50 yards (45 m) to join route at Haywood.)

① From station walk upstream on right side of Padley Gorge, following main path through the oak wood, over bridge half-way up, and on to open moorland beyond, recrossing stream. Continue to 90 yards (80 m) before gate on to road at bend below the distinctively shaped Toad's Mouth Rock. ② Turn sharp right, ascending slowly to road. Cross and enter the Longshaw Estate. ③ Follow signposted footpath past the front of Longshaw Lodge, passing two wicket gates. ④ Turn right at the road and continue as far as the Grouse Inn. ⑤ Follow the footpath from behind the Grouse Inn and walk steeply down through the Haywood to join the B6521 at Grindleford ⑥ Turn right and cross the riverside meadows. ⑦ At small stream on right (Burbage Brook) cross, turn half right, and climb gently through fields to cross the railway line by a bridge. Turn right on entering lane; continue past Chapel to station.

🏠 Padley Chapel was once the gatehouse of a large manor house now demolished. During the persecutions of the Roman Catholics in Elizabeth I's reign, 2 priests who celebrated mass there were hanged, drawn and quartered in Derby.

↖ Carl Wark, ½ mile (0.8 km) away, and Burbage Rocks, ¾ mile (one km) distant.

※ Carl Wark is an Iron Age fort made of gigantic gritstone blocks.

🍺 Grouse Inn.

↖ Froggatt Edge and the Derwent Valley.

A later model of Arkwright's famous Water Frame, so-called because it was water-powered.

THE PEAK DISTRICT

Matlock to Cromford
2½ miles (4 km) Sheet 119 297601

Easy A convenient escape from the crowds in this holiday area; fine views and peaceful woodland. *Farmland; woods.*

Start Matlock; frequent buses and trains. **Car parks** in Matlock. **Return** to starting point by bus or trains; buses leave from the square, Cromford.

① From the centre of Matlock follow the Snitterton road past Williams Deacon's Bank to lane on left signposted Bridge Farm. Follow this. At farm, climb short flight of steps into field. Follow path uphill and fork left to cross fields by stiles. Enter wood. ② Turn right by St. John's Chapel and walk up the lane to signpost for Matlock Bath. This points to a track to left of a large house.

Follow this below Masson Farm as far as another signpost at which turn left through woods to join Upperwood Road below pleasure grounds of the Heights of Abraham. ③ Turn right along Upperwood Road. ④ At last house in the hamlet of Upperwood take the path signposted to Bonsall and Scarthin. Follow main path through the woodland ahead. ⑤ Above Cromford zigzag down by path to the cobbled way leading to Scarthin and continue to Cromford.

▼ A variety of pubs and cafés.

† Derwent Gorge, dominated by the limestone cliffs of High Tor. On the hillside above High Tor, about a mile (1.5 km) distant, is Riber Castle, built in 1852 by a local mill owner as a hotel. It now houses a European fauna zoo.

⛪ St. John's Chapel, a building with an almost Tyrolean appearance.

† Victoria Tower, on Masson Hill, is an excellent vantage point.

⛺ There are guided tours round the caves in the Heights of Abraham public recreation grounds.

🏭 Richard Arkwright, textile magnate and inventor of spinning systems, established his first water-powered mill at Cromford. It is preserved as an exhibition centre.

ⓘ Arkwright started his career as a wig-maker, turning his mind to spinning in the 1760s and beginning work on his first machine in 1764. It made thread strong enough to be used for the warp in weaving – the threads running length-wise on a loom, crossed by the weft. Earlier machines, such as Hargreaves' 'Spinning Jenny', produced thread suitable only for weft. Within a few years Arkwright was operating several factories. and had made cotton cloth manufacture Northern England's leading industry. The inevitable accolades, and wealth followed: he was knighted in 1786 and left a vast fortune. Horse-drawn boat trips can be taken on the canal that ends at the mill.

▼ Pubs and cafés.

THE PEAK DISTRICT

Lyme Park and Bow Stones Moor
5 miles (8 km) Sheet 109 964823

Easy An introduction to much that is typical and dramatic of the Peak District. Excellent views of the Cheshire Plain from the moorland around Bow Stones. The gardens of Lyme Hall and the rhododendrons in West Park are at their best in spring and early summer. *Parkland, moorland, meadow, woods; one climb; slightly boggy in section ⑤. If inexperienced at hill walking, avoid in poor visibility.*

Start Take the A6 to Disley and enter Lyme Park at signpost; buses and trains to Disley; transport in park from Parkgate. **Car park** at side of Lyme Hall.

① From car park follow path alongside Dutch Garden to lake in front of Hall. Turn right and walk through avenue of trees towards Knight's Low. ② Enter the pine woods on a wide track, turn left and walk through the wood to a stile over the boundary wall. Continue on path climbing open moor to Bow Stones Farm. ③ At Bow Stones turn right along lane. ④ At end of lane turn right through gate and follow rough path across open moorland of Sponds Hill. ⑤ Cross the lane and strike diagonally across field to a deep gully, then climb slightly into meadowland to a farm. Follow path to the chapel. ⑥ Turn right at the chapel and continue down the track to West Lodge. ⑦ At Lodge turn right into West Park woods and follow track to start.

🏛 Lyme Hall – Elizabethan with some fine later additions – is the seat of the Legh family (Lord Newton) and is now maintained by the National Trust and Stockport Corporation. There are some superb Jacobean rooms. It is one of the several houses where Mary Queen of Scots was held captive; she visited nearby Buxton to take the waters for her rheumatism.

🦌 A large herd of red deer have lived in the 1,320-acre (534 ha) park for centuries.

🔭 Extensive views over the Cheshire Plain.

❋ The Bow Stones are a pair of megaliths or monumental stones. Local legend holds that Robin Hood and his men used them for bending their bows.

Elton and Gratton Dale
6½ miles (10.5 km) Sheet 119 223610

Moderate Gives insight into some of the area's contrasting rock formations and their interesting effect on the surface pasture; also passes a hermit's cave. *Farmland, dry limestone dales, gritstone outcrops; one climb; mud.*

Start From the A6 take the B5057 to Winster, then minor road to Elton; buses. **Parking** in Elton – do not block entrances.

① From centre of village follow the road opposite the church S as far as the speed de-restriction sign. Turn right along cart track between pastures. At junction with an overgrown track turn left – the way is easy to follow even if the track is overgrown. ② At end of track turn right over stile and cross a series of fields by way of a grassy path. Continue as far as the Cromford-Newhaven road. Turn right and continue about 150 yards (137 m). ③ At an indistinct style by side of a square field turn right over style and follow field wall around rear of Mouldridge Grange Farm. Turn right into Gratton Dale and follow it as far as Dale End Farm. ④ Turn left on to road at Dale End Farm and almost immediately right by a gate. The field here is marshy and the correct line of the path is impossible to follow. Instead follow gravel farm track to top of field above the swamp. Follow the wall around to the right as far as a stile. Turn left and cross several fields by stiles eventually reaching the Elton-Harthill road. ⑤ Turn left along the road and walk on until opposite the turning to Harthill Moor Farm. ⑥ Turn right and cross fields aiming to left of the distinctive shape of the rock formations of Robin Hood's Stride. ⑦ Go downhill to the road and turn right, walking uphill to the minor road to Dudwood Farm. Continue to farm. ⑧ Beyond the farm turn right on to a field path slanting upwards to Elton village.

Elton's church had a unique Saxon font, whose worth was unappreciated, and which was thrown out during rebuilding in the 19th C. It turned up, however, in Youlgreave church (see page 212), where it now stands.

Interesting orchids and other plants which thrive on limestone.

There are remains of lead mines on Elton Common, usually detected by grassy humps. They were small-scale, being worked by one or 2 men only.

This section follows the Portway, a prehistoric way running from near Nottingham to the hill fort on Mam Tor.

The curious gritstone formation of Robin Hood's Stride is known locally as Mockbeggar's Hall because of the 2 'chimneys', which look particularly life-like at dusk. Rock climbers call them the Weasel and Inaccessible.

The hermit's cave has a crucifix carved in the rock at the rear.

The rock strata can be seen changing from limestone (S) to gritstone (N).

THE PEAK DISTRICT

Goyt Valley and Shining Tor Ridge
6½ miles (10.5 km) Sheets 118 and 119 012749

Moderate This is a safe walk from which to appreciate the solitude of wild moorland. The Goyt Valley is the first area of open country to operate a traffic-free scheme. Best in summer and autumn when the moor is dry. *Woods, moorland; 2 climbs; Cats Tor is boggy but avoidable.*

Start From the A5002 Manchester–Buxton road via Long Hill take the minor road into Goyt Valley from the summit; buses to Long Hill. **Car park** the Goyt Valley Car Park.

① From car park follow the forest trail to the stream below the ruins of Erwood Hall. Turn right, up towards the Hall. ② At Hall, follow track round the front and towards the far stream beyond the house. Follow this the whole way to the road. The lower reaches of the path are waymarked with white sticks: leave the waymarked route where the sticks turn sharp right and follow the path ahead. ③ At road turn left and walk almost as far as the Pym Chair Car Park at the highest part of the climb. ④ Turn off the road and walk forward on moorland following drystone wall or its remnants whole way to Tor. ⑤ At Shining Tor turn left and walk towards the far side of the valley. ⑥ Turn left down the smooth track back to the car park.

 Ruins of Erwood Hall, built by the Grimshawe family in 1830. The variety of rhododendrons in the pine woods is a reminder that of this large plant group – over 600 species – about half are able to thrive in the U.K. Gardeners and landscape artists have found them useful material because their fine roots do not grow to great depths, which makes them easy to move without damage. Azaleas are abundant, too.

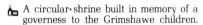 A circular·shrine built in memory of a governess to the Grimshawe children.

Shining Tor opens up superb views of the Cheshire Highlands. The conical hill is Shuttlingslow, 1,659 feet (506 m).

✗ Café. About a mile (1.5 km) S on the road to Burbage is the Cat and Fiddle, one of England's highest pubs at 1,690 feet (515 m), from where views extend to the Mersey on clear days.

Our most familiar rhododendron, the so-called wild species (R. ponticum), with its purple flowers, was introduced in 1763.

Castleton and Mam Tor

6½ miles (10.5 km) Sheet 110 151827

Moderate Interesting archaeological and geological features; fine views. *Dry dale, limestone moor, gritstone moor, grassy ridge; 2 climbs; take care on Mam Tor, which can be dangerously slippery if wet. Do not attempt in poor visibility.*

Start Castleton on the A625; buses to Castleton; trains to Hope, where there are buses to Castleton. **Car parks** in Castleton.

① From square in front of youth hostel enter Cave Dale by its narrow entrance between cottages. Climb up the dale and across the grassy moor on well-defined footpath. ② At crossing of 4 tracks turn right along the farm lane and continue past Rowter Farm. ③ Cross the road and enter the field opposite. Follow the track over Windy Knoll and cross

the Rushup Edge road. ④ Climb the steep field opposite and at the stile turn right to climb the well-marked path across Mam Tor. ⑤ At Hollins Cross turn right and follow the path downhill. This eventually joins a walled lane which leads directly to Castleton.

▮ Peveril Castle began in 1080 as a wooden stockade.

〰 The brown, rounded rocks beyond the gate at Cave Dale's head are remains of an ancient lava flow.

⌖ These are show caves.

❋ At earliest, a Bronze Age fort.

⌇ The Hope Valley.

⌇ Across Edale to Kinder Scout; down Hope Valley to the White Peak plateau.

THE PEAK DISTRICT

Lathkill and Bradford Dales
12 miles (19 km) Sheet 119 210643

Energetic A route through some of the most interesting and attractive dales in the Peak. Well-blessing at Youlgreave is a charming spectacle, performed annually. *Farmland, limestone dales, villages; 2 climbs; mud after rain; Cales Dale is slippery when wet.*

Start Youlgreave off the B5056; buses. **Car park** On Moor Lane, about 100 yards (91 m) E of ②

① From centre of Youlgreave walk up lane opposite the youth hostel as far as the car park beyond the old mineral workings. ② Leave road by stile marked with a 'footpath sign and walk across fields. The route is waymarked by posts painted with a yellow mark. ③ Go through Calling Low farmyard, following the signs, and cross a series of fields. ④ Descend steeply and cross Cales Dale on clearly defined path to One Ash Grange Farm. Continue on cart track. The walk may be shortened by turning right in Cales Dale and walking down it to join Lathkill Dale. ⑤ Where cart track beyond the farm turns sharp right at gate, go through gate and immediately turn left to follow wall up side of field. At top of field cross stile and follow path through series of fields. Eventually the path joins a walled, grassy lane; follow this the whole way to Monyash. ⑥ Follow the road through Monyash village, turning right at the green opposite The Hobbit. Leave village on the Bakewell road. ⑦ In dip in road beyond Monyash turn right at the signpost 'To Lathkill Dale'. Follow the dale, keeping to the only path, which is on the N bank of the stream. Continue as far as the road bridge at Conksbury. ⑧ Turn right across bridge and walk up road as far as gate with yellow arrow on left. Follow this path to the road at Alport. ⑨ Cross the road and enter Bradford Dale on wide farm track. Continue ¾ mile (one km). ⑩ Cross road and continue along the dale on path on N side of stream. At a clapper bridge, cross and continue up the dale, passing a series of trout pools. ⑪ Below the final pool turn right and cross the stream on wide stone bridge. Climb steeply through the woods to Youlgreave.

🏰 The church is one of Derbyshire's loveliest, with a fine 15th C. tower and a late medieval chest tomb. The centre of interest, however, is the Saxon font. It has a curious side projection, the use of which is the subject of controversy; possibly it is a container for holy oil. More controversial still, to local people, is where the font belongs. During the 19th C. it was carried back and forth between here and Elton church, whose property it was: a saga of village rivalry.

✕ Calling Low Farm sells non-alcoholic drinks, including milk.

🏢 One Ash Grange Farm has a considerable main building, which in medieval times was a place of correction for erring monks.

🍺 The Hobbit: real ale and good pub food.

The River Lathkill flows out of a cave here when it is wet. In dry weather the upper reaches run underground.

Clear trout pools in the Lathkill.

Ruins of a pumphouse which served Mandale Mine.

Lathkill Dale Nature Reserve.

Lathkill Dale.

The pub serves food.

The ancient local ceremony of well-blessing takes place in late June each year.

Several pubs and tea rooms.

The Delamere pine forest, off the B5152, has waymarked walks radiating from the car park and visitors' centre.

Edale is an excellent starting point for walks in most directions.

Longshaw, 3 miles (5 km) SE of Hatherage via the A625, gives access to paths with fine views leading to the Rocking Stone and Frog's Mouth Cave.

Congleton Edge provides a 3-mile walk with spectacular scenery. Approach on the A527 from Biddulph.

Well to the S there is Cannock Chase (lying SE of Stafford) with its network of secluded woodland paths.

Dove Dale's riverside and woodland paths deserve further exploration, preferably out of holiday season.

NORTHERN ENGLAND

LANCASHIRE, THE SOUTH PENNINES, YORKSHIRE WOLDS, YORKSHIRE DALES, NORTH YORK MOORS, CUMBRIA AND THE LAKES, NORTHUMBERLAND

LANCASHIRE

Some think that this county's charm was lost to the walker when its corner of the Lake District, Furness and Cartmel, went to Cumbria in 1974. At the same time, Lancashire gained a slice of Yorkshire containing the whole of the wild, fell-walking terrain of the ancient hunting Forest of Bowland.

The Forest is one of three hunks of the Pennines which thrust westwards into Lancashire. Next, to the south, is Pendle Hill, and then, across the Calder Valley, the fells of Rossendale. From both, the walker looks down on the milltowns. You do not, however, have to live in Burnley, Accrington, Nelson or Colne to feel the release of these uplands; the inhabitants of the intensively farmed flatlands behind Southport and Blackpool are thankful for them, too.

W. G. Hoskins, the great landscape historian, has noted that in the Ribble and Lune valleys ancient enclosures have produced almost Devonian scenery of winding lanes, stone farms and hamlets. These rivers debouch on the county's other great asset, a coast of wide strands and bird-haunted estuaries.

Wyresdale
5 miles (8 km) Sheet 102 551545

Easy Varied walking with excellent views of the fells. *Farmland, river, woods.*

Start The church (obscured by trees) 2½ miles (4 km) E of Dolphinholme on the road to Abbeystead. **Parking** opposite church.

① Go through churchyard to single gate on far side. Drop to footbridge and climb over double stile on right. Cross field, climbing hill and heading for farm. ② Turn left in yard through gates and stile alongside barn. Continue towards wood, and enter it over ladder stile at bottom of hill. ③ Over iron bridge, bear right, then left to footbridge over tributary. Leave wood over stile and turn right; climb track. Fork left beyond Catshaw Hall past Little Catshaw. ④ Track bends decisively right; leave it to follow reedy ditch. Bear slightly right after footbridge. Bear right in wood, descending to locate drained mill pond. Follow embankment, then descend to footbridge which points out of wood uphill to farm (not in view at first). ⑤ Follow farm track to tarmac road; turn left. ⑥ Leave road at first gate on left after farm. Descend through 3 fields on left of wooded stream. Track leads through wood, downhill to footbridge and then to lane at bridge. Turn left over bridge, shortly joining road at Stoops Bridge. Cross this also and go right over wall stile. ⑦ Track through riverside fields to road at Grizedale Bridge. ⑧ Leave road immediately at wall stile on left. Climb to foot-

Wyresdale Church: shepherds probably hung their crooks on the porch's iron hooks.

bridge and continue until barn is 100 yards (91 m) to right. Keep to top of slope. Stiles waymark route straight ahead to road. ⑨ Cross stile opposite, then make for small gate. Turn right to ①.

⌂ The (18th C.) stone building once stabled churchgoers' horses.

⊞ Abbeystead House, formerly owned by Earls of Sefton, renowned for shooting hospitality: a record bag was 2,929 birds.

LANCASHIRE

Pudsay's Leap
10 miles (16 km) Sheet 103 776466.

Moderate A refreshingly lonely stretch of the popular Ribble Valley. *Riverside, farmland, woods; mud; slippery in parts.* ② to ⑤ is waymarked R for 'Ribble Way'.

Start Sawley, off the A59 NE of Clitheroe.
Parking opposite Spread Eagle Hotel.

① Take minor road opposite Spread Eagle. Fork left. Go through 2 gates on left just before second gateway to Sawley Lodge. ② After footbridge, follow ditch to stile and footbridge; further stiles lead to river-bank. Continue mainly by river about 1½ miles (2.5 km). ③ Climb track and fork right to go above riverside wood. Turn right over stile at corner of fence and wood, heading for next corner, where look carefully for rail. Cross and continue left of fence, over stile and changing to right of fence at barn, to join access road. ④ Follow access road from farm, then go through gate on left of isolated barn. ⑤ After crossing steep-sided stream to gates, over field to stile by house; right and left into drive and straight ahead to road. Turn left and continue 1¼ miles (2 km). Where road turns right, continue up Park House drive. ⑥

Enter field on right of farm but keep left to descend to footbridge. Cross stile on left. Turn right, uphill. ⑦ After plantation, follow right-handed boundary to Fooden Farm. (If bull in field, the farm track to right is a safer way to the road.) ⑧ Turn right at house. Leave yard at top end by building with curved roof. Bear left to gate in fence. Aim for left end of long plantation to stile in corner. ⑨ Cross 2 fields to join road to right of white house and follow through village. After crossing bridge, fork left into surfaced track. ⑩ Cross stile on right at bend of road. Climb slightly left past oaks, and descend to stile. Leave next field at far left corner. ⑪ Continue ahead through kissing-gate and stile. Cut across bend of stream on right before crossing at footbridge. Half left to next stile and continue on this line. ⑫ Gradually close in on River Ribble (on left), then follow white stones, ⑬ crossing stream on right. Head for Sawley Bridge.

Ruined Cistercian monastery (1147).

Pudsay's Leap: 16th C. squire jumped the river on a horse with a magic bit to escape arrest for (magically) minting silver from lead.

Chipping Fells
7 miles (11 km) Sheet 102 or 103 622433

Moderate Accessible, yet crowd-free at any season; constant changes of view. *Sheep and limestone country; 2 climbs.*

Start Chipping, N of Longridge and the B5269; buses from Preston to Chipping bus terminus. **Public car park** near the church, Chipping.

① From church, take the road N–the weather vane on the spire points the way. Then fork right. ② Midway along millpond, turn right to stile off track. Climb hillside with back to pond. Keep parallel to valley, then bear right of quarry ahead to stile. Aim to left of Birchen Lee through 2 reedy fields. ③ Follow track past Birchen Lee and turn left at first junction. At bridge in dip before next farm, walk a few yards upstream to join faint track at ford. Climb far bank to gate. Skirt to left of low hill and join stony track; go right. ④ At Lickhurst Farm follow road round to left. Cross footbridge at bottom of hill. Climb to stile. Join faint, rutted track on left of limestone hill. At first head well to left of Dinkling Green Farm, ahead, then

directly towards it with fence on left, leading to clear track and gate in corner. ⑤ Pass right of building with carved face over door. Follow farm road for ⅓ mile (0.5 km), leaving it where track turns half right by gate on left. Climb over ridge and descend to stile-gate at road. Turn right, and left at telephone box; in 230 yards (210 m) ⑥ turn right on to farm road. Follow this for ¾ mile (one km), passing Higher and Lower Greystoneley to reach isolated barn. Go through gate, fork right past old lime-kiln and quarry, then continue to stile in tree-lined fence 110 yards (100 m) left of wood. Drop to footbridge, then follow right-hand boundaries of several fields straight ahead. At end of boundaries, straight ahead to farm road near wood boundary wall. Turn left, then right at road.

🏴 Chipping means 'market', which was the town's former role.

🏭 Berry's Chair Works, once a cotton mill.

🏠 The Windy Street almshouses are still used charitably, housing 2 people.

🏠 Upland sheep rearing is taught here.

LANCASHIRE

The Ribble Valley at Ribchester
3 miles (5 km) Sheet 103 653355

Easy A historically fascinating part of the Ribble Valley. *Farmland, woods; one climb; mud after rain.*

Start The Ribchester Arms hotel, outside Ribchester on the B6245 (Blackburn road); buses stop by the hotel. **Parking** near the hotel.

① Take Stydd Lane, between hotel and bridge, but turn right after a few yards through gate with stile. Continue to follow stream after crossing stone bridge. ② Cross stile on right, then footbridge. Bear left and continue through 3 fields passing about 150 yards (137 m) to left of farm. ③ Cross stile in corner of field and stile on immediate left. Bear right to stile up bank on to road. Turn left and go to gate on left at S-bend. Cross middle of field to stile; follow raised track to enter Duddel Wood. Follow path through wood. Cross second footbridge on left *after* passing ruins of comb mill. ④ Path climbs to leave wood at stile. Cross stile on right after ruined barn. Leave next field in diagonally opposite corner. Make for summit of Duddel Hill. ⑤ Face across Ribble Valley. Descend to stile by short length of stone wall. Continue in same direction to cross stile, footbridge and stile (on right) in turn. ⑥ Pass through yard of Stydd Manor Farm. Follow lane to point ①.

🏛 Ribchester was the Roman cavalry fort, Bremetonacum; museum has relics .

🏚 The extraordinary Stydd Almshouses, with Roman pillars set into the porch, similar to those at the White Bull in Ribchester.

Dunsop Fell
12 miles (19 km) Sheet 103 659501

Energetic Insight into the wild beauty and enchanting softer aspects of Bowland. *Riverside, undulating sheep country; one climb; do not attempt in poor visibility – compass recommended.*

Start Dunsop Bridge, 2 miles (3 km) W of Newton and the B6478. **Car park** at E end of village.

① Cross bridge and take private road at war memorial. After 2 miles (3 km), cross first half of concrete and iron bridge. Continue on track uphill. At junction fork right. ② Turn right on nearside of farm. Take rough track beyond barn to climb Dunsop Fell. After second elbow bend, path is indistinct, but the route is directly uphill, in direction of cairns and post on skyline. (Waymarked by posts with yellow discs, arrows, or bands.) Approaching fell-top fence, follow path as it bears right to small gate in wall. ③ Beyond wall leave waymarked track: turn right, and gradually bear away from wall (beware of false tracks – made by sheep). When valley comes into view, descend near top of ridge on *right* side of valley. Turn right near bottom, and go through second gate (in a dip) in wall on left. Make for Burn Side (farmhouse), looking for waymarks (blue arrows) as you approach farm. Follow access road to road and turn right ④ Enter field from yard of Laythams (name on house). Then aim for farm ahead (Parrock Head), but bear left at first, then along wall and over stile. ⑤ Leave Parrock Head farm yard on near-side of main buiding. Aim for Pain Hill Farm, reached over footbridge hidden in dip. ⑥ At Pain Hill Farm cross wall-stile on right of buildings, turn right then follow wall to left. Climb next field, looking carefully for stile in left-hand wall, at corner of adjacent field. *Do not cross stile*, but angle away, aiming to left side of tree-lined water hole. This puts you on target for a wall-stile 500 yards (457 m) distant. This stile is on right of kink in wall, hardly visible until wall is reached (the same applying to the next 2). Cross next field directly to wall-stile. Bear partly right in next to stile on to road (on left of pond). Continue to right about 250 yards (229 m) to ⑦ a walled, rutted track (Bull Lane). Follow it to end (after right and left bends). Bear slightly right to gate that comes into view. Descending to Rough Syke Barn, note position of

Back of Hill Barn beyond. Bear slightly right with track after Rough Syke Barn, down to bridge over stream. Pass through gate on left, ford a stream, and climb in direction of Back of Hill Barn. ⑧At barn continue ahead, then bear right at track. Beyond farm and Beatrix, leave track when fence on right stops. Continue parallel to overhead wires on right. Pass over hillside and descend to wall-stile 40 yards (37 m) to left of wires. Descend to river; turn left through yard to ①.

\⚡/ Interior of the Forest of Bowland.

🔟 A superb, alternative approach to Dunsop Bridge is through the Trough of Bowland, a dramatic valley route.

Ideal for improvised walking in this area are the banks of the Lancaster Canal, one of the country's most pleasing waterways. Do not overlook the branch to Glasson, an attractive harbour on the Lune estuary.

Across the estuary there is a fine walk around Sunderland Point. Check time of high tide first – approach to Sunderland may be flooded.

Pendle Hill is a favourite climb, but not to be undertaken lightly.

A leaflet showing access areas in the Forest of Bowland is available.

THE SOUTH PENNINES

Why should this end of the Pennines be despised? It often is and by walkers who ought to know better. They think of this region as a nondescript patch of largely industrialized hill country which intervenes between the northern boundary of the Peak District and the southern boundary of the Yorkshire Dales national parks. But attitudes are changing and these days ramblers are readier to see the charms of the country on their back doorsteps.

The landscape is seamed with canals, railways and now motorways which link the conurbations on either side of the Pennine chain. In fact the close juxtaposition of industry and nature makes for exciting contrasts. Huddersfield's centre, for instance, is within three miles of the moors and the nearby bluebell-filled Mollcar Woods. From Ainsley Top the walker has before him a sweeping view of the Calder Valley and Halifax.

The smaller textile towns and mill villages are living records of an industrial era now fading. Howarth was the home of the Brontë family and the surrounding moors provide a setting fully worthy of the great novels that were written here. Indeed, Withins Moor is supposed to be the model for Wuthering Heights. Through all this the Pennine Way weaves steadily northwards. Those who walk this first of our long-distance paths should pause to explore this robust, working terrain.

A lost village
3 miles (5 km) Sheet 109 911176

Easy Spectacular views across the Pennines, and over the Roch valley. *Pasture and rough grazing; one climb; mud after rain.*

Start From the A58 between Rochdale and Littleborough take road at Sandknockers Inn to Wardle. Continue through Wardle to Wardle Fold, and on to where lane ends below reservoir gates; frequent buses to Wardle. **Parking** by side of road in lane, not causing an obstruction.

① Go through the reservoir pedestrian entrance, following the main track around and to the right up to the reservoir dam. ② Continue along track around reservoir wall, through gate and around E side of reservoir. ③ Where track joins old, cobbled street, follow street N uphill. ④ Where lane bears right at ruined farm (gatepost on left), leave it left to descend to stream at head of reservoir. ⑤ Ford stream and follow line of old wall above little ravine ahead. Go through gap in crossing wall to next wall ahead. ⑥ Turn left along wall, keeping ahead across open pasture to join old, walled, grassy lane ahead. ⑦ Follow grassy way downhill curving right to ruined farm. ⑧ Cross open pasture above scattered trees, keeping about 100 yards (91 m) above reservoir and making for wall directly ahead and parallel with reservoir. ⑨ Descend to reservoir dam past old quarry – bear left towards gate. ⑩ Go through pedestrian gate and along top of reservoir dam. At end of dam turn right through reservoir gates.

🏠 Wardle Fold, a former weaving hamlet, has several 3-tiered cottages with the typical Lancashire weaving

Watergrove Reservoir: access around the edges is unlimited

loft to accommodate the hand-weaving loom.

🔟 The weaving hamlet of Watergrove was drowned in 1935 to make the reservoir. The cobbled lane between Wardle Fold and Watergrove disappears beneath the dam, and it can be seen going under water at the reservoir's E edge. If the water is low, the hamlet's foundations are visible. The reservoir is Rochdale's principal water supply.

🔟 Small quarries and coal pits bear witness to this derelict area's former livelihood, as do the farms, emptied to avoid pollution of the reservoir.

THE SOUTH PENNINES

Wycoller
4 miles (6.5 km) Sheet 103 926395

Easy An attractive 'hidden' hamlet; views giving insight into typical local scenery. *Pasture; mud after rain.*

Start From Trawden, 2 miles (3 km) SW of Colne, follow signs to Wycoller; frequent buses from Keighley and Colne stop at Laneshawbridge – get off at crossroads and join walk at ⑨. **Car park** 440 yards (400 m) W of Wycoller hamlet on road from Cotton Tree and Colne – cars not allowed beyond.

① From car park walk down lane into Wycoller, keeping on lane through hamlet. ② Cross beck (stream), right, by ancient 'clam' footbridge, and follow wall uphill to crossing wall above. Follow track above this left to barn at Bank House. ③ Follow path round Bank House, then down slope on grassy way. Cross hurdle stile and footbridge below, then go uphill to gate and Dean House Farm. Walk between farm and barn to stile behind farm, over field and through gate to Parson Lee Farm. ④ Over stile to left of barn, cross lane, over beck at stepping stones and bear left uphill to white farm (Foster's Leap) ahead. ⑤ Follow path in front of farmhouse, then through series of stiles (some gaps) in narrow fields, keeping same height, then descending slightly to the left. ⑥ At gate, path joins sunken, metalled track; follow this downhill, through stile and down steps back to Wycoller Hall. ⑦ Keep right along track above Hall and behind hamlet, entering field

by gap on right. Over stiles to join track in front of old Pump House. ⑧ Follow track into fields, keeping same direction to junction of paths. Ignore stile straight ahead, crossing stile, left, and taking path between wall and beck. Cross stiles and take path on higher land above beck ahead to Covey Bridge. ⑨ At lane cross bridge and walk uphill. ⑩ Turn left at tall step stile, following wall for 150 yards (137 m), through stile on left, and at next stile bear diagonally right downhill across beck, going uphill, over stiles, to Slack Farm. ⑪ Follow track round outside of farm, go through gate on left beyond farm, then alongside wall and straight on through gates to lane just above car park.

🏠 Wycoller was a farming and weaving community which declined after the 1820s, the peak years of handloom weaving. The ruined Hall is reputedly the model for Ferndean Manor in *Jane Eyre*. Picnic site; refreshments at Oak House.

⌒ The hamlet was the meeting point for several cross-Pennine packhorse ways; the double-arched packhorse bridge may be 13th C. Nearby is the clapper bridge, made of 3 slabs, between 1,000 and 2,000 years old. The next upstream, a 'clam' bridge, is older still, the most primitive form of permanent bridge.

🏠 The unique walls of upright slabs were probably erected between 1100 and 1400 as enclosures for local cattle-rearing farms.

Ponden Clough

6 miles (9.5 km) Sheets 103 and 104 007382

Energetic An unusual walk on the fringe of the much-visited Brontë country, with superb views over the Oakworth, Haworth and Keighley areas. *Farmland, moorland; one climb; mud. Do not attempt in poor visibility.*

Start Unclassified road from Colne to Keighley. **Car park** at Hare Hill Edge, 1½ miles W of Oakworth.

① From car park walk W along road to signposted, enclosed path by water filtration works. Follow it to Oldfield School. ② Turn left in village, then first right along farm track. Below farm, continue along grassy way, which becomes a field path, going through gate and downhill to Griff Mill. ③ Cross beck (stream) at footbridge, turn right to go outside mill, climbing along enclosed, grassy track to Stanbury. ④ Through gate behind farm and into back lane, keeping right through village to Hob Hill (bus terminus); bear left up minor lane. ⑤ At junction of lanes, bear right above farms and cottages along quiet lane and track. ⑥ At last farm, keep left around outside wall on moor edge, through wicket gate. Where wall swings right, maintain height, keeping ahead to pick up faint track through heather. ⑦ As path nears end of short valley, bear right to path downhill to cross stream at small dam. Follow path downhill by beck, walk down rocky steps with handrail (extreme care

required if wet) and past waterworks retaining wall. Go left along clear path to next waterfall. ⑧ Continue along grassy footway, rising to Upper Ponden Farm. ⑨ Turn left immediately before farm, round farm and down to white notice by gate below. Turn right through gate and continue along track to junction. Right again for Ponden Hall. ⑩ From Ponden Hall retrace to junction, keeping straight ahead, then bearing right to track round reservoir, and climbing up to road. ⑪ Left along road for 100 yards (91 m), then right over stile (Pennine Way), climbing pasture to farmhouse, where turn left up farm track. Bear left along side of wall to track at Crag Bottom. Turn left along road. ⑫ Go 200 yards (183 m) along road, then right along track (Pennine Way) uphill. Continue ½ mile (0.8 km), crossing 3 substantial stiles. ⑬ At obvious junction of tracks, go right along path outside fell wall (avoiding boggy places) to wall corner. Follow track to pinewoods, then continue along well-defined farm track to road. Continue ahead to car park.

ⓑ Timmy Feather, the last Yorkshire handloom weaver, worked in Stanbury.

〰 Ponden Clough – a steep-sided valley.

🏭 Ponden Hall, dating from 1634, now a craft mill and shop, has changed little ▬ since the time of the Brontë sisters, who lived nearby at Haworth. It may be the model of Thrushcross Grange in ✕ *Wuthering Heights*. Tea shop.

THE SOUTH PENNINES

Bretton

5 miles (8 km) Sheet 110 296124

Easy Fine parkland surrounded by industry, close to the M1; an interesting contrast to other routes in this section. *Parkland, farmland.*

Start The Country Park one mile (1.5 km) S of West Bretton on the A637 – adjacent to M1 junction 38; frequent buses from Barnsley, Huddersfield and Dewsbury pass Park entrance; connections possible with Wakefield-Huddersfield service at Bretton roundabout and Wakefield-Holmfirth at West Bretton village. **Parking** by Visitor Centre at entrance to Park on A637. The Park opens at 10 am and the car park gates are locked at 6 pm. Alternative parking at W side of park on High Hoyland Road 220 yards (200 m) N of point ⑨.

① From car park and picnic site cross to entrance of Country Park, through gate and follow broad, well-defined path towards lake. Follow river-bank to Bretton Park Bridge (good view of lake from bridge). ② Follow bridleway uphill from bridge directly away from lake. ③ To visit Sculpture Park and gardens turn right at junction of tracks, making for Sculpture Park car park behind College buildings, passing through car park to the drive with sculptures either side. Return by track leading left past bungalow just S of main entrance. Follow signposted path leading from track

N of row of lime trees along edge of field to stile, then downhill to footbridge. ④ Over footbridge, then bear left around corner of fence to gate, then half-left to stile on to Hoyland Road. ⑤ Cross stile opposite and bear slightly left towards stream and woods to cross 2 wooden stiles. Cross field to stile on to farm track. ⑥ Left at farm track, and climb past sewage farm to Clayton Hall Farm. ⑦ At NE corner of farm buildings, go through gate and keep fence on left. Go downhill through long field to stile and footbridge, crossing both to climb next field to stile on to road straight ahead. ⑧ Left for 50 yards (45 m) then right over stile before farm. Along field, over next stile and into Bretton Park. Descend towards far end of lake crossing main track after dip, keep at same level and make for a red-topped post on ridge. ⑨ Cross stiles into wooded area, go down slope to E edge of lake and back to car park.

🏕 Waymarked trails in the Country Park, with wildlife and botanical interest, are
🦌 given in leaflets on sale at the Visitor Centre. Keep dogs on leads at all times in the Park.

🏘 Bretton Hall, built in 1720 in the classical style, was extended in Regency times. Now a college of higher education, it is not open to the public. The Sculpture Park features work by Barbara Hepworth, born in Wakefield.

THE SOUTH PENNINES

The Towpath to East Marton
7½ miles (12 km) Sheet 103 932543

Easy Involves sections of 2 long-distance paths, the Pennine Way and the historic Leeds-Liverpool canal; plenty of activity on canal in summer. *Canal-side, pasture; mud after rain.*

Start Gargrave, off the A65 NW of Skipton; frequent buses; frequent trains to Gargrave station on the Leeds-Morecambe line. **Car park** in West Street, Gargrave (turn right by old Swan Inn); a second car park at junction of Broughton Road and A65.

① From the car park on West Street turn right up lane to the canal bridge. Follow towpath past moorings and wharves for one mile (1.5 km), crossing under A65 and railway. ② At Priest Holme Bridge, cross canal with towpath. Go along lane, then pick

up towpath at wooden gap stile on left. Continue past locks and Bank Newton boatyard. ③ At next bridge do not continue through stile on same side; cross canal, walk down lane and find entrance to towpath at wicket gate. Follow it for 2 miles (3 km) around deep bends to East Marton and double bridge. ④ Continue on towpath under A59, then take bridge on right to church. Follow path right alongside churchyard to main road at East Marton and make for Cross Keys Inn. ⑤ Follow lane beyond Cross Keys down to cross canal at Williamson Bridge. Continue on lane. ⑥ At stile (signposted) turn right to pick up Pennine Way into field. Continue past wood and back into lane. Follow lane. ⑦ Cross next stile, on right, and cross field to footbridge and stile. Bear left along beck (stream), crossing stiles. ⑧ One hundred yards (91 m) beyond wood, where beck bends E, keep straight on through gate and over bridge. Continue ahead along field edge, over stiles, across field corner and up Scaleber Hill. ⑨ Keep directly ahead to farm track below leading over railway bridge. ⑩ Over ladder stile on right. Follow path across fields and stiles to stile on left by old school.

Oldest and largest of the 3 trans-Pennine canals, the Leeds-Liverpool was built in 1770-1812, and remains the only one in working order. The old wharves, warehouses and locks at Gargrave are fascinating, as are the boatyards at Bank Newton. This is a contour canal, preferring to use the natural lie of the land rather than locks, expensive to build. The canal follows an extraordinary loop S of Newton to avoid a climb and fall.

Cross Keys – real ale and good food.

The double-arched bridge was built this way for extra strength; 200 years later it is standing up to juggernauts.

Although only a linking section of The Pennine Way long-distance path (see pages 328-334), this is nonetheless green and attractive.

Gargrave is a former coaching village with a splendid coaching inn, The Old Swan. The village was also an important port on the Leeds-Liverpool canal, where lead from the Wharfedale lead mines on Grassington Moor was embarked.

227

THE SOUTH PENNINES

Harewood
7 miles (11.5 km) Sheet 104 326432

Easy A gentle but rewarding route; fine views over Lower Wharfedale and Pennine foothills. *Farmland, parkland; mud after rain.*

Start From the A61 between Leeds and Harrogate take the lane to Wike, making for SW gate of park; frequent buses to lane corner by start of walk. **Parking** on broad verge in lane between A61 and Lofthouse Farm.

① From parking walk along lane 700 yards (640 m) and take unsurfaced track branching left by wood. ② Turn left at field gate on to track alongside hedge. Continue along edge of fields to Spring Wood. Bear left with path downhill, past wood, then climb to Hollin Hall ponds ahead. Make for Hollin Hall Farm. ③ Go directly between farm buildings; leave farm track as it bends left to reach gate by hedge straight ahead. Cross bridge, and continue directly ahead along track to New Laithe Farm. Continue along farm drive to road. ④ Cross road with care, turn left, and walk 400 yards (366 m) to gate by edge of field on right. Follow path along edge of field to gate and stile. ⑤ Cross stile and join track to left, following it into village. ⑥ Cross A61, go along Church Lane ahead and slightly right. Continue for one mile

(1.5 km), past church to where lane descends; meet junction. ⑦ Turn left along farm road towards Stank – pass farm and rear of gardens. Where track turns left, keep on narrower track alongside wood to cottage ahead. ⑧ Follow path by ruined cottage (Carr House) to track above. ⑨ At junction, turn left into wood, bearing right and ignoring track on right to Stub House. Keep ahead into woods. ⑩ Follow main track to beck (stream). Cross small bridge and turn left. Follow track to main stream and cross at bridge. Follow track uphill to lodge gates.

🏠 John Carr stayed at Carr House while Harewood was being built.

⚔ To ruins of 14th C. Harewood Castle.

🏛 Harewood, one of the greatest of
✗ Yorkshire's great houses, was designed by the York architect John Carr and built in the 1760s. Interiors by Robert Adam; park landscaped by Capability Brown; home of the Lascelles family. Open April-November.

🦆 Best views of waterfowl on lake are from the gardens, via official entrance.

🏠 The village stood in the park until a Lascelles had it removed and rebuilt to designs by Carr as a 'model' village.

Stanedge

7½ miles (12 km) Sheet 110 047116

Energetic Involves one of the most
spectacular stretches of the Pennine Way
and some generally underrated walking
country, rich in industrial and cultural
history. *Canal-side, moorland; one climb;
mud. Do not attempt in poor visibility.*

Start Marsden, on the A62 between
Huddersfield and Oldham; frequent buses;
frequent train service from Leeds. **Parking**
in Marsden, near the church.

① From Marsden church, follow lane N of
church, over packhorse bridge and up
narrow, enclosed way. ② Turn right at top
and cross to gate on left giving access to
towpath of Huddersfield New Canal. Follow
canal to canal basin and entrance to
Marsden Tunnel. ③ From tunnel entrance
climb to Junction Inn and left along lane past
canal reservoir to Hey Green hamlet. ④
Where road bends left, look for iron gate,
left, leading to narrow path between wall
and river. Follow this to Eastergate
packhorse bridge. ⑤ Cross bridge, do not
take obvious paths left or right by beck
(stream), but follow way up steep tongue of
land between the 2 becks. This climbs to
open moorland, and a more obvious track
marked by stone pillars (most fallen) which
bears right to cross beck and then climbs

open moorland ahead. ⑥ Keep clough (steep
valley) and stream to left, and follow path
due W to join A640 at layby S of the
distinctive shape of March Hill, half right. ⑦
Do not reach A640, but turn S along Pennine
Way up steep and (often) muddy track,
marked by cairns. ⑧ Go past trig. point and
last of fallen walls (with road in sight) and
bear left on sheep track to find broad,
shallow, grassy track over moor. ⑨ As track
nears wire fence, turn right along top of
reservoir culvert (channel) to reach A62 just
E of Great Western Hotel. ⑩ Cross road, and
enter Red Brook Reservoir by gate; follow
path along embankment and over white
footbridge, keeping same direction, then
slightly left to join road by shallow clough. ⑪
Bear left at junction and follow lane with
broad, verge down to Marsden centre.

🚣 The canal tunnel cuts through 5,416 feet
(1,651 m) of Stanedge at 644 feet (196 m)
above sea level; built 1798-1811.

🏰 The line of crags gives Stanedge its
name – 'stan' means stone in Anglo-
Saxon. Until the work of Metcalfe and
others, it was a major barrier to E-W
Pennine communications.

🏰 The grassy way is a survival of Jack
Metcalfe's road over Pule Hill and
Stanedge. The great road-builder, born
1717, was blind from childhood.

THE SOUTH PENNINES

Hebden Bridge and Heptonstall
7 miles (11 km) Sheet 103 993272

Moderate Includes a section of the Calderdale Way and 2 famous Pennine spots. *Canal-side, farmland, woods; 2 climbs.*

Start Hebden Bridge, between Halifax and Todmorden on the A646; frequent buses; frequent trains stop at Hebden Bridge (Manchester-Bradford-Leeds line). **Car parks** signposted at centre of Hebden Bridge, and one just E of point ①.

① Cross the small park on the main road in the centre of Hebden Bridge, go over the canal bridge and turn right alongside the canal. ② Cross bridge back on to canal towpath, and follow towpath across aqueduct over river; continue along towpath for nearly 2 miles (3 km). Continue past millpond. ③ After waterworks, where road comes in from left over canal, turn right over river and past mill to main road. Turn left at road. ④ Follow lane on right which goes under railway arch – signposted Calderdale Way, and Great Rock. It becomes a stony track, climbing zigzag through woods and past Eastwood Old Hall to Great Rock. ⑤ Follow path left of Great Rock, alongside wall ,and descending over ladder stile to Hippin Bridge. ⑥ Cross bridge and take track forking right in front of Hippins Farm. Follow it between buildings to stile. Continue ahead to farm. Cross track to stile on right and go along path by wall to more buildings. Continue along track, bearing left to gate into Blackshaw Head. ⑦ Take path over stile opposite post office, bear right to stile and keeping same direction descend diagonally across fields, over stiles, to Shaw Bottom. Turn left along metalled track, then sharp right along another metalled track which soon becomes stony. ⑨ At Pennine Way turn left down steps and right over Hebble Hole Bridge and Colden Water. Climb bank and continue along paved way to stile at corner of wood. Cross to next stile, then right over a third stile and cross several fields to broader track. ⑩ Turn right at junction, go past cottages and along paved way. Keep ahead at next junction on wide track to road at Lumb Bank. ⑪ Where road bends left, turn off right on to path which follows edge of Eaves Wood above crags, soon alongside wall. ⑫ Turn left at corner of wall into narrow lane which leads into back of Heptonstall village. Cut through churchyard,

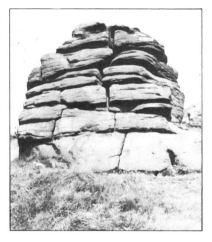

The Great Rock near Hebden Bridge, landmark and stopping place for walkers, is millstone grit – coarse sandstone – like limestone, highly characteristic of the S Pennines. Stoodley Pike, seen across the valley, is a famous local landmark commemorating the Battle of Waterloo.

past ruined church. ⑬ From Heptonstall follow main road downhill towards Hebden Bridge. After 250 yards (229 m) take steps on left to road below. Keep ahead past track on left to where steep, paved way with handrail leads down to centre of Hebden Bridge.

🏠 Hebden Bridge is regarded as the capital of the S Pennines. The 'double-decker' houses are built one 'on top of' the other to take advantage of the steep hillside and minimize waste of space.

🚶 The Rochdale Canal, running from Manchester, Rochdale and Littleborough to Sowerby Bridge, was opened in 1804. A superbly engineered waterway, it is one of 3 trans-Pennine canals. Competition from the railways forced closure in 1952, but there are hopes of having it re-opened for pleasure use.

📖 A section of the Calderdale Way, the 50-mile (80 km), unofficial long-distance route in the S Pennines (see pages 328-334). The route is a focal point for the revival of interest in the landscape of the area.

This is a good specimen of late 17th C. or early 18th C. Pennine farmhouse. 'Hippins' means stepping stones.

Blackshaw Head was an important meeting point of several packhorse ways crossing the Pennines.

Lumb Bank House is the former home of the poet Ted Hughes. The house now belongs to a foundation and is used for courses in writing and the arts.

Heptonstall was the focal point of the surrounding weaving community. The 13th C. church, dedicated to St. Thomas à Beckett, fell to ruin after suffering storm damage in 1847; it stands in the graveyard of the 19th C. church which replaced it. The 17th C. grammar school is a museum, open at weekends.

The Leeds-Liverpool Canal towpath provides splendid walking all the way from the centre of Leeds, through the Aire Valley and into industrial Lancashire. Though the towpath is not a public right of way, walkers who wish to make use of it have the full support of the waterways board.

There is more excellent canal walking in the Calder Valley beside the Rochdale Canal. Most of the canal can be followed from Rochdale to Sowerby Bridge. Parts of the Huddersfield New Canal can also be walked.

The Eccup Reservoir, north Leeds, is yet more easy waterside ambling, with paths mostly smooth and dry enough for prams or wheelchairs.

YORKSHIRE WOLDS

These hills are the quiet ending of the chalk lands which cross Britain from Dorset, via Wessex and the Chilterns, marching on through Cambridgeshire and Lincolnshire. At last, north of the Humber, the chalk expires in this crescent of low hills which reaches the sea with some drama at Flamborough Head. They lie mostly between the 400- and 600-foot contours (122 and 183 m), but top 800 feet (244 m) at Garrowby Top.

Until the end of the 18th century, the downs and their dry valleys were mostly sheep-walks, but today the land is nearly all arable. At best it is an airy, upland landscape, at worst, bitterly cold. When the wind is from the North Sea, it comes unobstructed by any higher ground between there and central Russia.

Public paths are relatively sparse. Much of the area has suffered because the old East Riding County Council dragged its feet when making the required map of rights of way. The Wolds Way is some compensation, but would be better if farmers and landowners had not opposed its proper route. At the north, the Way joins the Cleveland Way and at the south, walkers can cross the footway of the impressive new Humber Bridge to join the Viking Way. And the Humberside City Council has recently been congratulated on its progressive attitude to improving the right-of-way network.

Settrington
6 miles (9.5 km) Sheets 100 and 101 835707

Moderate Follows some relatively recently agreed 'new' rights of way and a typical stretch of the Wolds Way official long-distance path. Excellent views of the N York Moors and the Dales. *Village, wooded hillside, woods, farmland; 2 climbs. Around ⑫ path crosses field, which may be cropped. Follow directions carefully.*

Start From Malton take the B1248, turning left for Settrington in about 1½ miles (2.5 km). **Parking** in village.

① From the bridge at N of village walk S along road by the stream crossing the footbridge near a ford, and at road junction keep left to T-junction. Here turn left uphill, past Settrington House. ② At first farm track turn right and continue to Low Bellmanear Farm, going through 3 gates. ③ In front of Dutch barn turn left, soon following a track past a building on left to reach a gate and stile. ④ From gate follow track up hillside to right. Keep to the right-hand track and head towards gate at wood edge. ⑤ At end of wood cross stile and continue left of fence to the wood ahead. ⑥ Turn left and walk along the well-defined track. ⑦ At road turn right and in 20 yards (18 m) left through gate to forestry track. ⑧ Follow track as it turns right (waymarked) and at its next right turn, turn left along a grassy track to emerge on Thorpe Bassett Brow. Continue on this track to bottom of Brow. ⑨ Turn left and follow the track along the hill bottom, soon going

through bridle gate, after which the track is less distinct. ⑩ Follow faint track up the hillside diagonally, heading for electricity poles in plantation between 2 woods. Track becomes more obvious before reaching a gate. ⑪ At gate follow track through plantation and past ruined farm, turning left and right at the end of the building to follow field edge path (hedge on left). ⑫ Cross stile and follow waymarked route across the field to telegraph pole at entrance of Wold House Farm. Continue down drive. ⑬ Just in front of farm, turn right, then left just past a shed. Continue down the valley keeping left of trees. ⑭ At gate bear slightly right, soon crossing stile in near field corner. Bear left and gradually climb the hill. ⑮ In corner at top of field cross stile to left of gate and follow the field edge to pick up a track. Follow this to the road, where ⑯ turn left and walk downhill into Settrington.

🏠 The village owes its attractiveness and uniformity to being purpose designed (in 1800) as an estate village. Most of the stone cottages stand well back from the stream, and are built on the blueprint of 2 windows and a doorway at ground level, and 2 more windows above.

⛪ Though much restored, All Saints retains its 13th C. character.

🏛 Settrington House, designed by Francis Johnson about 1790 as a 3-storey mansion, was partially gutted by fire in 1963.

YORKSHIRE WOLDS

Watton Priory

6 miles (9.5 km) Sheet 106 018500

Moderate A walk for savouring wet places – springs, streams and a small lake – with attendant flowers and birdlife. Also, pleasant views of the Wolds, and a sense of history at Watton Priory. *Streamsides, woods, farmland; mud; some sections tend to be overgrown in summer, especially near ③ and ⑩.*

Start Watton, on the A164 between Driffield and Beverley; frequent buses. **Parking** on lay-by to E of Watton village. Walk can be shortened by catching bus back to Watton just N of ⑪.

① From lay-by cross A164 into village and turn left past the first pair of council houses, down a track and across the meadow ahead. ② Go through gate and past the old mill cottage, turning right along the beck (stream) bank after the stile. ③ Once in woods, turn right over the first bridge and then left to follow the other bank, still going W. Pass one bridge on left and cross a small plank bridge and stile. ④ Cross bridge and continue along stream (on left) until stile and bridge are reached. To visit Kilnwick, cross these and follow path. To continue, bear right across meadow to far corner. ⑤ Cross stile and turn left following path which turns left at

'Private' sign. Reach gate and continue ahead, following field edge to road. ⑥ At road turn right and in 10 yards (9 m) left up farm track, climbing steadily. ⑦ Where track finishes, continue ahead across fields to Burn Butts. After the gate turn right along the gravel track to the road. ⑧ At road turn right and at first junction left, soon turning right at the entrance to Bustard Nest Farm. ⑨ At bend continue ahead along field path with hedge on left, soon following farm track. ⑩ Where track leaves the hedge, continue ahead up edge of industrial area to main road. Turn left and in 100 yards (91 m) right. ⑪ Turn right across bridge and follow path along field edge into second field, where turn right when stile is reached. Continue across the meadow diagonally. ⑫ Cross stile and turn right along road, soon continuing ahead along field edge path until bridge. Cross. ⑬ After bridge turn to walk E and after gateway turn right, following the dyke to stile. Cross on to a farm road. ⑭ Cross road and after stile walk straight ahead to Watton Priory. ⑮ At the abbey buildings turn right and from the end of the building continue to white gate, where 2 stiles give access to track. Follow this back to lay-by.

🏛 All Saints is substantially Norman with a fine font and an interesting monument to the Grimston family.

🏛 Site of 18th C. Kilnwick Hall, seat of the Grimston family. All that remains of the old house is the huge brick wall that enclosed the kitchen garden, and a colonnaded well-head.

🚶 Towards Middleton (946504) and South Dalton (967464).

🍺 White Horse – hand-pumped ales and
✕ bar meals.

🏛 The site of Watton Priory, founded in 1150 by Canon Eustace Fitzjohn. Among monastic communities it was unusual in that it had male as well as female members. They lived separately, prayed in separate churches and their grounds were divided by high walls so that they never saw each other. There are few visible remains.

Thixendale High Wolds
*4 or 6½ miles (6.5 or 10.5 km) Sheet 100
844610*

Moderate Offers a true feeling of the high Wolds, fine views and an extension to visit a deserted village. This part of the Wolds receives some considerable snowfalls, which transform the landscape. *Hillside, valley, farmland; 2 climbs. Combines sections of Wolds and Centenary Ways.*

Start From the B1248 at Wharram le Street take the minor road past Bella Farm and access point to Wharram Percy. At Burdale pond turn right to Thixendale. **Parking** at edge of road near Cross Keys.

① Walk to the W end of the village and 100 yards (91 m) past the telephone box turn right up chalk track signposted 'Wolds Way'. In 40 yards (37 m) go through gate. ② Before farm buildings take the left fork soon crossing ladder stile and when fence is reached cross by the stile; turn left and walk around 2 sides of this field. ③ At fence cross stile and follow the path down the valley side. Before the dale bottom, turn left over a stile in a small depression. ④ In valley bottom cross stile and follow path up the valley ahead to an ancient earthwork. Follow this along side of field. ⑤ Join the Aldro bridle road and turn right. ⑥ For shorter walk, at end of wood on right opposite a farmstead across the valley leave Wolds Way and turn right heading towards ruined farm waymarked CW. ⑦ To visit Wharram

Percy, continue along side of valley, bearing left at end of next wood and later down to ruined church. Retrace to ⑥ and turn left. ⑧ About 50 yards (46 m) past Wold House ruins turn left along the track which soon bears right. ⑨ Where the track turns left and right (near a pond), turn right and follow the hedge on right. ⑩ Go through the bridle gate and turn left following the valley top. ⑪ At gate and fence, turn right and in 20 yards (18 m) go through the bridle gate and continue across track and along top of bank to waymarked stile. ⑫ Cross and continue across the field to left of trees and descending bank to a gate, entering village near Cross Keys.

🍺 Cross Keys – hand-pumped ale.

🏛 Wharram Percy is archaeologically the most interesting deserted village site in East Yorkshire, although apart from the restored Norman church there is little above ground to show for this.

Pocklington Canal

12 miles (19 km) Sheet 106 803487

Moderate An absorbing towpath walk over heathland, with the remains of 7 locks. The last mile (1.5 km) across an old airfield has the entertainment of gliders taking off, and there is a *Good Food Guide* restaurant on the route. *Pasture, streamside, canal-side, farmland, wooded common, heath; path between* ⑮ *and* ⑯ *has been reported ploughed out.*

Start Pocklington on the B1246; frequent buses. **Car park** next to old station in Pocklington (now used as sports hall).

① From car park walk E and turn right opposite fire station along a narrow path to a lane, where turn left and continue to the cemetery entrance. ② Go up a grassy path to cross a stile and continue to cemetery corner. Cross stile and bear nearly half left aiming for stile in the far corner. ③ Cross stile and go through gate opposite to walk up centre of field to a stile. ④ Cross stile, then bear right and after a field follow the streamside, crossing several stiles until reaching a farm. Go through 2 gates to the main road. ⑤ Turn right on to the A1079 and in 50 yards (46 m) left into the canal head area. Walk along the canal towpath past 7 locks and 3 road bridges. ⑥ At the second farm bridge after road bridge number 3, turn right across meadow to dyke. Cross by plank bridge. ⑦ After crossing stile walk up field to gate, where turn right on to a sandy track. Track soon bears left. ⑧ Follow track over a road to Thornton Grange. Walk through farmyard and continue in same direction on another farm track. ⑨ After passing 3 fields on right, turn right and follow the field edge (on left) to the road. Turn left towards the wooded Allerthorpe Common. ⑩ Through bridle gate (next to a large gate), bear right, soon taking the right-hand track to walk along the S edge of the common. ⑪ Where track reaches edge of wood turn left, entering trees again. ⑫ After 2 tracks have joined from left, continue ahead through gateway at crossing of tracks. ⑬ At end of wood, follow rough road as far as Allerthorpe village, where turn right then left to walk up main street. ⑭ At main road turn right, continue 250 yards (228 m), then left along road. In another 250 yards take track leading to old airfield. ⑮ Turn right along the perimeter track, following this across a runway, soon joining

path on right which leads left of a cream building. ⑯ At road turn right and in 200 yards (183 m) right along metalled path following the dismantled railway. At the road turn left and right back to car park.

🍴 Feathers Hotel, a former coaching inn, serves bar food.

✿ The gardens of Burnby Hall are renowned for their collection of waterlilies. The house, open Easter until May, contains a collection of memorabilia from world travels.

🍺 Wellington Oak – hand-pumped ale.

⚓ Opened in 1818, at a cost of £35,000, the canal carried traffic up to 1934, then lay deteriorating until 1968, when restoration began. Only 9¾ miles (15.5 km) long, with 8 swing bridges and 9 locks, it was one of the smallest commercial waterways. Birdlife along the banks includes herons, swans and many species of duck. Fish include pike, perch, roach and trout.

🍺 Cross Keys.

🌸 Allerthorpe Common is a boggy heath harbouring, among other plants, the rather rare marsh gentian (flowers July-Sept.) and the carnivorous sundew (June-Aug.) with sticky red hairs for catching insects. Nightjars, curlews and whinchats may be seen.

🌲 The Wolds.

✕ The Plough has a *Good Food Guide* entry.

YORKSHIRE WOLDS

Welton Dale

7½ miles (12 km) Sheet 106 957273

Easy A happy mixture of dales, woods and field edge paths: Welton Dale is peaceful and unspoilt. The route passes a church in an exceptionally beautiful situation. *Valley, woods, farmland; one climb.*

Start From A63 take turning marked Welton and follow signs into village; frequent buses – alight at the Green Dragon. **Parking** on roadside opposite Green Dragon or by church 50 yards (46 m) away.

① From the church walk up Cowgate, then Dale Road, passing old mill buildings on right. ② At entrance to Dale Cottage continue on track past cottage and over stile next to white gate. Walk up the dale. ③ At the waymark bear right off the track and through the woods. ④ At end of woods, cross the road using the 2 stiles and turn left along the bridleway to the road. ⑤ At road turn left and enter the woods at the footpath signpost. ⑥ At the junction of paths turn right, following the path downhill to the road. Turn left. ⑦ Just before some untidy buildings turn right, soon turning left up short, steep hill. ⑧ At the track cross over and follow the well-defined track through the woods. ⑨ To visit Brantingham church, village and pub, walk down the hill. Otherwise, at the road turn right, continuing ahead after it has become metalled. ⑩ At the junction, follow the rough track ahead into the woods. ⑪ At the junction of paths turn right through the hand gate and follow the field edge ahead. ⑫ Just past the farm cottages turn left and in 20 yards (18 m) right at the pond, walking ahead with first pond, then wood, on right. ⑬ At junction of paths turn left and in 20 yards right over a concrete road and into trees ahead. Follow field edge path. ⑭ At quarry gate turn right and follow road into Welton.

The white-fronted Green Dragon Inn was a favourite haunt of John Palmer, alias Dick Turpin, who was arrested here in 1739 and taken to York Prison, later to be executed.

St. Helen's churchyard is the resting place of a local 18th C. philanderer, Jeremiah Simpson, who, as his headstone records '. . . hath eight times married been but now in his ould age he lies in his cage under the grass so green'. The church's chancel is 13th C.

Triton Inn – hand-pumped ales and a restaurant serving good, plain food.

As far as the Humber Bridge, largest single-span suspension bridge in the world.

Wauldby Manor, and its chapel dated 1844; site of lost village S of church.

The disused railway from Beverley to Market Weighton is a 'walkway': access from Molescroft near Beverley.

The 23-mile (37 m) Holderness Way from Hull to Hornsea divides into 3 short sections, Hull-Beverley, Beverley-Leven and Leven-Hornsea.

There are short linear and circular walks incorporating sections of the Minster Way (Beverley Minster to York) and the Hull Countryway.

The Beverley 20, 20 miles (32 km) from Hessel to Beverley, has extensions forming the E Riding Heritage Way.

Leaflets and guidebooks describing these routes, mostly fully waymarked, are available from local officers of the Ramblers' Association.

All Saints, Brantingham, in its wooded setting; inside is an early 13th C. font.

YORKSHIRE DALES

No other English landscape so closely unites the wild and the domestic. The peat and the bent grass of the sheep-dotted fells butt directly on to the enclosed beauty of the dales them-selves.

The most exhilarating moment of a typical dales route is when starting to descend from the 'tops' into the next dale, spread below like a map. Towards its head are just scattered farms, with, it seems, grey-walled barns at the corner of almost every field. Further down, the dale widens to accommodate villages and meadows. Further still a great castle or abbey such as Richmond or Fountains may well command the broad skirts of the valley. Linking all will be a tawny river, possibly with dramatic falls and rapids – of which Aysgarth Falls on the Ure and the dangerous Strid at Bolton Priory on the Wharfe are only the most famous.

The tops themselves are criss-crossed by paths and green lanes – grassy tracks once used by drovers and packhorsemen. Around the Three Peaks (Ingleborough, Penyghent and Whernside) especially, the limestone of the area forms immense 'pavements', a stark landscape, but with the occasional rare plant growing in its 'grykes', crevices a few inches wide and many feet deep.

Pikedaw Hill and Malham Cove

5½ or 3½ miles (9 or 5.5 km) Sheet 98 900627

Moderate An unusual, richly interesting walk taking in famous Malham Cove. In winter the ancient field patterns are revealed after light snow. *Moorland, limestone terraces; one climb. Do not attempt in poor visibility.*

Start Malham, N of the A65. **Car park** behind information Centre.

① From car park entrance turn right on to a stony track, then first right along track behind car park. ② Left at junction, following track uphill. ③ Left at next junction uphill past barns, then drop to stream. ④ Just past stream and footbridge, go through gate (with signpost) on right; follow path across field to stile to right of barn seen ahead. Then continue on same line, crossing a ladder stile under a line of crags and heading for their left end. ⑤ After passing the crags, at another ladder stile do not follow obvious track ahead, but bear half right, climbing to a plateau with limestone outcrops and reaching grassy track at signpost with 3 arms. (If you arrive at wall, gate, and one-armed sign, you have taken a short cut to ⑦.) ⑥ Turn left along grassy track, 'BW Settle', past mineshaft to gate in wall ahead. (For 3½-mile version, turn right along green lane, 'BW Malham', down to Cove Road for Malham village.) ⑦ Follow wall (signpost 'Langscar Gate') past cross-

shaft, where wall bears right; continue (always towards Malham Tarn below) through 3 gates and across field to corner to meet grassy track. ⑧ Turn right along track, later bearing left to rejoin wall, to cattle grid on road. ⑨ Cross road, over stile, downhill to stile and along the 'Dry Valley' to Malham Cove. ⑩ Cross limestone pavements with care, bearing right to stile leading to steps down side of Malham Cove. Take well-defined path through kissing-gates back to village.

[b] In the Middle Ages, this was the monastic settlement, later the sheep fair, then the lead and zinc mining.

The beck (stream) down Pikedaw follows roughly the line of the Mid-Craven Fault, a major shift in the earth's crust.

A 'level', or entrance to part of Pikedaw lead mines, busy from the late 18th to late 19th C., now exhausted.

New Calamine Shaft, 60 feet (18 m) deep, covered by a manhole, was access to the calamine (zinc) mines.

The shaft of Nappa Cross, raised by monks of Fountains as a guide-post.

The Dry Valley, carved by melting waters of the most recent Ice Age.

The limestone face of Malham Cove, 300 feet (91 m) high, was the site of a great waterfall, fuelled by melt-waters of the Ice Age.

YORKSHIRE DALES

Watching a dipper feed underwater is as absorbing as any of the sights of a fast-flowing river. The bird looks silvery-grey underwater, and uses pebbles as anchors.

Grassington
3 miles (5 km) Sheet 98 003637

Moderate A short but varied walk from one of the most interesting Dales visitor centres; best in spring – clear, open views and possibility of snow on tops. *Farmland, woods, pasture; one climb.*

Start Grassington on the B6265 N of Skipton; frequent buses from Skipton; trains (Parklink through tickets available) from Leeds and other stations. **Car park** off the B6265, 220 yards (201 m) E of the Square.

① From car park walk along B6265 towards square. Walk up the main street, past square, to the Town Hall, where ② turn right along lane climbing past cottages. Take the first fork left past bungalow along walled track. ③ Look for a gap stile on left by a gate. Follow path over a second stile in wall on right. Continue on path, crossing a series of stiles, and diagonally over fields, climbing in same direction throughout. ④ Turn right where path meets track. Follow track uphill to point beyond radio mast at gate and ladder stile on right. ⑤ Cross stile and bear slightly left downhill above hospital towards pine woods. Make for wall. ⑥ Follow wall downhill, cross stile and continue alongside hospital. Continue straight on through woods to stile at end of woods. ⑦ Turn right over ladder stile, along edge of wood, then left at sign alongside tiny beck (stream) to ladder stile at road. ⑧ Cross

road and pick up connecting path through fields, cutting diagonally across, over stiles. Cross track and head for left of barn (Ray Lathe) ahead. ⑨ Cross stile behind barn, continuing downhill. At second stile take path towards riverside. ⑩ Go through kissing-gate and along track by converted mill, through stile on left as track climbs, then follow field path, crossing stiles, to Tin Bridge. If river is low, cross stepping stones and go directly to Linton church. ⑪ Cross waterfalls by Tin Bridge; by mill bear left up to road. Left along road to church. Retrace to Tin Bridge. ⑫ Climb narrow, enclosed path to Grassington village and car park.

🏚 Grassington's history goes back to the Iron Age, with evidence of ancient settlements visible on the hillside terraces. The present village is mainly 18th and 19th C., when it was a mining centre, dependent on rich lead deposits of Grassington Moor. Museum; pubs.

↖ Across Wharfedale, and (clear days) as far as Pendle Hill, Lancashire.

⛪ This simple but fine Norman church ('the cathedral of upper Wharfedale') is on the site of an even older one.

〰 Linton Falls, with the limestone eroded into attractive shapes by the River Wharfe. The footbridge is known as Tin Bridge because of an earlier, tin-clad bridge on the site. Dippers; wagtails.

West Burton
6 miles (9.5 km) Sheet 98 011887

Moderate The typical limestone scar scenery of Wensleydale, with an outstanding village and fine waterfalls. *Farmland, riverside; one climb.*

Start Aysgarth Falls, signposted from Aysgarth, which is E of Hawes on the A684; frequent buses from Darlington; infrequent, seasonal service from Leeds via Ilkley. **Car park** at Aysgarth Falls.

① From W end of car park follow tarmac path to Aysgarth Bridge. Cross bridge and take steps by Carriage Museum past church to main road. ② Cross road and take path by stile ahead. It crosses a shallow gill (valley). Continue in same direction through stiles and gates, aiming for Eshington Bridge, below. ③ Cross, over stile on right, and across field. Go to stile on left of gate, cross two stiles by the river and up through two fields to road. Cross road and follow steps ahead into West Burton village. ④ Go right to village centre, then left down the green. At end continue along path to footbridge below a waterfall. Over stile turn right and follow wall uphill, then cross pasture to wood. Follow path uphill through wood to stile at top. Continue more or less directly up the steep slope, looking for stiles then yellow-topped poles marking a zigzag path. ⑤ Where slope moderates, cross stile and half right, past last post to moorland wall ahead

at gate. Turn left along wall to gate which enters enclosed lane. Follow clear track for nearly 1½ miles (2 km) further. ⑥ 220 yards (200 m) after gate across track turn left through gate to track. Take path which leads off left at bottom of 'S' bend in track, making for gap between woods ahead. Head for small, enclosed ruin (chantry). ⑦ Through gate, descend through wood and along field edge to road. Turn left and continue over river bridge. ⑧ Over stile at farm drive entrance then follow stiles ahead to riverside. ⑨ Keep to top side of wire fence, then bear left to stile into plantation crossing to church and ①.

🏠 Aysgarth's Victorian church, serving a scattered parish; notable Tudor screens.

🏞 Aysgarth Falls are some of the Dales' finest. The Upper Falls are spectacular – best view from the (Tudor) road bridge. Middle and Lower Falls are also worth seeing.

🏠 Carriage Museum, in former cotton (later flour) mills, open daily in summer.

🏚 Picturesque West Burton was a manufacturing village, with a reputation for its wool combing.

🏚 This track, known as Morpeth Gate – 'gate' meaning road or highway — is the ancient way along Wensleydale.

🏠 12th C. chapel of the Knights Templar.

YORKSHIRE DALES

Lower Dentdale

6 miles (9.5 km) Sheets 97 and 98 657922

Moderate A comparatively unvisited area of the Dales, and a fine section of the Dales Way. Best in spring – possibility of snow on the tops – or autumn, for colouring on the fells. *Farmland, riverside; one climb.*

Start Sedbergh, on the A684; infrequent buses; Dales Rail Buses serve Sedbergh from Garsdale Station on certain weekends. **Car parks** (signposted) on Main Street (by National Park Centre), or on Dent Road.

① From car park walk W along Main Street to church. (From Dent Road car park cross road to church.) ② Follow metalled path behind church by school cricket pitch, following path left through school grounds. ③ Continue in same direction, crossing road at kissing-gates. Follow path through another kissing-gate downhill and around garden fence to lane. ④ Turn left into lane, and in 150 yards (135 m) right through stile to follow signposted path, going straight on over 3 further stiles and under old railway line. Then bear slightly left over 2 more stiles to Brigflatts Meeting House. ⑤ From Brigflatts follow lane right to A683. Turn left along road to riverside path. ⑥ Follow riverside path back past disused railway line (walk along foot of embankment to steps) and meeting of rivers to Birks Mill. ⑦ Cross river at footbridge, double back and follow path uphill through wood to stile. Keep ahead through next 2 stiles, and right into lane downhill to Abbot Holme Bridge.

⑧ Cross bridge and stile on left; follow path by river, then uphill above narrow gorge across neck of bend to stile into lane. Straight ahead along lane. ⑨ Turn left over Rash Bridge, then right on to road. ⑩ At second gate on left (signposted) follow Dales Way uphill, bearing left along wall to join grassy track at second stile. ⑪ Turn left along grassy track, continuing straight on over brow of hill (take either branch) and dropping past golf course to Millthrop. ⑫ Go through Millthrop, left to main road and over Millthrop Bridge towards Sedbergh. ⑬ At '30' sign turn right through stile and along path uphill through two more stiles, then down through kissing-gates to drive by playing fields and into town for car parks.

🏠 Sedbergh, with the public school of the same name, is a fell walking centre.

🏠 Brigflatts Meeting House is one of the country's oldest and best-known Quaker meeting houses, dating from 1675. George Fox stayed in the vicinity before giving his famous sermon on nearby Firbank Fell to more than 1,000 people – generally accepted as the launching of the Quaker movement.

🏠 Catholes Bunkhouse Barn was converted to simple accommodation for walkers by the Countryside Commission as an experimental use for redundant barns which would otherwise go derelict. It is proving popular.

🏠 A section of the Dales Way: see pages 328-334.

YORKSHIRE DALES

Hell Gill
9 miles (14.5 km) Sheet 98 787919

Energetic Some of the Dales' most dramatic walking. *Farmland, fells; 2 climbs; do not attempt in poor visibility.*

Start Garsdale Station, off the A684 W of Hawes; infrequent buses; infrequent, seasonal trains from Leeds, Preston and Carlisle. **Parking** on verge (not causing an obstruction) of approach road to station.

①Cross A684 and follow path from stile and signpost uphill and slightly left to gate ahead. Follow path round at top of steep slope to farmhouse. ② Cross next stile, to right of farmhouse, and drop with path, crossing stile left of nearest building, and

another stile to join lane at Moor Rigg. ③ Follow lane past East House and steeply uphill to T-junction. ④Turn right and in 120 yards (110 m), leave track to climb directly up open fell. Head for the col between Turner Hill (to the right) and the shoulder above it, reaching a wire fence on the ridge. Go through gate and head half left, descending the slope obliquely, and make for a building and trees that come into sight high on the slope. ⑤ Through gate and right of building, then follow walls, continuing straight on through gates to join road at Aisgill. ⑥ Follow track to right of Aisgill Moor Cottages to Hell Gill Force (waterfall); retrace a few yards and go uphill alongside beck (stream) to farm. Beyond farm gate, make for bridge. ⑦ Cross bridge, through gate and along grassy track. ⑧ After about 200 yards leave well-defined grassy track sloping down to West End, bearing left above a stone enclosure ahead. Pick up grassy track (High Way) above inclosure wall and follow past ruined farm (High Hall). In about ½ mile (0.8 km) ⑨ look for stile on right immediately before gate and wall ahead. Descend field, bearing left down sunken track, to pass above Shaws. Descend by gill, cross footbridge, drop by winding path passing Lunds church, and cross river by ford or footbridge. Follow drive between pines. ⑩ Look for stile on left as drive dips after a climb. Follow path through plantation and across fields over stiles to road. Go left along road. ⑪ Opposite footbridge over railway look for indistinct path from stile leading to bridge (or use track). Cross footbridge and continue over stile on left, bisecting angle of wall to cross ruined wall and continue to ladder stile. ⑫ Cross stile, and gap stile in next wall ahead and to the left. Cross a third stile and drop to stile opposite cottages on road E of Carsdale Head; turn right to ①.

🚃 The Settle-Carlisle line, the highest mainline railway in Britain.

〰 Hell Gill: the deep, limestone gorge is gouged by the River Eden, whose source is Hell Gill beck (stream). The Eden flows N (unique among major English rivers) into the Irish Sea. The Ure enters the North Sea.

🔟 The High Way was in regular use from the Bronze Age to the 19th C.

⛪ The remote Lunds chapel is 18th C.

YORKSHIRE DALES

Richmond and Swale
7 miles (11 km) Sheet 92 168007

Easy The lovely old Dales town of Richmond, and a fine section of the Coast-to-Coast Walk. *Woods, farmland, riverside; one climb; mud after rain; walk single-file on paths through riverside meadows.*

Start Richmond, on the A6108; frequent buses from Darlington and Leyburn. **Public car parks** at Richmond Green (signposted 'Coaches'), near Richmond Bridge, or Nuns Close, N of town centre (signposted 'Cars').

① From Richmond Green car park walk down to bridge. From Nuns Close, leave by corner near church, right for a few yards, then down Cravengate to bridge. Cross bridge and taken opening on right down to river bank. ② Follow track into Hudswell Woods, soon climbing steps. Where path divides, take lower fork to right. Keep straight ahead at next fork and continue to end of wood. Cross wooden stile on right ③ and continue with path over pasture, scar and between wooded knoll (Round Howe) and river. ④ Cross river by footbridge to picnic site and turn left along A6108. ⑤ Take first track on right, ignoring junction on right. Straight on to farmhouse. ⑥ Go through small gate on right just before farm and follow waymarks to stile into wood. Follow cart-track to within sight of gate at end of wood, then take waymarked path to right and shortly over stile into field. ⑦ Follow path along beck (stream) to meet riverside beyond ruined wall and continue along bank to stile. Continue straight ahead to edge of meadow, then right to stile. ⑧ Through stile keep straight along right edge

of meadow to gate. ⑨ Climb past ruined house and continue in same direction to gateway under Low Applegarth, where turn half right and over stile by iron gate. Climb 100 yards (90 m) uphill to join Coast-to-Coast Path. ⑩ Look for waymarked stile on right above farm. Then through 2 more stiles to join drive to East Applegarth Farm. ⑪ Through gate, left at once and around farm to join track leading towards Whitcliffe Wood. ⑫ Through gate and stile into woods. Carry straight on at far end of wood to join lane to Richmond. ⑬ Look for parkland (West Field) above Richmond – enter by stile and walk through it, parallel to road, into town. ⑭ After joining A6108 turn right down Cravengate or left through opening to the respective car parks.

🏰 Richmond is a fine old town clustered round the Norman castle started by Alan
🏠 the Red in 1071. The keep (12th C.) is well preserved. Interesting walks around
✕ castle walls. The town has some fine 18th C. buildings; military museum;
▮ cafés; pubs. Richmond Bridge (1879) may
∩ be by John Carr, the celebrated York architect.

\†/ Hudswell Woods, beautifully situated along limestone scar above the Swale,
**�# ** give good views back to bridge, castle and town. Picnic site at W side.

🔟 This is a section of the Coast-to-Coast unofficial long-distance path pioneered by the late W. A. Wainwright.

🔟 The memorial to Robert Williance's 'Leap' (1606) is some way up the hill.

🌲 Fine woodland, mainly larch and spruce.

Stean, Middlesmoor and Nidderdale Edges

8½ miles (13.5 km) Sheet 99 098734

Moderate Spectacular limestone features and first-class moorland views. *Farmland, moorland; 2 climbs; mud after rain.*

Start Stean, about 7 miles (11 km) NW of B6265 at Pateley Bridge; infrequent, seasonal buses from Skipton. **Car park** E of Stean bridge.

① After visiting gorge, continue up the road from café. Shortly before village, turn right over stile ②, signposted 'Middlesmoor' and 'Nidderdale Way'. Cross footbridge and climb steps. ③ Bear right after steps to wall and stile; then follow side of wall uphill. At road turn left through Middlesmoor. 50 yards (45 m) past Post Office, go through stile on right, heading for left end of wood in dip. Continue through stiles (mostly marked with yellow arrows) to join farm road beside wood, and through gates to next wood. ④ Turn sharp right downhill, bearing left to cross stream, then over wood and stone stile by tree ahead. ⑤ Half left to next stile stone steps (about 15 yards (13 m)) from field corner, then on the same line over 3 more stiles to lane. Turn left and follow the lane for ¾ mile (1.2 km). ⑥ Enter drive to Summerstone on the right, across bridge and immediately turn left along river. Where the river bends left, follow track to right, up hill and ⑦ turning back to the E under The Edge. ⑧ Before track zigzags downhill at a farm, fork left up a lesser but clear track above conifers, joining another at the top and following S over Lofthouse Moor. ⑨ From shooting lodge go downhill to gate; through it, turn left to pick up grassy track to wood where bear right downhill. ⑩ At Thrope Farm turn left through gates along grassy lane, then ahead through gates to Lofthouse.

〰 How Stean has been called Yorkshire's Little Switzerland. There are remark-
🔲 able walks under the overhangs of the limestone ravine. Tom Taylor's Cave is
✕ 50 yards (46 m) long. The excellent café at the entrance serves hot meals; modest entrance fee to gorge.

🏠 Middlesmoor is a rare example of a Pennine hill village on the spur of a ridge.
🍺 Unspoiled pub; fine views down Nidder-
🔽 dale from churchyard.

ⓑ The lane from Lofthouse to Angram and

New Scar House follows the line of the former Upper Nidderdale Light Railway, built to carry men and materials to construct the reservoirs.

🎯 Lofthouse, first-class grouse moor, with a typical Edwardian shooting lodge.

How Stean: a natural sculpture.

YORKSHIRE DALES

Ingleborough
11 miles (17.5 km) Sheet 98 693733

Energetic An unusual way of climbing this considerable English mountain; some fascinating limestone pavements. Best in spring and summer – clear views, possibility of snow on tops. *Fells, rough grazing, grassy slopes; 2 climbs; do not attempt in poor visibility – for experienced hill walkers – 1:25,000 map and compass recommended.*

Start Ingleton, on the A65 N of Settle; frequent buses from Skipton, Settle and Lancaster. **Car parks** (signposted) at Ingleborough Community Centre, Ingleton, or (fee) at entrance to waterfalls near bridge.

① From entrance to Falls (fee) go through kissing-gate and along path up gorge to head of Falls. ② At last fall, Thornton Force, follow path up steps, across beck (stream) and up further steps to join track (Twistleton Lane). Turn right. ③ Look for grassy track coming in from left, and follow it zigzagging uphill to limestone gap or 'nick' through Twistleton Scar End. Follow path straight ahead across edge of limestone pavements. ④ Do not follow wall, but keep slightly right over moor to pick up faint track, later turning to path. Follow it under steep side of hill and drop to Ellerbeck Farm. ⑤ Follow farm drive downhill by woodland to Chapel le Dale. ⑥ Cross road and follow path through stiles to Souther Scales. Continue with path through gate behind farm, uphill. ⑦ Follow well-defined path uphill through gate and along becks to saddle of Ingleborough. ⑧ On summit ridge turn right to summit shelter and trig. point. ⑨ Follow main track SW off summit, across area of large stones and boulders to broad track down fell. ⑩ Follow enclosed, stony lane directly back to Ingleton.

📖 Ingleton was a coal-mining town.

〰 These are the most impressive series of waterfalls in England – 4½ miles (7 km) of gorges and glens filled with raging torrents. Ancient stone – pre-Cambrian rocks, Ordovician slates and Carboniferous limestone – are exposed at several points. The ravines are dangerous – keep to the hand-railed paths. A short-cut (4½ miles) runs back from Beezley Falls, below Beezley Farm.

Ingleborough's geology; the base is ancient, Pre-Cambrian/Ordovician rock. Then comes 600 feet (183 m) of limestone, then 3 layers of shale and sandstones, seen mainly as crag and scree. The cap is millstone grit. The summit reveals (left to right): the site of a hospice (triangle); a wind shelter (cross) with the view indicator and trig. point close by. Next are primitive hut circles, then remains of Iron Age walls.

📖 This ancient track, known as Kirkby Gate (gate meaning road or highway) was a prehistoric trading route, and in medieval times a packhorse way to Kirkby Stephen. The narrow nick through the limestone at Twistleton Scar End is a typical feature of ancient hill routes and may be partly man-made to indicate the line of the path.

📷 The intriguing settlement of Chapel le Dale is close to 2 huge potholes – Hurtle Pot (seen from track) and Jingle Pot (seen from near track). Weathercote Cave, nearby (painted by Turner), is closed to the public. The sculpture by the road is intended to complement the natural, weathered limestone. More than 100 navvies, who died in epidemics when building the Ribblehead Viaduct, are buried in the graveyard.

〰 Ingleborough was long considered England's highest peak; in fact, at 2,372 feet (723 m), it is the second highest of The Three Peaks; Lake District NW.

Alum Pot and Crummack Dale
14 miles (22.5 km) Sheet 98 808726

Energetic The Dales limestone country at its best – fell walking on the grand scale. *Moorland, rough grazing, limestone 'pavement'; 2 climbs; do not attempt in poor visibility – for experienced hill walkers.*

Start Horton, N of Settle on the B6479; frequent buses from Settle, infrequent seasonal service from Giggleswick station. **Public car park** in Horton; if full, use a verge.

① From car park walk NW to end of village and take track (Pennine Way) which starts at Crown Inn. Follow it N for 3 miles (5 km). ② Follow Pennine Way W over ladder stile to join surfaced track leading to Old Ing. ③ Leave Pennine Way at Old Ing, keeping along farm track down to High Birkwith Farm. ④ Turn right at High Birkwith over stone stile, cross stile by wood and 2 more stiles to reach Low Birkwith Farm. Pass to right of building and keep same direction with Coppy Gill beck (stream) on right, crossing stiles to footbridge over River Ribble. ⑤ Cross bridge, round hill to ladder stile and into grassy lane leading to road at Selside. ⑥ Turn right through hamlet, taking first track left up to Alum Pot. (To visit Pot pay entrance fee at Selside Farm, the white building on the right as you cross under the railway path to Pot through gap stile from lane corner ahead to clump of trees.) ⑦ Follow track round corner to gate, along wall for 200 yards (180 m) and half left to a ladder stile; then across fields and 2 more stiles. ⑧ Join track going half right (parallel to wall on right). After a gate the track continues on a terrace to a signpost on the plateau of Sulber: continue on the path towards Clapham, shortly going through Sulber Gate. ⑨ ½ mile (0.8 km) on, fork left at a low cairn, on a grassy track soon bearing steadily left downhill into Crummack Dale. Then right through gates to join farm track SW of Crummack Farm. ⑩ Follow lane downhill to next junction; bearing left along stony track to small ford and footbridge. Cross and continue to next junction. ⑪ Turn sharp left along Moughton Lane, a narrow, unsurfaced track. Follow to gate, then grassy path forming natural 'pass' over hillside. After zigzag at the top continue in former direction to track marked by cairns, along a line of stone grouse butts. ⑫ Cross top wall at stile, then left along wall, over

The limestone 'pavement' of this area makes stern, but fascinating walking.

another stile and half right, joining path from Ingleborough to go through gap in wall. ⑬ Follow fairly well-defined path marked by occasional cairns, posts, and yellow dots to cross railway line at Horton Station. Straight on to village.

▣ Jackdaw Hole and Sell Gill Holes, deep, natural shafts giving access to the area's underground cave system. Alum Pot's spectacular, spray-blown entrance, with smaller potholes above.

▩ Limestone pavements.

♠ Moughton (pronounced Mooton) Scars has the remains of pre-Ice Age tree cover – the ancient dwarf juniper trees still clinging to the limestone pavement.

▩ Crummack Dale is one of the remotest dales, its upper reaches only accessible on foot.

✕ Horton in Ribblesdale, a popular walker's village, with a café, and the

▮ Crown Inn, conveniently placed on the Pennine Way, Britain's original long-distance path, (see pages 328 – 334).

There are miles of easy tracks, mostly traffic-free, and many suitable for wheelchairs or prams, in the Studley Royal/Fountains Abbey estate.

A walk round the perimeter of Washburndale Reservoir is also a feasible expedition for those with young children. Other reservoirs in the Dales with paths or tracks and easy access are Nidderdale and Fewston.

York is not strictly speaking in the Dales, but its superb walls are an intriguing circuit.

NORTH YORK MOORS

'Grand' is the Yorkshire word for these moors. Once up on the flat plateau-tops, the heather stretches for miles. The Cleveland Hills, backbone of the region, rise to their summit at one and a half thousand feet (457 m) on Urra Moor. From Cringle Moor, on the Hills' escarpment, some have been able to make out Cross Fell, nearly 60 miles (97 km) away in the Pennines. The intersecting dales are more gently cupped than the Yorkshire Dales further west.

Expect some energetic walking. Off the beaten tracks, the heather stems make a stiff, calf- and thigh-straining barrier. Wind and rain penetrate icily; there is no shelter to speak of. The Cleveland Way offers superb cliff-walking, but watch for the sea frets – banks of fog rolling suddenly inshore. They are disconcerting and unpleasant.

The Moors carry the scars of digging for alum and jet, and the course of the railway that transported Rosedale's ironstone. Today's industry, despite the decline of small farms, is basically sheep, though the gloomy conifer forests have swallowed too much of the open land. The huge golf balls of Fylingdales early warning station are another intrusion, but at least they have their own eerie magic.

Rievaulx
3 miles (5 km) Sheet 100 575845

Easy Haunted by changing views of the centre of interest – the abbey ruins. *Woods, riverside, farmland; one climb; mud after rain.*

Start 1½ miles (2.5 km) from Helmsley on the B1257 bear left on to the road signposted Scawton and Old Byland. Continue downhill to river and turn right before bridge. **Parking** area on left in trees 300 yards (274 m) after right turn – do not use Abbey car park.

① From parking area* turn right back to bridge. Cross and continue to next right turn where ② cross stream to Ashberry Farmhouse. Behind this cross stile and continue on path uphill along edge of wood. ③ Leaving wood keep to edge of open land near woods. Continue to ④, gate on to rough road. Through it, cross diagonally right, over stile and take footpath signposted Hawnby. Follow it (later beside river) to where fence obstructs progress. Turn left along fence to ⑤ gate on to road; turn left. In 750 yards (686 m) ⑥ fork left downhill on track. Soon cross outward route. ⑦ Cross bridge and continue uphill on farm road. After gate continue downhill. ⑧ In village opposite church turn right and continue to ①.

🌢 Ashberry Nature Reserve fosters interesting plant specimens, including bird's-eye primrose and globe flower.

Rievaulx, the Moors' justly famous collaboration of lovely ruin and setting.

🏚 Monasteries owned farmland and these fields were probably worked by monks.

🗡 Rievaulx (pronounced 'Ree-vo') fell into ruin after Henry VIII looted and shut down the Roman Catholic monasteries.

🏚 Rievaulx Terraces – landscaped hillside – and Twin Temples were created by a local landowner; views of the ruin.

NORTH YORK MOORS

Lastingham and Hutton-le-Hole
4½ miles (7 km) Sheet 100 728905

Moderate Particularly fine views of the Tabular Hills – flat-topped, limestone headlands which are a major feature of the S edge of the Moors; visits 2 attractive and flourishing moorland villages. *Woods, farmland, village, moorland; one climb; mud after rain.*

Start From the A170 turn N at Keldholme for Hutton-le-Hole and turn right (past car park) to Lastingham. **Parking** in wider parts of village street, or park at Hutton-le-Hole and start walk at ⑥.

① Leave village by steep road to Appleton-le-Moors and turn right to Spaunton. ② Left at end of village into lane between fields. Continue straight on for ¾ mile (one km), then bear right at fork. ③ At corner of wood: turn right through gate into wood; follow path along edge of wood and into lane. ④ Turn right on to road coming from farm at left and follow it through fields. ⑤ In Hutton-le-Hole find Public Footpath sign by wall opposite village hall and follow path across fields and through woods. ⑥ Join road from Hutton-le-Hole to Lastingham and continue on mostly wide verges to ①.

🛐 St. Mary's church is unique among English parish churches for the scale of its crypt. This is almost a complete church below the main structure, with an apse (semicircular domed roof), chancel nave and side aisles. The first church on the site was built in the 7th C. by St. Cedd. It was reconstructed by Abbot Stephen of Whitby in 1078. A planned great church was abandoned in 1228 and the remains converted to a general parish church in the 13th C. The tower was added in the 15th C.

🍺 The Blacksmith's Arms.

🔟 Site of ancient manor house, home of lords of the manor of Spaunton.

✗ Tea shop.

🍺 The Crown Inn; restaurant.

🏛 The folk museum contains local archaeological finds and an impressive collection of implements, tools and household items made in the area; also ancient house reconstructions.

Broxa Forest
7½ miles (12 km) Sheet 101 965944

Moderate Views of the Moors without being on them; an unusual variety of landscaping for woodland, with a singular, remote, sheltered valley. *Woods, riverside, farmland; one climb; mud.*

Start From Scarborough, go through Scalby and steeply uphill; turn sharp right and continue on straight road through Silpho Forest. **Car park** on top of Reasty Bank at edge of Silpho Forest.

① From car park walk W on road along top of escarpment, following the blue hiker signs (Allerston Forest Walk), and continuing past barrier where forest road bears left. 165 yards (150 m) after turning a sharp bend, double back down a steeply descending track. At cross-tracks (marked by a white-topped post) continue in the same direction, down a slightly overgrown path; later bear left and descend steeply again to river bank. ② Continue downstream, keeping to the left bank. (The path occasionally diverges from the bank, by not more than 100 yards.) ③ At footbridge in about a mile (1.7 km) leave riverside and bear left on uphill path (keeping left at cross-tracks). ④ Reaching level ground at top of slope, follow path at edge of wood to road. (Fifty yards (46 m) after ④ a broad forest ride joins from the left. This is the S end of the escarpment walk which was left at ①. After rain the riverside path is often severely muddy and this alternative route from ① to ④ is likely to be dry.) Turn right on to road; fork left at Broxa Farm and take signposted path over stiles across field and ⑤ along top edge of wood for 500 yards (450 m) before going down through wood and down end of field to reach road. (At ⑤ an alternative track leads downhill at the wood's edge. It is steep, and the last 200 yards (183 m) are rough.) ⑥ At road turn left. Cross stream, over stile and into field. Follow path towards farm. ⑦ Through farm, across streams and continue along valley of Whisper Dales, uphill about 2 miles (3 km) to ①.

Birds include the tawny owl, the most familiar owl, with short, rounded wings and a head that looks oddly large for the body; also the sparrowhawk – broad wings with rounded ends, squared-off tail and a small head.

Roe deer may be seen.

The ruins of Barnscliffe Castle. This is the approximate site, and the few remains are difficult to find.

An excellent example of modern creative forestry. There was woodland here before Bronze Age man began its destruction by farming land. The soil remained rich if replenished by annual leaf fall, but clearance continued and the exposed soil became acid and hard for 2 feet (0.6 m). In the 1950s, deep ploughing broke the hard layer, allowing new seedlings to root and aiding drainage. The present woodland is mainly larch and Scots pine.

A parish boundary stone: SIL is written on one side, marking the boundaries of Silpho and Suffield cum Everley.

NORTH YORK MOORS

Kirkdale

4, 4½ or 6 miles (6.5, 7 or 9.5 km) Sheet 100
675855

Easy A winding, sheltered valley, fine
woods, mellow buildings. *Farmland, woods,
riverside; mud after rain.*

Start From A170 between Helmsley and
Pickering about 1¼ miles (2 km) W of
Kirkbymoorside, turn N and continue about
¼ mile (0.5 km) crossing disused railway,
to T-junction. **Parking** on roadside in vicinity of T-junction (not in church car park).

① Walk down to right from T-junction, and
left to church. From church car park go
through gate into meadow and cross stream.
In about 450 yards (400 m) ignore track
leading right and continue on path just
inside wood. ② At mill do not cross river; go
over stile or through gate to keep on track
near river. ¾ mile (1.2 km) from mill there is
a line of hawthorn trees across the field:
cross stile on the right and continue just
inside wood. ③ In ½ mile (850 m), opposite
stile on left, turn half-right to ascend sunken
track. In ¼ mile (400 m) ④ turn back sharply
right on to well-constructed forestry path,
first maintaining height, then descending,
eventually joining outward route at ②.
Retrace to ①. Extensions: from ④ continue
300 yards (274 m) uphill to level track and a
further 250 yards (229 m) to meet road. Turn
right, continue ¼ mile, meet road from Fad-
moor to Welburn, turn right and follow road
for 1¼ miles (2 km) to 165 yards (150 m) past
farm ⑤ where follow path indicated by
public bridleway sign on right downhill.
Continue bearing left into woods, eventually
joining outward route and retracing to ①.
Or, from ②, cross bridge, follow farm road
to top, then turn left on to signposted
bridleway through wood. In 180 yards (160
m) go through small gate on right and
continue along field edge. Descend through
gate to road junction and turn right to ①.

St. Gregory's Minster: a church stood on
the site in the 7th C. was destroyed by
Danes in the 9th C. and rebuilt in about
1060.

The Hyena's Cave, discovered in 1821,
contained the bones and the teeth of not
only several hundred hyena but remains
of rhinoceros, mammoth and other pre-
glaciation animals.

*St. Gregory's Minster: Saxon sundial and
cross carved on outside wall.*

⑲ Skiplam and Wether Cote are probably
on the line of a medieval way.

The Bridestones

8½ miles (13.5 km) Sheets 100 and 101 845899

Energetic Takes in some of the finest and most varied countryside in the region. *Woods, moorland, valleys; 2 climbs; mud.*

Start From the A169 5 miles (8 km) N of Pickering take the road signposted left into Lockton; 3 buses daily to and from Pickering. **Parking** between church and cemetery.

① From parking cross main road on to track. Continue through the wood and gates beyond to the farm road. Turn left and in about ½ mile (0.8 km) where it joins another turn sharp right through farmyard of Low Pasture Farm. Follow direction of National Trust signs for about ½ mile. ② At foot of hill pass to right of cottage, then immediately left to follow grass track. Cross stream and turn left to stile and National Trust sign. Continue on track up valley; Bridestones visible high on right. Cross broad footbridge and climb paved path to ③ High Bride-stones. Curve right, crossing small valley to Low Bridestones. Climb to top of ridge and follow broad track back N, bearing right to keep out of the small valley. The path through heather becomes vague, but continue to join broad, cleared way – a fire-prevention belt – between edge of heather and forest. Continue uphill by edge of woods and at top join well-defined track; follow it left, going NW to reach A169 near car park. Turn right down road. ④ Cross road at sharp corner and follow wide path out on to open moor. Do not follow path left down to valley. Eventually reach gate into lane and continue to Levisham, then Lockton.

🏠 Lockton's church has a 15th C. tower.

🏔 The Bridestones, an outcrop of sand-stone in weirdly eroded shapes.

↑ Fylingdales early-warning system.

🍺 The Saltergate Inn, 550 yards N of ④.

🏔 The Hole of Horcum.

Above and Around Bilsdale
10 miles (16 km) Sheets 93 and 100   559994

Energetic A steady climb well up on to the Moors, from where most of the route can be surveyed; reaches the highest point on the Moors – superb views everywhere. *Farmland, moorland, craggy hills; mud.*

Start About 300 yards (274 m) S of Chop Gate on the B1257 between Helmsley and Stokesley. **Car park** 300 yards S of Chop Gate.

① From car park walk S along the B1257 to farm entry road with signpost 'Public Footpath to Bransdale'. Turn left and continue about ½ mile (0.8 km). ② Keep right in front of farmhouse, then left up lane between stone walls, continuing about ½ mile. ③ Turn left at T-junction of paths and after about 250 yards (229 m) sharp left. Then curve right, uphill, and follow contour. In about 1½ miles (2.5 km) ④ join track coming up from Bilsdale Hall and turn right. Continue about 1½ miles. ⑤ Near cairn turn sharp left to go downhill NW on well-defined track – the Lyke Wake Walk. Continue more than 2 miles (3 km). ⑥ After crossing road and climbing steps by wood edge, go left over fence and climb face of Hasty Bank. In about 1½ miles. ⑦ At the top of the second steep ascent, at a small cairn, turn left and continue S along the ridge of Cold Moor. ⑧ Where path divides take the left branch, going downhill to corner of moor and through gate into lane (likely to be muddy).

🍴 The Buck Inn; restaurant.

🔆 The Moors' most impressive earthwork or dyke, which runs for 3 miles (5 km) along the E side of Bilsdale on the edge of Urra Moor: mostly in good condition.

⛰ At 1,489 feet, the Moors' highest point.

📖 A section of the Lyke Wake Walk, which runs 40 miles (64 km) across the Moors.

🦋 In mid to late summer, beehives are seen dotted around Bilsdale and elsewhere on the Moors. Keepers bring them up to harvest the heather nectar.

📖 A stretch of the Cleveland Way long-distance path; see pages 328-334.

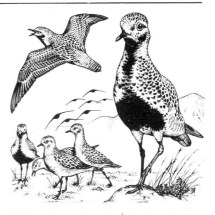

Golden plovers in typical standing, flocking and flight attitudes: they look solid, with their rounded heads noticeable in flight.

📖 Bilsdale hunt has a famous pack of hounds, based here. It is almost certainly descended from the 17th C. Duke of Buckingham's own pack, which hunted after retirement to Helmsley Castle. Old people in the neighbourhood can remember when Hunt fixtures were announced from Bilsdale church pulpit.

🦃 Golden plovers are seen here during their breeding season, February to July. The mating song, heard in early spring, is a beautiful, trilling sequence.

Bridestones Moor Nature Reserve has marked trails.

Sutton Bank, on the A170, is a popular starting point for walks, including marked trails.

The Roman road on Wheeldale Moor, part of Wade's Causeway, is well defined for 1½ miles (2.5 km). A signposted path leads to it from the hamlet of Hunt House.

Goathland, 7 miles (11 km) SW of Whitby on the A169 is a starting point for exciting walks.

A geological trail starts from the Wildlife Centre on the unclassified road from the A171 into Ravenscar.

Paths round Robin Hood Bay 5 miles (8 km) SE of Whitby are waymarked as part of the Cleveland Way.

CUMBRIA AND THE LAKES

Writers—and no doubt walkers—long ago ran out of adjectives for the Lake District, this unique 900 square miles (1,448 square km) comprising the highest mountains in England and the long, deep lakes between them. Millions of words have been written describing the finest views. Wordsworth was by no means the first to do so, nor will Arthur Ransom be among the last. For the first-time walker here the best advice is to ignore other people's ideas of the 'best bits'. That way a reasonable chance can be gained of finding privacy by a tarn, a fellside or waterfall, even in July and August.

The further east or west from the central Ambleside-Keswick axis, the lonelier the country. Treat it with the respect due to mountains. But do not neglect the rest of the county. What the locals call 'back o' Skidda' is a world of its own to the north of the lakes and there is the gentle Eden Vale to the east. The low hills of Arnside make excellent rambling and so do the tougher Howgills, a magnificent, miniature mountain range.

CUMBRIA AND THE LAKES

Mayburgh Henge Brougham Castle
5 miles (8 km) Sheet 90 519284

Easy A group of historical sites close to Penrith and the M6. *Minor roads, riverside; mud after rain.*

Start From Penrith head S on the A6. Cross Eamont Bridge (traffic lights) and take first right as for Pooley Bridge, then right on to narrow road. Follow it left and right. **Parking** at edge of this road, 150 yards (137 m) past henge, not obstructing houses.

① Walk back along road beside M6. ② Entrance to Mayburgh Henge is the signposted gate. Continue to A6, then right and first left. Follow road to castle. ③ Go down abandoned road N of Castle and continue to its end, where take riverside path back to A6. Retrace to ①.

🌿 Mayburgh Henge, a ritualistic monument, is probably late Neolithic or early Bronze Age. One standing stone remains. A second henge, obscurely named King Arthur's Round Table, is close by.

⛪ St. Wilfred's Chapel dates from the 14th C. and has beautiful wood carvings.

🏞 In the field can be seen the foundations of the Roman fort Brocavum. It guarded from the 2nd to the 4th C. A.D., what had

Primitive but powerful – the standing stone at the centre of Mayburgh Henge.

been an important crossroads since prehistory. Around it there is evidence of a large Roman village.

🏰 Brougham Castle grew with its successive owners from the mid-12th C. The last and greatest of them were the Cliffords; and of them the most formidable was Lady Anne, owner of vast estates, philanthropist and restorer.

261

Crosby Garrett Fell

3½ miles (5.5 km) Sheet 91 729096

Moderate Gives a succession of outstanding views of the W flanks of the Pennines and of Cumbrian countryside; outside any tourist area. *Grassy hillside and plateau; one climb; mud after rain; some misleading vehicle tracks on the plateau – follow directions closely. Sheep country – control dogs.*

Start Crosby Garrett, W of Kirkby Stephen, signposted via Soulby on minor roads. **Parking** in village.

① From parking make for the railway viaduct. ② Go under viaduct and continue up distinct track. ③ When the track nears its highest point, look right, up the hill, where what appears to be a ruin or broken wall should be seen on the crest. This is in fact a limestone outcrop. Walk up to it over the steep grass slope – no path. Take this slowly – if too steep, take the gully near track's highest point; however this entails a trudge back to the limestone outcrop after reaching the plateau. ④ From the outcrop, look SW towards Nettle Hill and identify what appears to be a square ruin, with a central chimney, on the highest point. Make for this, choosing a route on higher places where the grass is shortest. ⑤ From the ruin – a heap of stones and trig. point – head acutely right from the line of approach. This is due N. There is no distinct path and

the easiest way through the tussocks is to follow sheep 'trods'. ⑥ Do not be diverted by vehicle tracks. ⑦ Head to the right when the vehicle tracks come together to run towards the village. ⑧ The track heads towards the corner of a wall; do not follow the wall round, but take the track descending in direction of village from the wall corner. ⑨ The track becomes better defined and surfaced with hardcore; follow it down to the viaduct.

🔟 Ancient records show the village was
🏠 once called Crosby Gerard; who Gerard was is debatable, but Crosby means farmstead with a cross. In Christianity's earliest days, communities without churches made do with simple wood or stone crosses. Later, in Anglo-Saxon times, came a small church.

🔟 The limestone pavement is a good resting
🚶 place and viewpoint. The hill here is common land, where the villagers had grazing rights. Sheep farming brought what wealth there was to the area.

🔟 Nettle Hill – and not a nettle in sight; but
🚶 there probably was a nettlebed here once. Nettles, with various uses including dye for local wool, are a sign of earlier human settlement and these hills are covered with cairns and hut circles. N through E to SW are the Pennines; W and NW, the Lake District.

Long Meg and Lacy's Caves
5 miles (8 km) Sheets 90 and 91 566362

Moderate One of the finest Neolithic stone circles in the country, and a man-made cave in an idyllic situation; a beautiful river; all quiet. *Riverside, farmland; mud; may be overgrown between* ④ *and* ⑥.

Start From Penrith take the A686 in direction of Alston and turn left after crossing iron bridge over River Eden at Langwathby for Little Salkeld; infrequent buses. **Parking** in Little Salkeld without causing obstruction; alternatively NE of the village on grass verge in minor road leading to ⑭, starting the walk there.

① Walk W from centre of village to join surfaced track by railway. ② Continue on good-quality surface by railway line. ③ Go left on to concrete road. Turn sharp left by the transformer, then right at railway line to join narrow path leaving line, past old mine complex to riverside. ④ Watch carefully: Lacy's Caves can be overlooked. On reaching sandstone face, follow path on rock ledge to the left. After visiting cave, retrace steps to this point and follow the path up the bank onwards above the cave. ⑤ The path continues through lush growth and may be overgrown; some wet sections. ⑥ Follow the path beside river through fields. Make detours to avoid the worst of the mud. ⑦ Follow path through woodland to join minor road. ⑧ Follow road to Glassonby; look out for local drivers, who may not expect to meet anyone. ⑨ At Glassonby take the road right in direction of Little Salkeld. ⑩ After barns turn right on road to Addingham church. ⑪ Go through churchyard following paved path through iron gate S, then take track to access road. ⑫ Cross access road and go through gate; follow fence, using sketchy track. ⑬ Follow fence alongside plantation through two gates. Continue following fences and field boundaries to stone circle seen ahead. After stone circle, continue on road heading S. ⑭ Where road bends left continue heading S on track to join road again at Little Salkeld and starting point.

🔧 Long Meg mine produced anhydrite (for munitions) during the 1939-45 war.

〽 The River Eden can be approached here. It flows NW to the Solway Firth.

🏚 The extraordinary Lacy's Caves are a mystery. The Lacy family arrived in the neighbourhood in the 18th C. and may have created them as a folly. Grottoes, preferably complete with a hermit's retreat, were fashionable then.

〽 Long Meg and her Daughters date from Neolithic or Bronze Age times – more than 4,000 years ago. Originally there were probably 60 stones. It is assumed they had religious and astronomical significance. Viewed from the centre of the circle, Long Meg is in position for the setting of the midwinter sun. The day when the sun 'turns back', giving promise of spring, must have meant much to the farmers who depended on this valley for their living long before recorded history. Wordsworth was much struck by coming on the stones for the first time feeling 'A weight of awe not easy to be borne . . .'

CUMBRIA AND THE LAKES

The Black and White Combes
5 miles (8 km) Sheet 96 153847

Energetic A neglected corner of the otherwise well-trodden Lake District; some regard the climb as a dull slog over featureless moorland – but this way it is not. *Valley; heather hillside; moorland, tussocky plateau; one climb; mud (avoidable). Do not attempt in poor visibility, or under snow.*

Start On the A595, 2½ miles (4 km) NE of Whicham. **Parking** in lay-by at Beckside.

① From parking cross road with care and go up lane opposite. ② Follow grassy path above cottage and cross stile. ③ At the apparent fork, keep left to go alongside the wood. ④ Through gate, across bridge and then follow well-defined track up into valley of White Combe. ⑤ After passing the crags above and to the left, follow track as it leads slightly away from beck. Watch for the waterfalls above and forward to the left. Walk up from track towards the falls. ⑥ Cross beck below fall and walk up steep bank alongside it (no path). There is a slightly easier route to the right in a wet gully – but either way it is steep. Above the falls, on a slightly easier slope, look upwards and identify gap in crags ahead. Head for this; to most people, it looks worse than it is. ⑦ As the beck forks, continue uphill towards gap in crags. Beware of loose stones. (Parties should keep close together to avoid being hit by stones loosened by leaders.) Also watch for bog – identified by level area of bright green moss. Scramble through the gap and out on to plateau, continuing upwards and bearing left (no path). ⑧ The plateau is hard walking on tussocky grass. As the higher parts are reached some sketchy paths and tracks are seen. Follow any of them towards summit. ⑨ Follow the more evident tracks going to the right of the summit of Black Combe. ⑩ The obvious summit is crowned by an untidy cairn and a trig. point. From here retrace steps to ⑪ pathless plateau above the White Combe. ⑫ To avoid worst of bog, pick a route near to the fence. Turn to follow summit ridge SE. ⑬ From here the subsidiary summit marked 'White Combe' on the map can be visited. Otherwise descend to ⑭ a distinct path which zigzags comfortably down into White Combe. ⑮ The 2 bogs can be avoided to some extent by climbing above the path. ⑯ The path bends back to a beck; descend on outward track.

〰 Supremely clear water in this stream, the colour enhanced by light grey rock.

〰 The light grey rock gave the valley its name – White Combe – combe being the old word for a hollow. The rock is the oldest in the Lake District and known as Skiddaw slate.

🌢 A gardener would give much to reproduce the effect of the falls. The plant life is so profuse because the soil is enriched by minerals flushed to the surface by the water. There is a particularly large variety of mosses and liverworts. The dominant yellow flower is bog asphodel, flowering July-Sept.

\†/ The view is amazing; it is clear why mariners regard Black Combe as an important landmark. The Isle of Man is prominent; in best conditions one can make out the coasts of Ireland and the hills of North Wales and Galloway. All the higher central mountains of the Lakes are visible. Way out SE are the Pennines; S is Barrow and Walney Island with the Fylde beyond. Close to, the only ugly intrusion is Windscale Power Station. Wordsworth could truthfully write 'This height a ministering Angel might select . . .'

\†/ At last, the hollow of Black Combe.

CUMBRIA AND THE LAKES

Arnside Knott, Tower and Cliffs
7 miles (11 km) Sheet 97 454786

Moderate A walk of contrasts – viewpoints, historical interest and natural history. *Sea promenade, cliff top, woods, farmland, beach; one climb; mud after rain; cliff path may be slippery after rain.*

Start Arnside, approached from Milnthorpe on the B5282. **Car parks** in Arnside.

① From road end walk along promenade and surfaced footpath on sea shore. ② Watch for the gateway (no gate) by lifebelt; go up lane between cottages. Climb steeply and at the road turn right. ③ At second road junction climb steep road to left. ④ From view indicator on left climb directly uphill on gravelly path to another, walled, view indicator. ⑤ Turn left here and walk through woodland below summit for best views. Go to summit. ⑥ A number of paths lead off summit; descend SW (the bench-mark is on SW face of pillar). At bench marked '1923 CF 1985' turn left to descend steeply. ⑦ Join distinct track and continue left through woodland to descend to road. ⑧ Cross road with care and follow track towards ruined tower. Walk past this. ⑨ Take path on right through gate – woodland on left. ⑩ Go through green iron gate and skirt caravan site. ⑪ Look for double gate in fence to right:

go to its left and follow fence. ⑫ Go through wicket gate in fence and follow field paths towards road. ⑬ Cross road with care (blind exit) and go down surfaced lane opposite. ⑭ Follow spine road through caravan park. ⑮ At the end of park, where road bears right, continue on track towards shore. ⑯ Track becomes a cliff path; the surface varies. ⑰ Follow track as it turns left to White Creek; if conditions permit, continue on sands back to promenade. If the tide is too high, turn back having viewed White Creek and follow lane through caravan site to next bay. ⑱ Bear left at edge of wood. ⑲ At bay, continue on beach round next headland; if tide is too high, go inland on lane to join road into Arnside and signposted footpath to promenade on left.

↖ The best viewpoint is below the summit, slightly on the Arnside flank.

▣ Arnside Tower is 14th C.

❧ In midsummer look for the yellow rock-rose; also bloody cranesbill (red) and centaury (pink).

➤ In winter, waders, ducks and geese feed at the water's edge.

▣ The public road over Morecambe Bay from Morecambe to Kents Bank was once the only way into the southern Lake District and travellers needed guides.

265

CUMBRIA AND THE LAKES

Windermere to Grasmere
9 miles (14.5 km) Sheets 96 and 90 414987

Moderate Famous views; opportunity to visit Wordsworth's home, the cottage where he wrote his best work, the museum there and the poet's grave. *Grassy hillsides, farmland; 2 climbs; mud.*

Start Windermere station; frequent buses and trains. **Car parks** and lay-bys on the A592 N of Bowness (add 1½ miles (2 km) to the walk). **Return**: by bus from Grasmere.

① From station walk across main road with care and continue about 100 yards (91 m) in direction of Ambleside. Turn up tarmac lane signposted Orrest Head. Join track at top going right by wall. Pass through iron gate to high viewpoint. ② From Orrest Head viewpoint continue on grassy path N towards farm. Path does not reach farm; follow it along wall to stile on to road. Turn right. ③ Turn left off drive to circumnavigate buildings. ④ Across paddock to 2 stiles and on same line to the next. ⑤ Follow wall on right to next stile. ⑥ Half right to next stile. ⑦ After gate continue to cottage. Through gate and kissing-gate opposite, and follow wall on left to another kissing-gate. ⑧ Do not turn right, but go through gate towards barn and on behind it. ⑨ At farmyard corner bear right to follow tarmac lane. Cross minor road and ⑩ go over stile beyond cottages

and on to terraced, grassy path. ⑪ Join road, cross and continue on pavement. ⑫ Just *after* a road joins from right, go through gate on left and descend on track to cross 2 bridges. Continue uphill between walls. ⑬ Cross road and climb track opposite. Join another road and turn left; in about 80 yards (73 m) ⑭ climb track between walls. ⑮ Join level walled track. ⑯ Leave walled track by gate to follow path downhill. ⑰ Join track, over bridge and on past farm (High Skelghyll), following level track through woods. ⑱ Track becomes a surfaced lane and descends to minor road. ⑲ Follow road into Ambleside (Old Lake Road). ⑳ Leave Ambleside by Keswick road. ㉑ Join track through iron gates. Follow this fenced track about a mile through parkland. ㉒ Go between buildings behind Rydal Hall to join lane at T-junction. Turn right up slope. ㉓ Turn left on to walled track behind Rydal Mount. Later follow level path. ㉔ Join surfaced road to Dove Cottage. ㉕ Cross road with care and continue into Grasmere.

\|/ Orrest Head, one of the best vantage points in the district, takes in most of the central fells, but the glory is the long view over England's largest lake.

🏠 Town End is a worthwhile diversion: a 17th C. house belonging to a yeoman family, most of its interior is period, made

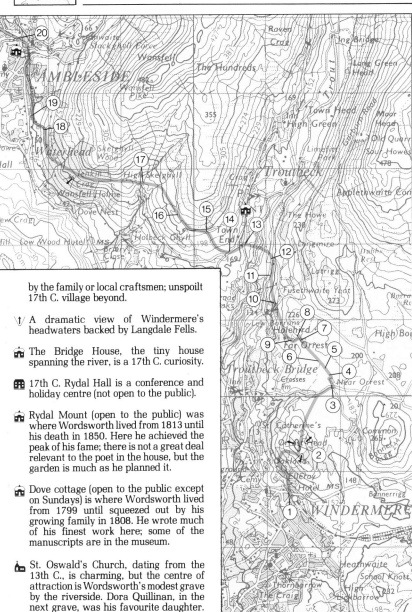

by the family or local craftsmen; unspoilt 17th C. village beyond.

A dramatic view of Windermere's headwaters backed by Langdale Fells.

The Bridge House, the tiny house spanning the river, is a 17th C. curiosity.

17th C. Rydal Hall is a conference and holiday centre (not open to the public).

Rydal Mount (open to the public) was where Wordsworth lived from 1813 until his death in 1850. Here he achieved the peak of his fame; there is not a great deal relevant to the poet in the house, but the garden is much as he planned it.

Dove cottage (open to the public except on Sundays) is where Wordsworth lived from 1799 until squeezed out by his growing family in 1808. He wrote much of his finest work here; some of the manuscripts are in the museum.

St. Oswald's Church, dating from the 13th C., is charming, but the centre of attraction is Wordsworth's modest grave by the riverside. Dora Quillinan, in the next grave, was his favourite daughter. Hartley Coleridge, son of the Romantic poet S. T. Coleridge, is close by.

CUMBRIA AND THE LAKES

Derwentwater and Lodore Cascade
3½ miles (5.5 km) Sheet 90 251213

Easy A delightful expedition, incorporating boat trips, and much opportunity for idleness; with a picnic lunch (the route is mainly on National Trust land) it could last all day. The ferry service operates between start of British Summer Time in March and the first Sunday in November. *Wooded lakeside, peat; parts flooded after rain.*

Start Hawse End, reached by regular boat service from Keswick boat stage; buses to Keswick. **Car park** in Keswick nearest the boat landing. **Return** to Keswick by boat (regular service) from Lodore.

① After picking up a timetable, board the Keswick Launch Co. boat going *anti-clockwise* for Hawes End – the first stop. ② Alight at Hawes End and go left along the shore path. ③ To avoid bog and scrub, the path continues through a stile and along a field edge. ④ Turn left with fence at end. Use the plank walk to avoid swamp. Follow the path along the shore again. ⑤ Ignore the path going steeply uphill to the right. Keep to the shore path. ⑥ Negotiate steps over rocky outcrop. ⑦ At the landing stage bear right. ⑧ At fork bear left and climb steps. ⑨ Go through kissing-gate and immediately left towards the land side of the boathouse. Continue between the boathouse and cottage; go through the gate. ⑩ At the fork, keep right (left track goes to a private house). ⑪ Enter Manesty Wood (National Trust sign). Go left with fence towards the shore. ⑫ To avoid worst of swamp, bear right, following path trodden by others for same purpose, to join a path sweeping down to the shore farther on. ⑬ Follow the path across the plank walk and over the bridge to the road. ⑭ Just before Lodore Swiss Hotel Entrance, go up lane on right to Lodore Cascade (waterfalls). Retrace to ⑭. Go up road and turn left for the boat landing. ⑮ Join anti-clockwise boat to Keswick.

⚓ The lake was an important highway. Boats carried ore from mines about the valley for smelting in Keswick, once a smoky industrial town. Friar's Crag, the viewpoint, is down the road and lane.

⚲ The shoreline's trees have particularly beautiful shapes. On St. Herbert's Island lived the saint of the same name, a close

friend of St. Cuthbert; in fact they were so close they died, in sympathy, on the same day.

⚲ One of the shore's many viewpoints: opposite is Wella's Crag, with Great Wood below.

⚓ This is the easily overlooked waste heap of what was Brandlehow Mine. The hillside, mined from ancient times, contains galena (lead), iron, silver, manganese, even traces of gold.

⚲ N. the Skiddaw range; forward, Shepherds Crag – watch for climbers.

⚲⚲⚲ Approach Lodore Cascade by paying a small fee at the hotel.

Opposite: photogenic Derwentwater.

Wastwater Screes Top and Miterdale

10½ miles (17 km) Sheet 89 143003

Energetic Wastwater Screes Top ranks high among the Lakes' great vantage points and Miterdale, unknown to many Lake District addicts, is magically peaceful. In winter, the route should be attempted only by experienced walkers with appropriate equipment. *Forest, hillsides, fell top, valley, riverside; one climb; a hard descent; mud.*

Start Eskdale Green, signposted from the A595; frequent trains – the narrow-gauge railway service from Ravenglass goes to Irton Road station, from where turn right to village centre for start. **Car park** near public lavatories in Eskdale Green.

① Take the walled lane from the telephone box and public lavatories uphill beside the Outward Bound School. ② Bear left at fork, between walls. ③ At junction with road cross road into wood, cross bridge and climb stony track. ④ Ignore crossing roads and tracks, continuing straight on, climbing on stone track. ⑤ After crossing upper forest road, the track becomes a path through heather; follow this, and climb the rocky steps. ⑥ When path eventually leaves forest, turn right to follow wall and keep climbing. ⑦ Cross stile over wall, and escape the bog by going right. ⑧ The path is poorly defined on wet ground. A steep ascent approaches; follow path, now more obvious. ⑨ Only peak-baggers will make for the highest point direct; discerning walkers will follow the pathless route on the cliff edges to view the lake 1,700 feet below. ⑩ From the summit, Illgill Head, follow the track downhill NE as if for Wasdale Head. If fog is approaching, return to start by the same route, keeping away from cliff edge, staying on the path. ⑪ Follow indistinct level path. ⑫ Pick up better-defined level path seen ahead. (The 'bridleway' marking is optimistic.) ⑬ With care, the boggy sections can be by-passed. ⑭ The 'bridleway' climbs vaguely away; keep to the narrow path at present level and head towards plantation fence. ⑮ At plantation descend carefully on extremely steep path to river. Cross to path and descend with river on right. ⑯ Cross bridge to ruined farm. If the river is in spate (full and flowing fast) at this point, go back over bridge after viewing ruin and continue downhill on path to ⑲. This avoids a ford. ⑰ From farm continue up walled pathway and

soon go left through wall gap. Continue on grassy track across fields. ⑱ Cross the ford. ⑲ Follow track past footbridge (not across it) through farmyard by riverside. ⑳ Cross bridge to road. Follow this. ㉑ Turn left to rejoin outward path. Alternatively, go straight on to join village road, a more direct route to Irton Road Station.

〰 Here the terrain changes from granite to the volcanic of the high central fells.

↑ Obvious signs of the geological change – hard volcanic rocks, which resisted glacial erosion – rise ahead.

↑ The lake, 1,700 feet (518 m) below is 258 feet (79 m) deep, with extremely clean water. The cliff (the 'screes') is unstable and sheds rock falls: it was undercut by the ice which ground out Wastwater over 10,000 years ago.

Towards the coast the contrasting geology is again evident: the sea plain is sandstone; the valleys are granite and the hills are volcanic.

↑ Better a few yards W.

🔟 The more level area around Burnmoor Tarn is once more granite country. Pollen analysis of the tarn bed shows that some 3,000 years ago the area was well wooded. Neolithic man's stone axes, made from the volcanic stone, probably cleared away the forest.

Skiddaw can be climbed from Keswick by the side of Latrigg and up the public bridleway.

Take a bus from Keswick to Rosthwaite and walk back via Watendlath, Surprise View, Ashness Bridge and Walla Crag on public footpaths.

From Ambleside to Grasmere along the S side of Rydal Water and then by Loughrigg Terrace is a fine walk.

On Ullswater, take the service steamer from Glenridding to Howtown and walk back on the lake shore paths.

An ascent of Coniston Old Man can be made in fine weather only from Coniston via Low Water. Return by Goats Water and Walna Scar. The mountain is scarred by copper mines, but the view superb.

NORTHUMBERLAND

From its north-east to south-west corners, North-umberland measures 70 miles (113 km): a big county, full of interest for the walker. There is a coast of great beauty, complete with wide, firm beaches, islands, seals, history in the shape of massively romantic castles, and some splendid cliffs. Inland is a coastal plain of pure enclosure countryside, a range of noble river valleys, ranging from the Tweed in the north to the Tyne in the south, and the low swell of the Simonside Hills.

The county incorporates an entire national park at its southern end, of which the best bit is Hadrian's Wall. This marches, Roman-fashion, relentlessly across the contours. It demands to be explored on foot, the mode of transport employed by the legions who defended it.

Further north in the park, the Cheviots loom over the rest of the county. These are the northern end of the Pennine chain and quite unlike the rest. They are more smoothly rounded, and the grass covering them is of a kind better to reflect the changing light and shade. They bring a new character to the hills just when the walker who has slogged up the Pennine Way is nearing the end of the trek.

Hareshaw Linn
4 miles (6.5 km) Sheet 80 840834

Easy A pleasant stroll near an interesting town. *Woods; mud after rain.*

Start Bellingham on the B6320; frequent buses. **Parking** at centre of Bellingham.

① From Bellingham walk along the West Woodburn road and turn left along lane by stream. Continue beneath the disused railway towards a row of cottages. ② Follow

Magnificent Hareshaw Linn, at its liveliest after prolonged rain.

the path directly ahead and into the wooded ravine of the Hareshaw Burn. ③ The path follows the E side of the stream about 1¼ miles (2 km), then swaps sides; for another ¼ mile (0.5 km) 5 plank bridges switch the route from side to side. As there is no right of way past the linn (waterfall), return by the same route. This is no hardship – the views are different each way.

🏠 The principal church in Bellingham (pronounced Bellinjam) has a 17th C. stone vaulted nave.

🏠 The Pennine Way long-distance path (see pages 328-334) goes through the town.

🌢 The woodland plants growing beside Hareshaw Burn do not need strong light: many of them flower in spring before the trees in leaf cut off too much sunlight. Flowering plants to be seen include foxglove, the source of the drug digitalis, used for the treatment of heart complaints, and the greenish-yellow wood sage, a herbal 'cure' for rheumatism. The first flowers June-Sept., the second July-Sept.

🏠 Hareshaw Linn, cascading over sandstone, is one of Northumberland's most famous waterfalls.

273

NORTHUMBERLAND

Along Hadrian's Wall
7½ miles (12 km) Sheet 87 753669

Moderate Follows the best-preserved and hence most interesting section of Hadrian's Wall, with a visit to Housesteads Fort and Vindolanda Roman Settlement. *Farmland, moorland, crags; 2 climbs.*

Start Bardon Mill, signposted from the A69; buses in summer. **Car park** at the Once Brewed Information Centre, signposted in village.

① From car park cross the B6318 and walk along the Steel Rigg road as far as the first cottage on the right. ② Immediately beyond Peel farmhouse turn right across a ladder stile and walk through the field as far as the Roman wall. ③ Turn right along Hadrian's Wall and follow it about 2½ miles (4 km) to Housesteads Fort (signposted at entrance). ④ Retrace steps from fort as far as Rapishaw Gap (pronounced dip in ridge) (the Pennine Way, clearly signposted, turns away from the wall at this point). ⑤ Turn left and walk downhill on faint path later becoming a track bearing slightly right through 2 fields to the road. ⑥ Turn right, cross and then left down the minor road towards Bardon Mill. In 1¼ miles (2 km) ⑦ turn right at Vindolanda car park, follow the lane past the museum and information

centre and ⑧ enter the ruins. Walk through Vindolanda and leave by the lane beyond the upper (W) car park. ⑨ At road right for ①.

> 🗺 The Romans built this great wall between A.D. 122 and 126 as a fortification, a raised military patrol route and a base for raids against the barbarians to the N. The wall used to stand up to 20 feet (6 m) high, with milecastles–patrol points–every 1,620 yards (1,481 m) and smaller turrets every 540 yards (494 m).

> 🗺 Housesteads (Vercovicium), probably the finest example of a Roman fort to be found in all Europe, includes barracks, granaries, a hospital, a mess-room with baths, and a latrine. The small museum contains interesting finds from the site.

> 🗺 Vindolanda (Chesterholme) was both a Roman fort, with a small garrison of 500, and a civilian community, a *vicus*. Excavation has already revealed houses, taverns, workshops, baths and temples, stone-built and well drained.

> 🍺 The 'Twice Brewed' pub, according to legend, got its name many years ago,
> ✗ when a customer complained that the ale wasn't strong enough and asked for it to be brewed again.

The Tyne Valley
4 miles (6.5 km) Sheet 87 910661

Easy A pleasing short walk through a little known area near Hadrian's Wall with excellent views of the S Tyne Valley. *Pasture, woods, riverside; one climb.*

Start Bridge End signposted from the A69; frequent buses; trains to Hexham, nearly 3 miles' (5 km) walk or bus ride from ①. **Parking** beyond the railway bridge near the Boat Inn.

① From the Boat Inn walk along the Warden road under the railway bridge and in about 60 yards (55 m) turn left along the path signposted to Quality Cottages. ② Turn right at the cottages and climb gently up through a small wood. Cross a series of fields on obvious track close to hedge, making for the wood ahead. ③ At the wood turn left and follow track past 2 sections of woods to a cottage. ④ Turn left at cottage and walk downhill (changing sides of wall) through a series of fields along track to Fourstones village. ⑤ Continue through the village and turn left at the crossroads. ⑥ Walk down the lane, over the level crossing and continue to the river bank. Turn left and follow the river. ⑦ In about a mile (1.5 km), ignore a stile leading left into a field and then continue ¾ mile (one km) along the river bank to the

paper mill. ⑧ At mill turn right along the road and walk back to the Boat Inn.

🍴 The Boat Inn serves food. The road from the inn leads to Warden, where the N ✕ and S Tynes meet.

\ The S Tyne valley.

ⓗ This country, through which the N Tyne flows, had a violent past. In the 12th C. Henry II agreed to the land passing into the care of the kings of Scotland, in return for their giving up a claim to inherit the earldom of Northumbria. A century later, nominees of the English crown, including Piers Gaveston, held the lordship of N Tynedale, and the resulting confusion between English and Scottish territorial power and influence made the area a lawless one, where outlaws could find sanctuary, protected by custom from arrest by law officers.

ⓗ In the Middle Ages the king's judges were met by the Sheriff of Northumberland at Fourstones when they travelled north. In those days the village was on the borders of N Tynedale and Hexamshire. The judges could well have used the Roman road Stanegate on their journey.

There is a pub in the village.

NORTHUMBERLAND

By the Pennine Way to the Border
9 miles (14.5 km) Sheet 80 764027

Energetic An exciting section of the Pennine Way, clearly marked by a fence, with incomparable views of the Cheviot hills. Path may be overgrown between ② and ③ but the firebreak is easy to follow. *Forest, moorland; one climb; mud.*

Start Byrness, on the A68; frequent buses. **Car park** in Byrness (signposted near Information Centre), or parking in lane parallel to A68.

① From car park walk along the lane parallel to the main road as far as the chapel – about ½ mile (0.8 km). ② Cross the A68 and walk along a drive opposite, then turn right at a gate to climb steeply up a firebreak (gap in trees). ③ Above the forest the path is well defined, and becomes less steep after a short scramble through a boulder field. On Byrness Hill turn slightly left to follow the path the whole way across the moor to the Border Fence. ④ At the fence, climb a stile close by the forest and turn left. There is no path on this section, but the route is easy to follow by keeping close to the fence. Follow the fence 1¼ miles (2 km) to a pronounced depression. ⑤ In the depression, turn left, crossing the low fence, and walk into firebreak (gap between trees). ⑥ Descend the firebreak to forest track. Turn left and at the junction with another forest track, turn right and follow it downhill through the forest, ignoring side turnings, to the main road. ⑦ Cross and return to Byrness.

🅱 The second-longest footpath in Britain, the Pennine Way runs 250 miles (402 km) from Edale in Derbyshire to the tiny village of Kirk Yetholm, once a gipsy settlement, just over the Border. (See page 328-334.)

\!/ The view SW takes in Kielder Forest, part of the 145,000-acre (58,681 ha) Border Forest Park created by the Forestry Commission in the last 50 years. Great plantations of trees, mainly sitka and Norway spruce, cover what was once sheep-grazing country, although the whole Border had been a forest in earlier times, before the Romans came.

\!/ To the NE is Cheviot Hill, 2,676 feet (816 m) high.

Craster and Dunstanburgh

4½ miles (7 km) Sheets 75 and 81 259198

Easy A coastal walk with a magnificent ruined castle as its focal point; interesting geological features; can be exhilarating in winter. *Sea shore, farmland, craggy outcrops.*

Start Craster, on minor road signposted from B1339; frequent buses. **Car park** in old quarry signposted on outskirts of Craster.

① From the car park walk towards the harbour and turn left; continue along road past cottages through gate on to coastal path. Follow the coast to Dunstanburgh Castle. ② After visiting the castle, leave by the main gate and turn right to follow the path around the golf course to Dunstan Steads Farm. Turn left through the farmyard and ③ follow the farm lane to Dunstan Square where, ④ turn left and walk downhill through a field towards the conspicuous crags – The Heughs. ⑤ Turn right and follow the path beneath the crags back to the car park.

✗ Craster's delicious kippers are reckoned the best in England: herrings from the North Sea are smoked over a fire of oak chips, and the results can be tried in the restaurant by the curing sheds.

🌿 Various seaside plants.

🏰 Largest of Northumbria's castles, Dunstanburgh was begun in 1313 by Thomas, Earl of Lancaster (and much altered in 1380-84 by John of Gaunt) for use as an outpost on the Lancastrian side in the Wars of the Roses. Turner included the castle in 3 of his paintings, and it is a magnificent spectacle, standing high above the sea on outcrops of the Whin Sill, the rock system which carries Hadrian's Wall.

Best preserved of the ruins are the gatehouse/keep and the Lilburn Tower.

🏠 This 14th C. tower house was titivated in the 18th C. Seat of the Craster family, it may once have been a watch-tower for Dunstanburgh Castle.

NORTHUMBERLAND

The Cheviot Foothills

12 miles (19 km) Sheet 75 992279

Energetic A solitary walk through contrasting countryside; some exposed moorland – avoid in poor visibility or bad weather. Superb views to the Tweed Valley and Scottish border country. *Moorland, valley, farmland; 2 climbs.*

Start Wooler, signposted from the A697; frequent buses. **Parking** in Wooler.

① From the Market Square walk up Ramsey's Lane. After about ¼ mile (0.5 km) its name changes to Common Road. Almost at the last house on this lane turn left on to a rough track to Waud House Farm. ② At the farm a stile by a gate leads to open country. Cross and turn sharply right to climb a small hill ahead on gradually improving path. Pass ramparts of a prehistoric settlement. Cross stile and walk through the young plantation. Continue towards Wooler Common Farm, seen ahead. ③ Go round the farm to the right and climb towards obvious gap between the 2 forests. Cross moorland – about 1¾ miles (3 km) – and descend to Carey Burn (stream). ④ Follow Carey Burn and at the junction of 2 streams follow the track climbing steeply above the stream on left. When the buildings of Broadstruther come into sight, follow path which veers slightly left and towards them. ⑤ Keep slightly left beyond the ruins of Broadstruther and continue on faint path across moorland towards the dip in the ridge ahead. ⑥ At the fence cross a stile, continue uphill about 100 yards (91 m) then descend by an improving path to Hawsen Burn and the Langleeford road, where ⑦ turn left and continue to Langlee Cottage. ⑧ Cross the burn (stream) by bridge on right; pass in front of Langlee Cottage and climb steep hill beyond. ⑨ Descend Brands Hill by a path which joins a farm track past the deserted farm at Middleton Old Town. Continue to North Middleton. ⑩ Turn left along the road and cross ford in Happy Valley. Follow road for about 1¾ miles and take the second turning right beyond the Happy Valley. ⑪ Follow lane to Earle Mill and then signposted path behind the mill to Wooler.

🏛 Until 1251 Wooler was the seat of a barony with a castle (now in ruins). It was known for its sheep and cattle fairs and still holds the Trinian Fair, on September 27th.

🍴 There are plenty of pubs and cafés from which to choose in the spacious main street.

🗻 The granite Cheviots are ancient: they were high ground before the ice ages, and when the glaciers came, the hills blocked their movement. Forced to change direction, the ice marked out the river courses – and therefore the lines of communication – that have made and influenced the history of Britain.

🏛 In the Cheviot foothills, the first settlers in Northumbria built their round huts and struggled to make a living from the land. The highest hill of the Cheviots is The Cheviot, 2,676 feet (816 m). It can be climbed in about 2 hours, starting from Langleeford.

Attractive, waymarked forest walks start from a picnic site near Stonehaugh. Follow the signpost off the B6320 N of Chollerford.

A forest track over the Simonside Hills, by Lordenshaw 2 miles (3 km) S of Rothbury off the B6342, leads to the dramatic vantage point of Tosson Hill.

Nature trails on the beautiful Farne Islands – with their superb seabird populations – can be reached by a short boat trip from Seahouses, 15 miles (24 km) N of Alnwick.

The secluded paths of Coquetdale, across the bleak moorland of the Cheviots, can be reached from Alwinton, 10 miles (16 km) NW of Rothbury.

SCOTLAND

SW SCOTLAND

Somewhere in this region, Richard Hannay, fleeing London for his life, got off the train and took to the moors implacably pursued by the German spy-ring of *The Thirty-Nine Steps.* John Buchan was not the first romancer to set a tale here. Sir Walter Scott did so in *Guy Mannering* and *Marmion,* and those who explore the region on foot can still taste the romance, even if the mountains have not quite the drama of the Highlands.

Merrick, the highest point in southern Scotland, is quite an easy climb from the car park near the Bruce Stone. With the parallel Rhinns of Kells, it forms a granite complex geologically allied to the Highlands. In the area round Glentrool, the Forestry Commission caters elaborately for walkers, but the best bits of the Forest Park are the central, untamed hills which have been left unplanted.

There is an excellent coast which is perhaps finest along the Solway Firth. A small mountain called Criffel gives the best views across the shining strands of the estuary to the peaks of the Lake District. Further west along the coast is Burrow Head and the peninsula where Christianity was first established in Scotland.

Loch Skeen and White Coomb

6½ miles (10.5 km) Sheet 79 185145

Energetic One of the most dramatic walks of Scotland's SW, with a superb waterfall, moraines and expansive upland views. The route passes through a gorge, best lit in May-June. *Gorge, heather moor, moraines, ridge, grassy slopes; 3 climbs; mud after rain. Do not attempt in poor visibility – for experienced hill walkers only – 1:25,000 map and compass recommended.*

Start Take the A708 from Moffat or Selkirk to **car park**, conspicuous about 7 miles (11 km) NE of Moffat.

① Cross bridge at car park. Uphill on path with waterfall on left. *It is dangerous to stray from the path.* ② Keep on E bank of burn (stream) until near loch. ③ Cross burn by stones below loch. ④ Climb Prominent ridge. ⑤ Head for higher ridge (with wall on it) to W. The path is indistinct. *If cloud is low, and you are not equipped with a compass, or uncertain of capability, retrace steps.* ⑥ A wall and ridge lead off at right angles to route from ⑤ – difficult to miss. Turn left at wall, following ridge and wall SW, S and SW to Donald's Cleuch Head. ⑦ Continue by wall S to Firthhope Rig. ⑧ Go E following wall down to col and climb by wall to White Coomb. ⑨ Descend from ridge ENE by wall. ⑩ Go ESE then E past Rough Craigs by wall.

The slope is steep, but there are grass/heather routes on either side of the broken ground. ⑩ Continue by wall SE, E, SE and S to top of steep slope above road. ⑫ *Avoid dangerous slopes on left.* Bear right all the way down on edge of forest until flat ground is reached. Return along road.

〰 The Grey Mare's Tail Waterfall is a 200 feet (61 m) cascade of water, the Tail Burn pouring down a sheer cleft into Moffat Water.

〰 Loch Skeen (or Skene) lies at a height of 1,750 feet (533 m), surrounded by 2,383 acres (964 ha) of land acquired in 1962 by the National Trust for Scotland. At the end of the Loch are moraines – shale and rocks left behind in the wake of glaciers. The lonely country behind it is grazed by wild goats and sheep. The sheep (whose stone fold is called a 'stell') are not aggressive, but the goats should be left well alone. The hinterland of the Loch gave the Covenanters sanctuary, but in later days, when Sir Walter Scott was riding through it in a thick mist, he and his horse fell into a bog and only got out of it with difficulty.

〰 On White Coomb, 2,695 feet (821 m) high, the crescent of snow under the crest of the ridge generally survives well into May.

SW SCOTLAND

Craiglee
5 miles (8 km) Sheet 77 484949

Moderate Sensational views into the wild country of the Galloway Hills to the S. Best avoided in April-May as the route passes through a sheep farm. *Grassy slopes; heather and grass, rocky hilltops; 2 climbs; mud; coarse grass with boggy patches between ⑦ and ⑧. Do not attempt in poor visibility: 1: 25,000 map and compass recommended.*

Start One mile (1.5 km) SW of Dalmellington on the A713, take road signposted to Loch Doon Castle and continue to castle. **Parking** beside castle, but not in turning place.

① From castle go to gate nearby at foot of slope. ② Follow burn (stream) uphill and go through gate at top of field. Climb with plantation on right. ③ Turn corner and follow edge of plantation. ④ Leave plantation at its highest point and climb to summit. Continue along ridge and when convenient ⑤ descend to the col (pass) below Craiglee. Climb Craiglee to the trig. point. ⑥ Continue about 350 yards (320 m) along ridge. ⑦ Descend to left down prominent, grassy gully to head of burn (stream) and follow this to forest. ⑧ Follow forest edge to road. ⑨ Walk left along the road to the castle and point ①.

🏰 Loch Doon Castle, built in the 13th C., was first called Castle Balliol. In 1290 the throne of Scotland was empty and Edward I of England chose John Balliol, an Anglo-Norman with lands in Scotland, to fill it as his vassal, favouring him rather than Robert Bruce. The castle, a Balliol stronghold, first stood on an islet in Loch Doon; it was moved and rebuilt when the level of the Loch was raised in the creating of the Galloway Hydro-Electric Scheme, Scotland's first large power scheme.

🔟 Loch Doon, 5½ miles (9 km) long, a reservoir for the Hydro-Electric Scheme.

\†/ From Wee Hill the view N takes in 3 lines of hills: the Dungeon, Kells and Merrick.

\†/ Craiglee looks NW to the distant Island of Arran. Here Robert Bruce landed in 1306 on his way to begin the war to gain Scotland's freedom from England.

Rhinns of Kells
12 miles (19 km) Sheet 77 553863

Energetic Substantial, varied rambling in central Galloway, best in spring when the weather tends to be driest and insects fewest. *Farmland, woods, grassy slopes, boulder-strewn slopes, grassy ridges; 4 climbs; mud after rain. Do not attempt in poor visibility. For experienced hill walkers only. 1:25,000 map and compass recommended. Point ⑦ is difficult to leave in mist.*

Start Two miles (3 km) N of (St. John's Town of) Dalry on the A713, take road signposted to Forrest Lodge. **Car park** near end of road where it crosses burn (stream).

① Walk through gate beside car park into forest. Follow road past Burnhead. ② Keep straight on. Avoid right fork. ③ Follow firebreak out of forest. ④ Climb slope from edge of forest. ⑤ Follow crest of ridge and descend to lochans (small lakes) in col. ⑥ Climb ridge from lochans and follow crest to Corserine. ⑦ A difficult summit to leave in mist (wide and bare). Go right along top of scree cliffs until ridge narrows. ⑧ Avoid descent by Polmaddy Gairy by keeping right along ridge towards the forest and lochs. ⑨ Descend towards right bank of Loch Harrow, looking for guide poles above forest. ⑩ Descend between guide poles to firebreak which leads to forest road and start.

A golden eagle normally nests on a cliff, or in a tree. No other eagle soars on raised wings. Its size and obvious power set it apart from other comparable predators.

The Rhinns of Kells, rising to about 2,600 feet (792 m), form the SE side of Galloway Forest Park. They stand on the W of The Glenkens, the desolate country through which Mary Queen of Scots fled after the Battle of Langside in 1568 to Kenmure Castle.

Galloway Forest Park, 150,000 acres of forest, bog, loch, burn, moor and mountain, has much of the finest scenery in S Scotland and plentiful wildlife, including roe and red deer and wild goats. ('Galloway' comes from the Gaelic word *Gallwyddel* – 'stranger Gaels', the name given to the Celts who, until 1060, refused allegiance to the Scots crown.)

Among the Park's many birds is the golden eagle, the most magnificent of Britain's birds of prey, with legs fully 'trousered' by feathers and a wing span of 6-7 feet (1.8-2 m).

SW SCOTLAND

Heads of Ayr
3 miles (5 km) Sheet 70 322193

Easy A seaside walk near Ayr, with dramatic seascapes and views of the islands. *Sand dunes, rock 'platform', pebble beach, track; one climb; mud after rain.*

Start From roundabout at Doonfoot on the A719 2 miles (3 km) S of Ayr, take Earl's Way towards the sea; frequent buses between Dunure and Ayr. **Car park** on shore at foot of Earl's Way, frequent buses back to start.

① From car park follow shore line left to ②, where a path leading away from the shore starts just E of a small waterfall. Follow path. ③ Pass under old railway (site of bridge) and follow road past caravan site to A719. *Buses back to start pass road end near Low Glenayes. Get off at Earl's Way roundabout to return to car.*

◼ Greenan Castle was one of the strongholds of the Kennedy family, who dominated the lands along the Firth of Clyde for some 30 miles (50 km) S of Ayr from the 12th to the 17th C. On 11th May, 1602, Sir Thomas Kennedy was murdered on the Sands of Ayr, and the bloody feuds between the Kennedys and other powerful families, in which he had taken a leading part, came to an end. The space for the Kennedy coat of arms is beside the first-floor doorway into the castle and not, as was customary, above the basement door, since this was on the N face of the cliff and very difficult to approach. There has been a castle on

Greenan Castle (Ayr beyond), a stronghold of the Kennedys and scene of predictably bloody clan warfare.

this site at least since the 15th C. The present building – now a ruin – is a mixture of dates: the first work on the tall, stern tower probably began in 1603.

◼ Deil's Dyke, standing above shore level, may be followed seawards at low tide for several hundred yards.

\|/ The view W takes in Greenan Castle, high on its cliff top, and in the distance the Island of Arran.

◼ The Heads of Ayr are volcanic rock formations.

◼ Bracken Bay, 25 feet (7.6 m) above shore level, an example of a raised beach.

Criffel

6 miles (9.5 km) Sheet 84 957655

Energetic Fascinating views over the Solway Firth, where the tide comes in at remarkable speed. *Farmland, heather hillside, woods; 2 climbs; mud. Do not attempt in poor visibility; 1:25,000 map and compass recommended. In June-Sept. the firebreaks from ⑤ to ⑨ are overgrown and extremely wet. It is advisable to divert back to ① by following the burn (stream) right. Visit the monument by climbing directly up firebreak from close to ①.*

Start From New Abbey take road W from The Square, past hotel to mill pond. Fork left past pond and continue to where road divides by Public Water Supply sign (ignore track leading right). **Parking** on left.

① From parking walk left over bridge. Pass left of shepherd's cottage and through small gate. In 15 yards (14 m) turn left on to well-defined track. Follow this, ignoring branches. It is generally well defined, becoming greasy. Go through gate by corner of plantation and *bear left* (skirting bracken if overgrown) alongside plantation, making for stone wall ahead. At wall turn right and follow it along ridge uphill. Over half-way to summit ② carry straight on where wall turns left along edge of forest. ③ From first summit (Knockendoch) follow path round ridge to summit of Criffel. Return from summit to col between the 2 summits. ④ Leave ridge and descend slope to valley to W, noting the firebreaks (gaps between trees on opposite hillside). The route eventually goes up the straightest of them, but now head for the foot of the one to its immediate left. ⑤ Cross burn at corner of forest by stepping stones if river not too high; otherwise a long stride is enough. To reach the correct firebreak (whose start is hidden by the trees to the right) begin ⑥ up the firebreak immediately in front. Go right when a clearing opens out on right and join correct firebreak. Continue up hill to summit of hill and ⑦ follow it down other side and as it bends right. Continue until it loses height in this new direction and ⑧ follow new firebreak which opens up to the left. Continue uphill to the monument. ⑨ From door of monument take the right of 2 firebreaks running downhill to ①.

🏰 Sweetheart Abbey was founded in 1273 by Devorguilla Balliol, mother of John Balliol, England's candidate for the Scottish throne. She was buried here with her husband's heart, which she had kept with her for 16 years. She also founded Balliol College, Oxford, which in 1966 set up a memorial stone to mark the original site of her tomb.

🏰 Kirk Kindar, is an ancient church built on a crannog: an Iron Age, man-made islet made of a pile of stones on a wooden base, reached by boat or causeway.

\t/ The views from Criffel, 1868 ft (569 m) high, reach to the Solway Firth, the Lake District and the Isle of Man.

SW SCOTLAND

The Merrick
9 miles (14.5 km) Sheet 77 414803

Strenuous A safe 'visitor's' route up the highest hill in southern Scotland, followed by exploration of a wilder area on the return journey. As might be expected, the panorama from the summit is sensational; best chance of clear conditions are in spring and summer. *Woodland, upland meadow, forest, hillside, high-level plateau, rocky mountainside, moorland, stream-side path; mud after rain; section between ③ and ④ indistinct – see directions (possibility of alternative route); two stiff climbs; do not attempt in poor visibility – the Galloway Hills can be as demanding as the Highlands.*

Start From the A714 (Newton Stewart–Girvan road), branch north at Bargrennan and pass Glentrool Village. Continue to the end of the public road where there is ample free **parking**.

① From the car park walk E for about ¼ mile (0.5 km) along the road. ② Opposite the Bruce Stone turn left on to path marked The Merrick. ③ Path is muddy, rocky and indistinct in places. Keep close to the river on the right. (Alternative route indicated by arrow on rock: this leads through forest to Culsharg Bothy). ④ Keep to the outside of the forest. ⑤ On reaching ruined cottage (Culsharg Bothy) and memorial stone, go behind cottage and follow path N through woods. ⑥ Reaching forestry road, turn right across concrete bridge, then left on to path signposted Merrick. ⑦ Follow wall for first part of walk from Benyellary to The Merrick, then bear right to cross open hillside directly to summit. ⑧ Descend E towards shore of Loch Enoch. ⑨ Follow shore S until loosely built stone wall is reached. ⑩ Follow stone wall SW for ¼ mile. Note Grey Man on a rocky outcrop on the right – map reference 437846. ⑪ Walk SE from the Grey Man, ascend low ridge and turn right. ⑫ Keeping to the high ground, head for the gap between Buchan Hill and the Rig of the Jarkness. ⑬ Follow the path SW beside the Gairland Burn, which leads back to ①.

🏛 The Bruce Stone commemorates the Battle of Glentrool: Robert the Bruce, newly returned from Ireland, found himself and a small band of followers in the Glen of Trool, pursued by a considerable force of English. Bruce's men spent a day and a night on the hillside to the S of the loch, manoeuvring hundreds of boulders into position above the narrow road. As the English passed beneath, the boulders were rolled down the slope; Bruce's men followed. Hardly an Englishman escaped being hacked down by the Scots guerillas, or swept into the loch by the boulders – or so the story goes. Bruce, who had just had his famous encounter with the spider, felt encouraged to continue with his newly learned lesson of perseverance, and seven years later, in 1314, his campaign for independence culminated in the great victory at Bannockburn. The English were buried in the flat land at the east-end of Loch Trool, still known as the Soldier's Holm.

👁 Views S and SW from The Merrick's summit take in the great wilderness of the Galloway Hills and extend across the Solway Firth to the mountains of the Lake District; you may even be able to make out the Isle of Man.
Northwards there are the Galloway Hills and the long slash of Loch Doon, backed by a sweep of the coast. Moving W, there is the Firth of Clyde, the islands of Arran and Ailsa Craig, the Mull of Kintyre and at 60 miles (96 km), the Antrim coast.

🗯 The Grey Man of The Merrick is a natural rock formation with a striking resemblance to a man's face; many fail to find it, but it is not difficult to locate in clear conditions.

🏛 The inlet on the W side of Loch Neldricken was dubbed 'the murder hole' by S. R. Crockett in his Galloway epic *The Raiders*. It is quite an interesting feature, but unlikely to have been used for concealing dead bodies: the deep mud around the edges restricts access.

👁 The view SW from here is almost Alpine: Bruce Stone far below.

🌿 In summer the hillside here is covered by a pink blanket of tens of thousands of foxgloves.

SOUTH OF THE FORTH

Edinburgh's setting is as magnificent as the city itself. The Forth widens slowly but surely into a great estuary as it joins the North Sea. The coast offers ever-changing interest. There is the start of the Antonine Wall, the two great bridges, a variety of industry, fishing ports, sandy beaches and the port of Leith.

Inland there is just as much variety of scene. Immediately south of Edinburgh lie the city's own special hills, the rounded Pentlands, 16 miles (26 km) of elevated pastures intersected by wooded ravines. Further south are the equally appealing Moorfoots and the windswept Lammermuirs. None of these ranges are startling in height or rugged in character, but up here on the heights the walker can find a real sense of being away from it all.

Beneath, the lower land is as fertile and well-cultivated as any in Britain. It has been long settled and its place between Scotland's densely populated central belt and the border means that it is packed with history. Across it the drovers pushed their cattle on the way south from the great tryst at Falkirk to markets in England. Some of the old drove roads can still be traced, leading down to where the Cheviots rise to the border.

SOUTH OF THE FORTH

Tinto Hill

4½ miles (7 km) Sheet 72 964374

Moderate Arguably the grandest hill in the SW part of this section; its relative isolation means the views from the summit are truly extensive. The clear, cool air of winter and spring give the best visibility. *Hillside, moorland, streamside; one climb.*

Start From Lanark, follow the A73 SE towards Biggar and in 3 miles (5 km) cross Hyndford Bridge (traffic lights) and turn left. In 4 miles (6.5 km) turn right to Fallburn Farm (signposted); infrequent buses. **Car park** on left ¼ mile (0.5 km) after right turn.

① From the SW corner of the car park head towards the summit of Tinto Hill – a broad track is soon picked up. ② Follow the broad track E towards the lower summit of Scaut Hill. ③ Descend the N slopes of Scaut Hill (no path) to the valley of the Kirk Burn, then continue to Park Knowe. ④ From Park Knowe turn left after ½ mile (0.8 km) reaching the original track back to the car park.

The red felsite of Tinto seems to glow in sunlight, which may be why the lonely mountain is called 'hill of fire'.

Tinto's summit cairn is the remains of a Druid settlement.

The famous view from Tinto takes in 16 counties, from Bass Rock in the E to

The Pentlands, looking from Carnethy Hill towards Scald Law.

Goatfell on Arran in the W.

The remains lower down the hillside (marked on the map as a tower) bore the curious name of Fatlips Castle, home of a local laird and reputedly haunted by a brownie.

291

SOUTH OF THE FORTH

Bonaly and Flotterstone
7½ miles (12 km) Sheet 66 212675

Moderate An ideal introduction to the gentle Pentland Hills, and their lonely valleys: remoteness within 6 miles (9.5 km) of Edinburgh. *Woods, hillside, moorland; 2 climbs.*

Start From Edinburgh take the A70 to the Juniper Green crossroads and turn left. At Colinton post office turn sharp right, then second left (Bonaly Road); buses to Colinton post office, one mile (1.5 km) from ①. **Car park** at end of Bonaly Road.

① From car park follow track upwards through trees and on to open hillside. ② Cross stile and keep to track on right around the W side of Capelaw Hill. ③ The track becomes indistinct, but crosses gradually from the E to the W side of the valley. ④ On meeting road at gate, turn left and continue around the NE corner of Glencorse Reservoir. Follow the road down its E side to the pub at the main road. Turn left and continue. ⑤ Turn left off main road to Castlelaw Farm. ⑥ At Castlelaw Farm, turn right to Castlelaw Hill Fort (signposted). ⑦ Cross over to the E flanks of Capelaw Hill (no path), then keep around N flank of hill to regain the original track near Bonaly Reservoir. Do not stray N – a ravine bars the way back to the Bonaly track. It is not difficult or dangerous to negotiate, but may be tiresome.

🏠 Bonaly Tower, close to the route, was the home of the Scottish legal figure Henry, Lord Cockburn (died 1854).

\↑/ Capelaw Hill looks N to the W parts of Edinburgh and across the Forth to Fife. All the coastline from the Forth Bridge to Leven can be seen – a stretch of about 25 miles (40 km) – with the hill ranges of the Ochils, the Cleish Hills, Benarty and the Lomonds behind.

\↑/ The view up the Logan Valley is of the 5 hills of the Scald Law range: Turnhouse Hill, Carnethy Hill, Scald Law, and East and West Kip.

🛶 Glencorse Reservoir, capacity 368 million gallons (1,672 million litres), was constructed in 1822 by flooding the valley of the Logan Burn. The waters cover the ancient church of St. Katherine in the Hopes (built in the 14th C.).

🕸 Castlelaw Hill Fort and Souterain were occupied in Roman times by a tribe called the Goddodin. Skilfully restored, the underground chamber is much as it must have been 2,000 years ago. (Key and information board at the farm at the bottom of the road.)

🍴 Flotterstone Inn and Restaurant perhaps took its name from the large, flat stone, ╳ once at the entrance, on which ladies alighted from their carriages. Full meals and bar snacks are available.

Queensferry to Cramond
5 miles (8 km) Sheet 66 137784

Easy A coastal walk with much nautical interest, from warships to supertankers, and the mild adventure of a short ferry trip, propelled by a sculling boatman. The trees of Dalmeny Estate and Almond Gorge are splendid in autumn. *Woods, parkland.*

Start South Queensferry, near the S end of the Forth Road Bridge; frequent buses; frequent trains to Dalmeny, ½ mile (0.8 km) from start of walk by path and steps through woods to the N of the station. **Car park** on the sea front, South Queensferry. **Return** to start by bus.

① Beneath for Forth Railway Bridge, bear left, away from the main road, and keep to the unsurfaced road along the shore. ② In front of Dalmeny House, keep along the seaward edge of the golf course. After passing the golf course, keep to the right (landward) side of a clump of trees on the water's edge, and reaching stream, follow it inland about 100 yards (91 m) to reach a footbridge. Continue on path through trees. ③ At Long Green Cottages (on left), where path divides into 3, keep straight ahead on the centre path as it climbs through a tunnel of trees. ④ At Cramond, keep to the road and path along the E bank of the River Almond. ⑤ At the landward end of the River Almond path, turn right to cross the old Cramond Bridge behind the Cramond Brig Hotel. The bus stop for the return to South Queensferry is on the other side of the main road, opposite the hotel (½-hourly on weekdays, hourly on Sundays).

🚩 Hawes Inn, dating from 1683, was once the ferry-boat inn. The ferry itself was founded in the 12th C. by Queen Margaret – hence the name 'Queensferry'.

⌂ Forth Railway Bridge, designed by Sir John Fowler and begun in 1883. is 361 feet (110 m) high.

🏰 Barnbougle Castle was the home of the Rosebery family until the building, in the early 19th C., of Dalmeny House. The latter is open on summer weekends.

🖼 Cramond – 'Caer-Almond' ('the fort on the Almond') – was a Roman garrison town and the foundations of the fort have been excavated. There is a helpful display plan.

🚩 Cramond Inn was a haunt of Robert Louis Stevenson, author of *Treasure Island*.

⌂ Cramond Bridge, known as Jock Howie-son's Bridge, in tribute to a peasant who rescued James V from attack by some medieval muggers.

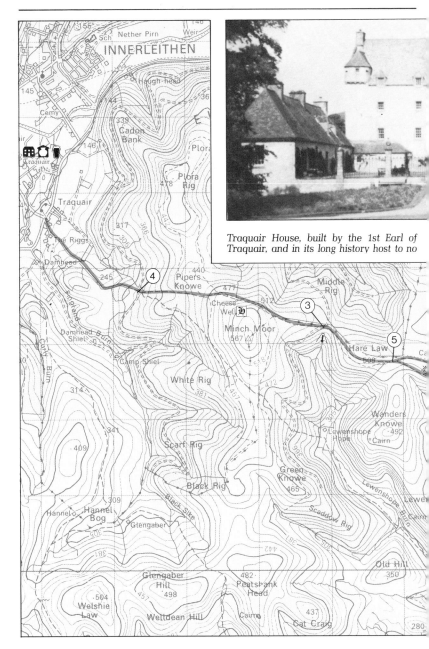

Traquair House, built by the 1st Earl of Traquair, and in its long history host to no *less than 27 monarchs. It is reputed to be the oldest inhabited house in Scotland.*

The Minchmoor
12½ miles (20 km) Sheet 73 407299

Energetic One of the best-loved and most outstanding of the Border drove roads: not only a cattle-driver's track, but a historic way, used by armies, highwaymen and monks alike. Offers the delight of walking on bright green, springy turf. *Hamlet, hillsides, moorland, woods, farmland; 2 climbs; mud.*

Start From Selkirk, cross the River Ettrick and turn left on to the A708. In 4 miles (6.5 km), at Yarrowford, look for Minchmoor Track signposted on right. **Parking** on roadsides at both ends of the walk. **Return** to starting point possible by the infrequent Border Courier minibus service between Yarrowford and Traquair (details from Eastern-Scottish Bus Co.).

① The starting point is 100 yards (91 m) W of the telephone box in Yarrowford village. Follow the street N, past houses, to its end. ② Go past the right end of the garages, and continue uphill, through trees, on stony track. ③ Continue straight across wide forest road. ④ Again, continue straight across wide, forest road. ⑤ If making the return journey, look carefully for junction of paths. The path is wet and eroded here, and the old drove road running off to the left is not immediately apparent. If in doubt, continue downhill on Minchmoor Road, then strike steeply uphill to the left at small stone marking Wallace's Trench. Then turn right, on to drove road, at N end of the trench. In ½ mile (0.8 km) ⑥ descend track on right into the valley of the Gruntly Burn. ⑦ Bear right on road back to main road.

※ Wallace's Trench, close to the route, takes its name from Sir William Wallace, but may be part of the Catrail, possibly a Pictish defensive earthwork.

\↑/ The view S is to the valley of the River Yarrow and the hills beyond.

🐟 At the Cheese Well, travellers used to leave cheese and other food to placate the local fairies and goblins.

🏛 Traquair House is, in part, 1,000 years
🏠 old, but the main section, in the style of a
French château, is 17th C. In the grounds
🍺 are craft workshops and a brew house, with the excellent strong ale on sale.

SOUTH OF THE FORTH

Scald Law Ridge
12½ miles (20 km) Sheet 66 164636

Energetic Of the many fine walks in the Pentland Hills, this is the most dramatic, with its high, undulating section along the broad, grassy ridge connecting 5 hills. Best in early spring, when there is some snow on the hills: in cold conditions the air is clearer and the views longer. *Moorland, hill tops; 2 climbs.*

Start From Edinburgh take the A70 towards Lanark and turn left for Balerno. In ½ mile (0.8 km) turn left at Balerno for Marchbank Hotel. Just past hotel, turn left on to minor road; frequent buses from Edinburgh to Balerno stop a mile from ①. **Car park** on right ½ mile from turning at hotel.

① At top of avenue of trees, turn right, then first left, through a gate and on to the wide track which climbs across the moor. ② Leave track, striking left on the short, steep climb to summit of West Kip Hill (narrow, faint path). ③ In the dip between Scald Law and Carnethy Hill, cross over track and climb to summit of Carnethy Hill. ④ From Turnhouse Hill descend SE towards the long, narrow clump of trees, keeping them on left. Make for monument on SE edge. ⑤ Descend from monument to road running past Rullion Green Farm, then turn left on to A702. ⑥ From the pub/restaurant at Flotterstone, follow road past Glencorse Reservoir. ⑦ Just past the farmhouse (known as The Howe) the road becomes a footpath. Follow this through gap between Hare Hill and Black Hill. ⑧ At top of avenue, turn right and descend road back to car park.

♣ Redmoss Nature Reserve – an area of raised bog.

\\!/ From Scald Law the view stretches from the Broughton Heights and Tinto Hill 20 miles (32 km) to the SW, to Largo Law 35 miles (56 km) to the NE. Beyond the Ochils and Lomonds to the N the mountains of Perthshire and the Cairngorms are visible nearly 80 miles (128 km) away. Nearer, to the S, are the Moorfoot Hills and the rolling hills of Tweeddale. The 2 Forth Bridges can be seen 15 miles (24 km) to the N.

🏠 The Kirk Road, which crosses the route at right angles, is an ancient footpath,

dating from the days when the parish of Penicuik took in much of the surrounding hill country. The church – or Kirk – was in Penicuik on the S side of the hills, and parishioners from the N side crossed the Pentlands by this pass.

⚔ The Battle of Rullion Green was fought on the SE slopes of Turnhouse Hill on 28th November, 1666. About 900 Covenanters making their way home from a gathering in Edinburgh were attacked and overcome by troops under the command of General Tam Dalyell, whom Charles II had, at his restoration, recalled from service with the Czar of Russia. Many of the Covenanters were slaughtered on the spot, others were hunted into the Pentland bogs, or taken to Edinburgh to be publicly hanged. Among those killed were women and children, shot out of hand, against the General's orders. So ashamed was he about the outrage that he retired from the army and was never again seen in public.

🚣 Glencorse Reservoir is one of 16 in the Pentlands which supply Edinburgh.

⛪ St. Katherine's chapel, covered now by the waters of the reservoir, was built in the 14th C. by Sir William St. Clair, who was given an estate in the district by King Robert the Bruce, in settlement of a wager. The submerged building lies at the dog-leg of the reservoir. The forbear of another ancient local family, the Clerks of Penicuik, won a grant of land from Robert the Bruce by rescuing him from a hunting accident.

All of the 32-mile (51 km) Union Canal (Edinburgh-Falkirk) is pleasant, level walking; outstanding is the 9 miles (14.5 km) from Linlithgow to Falkirk.

The Eildon Hills give fine views over the Border countryside.

In Glentress Forest, 2 miles (3 km) E of Peebles, there are 4 waymarked walks starting from the Forest Office.

There is a waymarked nature trail along the cliffs W of Dunbar harbour.

The Water of Leith Walkway is a pleasant walk through Edinburgh city and suburbs.

Aberlady to North Berwick is a superb coastal walk. At the end, climb Berwick Law for grand views of the Forth Estuary.

HIGHLANDS
AND
ISLANDS

Off the coast of Scotland are 610 islands and on those not unknown blue August days they dot a sea which looks more like the Aegean than the Atlantic. In this region, too, are Britain's only remnants of true wilderness, and its toughest mountains. There is, for instance, no easy way up the Cuillins of Skye. They are the preserve of experienced climbers. But any fit person can walk up Ben Nevis (at more than 4,406 feet (1343 m) Britain's highest mountain) by the bridle path from Achintee. Even so, it is a six- to eight-hour trek, not to be tackled in dirty weather or if ill-prepared. Alongside the lochs are days of comparatively gentle going.

One is generally free to wander at will on these moors and mountains, though it is a fallacy that there is no such thing as trespass in Scotland. Walkers are likely to be thrown off during the deer stalking season (roughly August to mid-October). Your main enemy, however, will be the dreaded Highland midge, which appears of a summer evening to torment human beings. There is no known defence.

The Lost Valley, Glencoe
2½ miles (4 km) Sheet 41 171568

Moderate, strenuous sections One of the easier short walks in Glencoe – the others being well-publicized nature trails. *Glen, gorge, valley; 2 climbs; mud after rain.*

Start The Pass of Glencoe, ½ mile (0.8 km) W of Allt-na-Reigh on the A82. **Parking** at the viewpoint in the Pass.

① From parking descend to the grassy, disused military road and continue about 250 yards (228 m) to where ② a path leads down to the river. Follow this to the bridge, cross, and continue on path leading up and into glen. ③ At large (bungalow-sized) boulder cross burn towards waterfall and continue along foot of rock face. ④ From the Lost Valley retrace steps. ⑤ Take path by trees towards burn (stream). Cross and walk downstream. Keep high to avoid wet sections. ⑥ Descend to join original path near mouth of gorge. Retrace to ①.

🐦 The pools below the car park are visited by black-throated divers. Alarmed, they submerge, heads only protruding.

ⓑ Glen Coe itself – wild, brooding – explains much of the notoriety of the massacre of the MacDonalds here in 1692. Forty out of 150 adults were killed; more fled, to die of exposure.

Glen Coe: the National Trust for Scotland owns thousands of acres in the area.

\↑/ Into Coire Gabhail – the Lost Valley, where MacDonalds hid stolen cattle.

\↑/ Bidean nam Bian, highest in the glen.

🌊 The gorge is a good example of hanging valley, created by a glacier.

🏚 Ossian's Cave, the 'home' of a 3rd C. bard: unlikely, as the floor is at 45°.

HIGHLANDS AND ISLANDS

Bracklinn Falls
4 miles (6.5 km) Sheet 57 626081

Moderate Some typical, wild gorge scenery in the Trossachs; Callander is busy in the tourist season, but unspoilt. *Woods, upland pasture, gorge, golf course; one climb.*

Start Callander; buses. **Public car park** in Station Road behind the Dreadnought Hotel.

① With car park on left follow road over old railway bridge then ② take path on left beside wooden shelter. Continue round fence and uphill to main track which leads to road. Walk up to car park then follow signposted track to Bracklinn Falls. On the far side of the gorge the path follows the river for a few yards then leads up to an old stone dyke, where ③ go through the iron gate, over the rail then through the wooden gate towards the farm. By-pass the fence at the back of the farm, then follow the right-hand wall to drop to the gate at the road. ④ At the cutting which carried the old railway bridge climb the embankment to the old railway track and follow this to Balgibbon Cottage. ⑤ Take the path by the cottage; this leads to the golf course; turn left and the path finally emerges on a side road just before the club house. Cross into Ancaster Road which leads to ①.

🏠 Callander, pleasantly situated near the foot of Ben Ledi, overlooks a once-

Rowan or mountain ash lines the gorge of Bracklinn Falls. Its bark is russet when wet, grey when dry.

important road junction. The scenery was immortalized by Sir Walter Scott in his epic poem, *Lady of the Lake*. The rounded mound by the Roman Camp Hotel is now known to be natural. The camp was at Kilmahog, 2 miles (3 km) W.

🏠 Rhoderick Dhu, in *The Lady of the Lake*, was 'brave but wild as Bracklinn's thundering wave'.

\t/ From Dumgoyne on the Campsie Fells to Stirling Castle.

🏠 Looking right, the second house was 'Arden House' in the TV series *Dr. Finlay's Casebook*. Callander was 'Tannochbrae'.

Kenmore
5 miles (8 km) Sheet 51 773455

Moderate An attractive village and varied walking country by one of Scotland's largest lochs, of which there is a famous view from the bridge. *Woods, riverside; one climb.*

Start Kenmore, on the A827 at the E end of Loch Tay. **Public car park** near the village square.

① From village square follow main road past church and over river. ② A few yards along the Tummell Bridge road turn left on to footpath which leads up to forest road. Turn left and continue on this, turning right at first junction, ½ mile (0.8 km) from gate. ③ At crossroads bear right to follow lower road for 2 miles (3 km), rejoining Tummell Bridge road. ④ Turn right then enter lane on left opposite cottage. Fork left to cross river by wooden bridge. ⑤ Turn right and follow old driveway which later joins main drive. Continue on this past Taymouth Castle. ⑥ From iron post keep to river bank path whole way to jetty. Take steps up to village.

🏠 The 3rd Earl of Breadalbane gave the
⌒ town its church in 1760, and in 1774 built the bridge, which bears a double-edged tribute to George III. He donated £1,000 towards its cost, but the money came from the estates he won in the 1745 Jacobite uprising.

🏠 The nearby island in the loch is Eilean nan Bannoamh, 'the Isle of the Lady Saints'. Alexander I, King of Scotland, founded a priory on it after the death of his wife, Sybilla, daughter of Henry I, King of England. The nuns were allowed out once a year to visit Kenmore Fair.

\↑/ Walk clear of the trees for a view NW up the Glen of Keltney Burn to the conical peak of Schiehallion.

※ Beyond the bridge on the left is Croftmoraig stone circle, whose origins and date are ancient, and uncertain.

↓ Red deer come down to the river from Drummond Hill, especially in winter.

🏰 The enormous Taymouth Castle, former mansion, hydro and boarding school, was built in the 19th C. to replace the 16th C. Castle of Balloch. From here the warlike Campbells of Glenorchy, later Earls of Bredalbane, ruled over one of the largest clan estates, with lands extending up to 100 miles (160 km).

🏠 The model dairy, Dairy Byre, is made of white quartz.

▌ The Boar's Head; also the Kenmore Hotel, where Robert Burns pencilled a poem extolling the view from Kenmore Bridge on a chimneypiece.

HIGHLANDS AND ISLANDS

The Cut
8 miles (13 km) Sheet 63 247721

Moderate The popular Renfrewshire Hills and a historic waterway. *Lochside, moorland; one climb.*

Start Leave the A742 W of Greenock and follow signposts to car park; frequent trains to Greenock Central. At rear of station take Lyndoch Street under railway bridge and join path; follow disused mineral line to steps on right, then path uphill to road. Join Cut at right side of filter station. **Public car park** at Cornalees Bridge.

① From Information Centre by car park follow road by Loch Thom Cottage to Iverton. (Those starting walk from Greenock join route here and from Cornalees Bridge continue to Overton, then retrace to Greenock.) ② Turn left over bridge (with '1827-1927' fountain) to follow path alongside Cut. ③ About 200 yards (183 m) beyond farm, follow the nature trail away from the Cut to descend into Shielhill Glen. Cross burn (stream) and continue up to viewpoint on disused waterway. Alternatively, follow Cut whole way back to Cornalees Bridge.) ④ Turn left and follow path to Cornalees Bridge.

⟱ Cornalees Bridge marks a corner of the Clyde-Muirshiel Regional Park.

ⓣ Loch Thom is named after Robert Thom, the engineer who built the Cut.

⟱ The Cut was built in 1827 to carry water 5½ miles (9 km) from the Loch Thom Reservoir to Greenock. Superseded by a tunnel in 1971, it is now protected by a conservation order.

⟱ Greenock, the Inverclyde town famed for ships and sugar, is also the birth-place of James Watt, improver of the steam engine. *The Comet*, Britain's first passenger steamboat, was built at nearby Port Glasgow in 1812. A replica is on show near Port Glasgow railway station.

⟱ Cowal Hills; NNW, Bute and Arran.

The Antonine Wall

4 or 8 miles (6.5 or 13 km) Sheet 64 693774

Moderate A few miles from Glasgow, this area of extensive Roman remains has a surprisingly remote atmosphere; may be bleak in winter. *Farmland, woods, rocky outcrops, canal, parkland; 2 climbs.*

Start Queenzieburn on the A803, 4 miles (6.5 km) NE of Kirkintilloch; frequent buses. **Parking** spaces on N side of A803. **Return** to starting point by bus from ⑨ or ⑪.

① From Queenzieburn follow side road towards Twechar. Cross canal bridge and continue to war memorial. ② Follow farm road left. ③ Just before drained water filter, enter field across stile and make for Bar Hill Fort. Take the path at the NE corner which leads to Castlehill. ④ Follow path alongside ditch to lane, then continue downhill to road. ⑤ Turn right, then left, then left again. Follow the lane by the lock-ups to rejoin ditch. ⑥ Follow the path uphill, then as it curves left alongside ditch by Croy Hill. ⑦ From uncut section continue to large boulders on higher ground, then follow edge of wood downhill and cross old mineral cutting. Descend by path through trees to Forth and Clyde Canal. Cross bridge, turn

right and follow bank for a few yards, then take path along far side of feed waterway. ⑧ Turn right in front of old stables; follow wall to stile. Cross and continue on path across disused railway, then follow stream to ⑨ the A803, where turn right, then first left along road and follow this as it curves right. ⑩ Just beyond cottage on left, take the path along the S bank of the reservoir. At far end turn right, then first left to follow feed canal whole way to Tak-ma-doon Road, Kilsyth. This leads to ⑪ the A803 – return to Queenzieburn by bus.

🚩 The Quarry Inn; real ale.

🚩 Fort built A.D. 142 on site of earlier one of A.D. 80 was one of the regularly placed strongholds on the Wall. Spanish, Balkan, even Syrian troops served here.

🚩 The defensive ditch on the N Side was dug out despite the rock.

🚩 The Forth and Clyde Canal, completed in 1790, had a major role in industrializing central Scotland.

🚩 Under the water is the site of the Battle of Kilsyth, 1645. Remains of an armed, mounted trooper were found in the bog.

Kinnoull Hill
4½ miles (7 km) Sheet 58 120231

Moderate A country walk in the Tayside area only a few minutes from Perth City centre. Crosses the Tay by a narrow catwalk beside the railway. *Town, woods, cliff top; one climb.*

Start Perth; frequent buses and trains.
Public car park at riverside across road from Tourist Information Centre.

① Walk under railway bridge and climb steps to footpath alongside railway line. ② A lane on the opposite bank joins Dundee Road, where turn right if visiting Branklyn Gardens (signposted); to continue, turn left and just before the hotel take Manse Road, which leads up to Hatton Road; follow this. ③ Where Hatton Road veers left, take the path on the right by the signpost. ④ At the first viewpoint, leave the path for a smaller one on the left. Follow this as it climbs to Kinnoull Hill and the view indicator. Follow the path along the cliff, down to a gate, then as it climbs gently to the tower or folly. Continue through the wood. Ignore the path to the left and continue on track as it winds round a glen overlooking Kinfauns Castle. ⑤ At Jubilee Car Park, the track curves back into the wood. Fork right at the T-junction, descend to a wicket gate, then join the road. Continue straight ahead, forking left, then going down Hatton and Manse Roads to

Dundee Road. Turn right then left over Queen's Bridge for ①.

🏠 The district where Perth now stands was known to the Romans, and later, in 846, the first joint capital of Picts and Scots under Kenneth MacAlpine was established at nearby Scone. Perth dates from the foundation in 1210 of the royal borough by William the Lion, King of Scotland from 1165 to 1214.
   Sir Walter Scott's novel *The Fair Maid of Perth* is set partly in the house of his heroine's father, on the site of the present 'Fair Maid's House', off Charlotte Street at the N end of the town.

✿ Branklyn Gardens contains a fine collection of plants, notably alpines. The garden is open from 10.00 am to dusk, March-Sept., and at other times by appointment.

🏰 Kinfauns Castle was the seat of the Earls of Moray. James Stuart, Earl of Moray, the illegitimate son of James V, became Regent of Scotland when Mary Queen of Scots, his half-sister, abdicated.

↷ Fine views over Perth, S across the Lomond Hills and E of the Tay winding towards the sea.

Worth the climb: the view from Kinnoull Hill is superb, and it opens out suddenly.

HIGHLANDS AND ISLANDS

Above Whiting Bay
4½ miles (7 km) Sheet 69 045262

Moderate The Island of Arran has been described as Scotland in miniature; this route, with its delightful variety, covers Arran in miniature. *Shore, glen, forest, hillside, farmland; one climb.*

Start On the A841 8 miles (13 km) S of Brodick; buses. **Public car park** at centre of Whiting Bay village.

① With car park on right take shore road through village. ② Just beyond bowling green, follow road uphill, ignoring side roads, past the houses of South Kiscadale. ③ Go through gate to join track winding up Glenashdale to join another forest track. ④ Turn right taking the track leading towards Lamlash to large, cleared area with viewpoint overlooking Holy Island. ⑤ From

viewpoint retrace steps a few yards to signposted path descending through forest to join narrow road, where ⑥ turn right, then take first left before the farm to join a rough track leading down to a narrow road ⑦ At road turn right for ①.

\↑/ An (interrupted) view to Glenashdale Falls, the island's largest with a vertical drop of 148 feet (45 m).

\↑/ Holy Island is associated with St. Molaise, a follower of St. Columba, supposed to have lived there after the discovery of ancient Runic inscriptions in the 'Saint's Cave'. Also to Goat Fell, towering above Brodick. This granite outcrop was once the molten margin of a now sunken volcano.

▦ Arran Gallery, selling local handiwork, is housed in a former church.

The High Track to the Cuillin
6 miles (9.5 km) Sheet 32 545173

Moderate Perhaps the best approach to Skye's notorious Cuillin Hills for the walker who wants to view them at close quarters, but who wishes to avoid the long climb from Glen Brittle over wet moorland on a path now badly eroded by walkers. A route through prime Highland scenery, well away from the well-trodden parts of Skye. Light effects on the hills at sunrise and sunset can be breathtaking, as indeed are the peaks when snow-capped. *High moorland, glen, shore; one climb.*

Start From Broadford on the Island of Skye, take the A850 in the direction of Portree, soon turning S on the A881 in the direction of Torrin and Elgol. Go round the head of Loch Slapin and in about 4 miles (6.5 km) pass through Kirkibost, then the hamlet of Kilmarie; in a hundred yards or so, stop where the road rises, with a small plantation on the right; **parking** in vicinity of the gate – beware of soft ground, and don't block the road.

① Go through gate, shutting it, and follow the well-defined track first through conifers, then across moorland. You pass a picturesque lochan (small loch) to the right, and then climb ② over the Pass of Am Màm. Follow the track as it zigzags down the hillside; where it bends sharply left ③, ignore the smaller path leading off N, continuing on the main track, which heads SW towards the sea. Continue on flat moor and grassland or on the

rocky/shingle beach and return at will from Camasunary ④ by the same route.

⚹ Remains of a Neolithic stone circle: the ground leading to it is usually wet and boggy. Such circles are often found by lochs and lochans.

🏚 Site of an old shieling: these rough structures were used as summer dwellings by crofters who brought their livestock here for summer grazing; hardy as these people were, the hut was probably used simply for shelter and overnight stops.

〳 From here are the best views to the Cuillin Hills, eroded and dangerous peaks which suffer some of the worst weather in the British Isles. Their pale brown crystalline rock makes compass readings unreliable, and has a magical power to reflect sky colour.

〴 Fine waterfall.

🏠 The house of Camasunary and the Strathaird Estate belong to Ian Anderson, lead singer and lyricist of Jethro Tull, the folk/rock band.

〳 A fine view out to the Island of Soay, once owned by writer Gavin Maxwell, famous for his book *The Ring of Bright Water*, and for exploits with otters. His association with Soay, however, pre-dates the otters: it was here that he set up his basking-shark fishery and his experiences of the coast hereabouts are recorded in *Harpoon at a Venture*.

19 Portree is the capital of Skye and its finest harbour. The name is a version of Port Righ – 'King's Harbour' – the name given it when James V of Scotland landed there. The inn where Flora MacDonald said farewell to Prince Charles Edward Stuart – 'Bonnie Prince Charlie' – is now part of the Royal Hotel.

\t/ Panoramic views from Beinn na Greine – 'Hill of the sun'; but remember that Skye is known as the Misty Isle, and its evocative Norse name, Skuyö, meant Isle of Cloud.

\t/ There are wide views N and E over Portree and the sea from Fingal's Seat. ('Fingal' comes from Fionn na Ghal, meaning Chief of Valour, the title given to the Celtic warrior Fionn MacCoul, who died heroically in battle against the Norsemen in 283.)

Beinn na Greine and Fingal's Seat
4½ miles (7 km) Sheet 23 472438

Moderate Superb panoramas within easy reach of Portree. *Moorland, peat; one climb; boggy; well landmarked, but do not attempt in poor visibility – the views are the point of the walk.*

Start Leave Portree by the A850, turn on to the B885 (signposted Struan). Continue steeply uphill about 550 yards (503 m) to a cattle grid; less than half an hour's walk from centre of Portree. **Parking** on track to left of cattle grid.

① Head for bothy (hut) on hillside to right of stream. ② Pick up path 10 yards (9 m) to left of bothy, and follow it about ¾ mile (one km) keeping to right bank of stream. ③ Just below meeting of the streams, the path leads off to the right. Leave it and continue along streamside to meeting of streams. ④ Follow the right-hand stream uphill. ⑤ When the stream finally disappears into the ground, head for the skyline in front, aiming for the left end of the line of peat hags – exposed outcrops of peat which encircle the hill. ⑥ At the saddle turn left and make for the summit of Beinn na Greine. ⑦ Return to Portree by following the hill's N spur (i.e., not the one used for the ascent) to Suidh Fhinn – Fingal's Seat – from where ⑧ turn away from the sea and descend hillside to rejoin stream and follow it downhill to ①.

The Falls of Glen Brittle Forest
6 or 8 miles (9.5 or 13 km) Sheet 32 384271

Easy Spectacular waterfalls; a useful alternative to the Cuillin Hills when the weather is bad. The extension opens up superb views of these hills. Waterfalls best after rain; much of the route is sheltered – suitable for winter, even a rainy day. Occasional views of Loch Eynort. *Forest, moorland.*

Start From Dunvegan turn on to the B8009 at Drynoch; continue to Carbost and follow signs to Glen Eynort. **Parking** by telephone box near bridge.

① From parking walk back along road and turn right at T-junction, crossing stream by bridge. Continue over cattle grid. ② Turn left off road on to track up hill. ③ Where track crosses stream, follow stream uphill a few yards to see waterfall. Retrace to track and continue. ④ At T-junction, turn right and follow around loch side. ⑤ At T-junction, turn right over stream. ⑥ At bridge over stream, turn right off track for view over edge of waterfall – but keep clear of the cliff edge. ⑦ At T-junction either follow track left up Bealach Brittle shoulder to view the Cuillins; or, go right, following track downhill to follow edge of Loch Eynort. It is about 2 miles (3 km) to ⑧ Forestry Commission buildings, through which follow the track to ①.

♨ It is worth coming here for the foxgloves alone in July-August.

↯ The Cuillins: these peaks take their name from the Old Norse *Kjöllen,* meaning 'keel-shaped ridges'. They are notoriously dangerous, precipitous and subject to some of British Isles' most changeable weather. The pale brown crystalline rock is magnetic, making compass readings unreliable. But for all its starkness and danger, it has what seems an almost magical power to reflect sky colour, from black and purple to blue, grey and fiery red.

🏠 Glen Brittle, broad and fertile, is flat enough in parts to have been used as an airstrip before World War II.

⛪ A village of well-designed houses for Forestry Commission employees.

A 3-mile (5 km) walk through the wild Nevis gorge starts at the car park where the road ends 6 miles (9.5 km) inside Glen Nevis. Access via the signposted turn-off from the A82 N of Fort William town centre.

From the lay-by on the B829 near Ledard Farm, take the path from the farm through the wood, then uphill. The remains of an iron fence at the base of the SE peak can be followed to the top of Ben Venue.

Opposite the Rowardennan Hotel on the West Highland Way NW of Balmaha there is a path easily followed to the summit of Ben Lomond.

From Lochearnhead, try walking the former Oban railway line above Glen Ogle, returning by the drove road through the glen alongside river.

FIFE REGION

Cut off by the sea to the east, the Firths of Tay and Forth to the north and south and by the Ochils to the west, the so-called Kingdom of Fife was essentially self-contained until the coming of modern transport. Walkers looking for dramatic scenery will be disappointed, but this is countryside in which to saunter and enjoy the lingering atmosphere of hundreds of years of Scottish life.

The towns and villages are exceptionally well-endowed with native architecture, especially so the burghs and fishing villages of the East Neuk ('East End'), though only Pittenweem still has a working fleet. They are set in rich farmland, which rolls gently, with a pleasant scatter of woods, except by coast.

The interior of the peninsula does not have much off-road walking, but there is more than adequate upland tramping (and vistas to match) on the three main hill ranges – the Lomonds, the Cleish Hills and the Ochils. The last are the chief of the three, a free-standing group which marks the limit of lowland Scotland. West and north is essentially highland territory. From the Ochils' highest point, Ben Cleuch, they say one can see 21 (old) Scottish counties on a clear day.

The Cleish Hills
4 miles (6.5 km) Sheet 58 100955

Moderate Hills which tend to be ignored because of their closeness to large towns: consequently they offer unspoilt, pleasant walking. Best in summer: the hollows between the hills are excellent for picnicking. *Loch-side, hills, moorland; 2 climbs; mud.*

Start From the B914 take the unclassified road N towards Loch Glow. In 1¾ miles (3 km) stop by gate on left, near highest point of road; buses to Gask, 1¾ miles S of point ①. **Parking** on roadside (anglers' car park at loch is private).

① At junction in Land-Rover track bear right towards Loch Glow and the hills. ② A quarter of a mile after crossing small dam on Loch Glow, leave track and climb to top of small hill on right. Keep going N over the hummocky terrain to reach the rocky top of Dummiefarline. ③ From Dumglow head back towards W end of Loch Glow. There is no track until the loch-side is reached, and it improves along the S shore.

Deer are seen S of the loch.

The lands round Loch Glow shelter many birds, including grouse, lapwings, owls and herons. Bewick's swans are winter visitors to the loch itself, while among its most common residents are coot, mallard

Benarty near Loch Leven – not Fife's wildest walking, but grand and remote nonetheless.

and eider.

From Dummiefarline the view E and NE is to Loch Leven and the Lomond Hills; to the S it takes in the Pentland Hills and the S side of the Firth of Forth, as far as the Bass Rock, nearly 40 miles (64 km) away at the entrance to the Forth.

Dumglow, 'the fort of the tumult', was the main Pictish hill fort in the area. From its summit the view W stretches, on a clear day, to Ben Lomond and the 'Arrochar Alps' in Argyll, 50 miles (80 km) distant.

FIFE REGION

Benarty
7 miles (11 km) Sheet 58 144967

Moderate Shows the 2 faces of Fife: to the S, the grimy former mining towns; to the N, the waters of Loch Leven, the clean lines of the Lomond Hills and the farming land around Kinross. Best in autumn for colour – purple (heather), orange (dead bracken) and greens; or in early winter for the thousands of migrating duck and geese. *Woods, hillside and ridge, pasture; 3 climbs.*

Start From the B996 S of M90 junction 5, turn on to the unclassified road towards Ballingry. Stop in ¾ mile (one km); buses to Lochran Farm, 1½ miles (2.5 km) N of Kelty. **Parking** on road, and at start of forest road.

① From road double back up wide, forest track. In 100 yards (91 m), track divides, and a noticeboard warns of firing on range below. (A barrier is drawn across if firing is in progress.) Follow the main track as it zigzags uphill. ② The forest road ends in a clearing. On the right (E) side, the embankment is worn by walkers' boots. Clamber up here and pick up path through bracken to wall. ③ Cross wall, turn left, and follow wall along side of forest. At end of forest, keep straight ahead towards 2 posts on hilltop. ④ On summit of first hill, turn right (E) and follow dry-stone wall. Beware of straying too far N of wall – the hillside ends in sheer crags. Make for Benarty

summit, marked by a white trig. point pillar. ⑤ Keep to right (S) side of wall. ⑥ Follow wall to where it ends, then continue 300 yards (274 m) until almost reaching the forest. *Do not descend at end of wall as the crags are dangerous.* When almost at forest, descend to left down steep, grassy slope and head towards electricity pylon ahead. On reaching wall in front of pylon, turn right and follow wall. ⑦ At end of wall turn left and follow fence down to main road at Findatie car park and picnic site. ⑧ At W end of car park go through gate giving access to loch-side. Follow path until it regains road, then continue W along road.

⑂ The Cairngorms, 50 miles (80 km) away.

※ Dunmore, 'the big fort', is one of the Pictish hill forts in the area.

⌁ The buildings below Loch Leven car park house the sluices, installed in 1826, which control the loch's water level.

⚲ Loch Leven is one of Britain's major wildlife centres. Wintering wildfowl include the whooper swan, pinkfooted and greylag geese, teal, wigeon, pochard, goldeneye and shelduck.

⚲ Vane Farm Nature Centre has static displays, a shop, an observation gallery (with binoculars) overlooking the loch and a nature trail.

Forth Bridges and Ferry Hills
4 miles (6.5 km) Sheet 65 129828

Easy For industrial surroundings, a surprisingly rural walk; magnificent views for little effort, sudden panoramas and impressions of immense space. *Town, hilltop, village, coastal path, industrial area; 2 climbs; mud; may be overgrown between ① and ②.*

Start From M90, junction 1, follow A92 (signposted Kirkcaldy). In ½ mile (0.8 km) turn right on to road leading to Inverkeithing square; frequent buses (stopping in square); frequent trains – station close to ①. **Parking** in Inverkeithing town square.

① At S end of lay-by on dual carriageway (A90), 35 yards (32 m) past R.A.C. box, turn sharp left and follow track uphill to top of road cutting. ② Cross open hilltop to meet tarmac path. ③ Turn right on to path and follow high fence to top of steps. Descend steps to bridge level, then continue downwards to road. ④ At road turn left and walk into North Queensferry. ⑤ In village, a steep road joins from left. At the bottom of this, and on opposite side, follow track as it climbs under the N approach viaduct of the Forth Railway Bridge. ⑥ Road alongside ship-breaking yard joins minor road. Continue on minor road until reaching railway bridge. Turn right at road, pass under small railway bridge, then turn right at road back to Inverkeithing.

🚢 Rosyth Naval Dockyard, one of whose roles is to refit, refuel and re-arm nuclear submarines.

⌒ Forth Road Bridge, the third longest suspension bridge in Europe. Walking its footpath is a worthwhile experience.

🌻 At least 40 species of wild flower are identifiable on the Ferry Hills.

🚜 Whinstone Quarry produces stone for road bottoming and other building work.

\⥮/ W and E, right across Scotland.

⌒ Forth Railway Bridge (always being painted) is the largest bridge of its type.

🚢 Much of the North Sea's oil is shipped from Hound Point Oil Terminal.

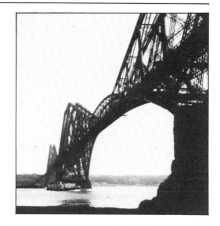

The Forth Railway Bridge, built for the North British Railway Co.; opened in 1890.

FIFE REGION

East Fife Coast
13½ miles (22 km) Sheet 59 613077

Energetic A taste of Fife's unspoilt coastline, well away from the tourist routes, with a picturesque fishing village and the town of St. Andrews, its golf courses and university. Best in summer for bathing, birdlife and delving into rock pools. *Cliffs, rocky shore, sandy beaches, dunes.*

Start Crail, on the A918 SE of St. Andrews: frequent buses. **Parking** in Crail. **Return** to starting point by bus from City Road bus station, St. Andrews, at 25 minutes past the hour; journey time to Crail, ½ hour.

Waymarked by posts with white tops; but some are missing, and some are not easy to spot. In general, keep to the seaward side of obstacles, or if in doubt about the path, near the shore. ① From Crail's main street, go down Shoregate to the harbour (signposted). ② Retrace from harbour to bend in road. At bend keep straight on up steps to Castle Terrace (sea-front walkway with viewpoint and indicator). ③ At E end of walkway, descend over grass to tarmac shore path and follow it E through caravan site. ④ Where fence crosses path, keep to seaward side of compound. ⑤ After coastguard station and lighthouse, keep to seaward side of golf course, following red posts. ⑥ At Cambo Sands car park, follow the road inland to Kingsbarns. (This diversion is necessary because it is impossible to cross the river up to ¾ mile (one km) W of Babbet Ness.) ⑦ Turn off road and go through village of Boarhills. ⑧ Just past the post office (on right), turn sharp right and follow farm roads back to shore. ⑨ Route climbs steeply to top of cliffs to avoid ravine. ⑩ At The Rock and Spindle go up steps to left. ⑪ Cross footbridge at harbour, then turn right. Go round seaward end of buildings, then turn right on path towards tall, square tower. ⑫ Follow railed path past castle on right, then along street for ¾ mile (one km) to golf clubhouse with flagpole. ⑬ Turn left towards road. Cross road and take first left (signposted Kirkcaldy). Bus station is at junction of first street on right. Buses for Crail (Dundee and Leven service) leave 25 minutes past the hour.

🏛 Crail Harbour, one of the loveliest old harbours in Scotland.

⚓ To the SW is May Island, one of whose uses is as a tracking station for birds.

✻ Dane's Dyke was built over 1,000 years ago as a defence against Danish raiders.

⚓ On Fife Ness there is an ultra-modern lighthouse and offshore, one mile (1.5 km) to the NE, is the beacon which replaced the lightship driven off station by a storm in the 1970s.

🍺 The Cambo Arms, tiny and friendly.

〰 Buddo Rock is sandstone, hence the weird shapes carved by the elements.

🏛 The beautiful ruins of St. Andrews Cathedral, founded in 1160, long the religious capital of Scotland.

🏛 St. Regulus's Tower was built in the cathedral grounds more than 800 years ago to house relics of St. Andrew brought to Scotland by St. Regulus.

🏰 St. Andrews Castle, started in about 1200, and famous for its bottle-shaped dungeon.

🏛 St. Andrews University, founded 1411, the oldest in Scotland.

⛳ The Royal and Ancient Clubhouse, mecca of the golfing world.

FIFE REGION

Dollar Glen and Ben Cleuch
11 miles (17.5 km) Sheet 58 963979

Energetic Uses the popular, and striking, Dollar and Tillicoultry Glens as access to more remote country. At best in spring – waterfalls at their most dramatic, clearer air giving longer views. *Wooded gorge, valley, hillside, ridge, town, disused railway, riverside; 3 climbs; mud. Advisable not to attempt in poor visibility.*

Start Dollar, on the A91; infrequent buses.
Car parks at top and bottom of road to Castle Campbell (signposted), or street-parking in Dollar.

① At top of Castle Campbell road go through gate marked 'Castle Campbell' and follow stream through picnic area. ② After entering woods, look for low building with blue door beside the stream. Take the upward path on right before reaching this building. ③ Path descends (look for chain handrail set into rock on right) to stream, then divides. Double back down and cross long, wooden footbridge which passes through gap in cliffs. ④ After climbing out of gorge, follow path across Burn of Sorrow by footbridge. Bear uphill towards Castle Campbell (on right). ⑤ Retrace from Castle Campbell to point where path at ④ joins the road in front of castle. Turn left off road and climb NW. Shortly join track which leads through upper part of gorge and into the open valley behind King's Seat Hill. ⑥ At head of valley, where streams meet, climb the grassy spur between the streams. From the top, look ahead (W) to a pointed hill and make across trackless moorland to the summit. (This is Andrew Gannel Hill, not named on the 1:50,000 map.) ⑦ From summit follow the fence towards the radio beacon (no path). ⑧ Pass radio beacon and continue along line of fence to the flattish summit of Ben Cleuch (indistinct path). Retrace from Ben Cleuch to radio beacon, bear right and ⑨ follow fence over summit of The Law. Pick up downhill path on S side of summit. ⑩ Cross the Daiglen Burn near where it joins the Gannel Burn, and pick up path running downhill through Tillicoultry Glen. There are a number of paths in the gorge, all eventually leading down to the town. ⑪ On A908 look for railway line crossing road, just before reaching the large, white, furniture warehouse. Turn left and follow the railway walkway E to Dollar. ⑫

Where B913 crosses old railway at Dollar, climb embankment to road – easiest ascent is on E side of bridge.

🏫 Dollar Academy, a private school, was given to the town by John McNab (died 1802), a poor local boy who went to London and prospered in shipping.

🌊 Kemp's Score, a high, narrow fissure where a long footbridge passes through the cliffs to a spectacular waterfall.

🏰 Castle Campbell, once the seat of the Earls of Argyll.

🔭 From Ben Cleuch, the highest peak in the Ochils, the view SW takes in the Wallace Monument and Stirling Castle. The winding River Forth is plainly visible, and so are the Pentland Hills to the SE.

Cairngorm peaks, to the N, are seen in good weather.

🔲 This wooden dam is a reminder that towns such as Tillicoultry were once thriving textile centres. Dams controlled the flow of water from the hills to provide constant power for driving machinery, washing cloth and so on.

🍺 The Woolpack is a free house, serving a range of beers, including the excellent local brew, McLay's.

✕ There are 2 tea rooms in Tillicoultry's main street, one each side.

🔲 Devon Valley Railway, opened in 1871 and axed by Beeching in the 1960s, linked Alloa and Kinross. Now it is used by walkers and riders.

The Lomond Hills' moorland and tracks offer much improvised walking. E and W Lomond are Fife's highest points. Access from car parks at 228062 or 252058.

An easy hill climb, with views right across Scotland, is Saline Hill. Start from Saline on the B913.

Tulliallan Forest has a variety of easy walks on forest roads.

Aberdour to Burntisland is a short walk around Hawkcraig Point, then along coastal path beside the railway.

Kincraig Point has a dramatic walk on 200-foot (61 m) cliffs, returning by chain walk along the cliff face.

A popular track runs through the Ochil Hills from Dollar via Dollar Glen and Glenquey to Glendevon.

DEESIDE AND CAIRNGORM REGIONS

As spectacular and dangerous as any mountains in Britain, the Cairngorms, with their sub-Arctic climate, can and do kill the inexperienced and ill-equipped.

Here, the granite forms great humps rather than peaks – some mountaineers find them disappointing – and there is endless loose scree. But between the great bulges run the 'mounths', the old public paths linking the settlements. Longest of these is the Lairig an Lui (Abernethy to Braemar, 37 miles [60 km]). Its name means calves' pass, and it was once used for cattle-droving. Other trails spread out from Loch Morlich and Glen More. With the climate go flora and fauna as near Britain can offer to the Alpine.

Despite the sprawling pressures of holiday and ski complexes around Aviemore, escape to near-wilderness, especially on foot, is easy. Above Glen More, for instance, lies Rothiemurchus Forest, a remnant of the primeval Scots pine forest once part of the Great Wood of Caledon.

The Cairngorm massif is the source of three main river systems: the Avon, the Spey and the 'snow-fed Dee'. The last starts in wild grandeur, descends in majesty, but never quite forgets its birth, for high ground hugs it almost to the sea at Aberdeen – providing marvellous, accessible walking for that city's inhabitants.

Bruar Falls

2 miles (3 km) Sheet 43 823661

Easy A short walk passing spectacular waterfalls, ideal as respite from the A9. *Woods, riverside; one climb.*

Start On the A9 between Perth and Inverness 5 miles (8 km) W of Blair Atholl; frequent buses. **Car park** signposted on A9.

① Walk the few yards W across the bridge and turn right up the path between the bridge and the adjoining hotel. ② In 300 yards (274 m), at junction, take the right branch. In a few yards go through tunnel under railway line, then over stile at fence, immediately taking the left-hand path. ③ In about 600 yards (549 m) note the point where the river bends right (gap in trees for spectacular view) and 100 yards (91 m) above this ④ take the left branch to the upper bridge, passing through rhododendrons and pine trees. ⑤ Follow path across stone bridge just above the Bruar Falls; at other side turn left up slope. Follow path as it turns right. ⑥ Follow path downhill to where forestry road joins from left. Ignore the road, go through gate and continue downhill with care – exposed tree roots and slabs of stone. ⑦ At the lower bridge re-cross the Bruar Water and descend by outward route to car park.

🗨 The Clan Museum tells the story of the local landowning families – Robertsons,

The best views of the main falls come between points ⑤ and ⑥.

Duncans, MacConnachies and others.

🔟 The banks of the Bruar Falls were first planted with firs in the late 18th C. by the 4th Duke of Atholl, in response to Robert Burns's poem, 'Humble Petition of Bruar Water'.

🏰 Five miles (8 km) to the E on the A9, is Blair Atholl Castle.

DEESIDE AND CAIRNGORM REGIONS

Glen Doll and Corrie Fee
5 miles (8 km) Sheet 44 284762

Moderate Getting inside a highland corrie (hollow) usually requires a long, hard walk; this is comparatively short. The area is famed for its alpine plants, at their best May-Sept. *Farmland, woods, grassy corrie; one climb; mud after rain.*

Start From the A926 take the B955 to Clova; continue 4½ miles (7 km) to Braedownie Farm, ¼ mile (0.5 km) beyond end of metalled road. Buses up the Glen from Kirriemuir. **Car park** (Forestry Commission) signposted near farm.

① From car park take the road leading to Youth Hostel and Glen Doll Forest. ② At Acharn Farm take the left branch of the 3-way fork (signposted 'Jock's Road' and 'Kilbo Path'). ③ In 300 yards (274 m) ignore the Kilbo Path as it branches off to the left and go straight on, through the gate. ④ In 200 yards (183 m) a track from the Youth Hostel joins from the right. Also ignore this. ⑤ In ¾ mile (one km) the drove road to Braemar – Jock's Path – branches off to the right. Ignore it and head down the gentle slope which leads, in a few hundred yards, to a concrete bridge over the Fee Burn (stream). ⑥ Just across the bridge take the right fork. ⑦ About ¼ mile (0.5 km) up the gentle slope a track goes off right. Ignore this

and continue straight on. In ½ mile (0.8 km) ⑧ the Land-Rover track ends but the route continues as a footpath. Follow it. Some sections may be muddy and careful footwork could be required. ⑨ At edge of forest climb high deer fence by ladder stile into Corrie Fee beyond. ⑩ The track is easy to follow for the next ½ mile up to the waterfall, where the ground is steep and sometimes slippery: take care. Return to ⑪, the concrete bridge over the Fee Burn, by the same route but instead of crossing it take the right-hand track. After about 500 yards (457 m) there is a bridge over the Burn of Kilbo and a junction of paths. Cross bridge and take the left branch, continuing downhill through trees. At the next junction do the same. turning left downhill. ⑫ At the crossroads turn left and cross the river by bridge. Turn right at the next junction and rejoin the outward route.

⑲ Jock's Road is an old drovers' – cattle drivers' – way.

♣ The floor of Corrie Fee is a habitat for alpine varieties of plants commonly found elsewhere, such as saxifrage, speedwell and cudweed.

⑲ The remote village of Clova, 4 miles (6.5 km) to the SE, and the rest of the Glen are worth exploring. It contains the 15th C. tower of Inverquharty.

Water of Ailnack

6 miles (9.5 km) Sheet 36 163174

Moderate One of the most spectacular walks in this locality, with a dramatic gorge. *Farmland, woods, moorland; 2 climbs. Do not attempt in poor visibility, or winter.*

Start At Tomintoul take the minor road in direction of Delnabo. Continue just past bridge over Avon. **Parking** in small area just beyond bridge: avoid obstructing the road.

① From the bridge take the road ahead towards Delnabo. In ¼ mile (0.5 km) ignore 2 junctions on the left. In a few yards also ignore road on right. Continue passing cottage on left and follow the Land-Rover track across bridge and as it climbs steeply to the left along edge of wood. ② Follow track along crest of small ridge with gorge on left and stream below on right. Continue towards wood, veer right through gate and after steep climb out emerge into open, flat country. In ¾ mile (one km) where the track turns left into a grassy field, walk to the edge of the gorge and follow a distinct sheep track. (Take care here, especially with children.) ④ At summit of a grassy rise (wooden pole at edge) rejoin the Land-Rover track and descend gentle slope towards lochan (small lake) on right. ⑤ About ¼ mile (0.5 km) past the lochan there is a small stream bed on the left and about this point the track becomes indistinct. It is advisable to cross the stream bed and join the sheep track near the edge of the gorge. ⑥ Follow path as it traverses edge of gorge and gradually descends towards the Water of Ailnack. (Short, muddy stretch here: because of the nature of the terrain, take extra care.) On rounding a corner of the river the path descends in a short, final steep section. ⑦ At the Ca-du Ford the water can be deceptively high: do not cross. Retrace to car park along outward route.

❧ In late summer and early autumn one of the pleasures of this walk is the sight of heather in bloom. Perhaps the most familiar species, properly called ling, has mauve, bell-shaped flowers and is distinguished by the quite substantial sprigs, which look like miniature conifer branches, sprouting from its stem.

The plant's scientific name, *Calluna vulgaris,* refers to one of heather's many practical uses. *Calluna* is the Latin for brush, and through the centuries, the plant has served for sweeping floors, thatching roofs, for bedding, fuel, basketry and making honey.

〟 The River Avon once formed a single river with the Don until the movement of ice carved a new valley for it.

\⎌/ The gorge is all the more magnificent for being unexpected

DEESIDE AND CAIRNGORM REGIONS

Cairnwell Ridge
3 miles (5 km) Sheet 43 142776

Moderate Short enough for a family picnic expedition, but with some spectacular views; opportunity to watch skiing and hanggliding. *Heather hillside and ridge, open moor; 2 climbs; boggy final section can be skirted; in winter miss out from end of ⑥ to ⑧ and return to start by the main road.*

Start The Cairnwell skiing complex on the A93 (Perth–Braemar road), 10 miles (16 km) S of Braemar. **Car Park** serving the Cairnwell skiing complex.

① From car park walk to fence which marks the border between the Tayside and Grampian regions. Follow the Land-Rover track which leads away from end of car park on left. It heads up a steep slope at right angles to the main road. In ¼ mile (0.5 km) ② at junction branch right. In about 400 yards (366 m) the path drops steeply to a watershed where ③ there are several huts connected with the skiing. Ignore paths leading to these and continue on track up steep section to crest of the ridge. ④ On top of rise the main track drops slightly into a small peat bog and then on uphill; do not follow this but turn right out along the obvious ridge. (If the main track is followed up the slope the summit of Meall Odhar is reached: only attempt in good visibility. ⑤ At end of ridge follow path as it runs right down an obvious spur to the junction of 2 streams and a small bridge. ⑥ Cross bridge and follow the track up to the main road. Walk downhill on road for about 200 yards (183 m), cross and go through metal gate on to section of former main road. In 100 yards (91 m) take the path which leads off parallel to the small stream entering from the right. ⑦ After ¼ mile (0.5 km) follow the path as it zigzags up the moderate slope to the top. The track may be difficult to find in places, but the flat ramp in the heather can usually be picked out. From the top follow the track as it contours easily back to the main road. (May be boggy.) ⑧ At road turn left to ①.

卌 Cairnwell Pass, 2,180 feet (665 m) high, is Britain's highest main road pass.

\↑/ The chair lift climbs nearly 1,000 feet (305 m) to the summit of Cairnwell, 3,058 feet (933 m) high, from where there are views, and a dry-ski run.

Glen Lui and Glen Quoich
9 miles (14.5 km) Sheet 43 066898

Moderate Through an ancient Caledonian pine forest with mountain plants in plenty. *Woods, grassy and heather hillside, gorge; one climb.*

Start From the A93 in Braemar take the road for Inverey and Linn of Dee. Continue 6½ miles (10.5 km). **Car Park** ¾ mile (one km) beyond Linn of Dee, signed at edge of road.

① From car park walk E along the metalled single-track road for 300 yards (247 m). ② At gate turn left on to Land-Rover track (signposted 'Public Right of Way'). Walk up track beside Lui Water for 1¼ miles (2 km) to bridge. ③ Turn left to continue up the track. In ¾ mile (one km) where a stream crosses the track ④ turn right from track on to a footpath up a moderate slope. The path

\↑/ Hang-gliding during summer.

🔟 The track here was once part of a military patrol route.

\↑/ There is a sweeping view of the Allt a' Ghlinne Bhig curving gently down.

✕ At the chair life a café provides snacks, tea and coffee.

is indistinct at first but better defined a few hundred yards up the side of the stream. Join the path and at the top of the slope follow it as it veers to the right away from the stream and contours round into another small valley, Clais Fhearnaig. ⑤ The sides of the valley become steeper with scree slopes either side of the path; reed-filled lochan (small lake) to the left. Soon enter Clais Fhearnaig proper, with crags on the left and boulder scree on the right. ⑥ Follow path past end of long loch and over large, grassy, 'island' in the heather. Continue on path down a gentle slope to the Land-Rover track. ⑦ At Land-Rover track turn right and follow it down the Quoich Water through pine forest. ⑧ About 300 yards (274 m) out of the woods turn left down footpath towards the Quoich Water. The path shortly drops to the river at point where river emerges from gorge. (The bridge is unsafe.) Walk back up the river about 100 yards (91 m) from

viewing Punch Bowl and Linn of Quoich and ⑨ join the Land-Rover track again which slopes gently through the trees on the left. At the top of the slope follow track as it veers right to join original track. Follow this to road. ⑩ At road turn right and follow it 2½ miles (4 km) to the car park.

🔭 The view takes in impressive Cairngorm peaks: Derry Cairngorm, Carn Crom and Carn a' Mhaim.

🌱 Plants of the locality include the butterwort (May-July), whose leaves can trap insects and alpine lady's mantle (June-Aug.), whose tiny flowers are green.

〰 The valley is part of a fault system.

〰 The cascading waters have worn cavities in the rocks. The almost circular one is 'the Earl of Mar's Punchbowl'.

Views of Lochnagar
12 miles (19 km) Sheet 44 215944

Energetic A safe and accessible route, but with a taste of remoteness; superb views of Lochnagar and Balmoral Castle. Avoid in the deer-stalking season (Aug.-Oct.); spectacular in spring when the peaks are still snow-covered. *Woods, farmland, moorland; 2 climbs. Do not attempt route in poor visibility.*

Start From the A93 (Aberdeen-Braemar) take the unclassified road at the Inver Inn signposted Aberarder. Continue 1¼ miles (2 km) on metalled road, then about ½ mile (0.8 km) on unsurfaced road to Y-junction. Buses to Inver Inn. **Parking** area at Y-junction, on left.

① Turn right at the junction and walk out of the wood towards stream. ② Turn right at the junction, cross stream, then continue uphill towards Balmore Farm. ③ Turn right through gate and down across field to stream. Cross bridge, turn sharp left and continue up easy slope through birch woods. ④ Keep straight on at junction near edge of wood through fields by ruined croft and then through gate in deer fence. ⑤ At bottom of the steep zigzag another road joins from the right. Keep straight on. ⑥ At junction of paths turn left. The path – indistinct at this

Balmoral – on Scotland's relatively dry E side – a much-loved royal retreat.

point – runs between the 2 large posts forming a gate at an angle to the fence. In ½ mile (0.8 km) the path becomes a Land-Rover track again, descending long, gradual hill. ⑦ Turn left at the junction near the stream. ⑧ Cross ford (should present no problems) at Feardar Burn (stream), then climb easy slope before descending to Auchtavan Farm. Continue on track across fields out on to open moor, where rejoin original path at edge of wood at ④. Retrace steps to starting point.

\|/ A convenient point for pausing to view Balmoral and the River Dee; further on, they are obscured. Prince Albert, consort of Queen Victoria, bought the Balmoral estate in 1852 and had the house rebuilt in the 'Scottish Baronial' style. The Royal Family were, and are devoted to the place. Queen Victoria described it as this 'dear paradise'. Guests have christened it the Scotch House, because it seems to have more tartan yardage on display than the London shop of the same name. And of course, the interior is also festooned with hunting trophies.

\|/ Deeside and Balmoral again.

DEESIDE AND CAIRNGORM REGIONS

Tullich, Morven and the Pass of Ballater
12 miles (19 km) Sheet 37 391975

Energetic A walk for getting the feel of the Ballater area, and from which further routes may be planned from excellent views of the surrounding country. Avoid in winter: deep snow. *Woods, glen, moorland, hilltops, thin woods; 2 climbs; mud after rain. Do not attempt in poor visibility.*

Start On the A93 (Aberdeen-Ballater) 2 miles (3 km) E of Ballater; buses to Ballater. **Car Park** at Tullich Church.

① From car park cross road and take track to Braehead of Tullich Farm. Do not turn right into farm but go straight ahead and through gate at end of field. Turn right, go through second gate and follow track. ② Follow track through birch woods and in ½ mile (0.8 km) pass small loch on right. For the next 3 miles (5 km) the track is easy to follow. ③ At head of glen cross fence and then stream. The track becomes grassy; after a few hundred yards cross Rashy Burn (stream) by easy ford. For the next ¼ mile (0.5 km) the track is indistinct. ④ The track joins another forming a T-junction. Turn left along grassy track. ⑤ At junction of tracks turn left towards Peter's Hill. Follow track gradually uphill. ⑥ At top of rise follow track slightly downhill past several small bog lochans (small lakes) on right. Just past these a track joins from right: ignore it and carry straight on. In 300 yards (274 m) also ignore track on left. ⑦ Follow track down to watershed with rock outcrop on left, then climb moderately towards Creagan Riach. ⑧ Follow track downhill towards Balmenach Farm. ⑨ At main road turn left and walk through Pass of Ballater about 2 miles (3 km) to ①.

🏛 In the Kirk of St. Nathalan, built about 1400 and now a ruin, there are Pictish sculptured stones.

🦌 Red deer and mountain hares may be seen in the area.

👁 Excellent views of the surrounding hills the Dee Valley and Glen Muick.

🦌 Monaltrie Animal Park.

The mountain or blue hare, so called because the mixing of its brown summer coat and white winter fur looks bluish.

ⓘ Ballater's existence as a resort is due to an old woman who, about 1760, cured herself of a skin disease by heeding a dream and bathing in a nearby pool which was later made the spa.

🦅 Birds of the area include the capercaillie (the male looking like a shaggy turkey), red grouse and siskins, which are tiny (smaller than sparrows) with long wings and short tails – all noticeable in flight.

Kirriemuir is an ideal centre for exploring the surrounding hills; 12 miles (19 km) N of the B955, peaceful paths climb to Lake Brandy.

Paths around Carnoustie climb the local cliffs and traverse the heath round the international golf course.

Aboyne, 20 miles (32 km) W of Aberdeen has marked trails to Glen Mark and, 5 miles (8 km) NE, to Macbeth's Cairn.

Cullen Bay, 13 miles (21 km) W of Banff has cliff-top walks.

The Linn Tummel Nature Trail, near the Pitlochry Dam, takes in a salmon pass and Faskally Reservoir.

Mountain walks, off the A951 near Aviemore, follow marked forest and upland trails. Advice on walking in the whole area can be gained from the Forestry Commission Information Centre at Glen More.

LONG-DISTANCE WALKS

NATIONAL TRAILS

This is an introductory briefing to Britain's astonishingly large network of national trails and long-distance footpaths.

National trail routes are designated by the Countryside Commission, and, together with long-distance paths, are maintained and signposted (and often substantially waymarked) by a Local Authority or local Ramblers' Association. Other paths and 'ways' exist more in the minds of the walkers who pioneered them than as geographical entities; an imaginative linking of footpaths, not all in walkable condition or waymarked.

Here, national trails and long-distance paths are given substantial entries. Other paths and 'ways' have a shorter entry, and are a selection of those which are generally maintained to an adequate standard, or fully described in a guide.

Actually to walk a trail or path requires the latest relevant guide. These publications are almost always modestly priced, give detailed directions and generous amounts of practical information, including accommodation and public transport links as well as general description. In the case of the 'unofficial' routes they are mostly produced by enterprising private individuals, and do not enjoy wide retail distribution.

Details of guide publications can usually be obtained from your local bookshop, or in some cases direct from the publisher. For information on Ordnance Survey guides contact their Information and Enquiries Branch, (0703) 792792. Leaflets and Fact Sheets relating to all trails, paths and ways may be obtained from the Ramblers' Association, 1–5 Wandsworth Road, London, SW8 2XX, or the Countryside Commission, Crescent Place, Cheltenham, Glos., GL50 3RA.

As in the rest of the book, numbers are given of the 1:50,000 sheets needed.

THE NATIONAL TRAILS

The South West Coast Path
518 miles (833 km)
This is the longest of the long-distance paths (formerly the South West Peninsula Coast Path). Here, for convenience, it is divided into 4 separate sections. Four guidebooks to the path are published by the Countryside Commission.

The Somerset and Devon North Coast Path: Minehead to Marsland Mouth
82 miles (132 km) Sheets 180, 181, 190.
This section is usually taken to be the start of the Coast Path, and considered the least arduous. It covers, however, as wide a variety of terrain as any. There are beautiful, picturesque villages. Parts lie in the Exmoor National Park, and others within an Area of Outstanding Natural Beauty.

The path is waymarked throughout with the standard coast path acorn. It is always wise to carry maps and guides.

Between Porlock Weir and County Gate it is beautifully wooded.

There should be no lack of accommodation, but during the holiday season bookings should be made in advance. Trousers are recommended, rather than skirts or shorts, as well as windproof and waterproof clothing. Distance calculations should be increased by 25% due to the frequent changes of levels and direction.

Highlights Selworthy Beacon; Culbone Church, claiming to be the smallest in England; Lynmouth and Lynton, twin towns of great beauty; Valley of Rocks, below Hollerday Hill; Saunton Sands, which have dunes up to 98 feet (30 m) high; Clovelly, with its steep and cobbled streets, where donkeys instead of cars are used for transport.

The Cornwall Coast Path: Marsland Mouth near Bude to Cremyll on the Tamar
268 miles (431 km) Maps 190, 200, 201, 203, 204.
Like the Dorset Coast Path, this section of the Coast Path goes mostly through an Area of Outstanding Natural Beauty. The walk goes across dunes, moorlands and cliff tops, often following the coastguard paths.

There is a wide variety of interest, from fascinating rock formations to the hunting ground of King Arthur at Tintagel; remains of tin mines; the artists' centre at St. Ives; the serpentine rock carving industry at the Lizard; and the china clay ports of Charlestown and Par, as well as the picturesque villages and beautiful views.

Conditions The path includes some sections regarded as easy and others as severe; the latter should not be undertaken unprepared. For example, Tintagel to Port Isaac, which includes one of the steepest parts of the whole Peninsula Coast Path; and St. Ives to Pendeen Watch, where there are 21 miles

(34 km) without a place for rest or refreshment. There are some ferry crossings, and even wading at low tide. Beware when there is a heavy mist, or when there are strong off-shore winds.

Trousers, rather than skirts or shorts, are advisable and distance calculations should be increased to allow for the changes in level and direction. Accommodation should not prove difficult, but this is a holiday area, and bookings should be made in advance. **Highlights** Many attractive villages and coves; Helford River Estuary, famous for its oyster beds; Looe, the shark-fishing centre.

Devon South Coast Path: Plymouth to Lyme Regis 93 miles (150 km) Sheets 192, 193, 201, 202. 1:25,000 Outdoor Leisure Map of South Devon, for the section between Bolt Head and Torbay

Most of the walk comes within Areas of Outstanding Natural Beauty, and several sections have been defined as Heritage coast. Though walkers have to make their way through Paignton and Torquay, much of the route offers spectacular cliffs, wide estuaries and remote bays, together with charming Devon villages. The number of river crossings adds to the variety.
Conditions The path should not be difficult for most walkers with the exception of the landslip at the Dorset end – there it is tough going, and should be left to the experienced walker, as, once started, there is no way off it. Maintenance and development have improved dramatically in recent years.

Between Budleigh Salterton and Sidmouth there is a long diversion through lack of a bridge, and though in exceptionally dry conditions it is possible to wade the river Otter, this is not recommended. Ferries have to be used on several sections, and times should be checked.

Allowance of about 25% should be made when calculating distances, owing to the changes in levels and directions of the paths in some sections. Stout footwear and trousers, rather than skirts or shorts, are advised. There should be no lack of accommodation, but as this is a holiday area, bookings should be made in advance.
Highlights Burgh Island, a miniature St. Michael's Mount; Hope Cove, with its spectacular cliffs; Salcombe Harbour; Slapton Ley, a freshwater lake, rich in wildlife and an angler's paradise; Brixham, fishing port and yachting centre; The Landslip, caused by a vast cliff slide.

Dorset Coast Path: Lyme Regis to Poole 72 miles (116 km) Sheets 193, 194, 195.

This is the shortest section of the South West Coast Path. With the exception of Weymouth, the whole path is in an Area of Outstanding Natural Beauty.

The area is famous for the fossils to be found along the cliffs, and dramatic examples of folded strata can be seen.
Conditions In general the path is well signposted, but the alternative route between West Bexington and Osmington Mills will require a compass and good maps. For 12 miles (19 km) of this stretch refreshment and accommodation are difficult, except at Portesham and Osmington. Otherwise these are readily available.

There are some problems in places with cliff slippage (for instance between Lyme Regis and Charmouth), and care must be taken to keep back from the cliff edge.

There is a badly neglected section between Abbotsbury and Weymouth. Firing takes place on Chickerell Range, and walkers must wait until given permission to proceed; and before setting out for the section between Lulworth Cove and Kimmeridge, a check should be made as to whether firing will be in progress; if so, the area must be skirted.

When calculating distances, allow an extra 25% for changes in level and direction. No special clothing is required other than strong footwear, but it is advisable to wear trousers because of overgrown sections.
Highlights Charmouth, a favourite town of Jane Austen; Golden Cap, the highest point of the South Coast, with spectacular views; Abbotsbury with its swannery; Lulworth Cove; St Aldhelm's (or Alban's) Chapel, dating from Norman days; Chesil Bank.

The South Downs Way: Eastbourne to Buriton, near Petersfield, and Winchester

80 miles (129 km) Sheets 197, 198, 199, 185.
The South Downs Way, as well as being a walk, is the only long-distance bridle way, so expect to see horseriders. In addition to the scenic beauty of this walk, with its superb views from such places as Beacon Hill, there is a profusion of wild flowers, birds and butterflies, and much to interest the archaeologist. Good public services make it ideal to walk in sections.
Conditions Even though the path is well

NATIONAL TRAILS

signposted, maps are essential. Strong footwear should be worn for protection against sharp flints. Public transport is available all along the route, but services are not necessarily regular, so do consult the timetables. Accommodation can be found in nearby towns or villages, but other than a few youths hostels there is little on the route. The extended section from Buriton to Winchester is not yet completely open.

Highlights West Dean, a flint village; The Long Man of Wilmington, carved from the hillside; Alfriston, with its timbered inns; the Norman Church at Southease, with its 13th C. wall paintings; the prehistoric fort at Devil's Dyke; hang gliding at Soper's Bottom.

The North Downs Way: Farnham in Surrey to Dover, Kent, with a loop to Canterbury

140 miles (225 km) Sheets 186, 187, 188, 178, 189, 179, 177.

The North Downs Way was officially opened by the then Archbishop of Canterbury, Dr. Donald Coggan, at the end of September 1978, and its route through South-East England offers plenty of variety – much of it along the crest of the North Downs, with its many beautiful and extensive views.

In parts it coincides with the Pilgrims' Way, so-called because it is supposed to have been used by pilgrims to the shrine of Saint Thomas à Becket at Canterbury.

There are many buildings of architectural and historic interest on or near the route, as well as attractive villages and major towns.

Conditions Being so near London, this walk has ample public transport. Special equipment is not needed, but walkers are advised to wear strong shoes and to take waterproof and windproof clothing. In several places negotiations are still taking place on rights of way, and the text of the guide books will indicate these.

In Surrey the route is marked by oak signposts, and in Kent by low stone plinths which are sometimes obscured by vegetation. Where there is some doubt, the acorn waymark is used to confirm the route. Finding accommodation should be easy.

Highlights The famous stepping stones over the River Mole; St. Martha's Hill, giving glorious views; Bluebell Hill, with fine views from its picnic site; the Crondale Nature Reserve; Chilham, claimed to be the prettiest village in Kent; Canterbury Cathedral; Dover Castle; and, on a clear day, France.

The Ridgeway: Overton Hill to Ivinghoe Beacon

85 miles (137 km) Sheets 164, 165, 173, 174, 175

The Path was opened in 1973. It lies entirely within the North Wessex Downs and Chiltern Areas of Outstanding Natural Beauty, and goes through the 5 counties of Wilts., Berks., Oxon., Bucks. and Herts. Much of it follows the ancient routes of the Wessex Ridgeway and Icknield Way.

At the start you see 5 round and 2 long barrows. A long and beautiful section is the downland patch passing by Segsbury Camp, close to Grim's Ditch, and down to the River Thames at Streatley. Leaving the river after some 5½ miles (9 km), the path wanders through woods to join the Icknield Way, and skirts Beacon Hill. Here you can visit the Rowant Nature Reserve. After crossing the Chiltern Hills the path drops down to the Union Canal. Having crossed this, you come to one of the loveliest sections over wood and grasslands to the Beacon.

Conditions This walk is not hard going, but sensible shoes should be worn against the sharp flints, slippery clay and chalk. Youth Hostel accommodation is plentiful, but other types are limited, so book ahead.

Highlights Bronze and Iron Age relics; Avebury Stone Circle; the Iron Age fortifications of Barbury Castle; Ashdown House, tiny and beautiful, owned by the National Trust; Wayland's Smithy, a chambered long barrow, with a fascinating legend; Coombe Hill, a high point on the Chilterns.

Pembrokeshire Coast Path: Amroth, Pembrokeshire, to St. Dogmaels, near Cardigan

168 miles (270 km) Sheets 145, 157, 158

The Pembrokeshire Coast Path gives magnificent views from the cliff paths of the beautiful coastal scenery. The coastline and the offshore islands are one of the greatest seabird areas, and there is much of archaeological and historical interest.

Conditions The path is well marked, but good maps are essential for enjoyment. Some sections are difficult and hazardous and should only be undertaken by the fit. Most stretches are however within the average walker's capabilities.

Sudden changes in the weather must be expected, and clothing should be appropriate. Altitude and direction changes during the walk should be taken into account when calculating distances.

Accommodation is available, but should be booked in advance during holiday times.

There is a stretch between Elegug Stacks and St. Govan's Head which is closed by the Ministry of Defence when firing is in progress, and enquiries should be made before setting out – there are inland detours.

The estuaries at Pickleridge and Sandy Haven can only be traversed at low tide; at other times it is necessary to make detours.

Highlights From Whitesands Bay there are views of Ramsey Island with its famous colony of grey seals; St. David's Cathedral, 12th C., said to be the resting place of David, the patron saint of Wales; the magnificent natural harbour of Milford Haven, now the largest oil port in the British Isles; Penally, noted for its old red sandstone rocks and carboniferous limestones; St. Govan's Chapel and holy well, dating from the 13th C.

Offa's Dyke Path

170 miles (270 km) Sheets 172, 162, 161, 148, 137, 126, 117, 116

The Offa's Dyke Path takes its name from the 8th C. earthwork dyke built by King Offa; it marks roughly the boundary between England and Wales. It is unique among designated paths in that it follows an archaeological route rather than a geographical one, and is considered by historians as the most interesting survivor of the Dark Ages, but note that the Dyke itself is only followed for about 60 miles (97 km).

The walk has become one of the best used of the long-distance routes, offering a particularly wide variety from the rough and lonely hill country and the steeply wooded valley of the River Wye to the lowlands and wide valley of the River Severn. Though there is no rock work, the walk is strenuous in places.

Conditions Though nearly all the path is well signposted, in some places the route may not be clear; directions are given in the guides.

A compass is recommended as the path covers some moorland stretches.

The road has been improved in recent years and is signposted throughout. Avoid the long ridge walk of the Black Mountains in bad weather and be prepared for no readily available accommodation or transport between Abergavenny and Hay-on-Wye.

Highlights Wintour's Leap; White Castle; Pen Twyn, an Iron Age fort; Telford's Aqueduct; Panorama Walk.

The Pennine Way: Edale in Derbyshire to Kirk Yetholm in Roxburgh District

250 miles (402 km) Sheets 74, 75, 80, 86, 87, 91, 92, 98, 103, 109, 110

The Pennine Way was the first of the long-distance walks to be established. It is the second longest in Britain, and remains the most challenging, passing through some of the remotest areas in the country.

There is much evidence of the past in the Roman remains, Norman churches and period houses. The Way goes through the heart of the Brontë country; there are splendid caves and potholes, spectacular views of rushing water. There is a profusion of plant life in the dales, and many varieties of bird can be seen.

Conditions This is a strenuous, high-level walk. It can be dangerous, indeed it presents some of the roughest walking in Britain. In bad weather it should only be undertaken by really experienced walkers, armed with maps and compass, and provided with correct clothing, equipment and supplies.

The frequent changes in level and direction make it necessary to add 25% when calculating distances.

Accommodation is obtainable in general – though it is advisable to check in advance; but there is a 27-mile (43 km) stretch at the end of the route, between Byrness and Kirk Yetholm, which must be accomplished in one day, unless equipped with tents.

Highlights Within's Height, with the ruined farmhouse-possibly the original Wuthering Heights; the Brontë Museum, Haworth 3 miles (5 km) off the Way; Pinhaw Beacon, giving panoramic views to all points of the compass; Pen-y-Ghent, offering fine views, and much loved by potholers; Hull Pot, where the Hull Pot Beck plunges spectacularly when in spate; Hardrow Force, and High Force waterfalls; Hadrian's Wall, and the forts of Birdoswald, Great Chesters, Vindolanda and Housesteads.

The Wolds Way: Filey Brigg to Hessle Haven on the River Humber

76 miles (122 km) Sheets 100, 101, 106

The Wolds Way is the latest of the long-distance routes to be designated by the Countryside Commission. The trail was approved in 1977, and the official opening was in October 1982. The walk links with

NATIONAL TRAILS

AND LONG-DISTANCE PATHS

the Cleveland Way, running along the chalk hills of the Yorkshire Wolds, crossing some of the prettiest of the dry dale sof the region, through farming country.

Conditions Waymarking is complete along all rights of way along the path.

The Cleveland Way: North York Moors and coast

93 miles (150 km) Sheets 93, 94, 99, 100, 101. The OS 1 inch to 1 mile Tourist Map of the North York Moors shows much of the route.

The Cleveland Way was the second long-distance walk to be opened in England and Wales. Its horseshoe shape is almost all contained within the North York Moors National Park, providing both moorland and coastal scenery – the latter being so outstanding that it has been defined as a Heritage Coast.

The path is well marked, but it is essential to carry maps and a compass on many sections. Accommodation is limited inland and it is wise to book well in advance.

Conditions There are frequent cliff slips, particularly in winter after rain, and the area is noted for its rapid changes in weather conditions, and for fog. Great caution is required, and suitable clothing must be worn. Always take an extra pullover and emergency rations.

Because of the climbs, and direction changes, distance calculations should be increased by as much as 25%.

This walk should not be undertaken alone, except by the most experienced – and even they would be ill-advised to do so.

Highlights The remains of the beautiful Norman Rievaulx Abbey; Botton Head, the highest point of the Cleveland Hills; Captain Cook's monument; the impressive remains of Whitby Abbey, at the picturesque resort; Robin Hood's Bay with its cliff-hanging cottages; the inlet of Cloughton Wyke, popular with geologists and photographers.

Peddars Way and the Norfolk Coast Path

50 miles (80 km) Sheets 132, 144

The latest National Trail to open. From Knettishall (Norfolk–Suffolk border) to Holme on the Norfolk Coast.

The Thames Path

214 miles (344 km)

Newly designated Trail due to open in 1994. From Kemble in Gloucestershire to the Thames Barrier, it follows the Thames from source to end.

LONG-DISTANCE PATHS

West Highland Way: Milngavie *(on the outskirts of Glasgow)* to Fort William

95 miles (153 km) Maps incorporated in the official guide.

The West Highland Way is the first of 3 designated Long-Distance Paths in Scotland. It starts at Scotland's largest city, passes its largest loch and ends at its highest mountain.

Conditions The route has been well though unobtrusively signposted with dark brown waymarks with a thistle symbol.

As the path progresses N, there are stretches through remote country with no shelter and some rough walking and scrambling. Scottish weather is unpredictable, and correct clothing and supplies should be taken. There is adequate accommodation, though bear in mind the remote stretches. In the tourist season it is wise to book in advance. Care should be exercised not to disturb livestock, and dogs should not be taken.

Highlights The whole route offers scenery second to none, but the shores of Loch Lomond and the rugged mountains of the western highlands (including Ben Nevis) are of course unforgettable.

The Cotswold Way: Chipping Camden to Bath

100 miles (161 km) Sheets 150, 151, 162, 163, 172.

A walk along the Cotswold Edge had been suggested as far back as 1953, and it was sponsored by the Gloucestershire County Council in 1970 in the hope that it would be taken over by the Countryside Commission as another long-distance footpath. By virtue of its popularity and excellent waymarking and condition it has become an 'official unofficial route'.

The route passes through many places of interest, the villages are beautiful, and plenty of time should be allowed to enjoy them and, of course, the great City of Bath. Because much of the route follows the top of the steep Cotswold Scarp, it has similarities with a cliff-top coastal path.

Conditions There should be no problems with this path. In wet weather suitable footwear must be worn to deal with the deep Cotswold mud; and, of course, waterproof gear. The path is largely over cultivated land, and care must be taken to fasten gates and not to disturb livestock. Dogs must be kept on leads. The path is waymarked using the Countryside Commission's system of coloured arrows supplemented by use of the white spot. Where there is need for careful navigation, the guide gives special warnings. Even so, maps are strongly advised.

Highlights Broadway, with its beautiful houses and the Lygon Arms Hotel; Stanton village; Stanway House, with its Inigo Jones gatehouse; the remains of the abbey at Hailes; Barrow Wake, giving superb views; Cooper's Hill – cheese rolling on Whit Monday; Horton Court, a medieval hall.

Avon

The Avon Walkway 13 miles (21 km) Sheet 172.
From Pill, following the River Avon, through the Avon Gorge, and the centre of Bristol, to Nethan Bridge. The walk can be continued to Bath, and is waymarked.

Buckinghamshire

The North Buckinghamshire Way 30 miles (48 km) Sheets 152, 165.
From Chequers Knap, through the Vale of Aylesbury to Wolverton. Here it joins the Grafton Way – see Northamptonshire.

Cheshire

Gritstone Trail 17 miles (27 km) Sheets 109, 118.
From Lyme Park to Rushton, linking with the Staffordshire Way – see Staffordshire.
The Sandstone Trail 30 miles (48 km) Sheet 117.
From Frodsham to Grindley Brook.
Wirral Way 12 miles (19 km) Sheets 108, 117.

Cumbria

The Dales Way 81 miles (130 km) Sheets 90, 97, 98.
From Ilkley to Bowness. This is a difficult path following the rivers Wharfe, Dee, Lune and Kent, and some of the Pennine Way.

Derbyshire

High Peak Trail 17 miles (27 km) Sheet 119.
From Cromford to Dowlow, connecting with the Tissington Trail this walk follows the route of the old Cromford and High Peak railway, and gives fine scenery.
Tissington Trail 13 miles (21 km) Sheet 119.
From Ashbourne to Parsley Hay, connecting with the High Peak Trail, following the old railway route, and offering fine and varied scenery.

Devon

Two Moors Way 103 miles (166 km) Sheets 202, 191, 181, 180.
From Ivybridge, Plymouth to Lynton, Barnstaple, linking Exmoor and Dartmoor.

East Sussex

The Forest Way 9 miles (14 km) Sheets 187, 188.
From Groombridge to East Grinstead, through to the Forest Way Country Park.

Essex

The Essex Way 50 miles (80 km) Sheets 187, 188.
From Epping to Dedham, in the lovely Constable countryside.
The Forest Way 20 miles (32 km) Sheets 167, 177.
From Epping Forest to Hatfield Forest, the ancient tracks of the forests opening out to large attractive areas.

Gloucestershire

The Heart of England Way – see Staffordshire.

Gwent

The Lower Wye Valley Walk 34 miles (55 km) Sheet 162.
From Chepstow to Ross through the varied Wye Valley Area of Outstanding Natural Beauty.
Usk Valley Walk 22 miles (35 km) Sheets 161, 171.
From Caerleon to Llanellen, providing both high superb views and quiet riverside walking.

Hampshire

South Wessex Way 117 miles (188 km) Sheets 197, 184, 185, 195.
From Petersfield to Poole; links the South Downs Way with the South West Peninsula Coast Path.

Isle of Wight

Bembridge Trail 15 miles (24 km) Sheet 196.
From Shide to Bembridge Point, through marsh and woodland.
Coastal Path 60 miles (97 km) Sheet 196.
Circling the coastline.
Hamstead Trail 8 miles (13 km) Sheet 196.
Hamstead Ledge to Brooke Bay, meeting the Coastal Path.

Tennyson Trail *15 miles (24 km) Sheet 196.*
From Carisbrooke to Alum Bay – offering varied downland and forest walking, and fine marine views.
Worsley Trail *15 miles (24 km) Sheet 196.*
From Shanklin Old Village to Brighstone Forest, giving a wide variety of forest, downland and high countryside.

Kent
Wealdway *57 miles (92 km) Sheets 178, 188, 198.*
From Gravesend to Uckfield.

Leicestershire
Jubilee Way *16 miles (26 km) Sheets 129, 130.*
From Melton Mowbray to Brewer's Gate, Nr. Woolsthorpe, linking with the Viking Way – see Humberside.

Lincolnshire
Jubilee Way – see *Leicestershire.*
Viking Way *140 miles (225 km) Sheets 141, 112.*
From Oakham to Humber Bridge.

London
London Countryway *205 miles (330 km) Sheets 165, 166, 167, 175, 177, 186, 187, 188.*
Complete circuit of London, with access by rail at several points.

Northamptonshire
The Grafton Way *12 miles (20 km) Sheet 152.*
From Wolverton to Greens Norton, linking with the North Bucks Way and The Knightley Way.

The Knightley Way *12 miles (19 km) Sheet 152.*
From Greens Norton to Badby, linking with the Grafton Way.

North Yorkshire
The Ebor Way *70 miles (113 km) Sheets 100, 104, 105.*
From Helmsley to Oakley. This links the Cleveland Way long-distance path and the Dales Way and goes via York.

Northumberland
Hadrian's Wall *73 miles (117 km) Sheets 85, 86, 87, 88 and the OS Hadrian's Wall Map.*
It is not possible to walk the whole length uninterrupted, but there are some fine unspoilt sections. (Proposed National Trail.)

Oxfordshire
The Oxfordshire Way *60 miles (96 km) Sheets 163, 164, 175.*
From Henley-on-Thames to Bourton-on-the-Water. This walk links with Chiltern and Cotswold A.O.N.Bs.

Powys
Glyndwr's Way *121 miles (195 km) Sheets 125, 126, 135, 136, 148.*
From Knighton to Welshpool, the walk, giving splendid scenic views, is divided into 16 strenuous sections.
The Wye Valley Walk *36 miles (58 km) Sheets 147, 148, 161.*
From Hay-on-Wye to Rhayader.

Staffordshire
The Staffordshire Way *32 miles (51 km) Sheets 118, 128.*
From Mow Cop south to Kinver Edge, connecting with the Gritstone Trail, North Worcestershire Path and the Worcestershire Way; it provides valley and hilltop paths.
Heart of England Way *80 miles (129 km) Sheets 127, 128, 139, 150, 151.*
Joins the Staffordshire Way at Cannock Chase with the Cotswold Way at Chipping Camden.

Surrey
Wey South Path *36 miles (58 km) Sheets 186, 197.*
Along the towpath of the former Wey and Arun Canal.

Thames
Thames Walk *150 miles (241 km) Sheets 163, 164, 174, 175, 176.*
From Putney to Thames Head.

West Midlands
West Midlands Way *162 miles (261 km) Sheets 127, 128, 138, 139, 140, 150, 151.*
Completely encircles the conurbations of West Midlands Metropolitan County.

West Yorkshire
The Calderdale Way *50 miles (80 km) Sheets 103, 104, 110.*
Making a circuit of Calderdale, by Ripponden, Todmorden, Heptonstall, Brighouse and Greetland.
Colne Valley Circular Walk *15 miles (24 km) Sheet 110.*
A circular path starting from Golcar.

INDEX

Aberdaron, 153
Aberdovey, 155
Acharn, 320
Alfriston, 99
Amesbury, 90
Arnside, 265
Ashbury, 89
Aylsham, 195
Ayr 286
Aysgarth, 243
Bala Lake, 156
Balerno, 296
Ballater, 327
Ballingry, 312
Bardon Mill, 274
Beckside, 264
Beddgelert, 162
Bellingham, 273
Betws-y-Coed, 152
Biggar, 291
Blackfield, 76
Blackheath, 109
Blair Atholl, 319
Bonaly Tower, 292
Bossington, 44
Bourton-on-the-Hill, 176
Bovey Tracey, 28
Brauncewell, 197
Braunston, 198
Brendon Two Gates, 53
Bretton, 226
Bridge End, 275
Bridgeham Heath, 193
Brockweir, 169
Brockenhurst, 75
Burghclere, 85
Burley, 76
Burnham Market, 189
Byrness, 276
Bwlch-y-groes, 107
Cairnwell Ski Complex, 322
Callander, 300
Camelford, 16
Carn Brea, 15
Castleton, 211
Cerne Abbas, 40
Chevening, 118
Chilgrove, 97
Chipping, 217
Chop Gate, 259
Clayton Green, 94
Coln St. Aldwyn's, 178
Colwyn Bay, 150
Conwy, 151
Cornalees, 302
Craignure, 307
Crail, 314
Craster, 277

Cremyll, 23
Crosby Garrett, 262
Crowfield, 141
Cwm-llwch, 146
Dalmellington, 284
Dalry, 284
Delnabo, 321
Disley, 208
Ditchling Beacon, 96
Dollar, 316
Dolphinholme, 217
Doonfoot, 286
Downs Ridge, 102
Dunsop Bridge, 221
Eamont Bridge, 261
Eartham Wood, 93
Edgeworth, 174
Errwood Reservoir, 210
Eskdale Green, 271
Farrington Gurney, 62
Flax Bourton, 56
Fovant, 83
Freshwater Bay, 69, 70-85
Friday Street, 106
Fritham, 79
Gargrave, 227
Garsdale Station, 245
Glentrool Village, 288
Godshill, 67
Gomshall, 113
Goyt Valley, 210
Grassington, 242
Great Kimble, 125
Great Yarmouth, 191
Grindleford Station, 206
Grwyne Fawr Valley, 143
Gwaun Valley, 138
Hare Hill Edge, 225
Harewood, 228
Harlech, 158
Hartshill, 184
Headley, 114
Hebden Bridge, 230
Henley, 129
Higher Bockhampton, 38
Hog's Back, The, 114
Holford, 51
Holt, 192
Horton, 251
Ilam, 205
Ingleton, 248
Inkpen, 86
Inver, 324
Inverkeithing, 313
Ivinghoe Beacon, 123
Kenmore, 301
Keswick, 268
Kirkdale, 256

Kirklington, 201
Lastingham, 254
Leatherhead, 105
Lee, The, 126
Lichfield, 185
Linn of Dee, 323
Little Black Hill, 142
Little Hampden, 126
Little Malvern, 170
Littlebredy Farm, 36
Little Salkeld, 263
Lizard Village, 20
Llangollen, 154
Llwyncelyn, 144
Loch Don, 307
Loch Doon, 284
Loch Glow, 311
Lockton, 257
Lough Pool, 168
Lucott Cross, 43, 49
Lullingstone Park, 118
Lydeard Hill, 50
Lydford, 26
Lyme Park, 208
Malham, 241
Marsden, 229
Matlock, 207
Meldon Reservoir, 30
Midsummer Hill, 167
Moretonhampstead, 27
Morvil, 136
Neuadd Reservoirs, 147
New Abbey, 287
Newborough, 157
Newlands Corner, 116
New Polzeath, 17
Northleach, 175
North Wootton, 56
Oakworth, 225
Osmington, 37
Otford, 121
Ozleworth Bottom, 173
Pass of Glencoe, 299
Pengegin, 139
Perth, 304
Pocklington, 237
Poldue Downs, 19
Porlock 48
Priddy, 57
Princetown, 25
Queenzieburn, 303
Reigate, 110
Ribchester, 220
Richmond, 246
Rievaulx, 253
Ringmoor Down, 29
Roche, 22
Rosebush, 135

Rostegue, 18
Rubery, 187
Rufus Stone, 73
St. Catherine's Court, 177
St. David's, 133
Shalford, 108
Sawley, 218
Sedbergh, 244
Settrington, 233
Sherringham, 194
Silpho Forest, 254
South Queensferry, 293
Stalham, 190
Stean, 247
Steyning, 94
Sticklepath, 33
Studland, 35
Symond's Yat, 171
Tanworth-in-Arden, 183
Tarpantan, 147
Tarr Steps, 44
Tenby, 134
Tetford, 203
Thixendale, 235
Tintern Parva, 169
Tinto Hill, 291
Tollard Royal, 92
Trefriw, 160
Turville Heath, 124
Ty-i-saf, 169
Tywyn, 149
Upton, 46
Walbury Hill Fort, 86
Walderton, 100
Wardle Fold, 223
Watton, 234
Webber's Post, 47
Wells, 58
Welton, 238
Wenallt, 146
Wherwell, 84
White Coomb, 283
Whiting Bay, 306
Winchcombe, 181
Windermere, 267
Winkworth Arboretum, 106
Winscombe, 60
Woldingham, 117
Wooler, 278
Wootton Bridge, 71
Worth, 58
Worth Matravers, 39
Wycoller, 224
Yarmouth, 68
Yarrowford, 295
Youlgreave, 212

ACKNOWLEDGEMENTS

Christopher Hall is editor of *The Countryman*, President of the Ramblers' Association and former Director of the Council for the Protection of Rural England.

David Platten Director, Bivvy Bug Design Associates Liz Prince *Walks in the Dartmoor National Park* (Dartmoor National Park Department) Anne-Marie Edwards *In the Steps of Jane Austen, In the Steps of Thomas Hardy, The New Forest Companion, New Forest Walks* (all available from Countryside Books, Newbury). David Butler (pseudonym of one of the Exmoor National Park wardens) *Exmoor Walks for Motorists* (Warne) the late E.M. Gould sometime Footpath Secretary, Mendip Ramblers' Association Ben Perkins *South Downs Walks for Motorists* (Warne) Janet Spayne and Audrey Krynski *Walks in the Surrey Hills, Afoot in Surrey, Walks in the Hills of Kent* Nick Moon *Chilterns Walks for Motorists, Southern and Northern Areas*-2 vols. (Warne) Chris Barber *Exploring the Brecon Beacons National Park;* Originator of the Three Peaks Trail, organizer of the South Wales Seven Peaks Marathon Walk, mountaineering instructor, caver James T. C. Knowles *Snowdonia Walks for Motorists* (Warne) Donna Baker *Tracking Through Mercia*-3 vols. (Express Logic) Richard Sale *A Guide to the Cotswold Way* (Constable) S.G. Wallsgrove Footpath Secretary, Warwickshire Area Ramblers' Association, Jeanne le Surf 'Rambler' of the *Eastern Evening News* Honorary County Footpath Secretary, Norfolk Area Ramblers' Association Brett Collier; walks columnist for the *Lincolnshire Evening Echo*, President, Lincolnshire and South Humberside Area Ramblers' Association, *Lincolnshire Rambles* (Countryside Books, in preparation) Brian Spencer *Dovedale and the Manifold Valley, The Derbyshire Wye, Matlock and the Upper Derwent, Castleton and Edale* (Moorland Publishing) the late Cyril Spiby *Walking in Central Lancashire, Walking in the Ribble Valley* (Dalesman) Colin Speakman *Dales Way* (Dalesman); Secretary, Yorkshire Dales Society Geoff Eastwood *Walking in East Yorkshire* (from 7, Highwood, Long Lane, Driffield, E Yorks); *The Minster Way*, with Ray Wallis and Alan Kilnwick (Lockington Publishing); National Chairman, The Ramblers' Association; Footpath Secretary, East Yorkshire and Derwent Area Ramblers' Association John Parker *Lake District Walks for Motorists* (Warne), *Observer's Book of the Lake District* (Warne), *Cumbria* (Bartholomew) Ken Andrew *Scottish Mountaineering Club Guide-Southern Uplands, with Thrippleton* (Scottish Mountaineering Trust) Dave Forsyth rambling contributor to *Dunfermline Press*; Angus and Fife section in *Walking in Scotland* Bill Brodie local walks leader F. C. A. Gordon Aberdeen Mountain Rescue Team, 1973-80.

PICTURE CREDITS

12-13 Janet and Colin Bord 15 Robert Roskrow 6, 21 Aerofilms Ltd 27 Jorge Lewinski 30 Janet and Colin Bord 35, 41 Mike Edwards 43 Jeff Haynes 67 British Tourist Board/Robert Harding Associates 73, 83, 84 Mike Edwards 87, 89 Aerofilms Ltd 98 Janet and Colin Bord 105, 110, 111, 113 Nigel O'Gorman 120 Allan Payne 124 Don Gresswell 130-1 Janet and Colin Bord 139 Roger Worsley 141 Glyn Davies 145 Chris Barber 149, 153, 161, 162 Mel Petersen 164-5 Nigel O'Gorman 167 John Bettell/National Trust 173, 174, 177, 179, 180 Nigel O'Gorman 189 Patrick Matthews/Robert Harding Associates 199 Janet and Colin Bord 205 Derek Widdicome/National Trust 217, 223, 230 Mel Petersen 239 Hull Daily Mail 251 Colin Speakman 256 Janet and Colin Bord 261, 269 Janet and Colin Bord 273 Richard Wylie 291 Ken Andrew 299 Scottish Tourist Board 305 Bill Brodie 311 Ken Andrew 313 Dave Forsyth 324 Scottish Tourist Board.

The help of the Countryside Commission in compiling the long-distance paths section is gratefully acknowledged; also of the Countryside Commission for Scotland. Thanks also to all the officials, County Councils and private individuals who have helped with the revision of this book.